Think you don't like fantasy?
Think again.

Praise for *Wish You Were Here*

★★★★★   Five Stars – Excellent Read

Vincent M. Wales has created a highly imaginative, yet believable world for his characters to inhabit, full of magic, wonder, danger, and intrigue. His writing style keeps the reader interested and entertained from one chapter to the next, making the pages fly by as if by magic itself. I highly recommend this book to anyone who enjoys the written word, because whether or not you are a fantasy genre reader, you will enjoy reading this book.

~ Sharp Writer Reviews

★★★★   Four Stars – Very Good, A Must-Read

[A] fun trip into a strange, magical world that is both much like and compellingly different from our own, everyday reality. [Wish You Were Here] is for anyone looking for a journey to a place that offers possibilities we've grown used to ignoring in our own reality: the adventures we long for, meaningful interpretations of honor and courage, and the capacity to become someone who matters significantly to a world and the people in it.

~ Scribes World Reviews

Wish You Were Here ... is a stunning novel. [T]his book combines a fantasy setting with some real earth issues to create an intelligent fantasy story. The humor is well done and often makes you take a step back and think about the way we live our lives and the values we have. If you want something that has the best of many styles, and is fresh, witty and exciting, give Wish You Were Here a go. Just make sure you've got time to read it all in one go - you'll want to!

~ BookNet.org.uk

ONE NATION
Under God

Bridget —
Hope you enjoy!

Vincent M. Wales

VINCENT M. WALES

DGC PRESS • SACRAMENTO

LCCN: 2003096608

ISBN: 0-9741337-0-1

Acknowledgments

My deepest thanks to Rich, for providing many insights, building my understanding of political matters, and for making sure I kept my facts straight. (But hitting me repeatedly with a rolled up copy of the Constitution isn't very respectful of our founding document.) Also to Thia, for another fantastic cover. And to my wife Lori, for everything, including tolerating my bouts of self-doubt and general bitchiness when the writing wasn't going so well.

Sincere appreciation also goes to:

★   Dan Barker of the Freedom from Religion Foundation for all the emails so kindly answered over the years, and for permission to paraphrase his "Easter Challenge," which appears in his book, *Losing Faith in Faith: From Preacher to Atheist.*

★   Bill Edelen of the William Edelen Ministries for his kind permission to adapt his essay, *The Sin of Silence,* for use in this book.

★   Jeff Clearwater of The Ecovillage Network for allowing me to adapt his vision of a futuristic ecological intentional community, which originally appeared in "Ecovillage 2015." (*Communities* magazine #111, Summer, 2001)

★   Cliff Walker of *Positive Atheism Magazine* for many enjoyable email conversations over the years, as well as his valued opinions on certain freethought issues and their ramifications.

My profound gratitude to everyone else who provided comments and contributions for this story, including: Austin, Christopher, Cyndi, Erin, Gary, Jennifer, Kelli, Kenneth, Lenny, Lori, Margaret, Margee, Michael, Sadie, Sandy, and Sonya.

And to Robert, who went peacefully into the Summerland July 6, 2004. Rest well, my friend. I'll miss our chats.

Special thanks also to:

★   Kaye Lynn and all at the Sacramento Valley School, Sacramento, CA
★   Larry and everyone at The Open Book, Sacramento, CA
★   Pam and the others at Southside Park Cohousing, Sacramento, CA
★   Frances and company at The River Reader, Guerneville, CA
★   Mike and the rest at Neptune's Corner, Rockaway Beach, OR

And to all the freethought activists I've known over the years, and my frequent visitors to *The Atheist Attic* – thank you for making a difference in my life.

Dedication

This book is dedicated to my wife, Lori, who so beautifully exemplifies the freethought mentality. Her ability to cast off dogmatic thinking and examine the world from outside the box is something I deeply admire.

Thank you for being you.

ONE NATION
Under God

Year One

2021

January 20, 2021

"Dear Diary..."

Boy, that's dumb. You don't write <u>to</u> a diary, you write <u>in</u> one.

So I asked for a DigiVox for Christmas, and naturally Mom has to get me this instead. I don't know why she likes these old paper things. What's wrong with a DigiVox? She's always getting me things I don't want instead of what I do want, in some weird attempt to make me like what she likes. I'll give it a try, though. It might not be too bad.

I can't believe my dad is President! Uncle Gene kept saying he'd get him elected. I didn't believe him. But he did!

I actually live in the White House! That's really cool and everything, but I already miss my friends. And I don't know how I'm going to make any here, because I'll be tutored instead of going to school.

And to make matters worse, Dad says I won't be able to use vidvox with chat, because of "security issues." So my friends won't be able to see my face or my room, or even hear my real voice. I'll probably have to use the keyboard instead of voice-rec, and that's just too dumb for words.

And with that stupid three-hour time difference between Washington and California, I'll be lucky to even be online at the same time as my friends.

Mom says I have to be extra careful. I can't let anyone online know I'm the President's daughter. She's pretty scared about the types of people you can meet online. I think she's just being silly.

I tell you what, though... This house is incredible! I had no idea it was so huge! My room is fantastic! And I can do whatever I want to it! Dad says they'll redecorate it however I want!

And there's the Lincoln Bedroom. I thought that meant Abraham Lincoln was the first President to sleep there, but actually, he used it as an office. Dad says it was in that room that Lincoln signed the Emancipation Proclamation in 1863. And now it's a guest room.

It's awesome to think that I stood in the same room where that took place. It's so freaky that I'm walking the same halls as all the Presidents who've lived in this house.

I hope one day some other kid will live here and think, "Wow... Paul Christopher, the greatest President ever, lived in this house..."

I hope my dad will be thought of that way by future generations. He's the greatest guy in the world!

God has been so very good to us!

"Good morning, everyone.

"I want to say first that it is a profound honor to have been elected your President. You have my undying oath that I will do everything in my power to convey that honor to the position I now hold. I will begin by breaking a long-standing tradition of what is 'supposed' to be done in an inaugural address.

"Decade after decade, Presidents have stood before the people and reiterated promises made on the campaign trail, promises to use the powers of their office to get this nation back on its feet, and so on and so forth. And decade after decade, they have broken those promises.

"Now, it's true that politicians are not in tune with Americans in general. They realize that promising to give the people what they want, whether or not they ever really give it to them, is how to get re-elected. Lying on demand is just a tool for saving face.

"George Washington is known as the President who could not tell a lie. But Washington was not a politician. We called them 'statesmen,' back then. Our founders were righteous men, and had little regard for the political posturing so common today.

"And like the father of our country, you will find that President Paul Christopher also cannot lie to the American public. Like George Washington, I'm not a politician, either. I've never gotten trapped in the messy cycle of greasing palms and knifing backs. And I won't.

"I'm a common citizen, just like you. I know what Americans want, and what they are and are not willing to sacrifice to get it. And I'm here to help us get it.

"Because we all want the same things. We want our children to grow up in a safer world than we did. We want a return to the solid morals that are the foundation of our country. We want to make this world a better place in every way.

"The great thing about this is that it's not only possible to do, but we don't have to sell our souls to accomplish it. In fact, what's needed is to *save* our souls. By heeding the word of God Almighty, we can turn this country around. Such is our duty to our fellow man, our duty to God.

"We've been saved once, two thousand years ago. But the sins being committed today are for us to atone for. We must save ourselves."

26 January 2021

When will the shock wear off? Since November, I've felt detached… as though I've been some disinterested observer watching someone else's life, like those voyeuristic television shows that Mary watches all the time.

I suppose the truth is that I never had faith that Gene could put me in the White House, as he always claimed. I under-estimated him and his "Family."

Still… over the past few years, I became convinced that it was a job I wanted, a job I could do. He kept telling me that political experience wasn't necessary, and I accepted that. But sometimes I still wonder if I'm truly up to the task ahead of me. I often catch myself questioning whether I did the wise thing in following Gene's urgings to run for office. After all, even aside from my lack of political experience, what real qualifications do I have? I keep telling myself that character, faith, and desire are the only things necessary. I hope that's true. Gene seems to think so. He keeps telling me so.

And why should I doubt? Gene is a man of God… one of the most respected, too. I must have faith in his foresight, no matter how little confidence I may have in myself. He's never steered me wrong, and there's no reason I should think he's done so in this.

And if it weren't for Sarah's constant support, I don't know if I could've even made it this far. She's such an incredible woman. Mary has been a great help, too. She has such faith in me. I suppose I was the same at her age, thinking my father could do no wrong.

It'll be difficult living up to her expectations, but by God, I intend to succeed.

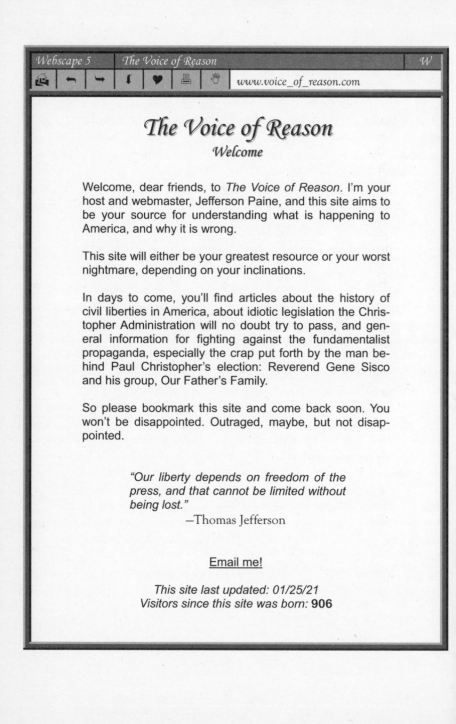

www.voice_of_reason.com

The Voice of Reason
Welcome

Welcome, dear friends, to *The Voice of Reason*. I'm your host and webmaster, Jefferson Paine, and this site aims to be your source for understanding what is happening to America, and why it is wrong.

This site will either be your greatest resource or your worst nightmare, depending on your inclinations.

In days to come, you'll find articles about the history of civil liberties in America, about idiotic legislation the Christopher Administration will no doubt try to pass, and general information for fighting against the fundamentalist propaganda, especially the crap put forth by the man behind Paul Christopher's election: Reverend Gene Sisco and his group, Our Father's Family.

So please bookmark this site and come back soon. You won't be disappointed. Outraged, maybe, but not disappointed.

> *"Our liberty depends on freedom of the press, and that cannot be limited without being lost."*
> —Thomas Jefferson

Email me!

This site last updated: 01/25/21
Visitors since this site was born: **906**

Recent letters to the editor in this fine paper have either lauded or condemned President Christopher's goal of bringing this country to God. Whether one likes the idea or not, it should come as no surprise that he has decided we should call upon God to save our country from its troubles. He's a religious man, after all.

But I can't help remembering other times in my life when there were identical urgings. The bombing of the Oklahoma City Federal Building when I was a child... the shootings at Columbine High School, where I lost my best friend... the unspeakable events of September 11, 2001... and so on up to the present.

After each and every horrific incident, there was a call for a return to faith. With every outbreak of violence, there was a call for prayer. Prayer, we were assured, would stop the next atrocity from happening.

But has it worked? Have we seen a decrease in terrorism or other violence? Have we seen an increase in charity or in common civility? No, we have not. Has the great sky god not heard these prayers, or worse, ignored these heartfelt pleas for clemency and kindness?

No. He has not ignored them, for he does not exist outside the minds of believers.

Doubtless this paper will be barraged with letters insulting me and defiantly proclaiming that their god is loving and does listen. But evidence does not indicate any truth to these claims.

It's time to grow up, America. It's time to quit hoping some make-believe father figure will fix things, and get on with the business of fixing them ourselves.

Eleanor Adams
President, Atheists USA

The Voice of Reason
A Peek at Paul Christopher

Religion: Raised Presbyterian by his now deceased parents, but in his teens, sought out more fundamentalist faiths. Now simply describes himself as "Evangelical."

Education: Attended Bob Jones University in South Carolina. (Yes, the same school that lost their tax-exempt status in 1983 due to their ban on interracial dating among the student body. The ban was lifted in 2000, but the school then required written permission from the interracial students' parents before allowing them to date!) Earned Bachelor's Degree in Bible Evangelism.

Experience: After graduation, he toured the country, studying prominent preachers including Billy Graham, Pat Robertson, Jerry Falwell, Benny Hinn, and others. Worked briefly for the Institute for Creation Research. During this time, he successfully lobbied to have evolution stricken from the curriculum of his high school alma mater.

Family: Met Sarah Schell at one of Gene Sisco's revival meetings. Married in 2008. Sarah continues to be active with a number of anti-choice and homophobic organizations. Paul has no siblings. Daughter Mary (born 2010) hasn't caused any trouble, yet.

Enter the Voice of Reason Archives

Email me!

This site last updated: 02/01/21
Visitors since this site was born: **1,129**

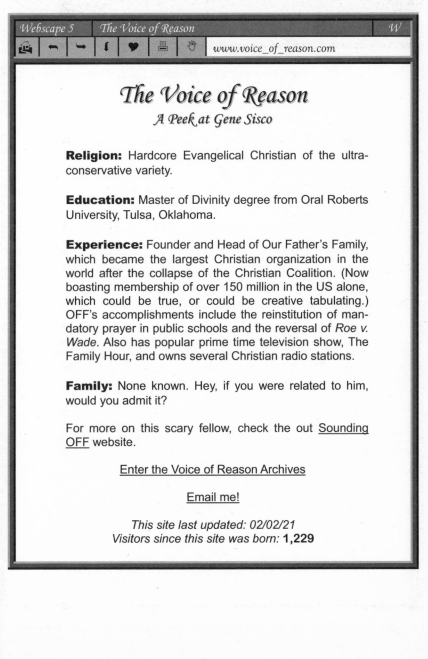

www.voice_of_reason.com

The Voice of Reason
A Peek at Gene Sisco

Religion: Hardcore Evangelical Christian of the ultra-conservative variety.

Education: Master of Divinity degree from Oral Roberts University, Tulsa, Oklahoma.

Experience: Founder and Head of Our Father's Family, which became the largest Christian organization in the world after the collapse of the Christian Coalition. (Now boasting membership of over 150 million in the US alone, which could be true, or could be creative tabulating.) OFF's accomplishments include the reinstitution of mandatory prayer in public schools and the reversal of *Roe v. Wade*. Also has popular prime time television show, The Family Hour, and owns several Christian radio stations.

Family: None known. Hey, if you were related to him, would you admit it?

For more on this scary fellow, check the out <u>Sounding OFF</u> website.

<u>Enter the Voice of Reason Archives</u>

<u>Email me!</u>

This site last updated: 02/02/21
Visitors since this site was born: **1,229**

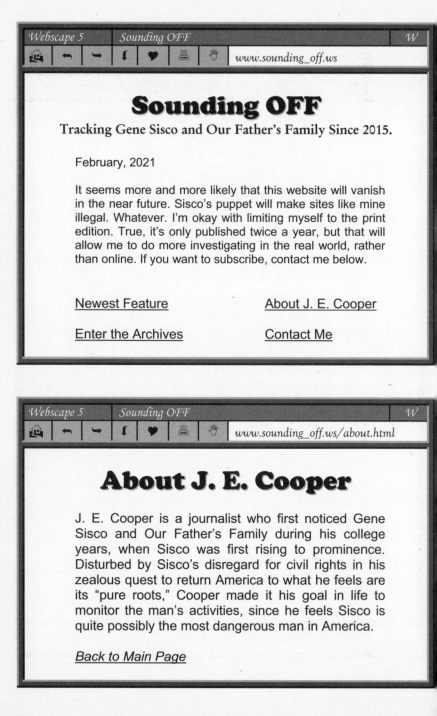

www.sounding_off.ws

Sounding OFF

Tracking Gene Sisco and Our Father's Family Since 2015.

February, 2021

It seems more and more likely that this website will vanish in the near future. Sisco's puppet will make sites like mine illegal. Whatever. I'm okay with limiting myself to the print edition. True, it's only published twice a year, but that will allow me to do more investigating in the real world, rather than online. If you want to subscribe, contact me below.

Newest Feature   About J. E. Cooper

Enter the Archives   Contact Me

www.sounding_off.ws/about.html

About J. E. Cooper

J. E. Cooper is a journalist who first noticed Gene Sisco and Our Father's Family during his college years, when Sisco was first rising to prominence. Disturbed by Sisco's disregard for civil rights in his zealous quest to return America to what he feels are its "pure roots," Cooper made it his goal in life to monitor the man's activities, since he feels Sisco is quite possibly the most dangerous man in America.

Back to Main Page

The Money Behind the Man

Gene Sisco's personal net worth is allegedly over a billion dollars. That's enough to put him in the bottom ten percent of the Forbes 400 this year.

Sisco has investments out the wazoo. Primarily, these are in commodities. Really valuable ones. Oil. Gold. Rumor has it that he owns a diamond mine, though I've been unable to verify this.

I can hear you saying, "But what about the ministry? How much does he bilk out of unsuspecting sheep every year?" You wouldn't believe me if I told you. Over 400 million a year. Now, that's not all profit, of course, but it's an amazing income stream.

So how much of this fortune did he invest into Paul Christopher's campaign? My research indicates a staggering fifty million dollars. Shit... Who *couldn't* win the presidency with that kind of outlay?

Of course, regular readers of this site know that I believe it was money spent not to elect a friend, but to ensure his own eventual seat in the Oval Office. Get scared, folks!

Enter the Sounding OFF Archives

Back to Main Page

Queer and Now

Editorial by
Polly Wright

As director of American Queers and editor of *Queer and Now*, I've been asked more times than I can count how I feel about what's happening in Washington, with regard to The Movement. My answer is always the same: "How do you *think* I feel?"

Let's sum it up. We've got a conservative religious nut in the White House whose most trusted advisor is an even more conservative religious freak. We have a virulently homophobic bigot as the Supreme Court's Chief Justice, a man who has already done more than enough damage to our cause all by himself. And the Republicans control the House and the Senate, which will make conservative legislation frightfully easy to pass in the coming years.

In short, the situation sucks rocks.

Now, it's true that "gay pride" hasn't been this high in all the years since the Stonewall riots. But we may well be in for some nasty years ahead of us. I'm not suggesting that we all go back in the closet. But we all need to be wary.

Some scary shit's coming down the pike.

Enter the March Issue   *Enter the Archives*

The Voice of Reason
Lies Your Government Told You!

"Studies Prove Prayer is Good Medicine!" Prayer can be useful for oneself, just as meditation or a positive attitude is useful. But no reputable study has ever shown intercessory prayer... prayer on behalf of others... to be effective. Reports stating otherwise are based on poor testing methods, faulty interpretations of data, and occasionally, outright fudging of the facts.

"Ten Commandments Reduce School Violence!" School crime in general had been dropping steadily for years before the 10 C's were illegally mounted in school classrooms, and there was no appreciable difference after they were posted.

"Homosexuality Can Be Cured!" Homosexuality isn't a disease. There's nothing to "cure." Brainwashing clinics like *The Camp* do not "cure" anything; they merely override behavior with intensive post-hypnotic suggestions. This almost always results in mild to moderate (and sometimes severe) psychoses. Almost 15% of those who "graduate" from these programs commit suicide within a decade.

"The only foes that threaten America are the enemies at home, and these are ignorance, superstition, and incompetence."
—Elbert Hubbard

Enter the Voice of Reason Archives

Email me!

This site last updated: 3/10//21
*Visitors since this site was born: **3,125***

March 12, 2021

I've been really sad, lately. I know I haven't even been here two whole months, yet, but I haven't made a single friend! And I hardly ever see anyone from home online. I knew they'd hate that I can't use vid-vox. I bet they avoid me because of it. They don't like having to actually read what I'm saying, and I don't really like having to type it, either.

If I had vid, they wouldn't mind as much, probably. And then I could show them how cool my room is. Just like Dad promised, we redecorated it. I got purple carpeting! It's so awesome!

Mom and Dad would freak if they knew this, but I've been visiting chat rooms online. I can't stand having no one to talk to. The online stuff is okay, but I really want a friend here to do things with.

I've hardly seen Dad at all. I know he's got lots of stuff to keep him busy, but I thought he'd be able to make time for me. He promised he would! Even Mom is busy with all kinds of things. I spend more time with my tutor than anyone else, and she's no fun at all.

I'm not sure about this whole tutoring thing. I mean, I swear I didn't have this much Bible study even at Holy Grove Academy back home! And it's not that I don't like Bible study. I do. But I like to read other things, too, and Arlene isn't having me read any other books. I don't like that. Or her, for that matter. She smells like medicine.

On the other hand, some of the things she's having me do are pretty cool. Like today we discussed faith healing. I've always thought that was awesome. But while I was doing some research online about it, I found a really terrible website. It said faith healing is baloney. Of course, it didn't give any proof. It also had articles that really upset me. They were very mean toward my dad and Uncle Gene.

What makes people so mean? It's not like my dad ever did anything to them! Sure, he's passed laws that not everyone will agree with, but that's tough! There's no sense getting upset about it. It's not like it'll change anything.

I swear I will never understand atheists.

Maybe I should do my own site. I don't know what I'd put on it, but it could be fun.

March 15, 2021

I've been reading all the articles on that "Voice of Reason" site. I just don't get it. How can he think such bad things about my dad? He doesn't even know him!

I've always hated when people judge others without knowing them. I've known lots of kids in school like that. And this Jefferson Paine guy is just like them. He lumps all Christians together and judges them as a group. All atheists do that. They're all the same.

I wonder if Dad has seen the site. I hope not. He's got enough to worry about with being President and everything. I'd like to talk to him about it, though, because I'd really like to understand why this guy thinks the way he does.

Uncle Gene's out of town, so I can't talk to him. I guess I could talk to Mom, but she'd probably just go on and on. She talks too much.

3/15/21

Mary and I had a nice mother-daughter talk this evening. I try not to be surprised when we do, but it's such a rare thing. Perhaps now that Paul's so busy with Presidential matters, she and I will have time to grow closer.

We talked about atheists. Mary wanted to know why anyone wouldn't believe in God. So I explained that most of them are really just too arrogant to admit that there's anything greater than themselves. Others are being deceived by the devil, and aren't strong enough to fight him off. And a few, I suppose, were raised to be atheists by atheistic parents, and never bothered to question whether this was true or not. So many people just accept whatever they're told, unquestioningly.

I certainly don't have to worry about that with Mary. Such an inquisitive girl. More than I was at her age, I'm sure. She's so much more like her father than like me.

15

Webscape 5 │ USAtheist │ W

www.USAtheist.ws/editorial.html

USAtheist

Editorial by Eleanor Adams

Chief Justice Mal Spencer displayed his ignorance of history on *60 Minutes* recently. He said the 'wall of separation' was an erroneous inference:

"While the Constitution is clear that government is to have no involvement in matters of religion, it does not say such non-involvement is meant to be reciprocal.

"The private writings of the founders, including Jefferson's letter to the Danbury Baptists, cannot be considered as founding documents. Privately held opinions have frequently differed from official policy. A uni-directional wall would better serve the interests of this country.

"Similarly, 'freedom of religion' is precisely that. It does not include 'freedom from religion.' Religious men founded America. It would be disrespectful of their memory and labors to pervert their wishes by eliminating religion from our government, even on the smallest scale."

Spencer implies that Jefferson's letter was no more politically significant than Sarah Christopher's recipe for banana nut muffins. But the letter was in fact an official Presidential statement, approved by Attorney General Levi Lincoln. While not a 'founding document' *per se*, it is most certainly not to be dismissed as irrelevant. And to turn Jefferson's Wall into a one-way wall is not only utterly inaccurate, but completely undermines religious freedom in this country.

The Call to Action

USAtheist

Call to Action

If any religion can freely influence the government, then *all* citizens are subject to the desires of that religion, whether or not they happen to subscribe to that religion's particular belief system.

Not everyone holds the same religious beliefs, and millions of Americans hold no religious beliefs at all. Perhaps Justice Spencer doesn't care about these particular citizens. Or worse, perhaps he agrees with former President George Bush (the first one), who stated that he wasn't even sure that atheists should be considered citizens!

I urge all Americans to contact their local chapter of the ACLU, who are planning a legal challenge if the civil rights of even one citizen are trampled if (when) these views find their way into a court ruling.

Freedom of religion *must* include freedom from religion, or it has no meaning whatsoever. Anyone not blinded by prejudice can see this, which apparently says a lot about our Chief Justice.

Eleanor

The Voice of Reason
HUAC, McCarthy and Reds. (Oh, my!)

In the 1950s, the U.S. and the U.S.S.R. (look it up) were the biggest military powers on earth. Each had its own ideologies, and both "knew" they were diametrically opposed to one another. As you can imagine, they were afraid of each other to the point of paranoia.

Senator Joseph McCarthy was quite vocal about the "Red Menace," as Communism was called. (That was the ideology considered insidious and dangerous to paranoid Americans.) He was also heavily involved with the House Un-American Activities Committee, a Congressional Committee put together to flush out any Communists in America, using antics not unlike the witch hunts of much older times.

To quote Committee Chairman, J. Parnell Thomas: *"The rights you have are the rights given you by this Committee. We will determine what rights you have and what rights you have not got."* (Makes you want to go to *that* party, doesn't it?) Because of McCarthy's vocal role in it, this witch hunt mentality was dubbed "McCarthyism." The HUAC hearings destroyed the lives and careers of many innocent people. It was an egregious abuse of Congressional power, and remains one of the darkest hours of our political history.

In fact, there was a virulent anti-Communist mentality after the First World War, too, possibly just as strong as after the Second. It could be that the lingering memory of this earlier "Red Scare" in many people helped fan the flames of the hysteria three decades later.

Enter the Voice of Reason Archives

Email me!

This site last updated: 03/17/21
*Visitors since this site was born: **3,243***

The Voice of Reason
America: Christian Just to be Different

Because America was insane with fear and hatred of the Soviets in the 50s, people felt we had to distinguish ourselves as being as *unlike* them as possible. One way to do this was for us to have opposite ideologies.

As it happens, the "official religion" of the USSR was atheism. (Never mind that atheism isn't a religion, nor that it doesn't matter diddly what the "official" anything is of a country. People will believe what they want.) And while Americans were under the mistaken impression that all Soviets were atheists, the Russian Orthodox Church kept growing and growing. It was, and still is, one of the largest Christian denominations in the world.

So, since they had atheism as *their* official stance, we had to have some sort of theism as *ours*. Yes, the Constitution forbade such a thing, but Americans are clever. To get around our own founding document, lawmakers did little things, like insert the words "under God" into the Pledge of Allegiance, and make "In God We Trust" our new national motto, replacing the Latin *"E Pluribus Unum."* It didn't matter that large numbers of Americans didn't even believe in a god, let alone put their trust in one. The phrase was printed on our currency, and minted onto our coins. Actually, it had been on and off the coins sporadically for quite a while, but after McCarthy's day, it was there to stay.

This should've been a sign of things to come. But we've never been the most observant people, have we?

Enter the Voice of Reason Archives

Email me!

This site last updated: 03/27/21
Visitors since this site was born: **4,919**

"Ladies and Gentlemen of the Press...

"For too many years, the liberal media have been free to run roughshod over factual reporting, to put whatever spin they like on matters they have no business doctoring. We have watched as the press has slandered fine Presidents such as Reagan and both Bushes, and defended morally bankrupt Presidents such as Clinton. No longer will the excesses of the media be tolerated.

"'Freedom of the Press' was never meant to provide the media with the ability to potentially destroy our nation's leaders. And no longer will they have this ability. A bill is now before the House of Representatives. It proposes that all media sources be monitored closely for any such un-American behavior. Guidelines have been drawn up that will pertain to the major media outlets and may be seen on the U.S. Government Internet website.

"The House votes on this bill tomorrow, at which point it will move to the Senate. I expect little opposition."

April 5, 2021

Yesterday was Easter, and today was the Easter Egg Hunt. It was huge! Dad said there were probably 50,000 people there! It was a lot of fun. One of Dad's secretaries was dressed up as the bunny. I forget her name. She's the one who always has a bucket of Red Vines on her desk.

There are a whole bunch of events we have to attend every year. Most of them sound boring. But Dad said maybe this year he'd let me light the White House Christmas Tree! That would be so cool!

I hate that I don't get to spend much time with him. He's always so busy. He gets up around five in the morning, every day, and has that briefing thing after he eats breakfast. Then he's off to do one thing or another, always surrounded by those Secret Service guys. They're creepy. But the worst is the guy (or guys – I think there are three or four of them who switch on and off) who has the case handcuffed to him. The creepy thing about that is what's in the case. Dad says it's a computer that'll let him launch nuclear weapons at another country if we're attacked.

That's scary. I mean, it's scary that we might be attacked, but to me, it's scarier to think that my dad would be the one to attack them back. The Bible says we're to turn the other cheek. So we shouldn't attack back if some country attacks us first. I don't think Dad should allow that guy to follow him around, anymore.

NPR: Our guest today on National Public Radio, Eleanor Adams. Eleanor, thank you for joining us. Now, you've been editorializing about Paul Christopher ever since he was given the Republican nomination. You've been particularly harsh when it comes to his vision for America.

Adams: Yes, I have.

NPR: What exactly do you think President Christopher means by a return to "family values"?

Adams: I see it as a desperate cry for a return to a largely mythical world of the past. My grandparents used to talk about these "good old days" all the time, and as near as I can figure, they were referring to the 1950s. And when you mention the 50s today, what do you think of?

NPR: Elvis Presley. Black and white sitcoms.

Adams: Right. And that's where the mythical element comes in. This period wasn't all Ozzie and Harriet. There was the fear and paranoia of the Cold War, rampant racism and sexism, not to mention Eisenhower's orgy of inflicting religion on the masses.

NPR: You're referring to the national motto?

Adams: Yes, changing it to In God We Trust, making it mandatory on our currency and coinage, and having "under God" inserted into the Pledge of Allegiance. He knew it effectively made the Pledge into a sort of prayer, thus violating the First Amendment. In fact, at the time, he said, "From this day forward, the millions of our schoolchildren will daily proclaim in every city and town, every village and every rural schoolhouse, the dedication of our nation and our people to the Almighty."

NPR: So you would say that this "Ozzie and Harriet" decade, ironically, is when everything started to "go wrong," in your view?

Adams: I'd say it took a great leap backward, at any rate.

NPR: But what about the 60s? Most would say this decade was liberal, free-spirited, and some favorable to atheists.

Adams: The decade when God was allegedly "thrown out" of public schools. The abolition of spoken prayer in public schools was definitely a step in the right direction, but it was only a temporary one. And despite the "summer of love" image that people seem to conjure up when they think of the 60s, it was a period rife with heinous things, too. Race riots. "Police actions." Political assassinations.

NPR: But despite such tumultuous goings-on, the 60s remain the decade of peace and love to most Americans.

Adams: Perhaps so, but then came Watergate. People then had proof that you couldn't even trust the guy at the top. The 70s certainly seemed to be a cold, impersonal decade, but it wasn't all due to Watergate. We had the Vietnam conflict, an energy crisis, rampant inflation...

NPR: But getting back to the decades and how they affected atheists, what happened, and when?

Adams: Well, in the 80s we were given Reagan and Bush the elder, both of whom were devoted to making religion a staple of American life. But at the turn of the century, Bush the younger did more to inject religion into government than anyone since Eisenhower.

NPR: And now we have President Christopher. I know you're not a political analyst, but how do you think he won? This was a man who'd never held any political office before.

Adams: Americans haven't cared about real qualifications for well over a century. Not enough people cared that he didn't have political experience. And too many cared only that he was tall, handsome, charismatic, well groomed, and loudly Christian. They loved his photogenic family, with his lovely wife and their pretty daughter. He's friendly, well spoken and an excellent debater. Of course, what comes out of his mouth is idiotic half the time and misinformed the other half. He's promised to return America to its religious roots, instill "family values" everywhere, and other lofty notions. No wonder he had a landslide victory.

NPR: "Family values" again. We've come full circle. So you're asserting that these "family values" of Christopher's are founded in religious teachings?

Adams: More accurately, he thinks "family values" can *only* be founded in religious teachings, and specifically in *his* religion's teachings. But as millions of Americans will attest, we don't believe that things such as racism, sexism, homophobia, and other bigoted views supported by these religious teachings should be considered "family values." Yet his religion can be – and is – used to justify all of these.

NPR: Given all this, why do you think the Republican Party felt he'd be a good Presidential candidate?

Adams: I don't know that they necessarily did. I think Sisco and his group used their considerable guile to get behind Christopher without the pols catching on, then blew in from nowhere to win the early primaries. The pols never recovered. And one thing you have to say about the Republicans is that they stand behind their candidates, even if they have misgivings. A friend of mine summed it up well: "When the runaway train comes through, you don't stand in the way." I think the already conservative Republican Party saw the train and decided to hop on board.

NPR: Can you blame them?

Adams: Of course not. Paul Christopher is a religious conservative's dream. The Republican Party would have been insane not to nominate him. The people love the guy. And some of them, it almost seems, practically worship him. If you don't believe me, take a look at all the conservative Christian groups who were raising such a fuss a quarter of a century ago. Groups like Christian Exodus wanted to move millions of like-minded Christians to South Carolina, establish a Christian theocracy, and secede. They even made some progress toward the first step of that, but today we don't hear a peep out of them. Why? Because Christopher is fulfilling their dream, on a national scale.

NPR: I'm afraid we're out of time. Thanks for being with us, today.

Washington—Hundreds of protesters are expected to participate in what is being called the first annual "Rights for Brights" march on the Capitol, scheduled for tomorrow.

The Brights are a loose-knit group of individuals self-described as having a worldview "free of supernatural and mystical elements." These non-theists are crusading under the banner of the First Amendment, which they claim demands total separation of church and state.

They hope to raise awareness of what they claim is the discriminatory nature of the current political climate in the United States.

City police are allegedly prepared for any violence, but state that they do not expect any.

12 July 2021

"Rights for Brights." Please. What rights should these infidels have? None, if I had my way. Frankly, I wish they'd follow the lead of Christian Exodus. Get all the atheists and pagans and whatnot together in one state. We'd be glad to be rid of them. Let them form their own little godless sinner nation unto themselves and quit corrupting American society. Maybe they should take California; it's already overrun by liberals and queers. But no. Too much prime real estate there. Maybe we can offer them the section of Nevada where all the nuclear testing was done.

But speaking of the would-be secessionists, Adams was right in her assessment. They have been remarkably quiet. Please, Lord, let them stay that way. The last time South Carolina tried to secede, the results were disastrous. Such political grandstanding is not something I want to deal with over the next several years.

Philadelphia—The Pulitzer Prize-winning newspaper, the *Philadelphia Inquirer*, resumed publication Monday, three weeks after a court order commanded the paper to stop its presses.

The paper had printed a harsh editorial in June, following the passage of the "Press Bill" by Congress. The editorial criticized not only President Christopher, but also Reverend Gene Sisco. As such, it violated the terms of the new law's restrictions on the press. Rev. Sisco's organization, Our Father's Family, immediately called for a boycott of the paper, resulting in tremendous numbers of cancellations by angry readers.

Many news publications contained criticism of the new restrictions. Newspapers and magazines around the country featured letters labeling them unconstitutional. Professors of history insisted that freedom of the press, as guaranteed by the First Amendment, was designed to do exactly what our current administration claims it was not designed to do. Many are of the opinion that the *Inquirer* was used as an example to others.

Frank Carver, publisher of the *Inquirer*, estimates it will be years before the paper again reaches its circulation prior to the shutdown, and possibly several years more before it recoups lost revenue.

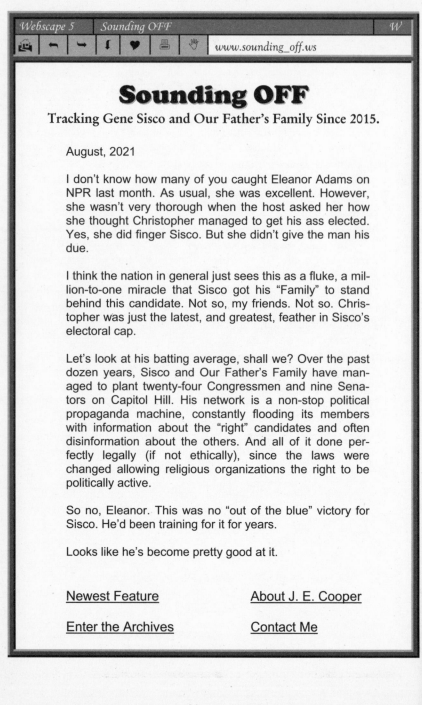

www.sounding_off.ws

Sounding OFF

Tracking Gene Sisco and Our Father's Family Since 2015.

August, 2021

I don't know how many of you caught Eleanor Adams on NPR last month. As usual, she was excellent. However, she wasn't very thorough when the host asked her how she thought Christopher managed to get his ass elected. Yes, she did finger Sisco. But she didn't give the man his due.

I think the nation in general just sees this as a fluke, a million-to-one miracle that Sisco got his "Family" to stand behind this candidate. Not so, my friends. Not so. Christopher was just the latest, and greatest, feather in Sisco's electoral cap.

Let's look at his batting average, shall we? Over the past dozen years, Sisco and Our Father's Family have managed to plant twenty-four Congressmen and nine Senators on Capitol Hill. His network is a non-stop political propaganda machine, constantly flooding its members with information about the "right" candidates and often disinformation about the others. And all of it done perfectly legally (if not ethically), since the laws were changed allowing religious organizations the right to be politically active.

So no, Eleanor. This was no "out of the blue" victory for Sisco. He'd been training for it for years.

Looks like he's become pretty good at it.

Newest Feature   About J. E. Cooper

Enter the Archives   Contact Me

Webscape 5   *The Voice of Reason*   W

www.voice_of_reason.com

The Voice of Reason
The Voices of Outrage

Many have emailed me, asking why there aren't more people speaking out about rights being taken away.

Truth is, people *are* speaking out. But who is going to showcase their concerns? Newspapers are getting shut down. Reporters are getting fired. And because this is a capitalist society, the media are concerned more with staying in business than in portraying the truth.

To hear what mainstream religion thinks of Christopher and Co., read some of their publications. They don't like what's going on, either. But they don't have the organizational clout that the fundies do, and the fundies are quite happy with the way things are going.

Non-religious organizations are being similarly silenced, and I don't doubt that the government intends to target them for total eradication in the near future.

And Mr. and Mrs. Public Citizen? They complain to their Congresscritters, which is akin to the Jews complaining to Nazi guards at Auschwitz.

(Click <u>here</u> to read snippets from various sources.)

In short, it's not a matter of people not protesting. It's a matter of having waited too long. The things being said now should've been said decades ago. Enough attention could've prevented this. Now we're stuck with the task of stopping it, and cleaning up afterward.

<u>Enter the Voice of Reason Archives</u>

<u>Email me!</u>

This site last updated: 08/7/21
Visitors since this site was born: **5,129**

The Voices of Outrage

Folks, these are all excerpts of letters or articles from recently published magazines. Judge for yourself how other segments of the public are feeling.

From *Christianity Today*:
"The truth is that many churches are afraid. They've come to rely on the funding they've gotten from the government and are afraid of losing it. It seems only the small churches, those not affiliated with mainstream sects or used to government handouts, have the guts to stand up and say that what Rev. Sisco and his President pal are doing is not truly Christian."

From *Tikkun*:
"Our community is about solidarity. The Bible commanded us to remember that we Jews were once slaves in Egypt. We believe that any oppression, whether of an individual or a group, is harmful and wrong... not just to that individual or that group, but to all humanity. And that is why we must oppose much of what is happening in America, even though many of us are not Americans."

From *Jet*:
"I think the African-American community is forgetting all the fighting we had to do to get where we are today. And especially, we're forgetting all those who helped us in those battles, including liberal Christians. And now they're the ones battling to retain their rights, and we need to stand with them."

From *Foreign Policy*:
"I was devastated by your bleak outlook for the economy under Pres. Christopher. Granted, our economy has been lousy for two decades, but if your analysts are right, we're headed for even worse. The middle class can't take more tax increases, especially for such idiocy as funding of religion."

Washington—The role of Big Brother, the government's special task force regulating the Internet, including the computer of the same name, has been expanded. The Internet will now be required to adhere to the same restrictions placed on conventional media.

Big Brother has been given the additional command to seek out and destroy any site that is considered "treasonous." That is, sites containing rhetoric that slanders the government or its actions.

Elwood Nutt, head programmer for Big Brother, stated, "Fruit flies will have longer life-spans than targeted sites, now."

Nutt, a graduate of the Massachusetts Institute of Technology, is the creator of the specialized "worm" programs used by Big Brother. His work has been on the cutting edge of computer technology for years.

New York—President Christopher was on hand for Patriot Day, as he joined New York City Mayor Ellen Bond and Governor John Larsen in leading thousands of people gathered in prayer.

The service was held in front of one the south reflecting pool near Freedom Tower, where the World Trade Center previously stood, built in memory of the thousands of people who died during the destruction of the New York landmark, which was leveled in terrorist attacks twenty years ago today.

President Christopher refused to answer any questions on the "War on Terrorism" declared by President George W. Bush after the terrorist attacks, a war that is still being fought today.

Libertarian Letters
Volume 6, Issue 4

It is no surprise that Christopher avoided questions regarding the War on Terrorism. Every President since the second Bush has avoided such questions whenever possible. The fact of the matter is that this "war" was designed from the start to be a perpetual struggle, allowing government to feed more and more money into the military and the industries that support the military. It has given "justification" for the sacrifice of individual liberties by all citizens, in the name of "national security."

Twentieth Century Senator William Proxmire said, "Power always has to be kept in check; power exercised in secret, especially under the cloak of *national security*, is doubly dangerous." These are words all of us should take to heart.

The USA Patriot Act, instituted during the Bush years, has been used (again, unsurprisingly) to designate many domestic activist groups as "terrorists." Any group that gives the impression of trying to "influence the policy of government by intimidation or coercion" can be so labeled. Many groups, such as Greenpeace, were not terrorists, except according to this definitely unpatriotic Act, which ultimately led to their disintegration.

I had hoped, two decades ago, that the American people would rise up in protest of the sweeping abuses of power that would certainly occur as a result of the USA Patriot Act. But such a protest has never happened, largely because of the perpetual ignorance of the American public... an ignorance that often, quite frankly, appeared to be voluntary.

Yes, there are organizations today who are protesting the loss of these freedoms. Voices from the public can be heard, if one listens. Even many religious organizations are protesting the actions of the Christopher Administration. But these collective complaints are too little, too late. Decades of complacency have allowed us to become a nation accustomed to having our rights trod upon, to being spied upon. We're so used to being without certain rights of privacy, for example, that we think little of their absence.

It was complacency such as this that permitted the success of the attacks twenty years ago in the first place, as well as all the lesser attacks upon us since then.

And unless we wish to allow further atrocities to be committed, we must end the complacency. We must insist on having our rights restored. If we do not fight for them, we don't deserve them.

Michael Lee
Political Director
Libertarian National Party

17 September 2021

My Chief of Staff advised me to keep abreast of the activities of those who could pose a threat to me in four years. And I'm glad he did, for it's important to know what they're saying about me even now. Still… I never would have thought a Libertarian would be among those who condemn me.

However, Michael Lee's comments are truer than he knows, in one respect. I'm very uncomfortable with what's still going on in the Middle East.

It truly does seem as though the whole affair were designed by my predecessors to be an "eternal war." History seems to shine favorably upon wartime Presidents, so maybe that was the rationale behind it.

Ostensibly, George W. Bush was committed to establishing democracy in Iraq. At the time, the only force in Iraq that could have commanded broad support in democratic elections was the Shi'a clerics. But Bush (wisely, in my opinion) said that we wouldn't permit any sort of non-Christian, cleric-dominated government.

In the years since then, we've established a tenuous democracy in Iraq. But of course, it couldn't survive without our troops there to keep it from collapsing. It seems every administration since then has found it necessary to continue this support, whether out of loyalty to our Iraqi allies, out of fear of the alternatives, or even simply to avoid disorder.

But the whole affair reminds me too much of Vietnam. It's a nightmare, but one of our own making. No wonder there is resistance to it. There is anti-American resistance, pro-Islamic resistance, and even Iraqi patriot resistance to this foreign occupation of their country.

And of course, there are constant protests domestically, too. Protesting our presence in the Middle East, protesting our methods of fighting terrorists, even protesting the base we're building on the moon.

Actually, I can in some ways understand that last one. As a boy, I dreamed of a Star Trek-like future, of exploring other worlds. A lunar base, in my dreams, was never primarily a huge array of military lasers and inter-planetary ballistic missiles.

The road to Hell is, indeed, paved with good intentions.

George Orwell is Spinning in His Grave
WIRED Looks Back...and Forth

In 2001, the Office of Homeland Security was created in response to the terrorist attacks perpetrated on America that September. Allegedly, its purpose was to safeguard the home front against future terrorism. Of course, not all terrorism is from foreign sources, and before long, the group was turning its eye on Americans themselves.

By 2010, the expanded Department of Homeland Security had assembled the ultimate computer surveillance technology: Big Brother. It was an expansion of Cyber Knight, the notorious FBI program that spawned such computer snooping efforts as Carnivore (DCS1000) and Magic Lantern a decade earlier. The tremendous leaps in computer technology over the ensuing ten years made it possible to track virtually everything in cyberspace. And eventually, the DHS was able to take over computers and satellites previously used by the CIA and various military branches, making the Big Brother operation staggering in its abilities.

Whenever a new Internet domain is registered, Big Brother's computers are alerted. Using sophisticated search techniques, they scan all web sites for key words, looking for anything offensive or dangerous. What qualifies as dangerous? Quite a lot. Pornography, of course. Excessive profanity. Anti-government or anti-religious sentiments. Anything that seems at all supportive of homosexuality or other alternative lifestyles. All of these, by their very nature, are subjective, but it doesn't matter. All protests have been ignored.

If the targeted site is located outside the US, the host's Internet Service Provider is ordered to make the site unavailable to computers within the States. If they refuse, they suddenly find their servers crashing over and over again. But if it is within the US, computer viruses known as "worms" are sent to destroy all data in the files. Simultaneously, the site owner is identified, and the ISP is alerted to the illegal site. The owner's name is added to a database, and if he/she registers any domains elsewhere with illegal content, they are arrested. If the previously notified ISP actually allows the party to put up another illegal site, the ISP is shut down.

Even more than sixty years after the publication of George Orwell's classic novel 1984, people were appalled that the government would even consider naming something "Big Brother." Today, what's truly appalling is that we're coming closer and closer to making that fictional hell a reality.

Date: 9/22/21
To: T. Bannister, CO BB Proj.
From: E. Nutt, CP BB Proj.
Subject: Trouble

No doubt you have heard rumors about a site that Big Brother has been unable to shut down. Here are the facts:

- On 10 April, BB detected a site (www.voice_of_reason.com) which contained inappropriate material. It was assigned a medium-level priority.
- Attempts to contact the host provider were fruitless.
- Our hacking has repeatedly failed, producing an automatically generated reply with insulting verbiage.
- Attempts to view source code result in a page reading, "Life is more interesting with a little mystery, don't you think?"
- The site appears to be hosted on a non-commercial computer tied directly into the Internet. Further, a random URL director is apparently scripted into the site's code, throwing the visitor to any of a hundred different "mirror" hosts.
- Attempts to shut down these mirror host ISPs have proven to be wastes of time. Whenever one is shut down, the site automatically routes to another. It is likely that the webmaster is adding new mirrors regularly.

Whoever scripted this site is a smart cookie. Not of my caliber, of course, but very capable. Possibly with a host of psychological maladies, but I shan't speculate on those.

I am certain I can shut the site down, given enough time. However, this will limit my available time for upgrades to BB itself. I await your recommendation.

I see nothing serious to worry about. The site is mindless babble aimed at the Christopher Administration. Irritating, I'm sure, but hardly dangerous.

I suggest keeping a lid on this site's existence. If given the green light, I can use more direct actions and have this site shut down before 'net lists can catalog it for search engines.

Washington–President Paul Christopher announced today that new federal guidelines from the Department of Education would require all public schools to teach classes in morality to their students, effective next fall. Schools have until May 30, 2022, to submit their proposed course outlines to officials at the state level. No course may be taught without approval of the outlines, including textbook selection. Private schools are exempt from this new legislation.

Swarthmore–Roughly 250 students of Swarthmore College engaged in a vocal protest over recent policies of the Christopher Administration yesterday. Swarthmore is the latest of dozens of colleges and universities around the country to voice displeasure over what they see as gross civil rights violations.

Considering the Administration's most recent legislation, that public schools should be teaching morality, it would not be surprising to find these protests increasing, despite the assurances of those who claim that it's all in the best interests of our children.

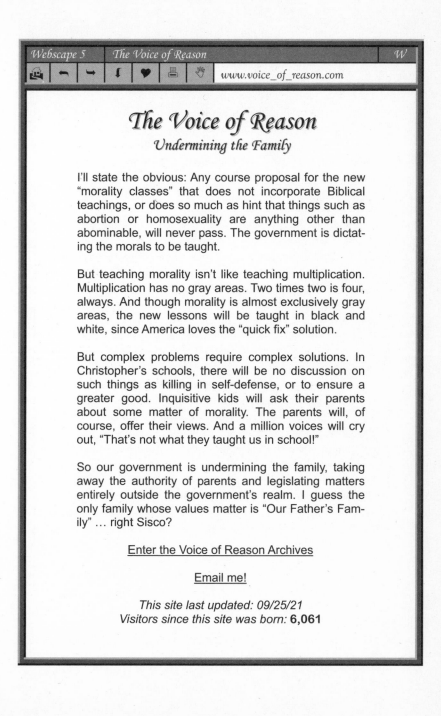

The Voice of Reason
Undermining the Family

I'll state the obvious: Any course proposal for the new "morality classes" that does not incorporate Biblical teachings, or does so much as hint that things such as abortion or homosexuality are anything other than abominable, will never pass. The government is dictating the morals to be taught.

But teaching morality isn't like teaching multiplication. Multiplication has no gray areas. Two times two is four, always. And though morality is almost exclusively gray areas, the new lessons will be taught in black and white, since America loves the "quick fix" solution.

But complex problems require complex solutions. In Christopher's schools, there will be no discussion on such things as killing in self-defense, or to ensure a greater good. Inquisitive kids will ask their parents about some matter of morality. The parents will, of course, offer their views. And a million voices will cry out, "That's not what they taught us in school!"

So our government is undermining the family, taking away the authority of parents and legislating matters entirely outside the government's realm. I guess the only family whose values matter is "Our Father's Family" … right Sisco?

<u>Enter the Voice of Reason Archives</u>

<u>Email me!</u>

This site last updated: 09/25/21
Visitors since this site was born: **6,061**

For those who don't know me, I run a halfway house for troubled teens in Los Angeles called The Bethlehem Inn. I also give lectures locally about the problems with religious fundamentalism. And now I have another segment to add to my lecture: to point out the flawed mentality behind President Christopher's latest edict, of forcing our public schools to teach morality.

Readers of *The New Anglican Review* will understand, of course, that the morals being taught will be those of Reverend Sisco's literal interpretation of the Bible. And this is something our order has long fought against, as have other non-fundamentalist Christian groups.

It is this kind of mentality that caused us to break away from the Old Episcopal Church in the first place. The Old Episcopal mentality was fundamentalist at one time, too. We New Anglicans should be outraged at the very prospect of forcing one set of values upon one and all.

We value free will above almost all else, and Sisco's literalism leaves very little room for free will in our nation's children. The sad fact is that I'm sure Sisco realizes this, even desires this. Evangelicals, as any student of the human mind will tell you, have a psychological *need* to control and coerce others.

I urge all New Anglicans to speak out against this new law. Even if your children are in private schools, or if you have no children, think of the children of others. These lambs will not be allowed to graze in the open air of liberty, but will be raised in a box of evangelical fundamentalism, as a veal calf unable to move more than a few inches in any direction.

Our love for one another cannot allow this to occur.

Fr. Emilio Montoya

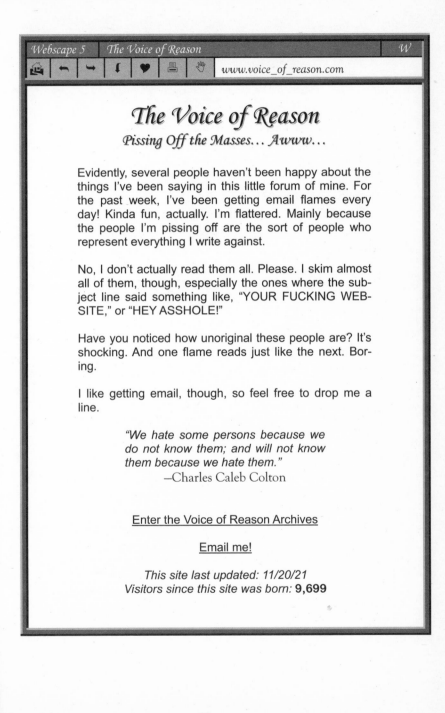

The Voice of Reason
Pissing Off the Masses... Awww...

Evidently, several people haven't been happy about the things I've been saying in this little forum of mine. For the past week, I've been getting email flames every day! Kinda fun, actually. I'm flattered. Mainly because the people I'm pissing off are the sort of people who represent everything I write against.

No, I don't actually read them all. Please. I skim almost all of them, though, especially the ones where the subject line said something like, "YOUR FUCKING WEBSITE," or "HEY ASSHOLE!"

Have you noticed how unoriginal these people are? It's shocking. And one flame reads just like the next. Boring.

I like getting email, though, so feel free to drop me a line.

> *"We hate some persons because we do not know them; and will not know them because we hate them."*
> —Charles Caleb Colton

Enter the Voice of Reason Archives

Email me!

This site last updated: 11/20/21
*Visitors since this site was born: **9,699***

November 26, 2021

Yesterday was Thanksgiving. Boy, do the cooks here know how to make a turkey! It was just so much better than Mom's! It was all moist and just perfectly golden brown! No lumps at all in the mashed potatoes. And the pumpkin pie was absolutely to die for! I'm eating a piece right now and the smell of cinnamon and clove is making me drool.

Of course, maybe Mom is just a bad cook.

It was weird having Thanksgiving with a bunch of strangers. I don't even know who they all were. People from Congress, I think.

I was hoping Grandma and Grandpa could come, but I don't even think they were invited. We haven't seen them since moving here, which really stinks. But Mom says maybe we'll have them out for Christmas.

I wish my Dad's parents were still alive. I wonder what they were like. Mom says Dad is just like his dad was, so I guess I'd have liked him.

Christmas is only a month away, and I'm not even excited, yet. I guess because I'm homesick. It just won't be the same without being able to visit my friends and see what they got and show them what I got.

I hate not having any friends, here. Maybe Mom will let me go to a real school someday and not have to be tutored anymore. She says I'll get a better education with a tutor, and maybe she's right, but I'm not making any friends! That's important to me, even if it isn't to her.

Dad warned me that things would be really different after he was elected. I guess I didn't realize just how different he meant.

Date: December 22, 2021
To: jefferson_paine@voice_of_reason.com
From: eadams@atheistsUSA.org
Subject: Your wonderful site

Mr. "Paine":

Please accept my unabashed admiration of and gratitude for your incredible site and all your freethought efforts. I am amazed your "Voice" hasn't been reduced to digital dust by now, and hope this is not simply a temporary state.

I absolutely MUST speak with you privately. Please contact me soon. You can download my public key at http://cryptkeys.org/19366/. I'm sure your email is safe against hackers, but I don't think the same can be said for mine.

Looking forward to hearing from you.

E. Adams

Year Two

2022

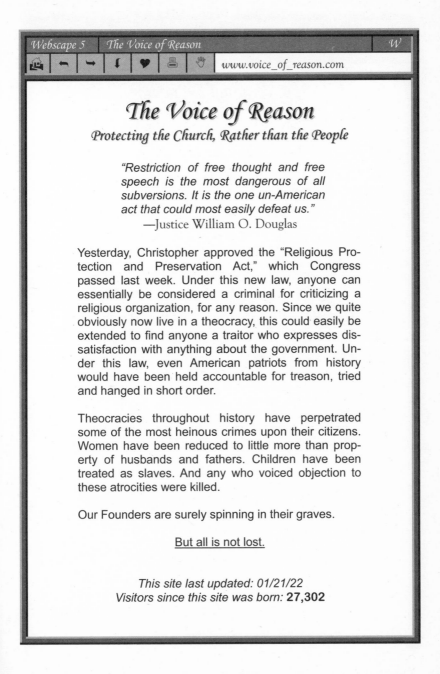

Webscape 5   The Voice of Reason   W

www.voice_of_reason.com

The Voice of Reason
Protecting the Church, Rather than the People

"Restriction of free thought and free speech is the most dangerous of all subversions. It is the one un-American act that could most easily defeat us."
—Justice William O. Douglas

Yesterday, Christopher approved the "Religious Protection and Preservation Act," which Congress passed last week. Under this new law, anyone can essentially be considered a criminal for criticizing a religious organization, for any reason. Since we quite obviously now live in a theocracy, this could easily be extended to find anyone a traitor who expresses dissatisfaction with anything about the government. Under this law, even American patriots from history would have been held accountable for treason, tried and hanged in short order.

Theocracies throughout history have perpetrated some of the most heinous crimes upon their citizens. Women have been reduced to little more than property of husbands and fathers. Children have been treated as slaves. And any who voiced objection to these atrocities were killed.

Our Founders are surely spinning in their graves.

But all is not lost.

This site last updated: 01/21/22
*Visitors since this site was born: **27,302***

The Freethought Underground

I put this site online to fight the propaganda of the wackos in the White House. But I'm way outgunned. There's no way I can keep up with the rhetoric constantly spewed out not only by Christopher, Sisco, and the conservatives in Congress, but by conservative radio and TV, and the many fundamentalists online who agree with them.

Sometimes, I feel totally hopeless in the face of such overwhelming odds. I'm mortified by the fact that the country I love is going down the drain. A lot of what's going on, I can't even believe! But maybe this is a common feeling. America is a land of extremes. For every ultra-conservative, there's supposedly a screaming liberal. So where are they? Are they all in the same state of disbelief? Are they stunned into inaction by all this crap? I wouldn't be surprised, but what will it take to snap them out of their stupor? Or is it already too late?

I am happy to say that there are those out there who remain true to the ideals of our Founders. They are The Freethought Underground, and they are traveling the country even now, educating people about our real history and assisting those in need of protection from our new theocratic dictatorship.

I have been asked to be their online recruiter, message center, and coordinator. For anyone interested in this, and willing to assist in a hands-on way, just contact me. I'll see to it that you're hooked up.

And if you encounter them, make sure you let them know their efforts are appreciated.

<u>Enter the Voice of Reason Archives</u>

<u>Email me!</u>

January 20, 2022

A year ago today, dad became President. It's weird. The year has flown by and dragged at the same time. It seems like just yesterday that we moved into the White House. But it seems like a million years ago that I last saw my friends back home.

Last night Mom and I talked about it. She says she's seen that I'm not very happy here. I told her how much I miss my friends. She said everyone eventually loses touch with their childhood friends. She says we might think that we'll be friends forever, but life gets in the way. For me, it's because Daddy was elected and we moved to Washington. We'll be here for four years at least. More likely eight. And she said that so many things change in eight years. By that time all my friends back home will be going off to college. And so will I.

She tried to make it seem not so bad by saying I'd make new friends in college and that those friends would be the ones I'd keep with me for the rest of my life. She told me how she lost touch with all her childhood friends after high school.

But I'm not her. I won't forget all my friends back in California. After our talk last night, I decided to write letters to my closest friends. I'll do it later this week, maybe. Or next week. I know they'll write back. When they see that I care enough to hand-write letters on paper to them, they'll know I think about them and they'll write back. I know it.

Date: 2/2/22
To: E. Nutt, CP BB Proj..
From: T. Bannister, CO BB Proj
Subject: VOR site

I see that your efforts have had less than desirable results. The website is not only still in existence, but is now acting as some sort of recruiting agent for these filthy atheists.

And its popularity is growing. It is easily found through search engines in any number of ways. I, myself, have located it quickly on searches for such things as government, religion, abortion, homosexuality, and others.

Isn't this the exact opposite of what we were aiming for?

I trust you will correct this situation immediately.

TB

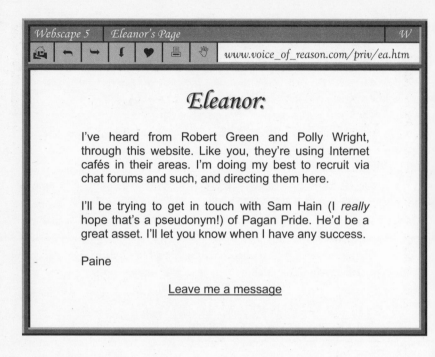

Webscape 5 *Eleanor's Page* *W*

www.voice_of_reason.com/priv/ea.htm

Eleanor:

I've heard from Robert Green and Polly Wright, through this website. Like you, they're using Internet cafés in their areas. I'm doing my best to recruit via chat forums and such, and directing them here.

I'll be trying to get in touch with Sam Hain (I *really* hope that's a pseudonym!) of Pagan Pride. He'd be a great asset. I'll let you know when I have any success.

Paine

Leave me a message

Dear Lindsay,

I haven't heard from you in a while, and so I thought I'd write you a real letter, instead of another email. I'm sorry I'm not allowed to have vid-vox here. It really stinks, but I can't do anything about it.

But aside from that, it's really cool living in the White House. Did you know that I can get brand new movies here? Even ones that haven't been in theaters, yet! The White House has its own theater! With popcorn and everything! It's awesome!

Dad is really busy, of course, but he says he's got a really big surprise for my birthday this year. That's great, but what I really want is to have a party with all my friends, just like we used to do all the time.

I miss all you guys, but especially you. I wish you could come visit. That would be fun. I'm writing to the whole gang. It will be great to hear back from you! Take care!

Love,

Mary

The Voice of Reason
Butler Blather

In her latest conservative tirade, right-wing political pundit Pam Butler said, *"Americans should stop whining about the so-called harshness of recently passed laws. We make them harsh in anticipation of being whittled down a little later on. It's no different than lawsuits which ask for outrageous sums of money in damages. The lawyers know the actual amount of the award will be less. It's whittled down in the bargaining process."*

I guess she hasn't been paying attention over the years. Many people said the same thing two decades ago, with regard to the Patriot Act. But it hardly got whittled down at all. And Patriot Act II followed with even more invasions of privacy, such as increased surveillance on US citizens, nationwide search warrants for non-violent acts, and the ability to suck information about citizens from businesses, 'net providers, even friends and family.

And in case Ms. Butler hasn't noticed, our policymakers aren't "bargaining" with anyone. What they command is what comes to pass. There hasn't been a major law passed in over a decade that has been challenged to the point of lessening its impact.

C'mon, Pam. You're not a stupid woman. But you're certainly arrogant in thinking that the rest of us aren't smart enough to see through your bullshit.

<u>Enter the Voice of Reason Archives</u>

<u>Email me!</u>

This site last updated: 03/18/22
*Visitors since this site was born: **39,443***

May 1, 2022

Dad's birthday surprise for me was that he invited the Sidestreet Girls to come here! I got to meet them, and they did a show for us in the East Room. They were awesome! My dad is the best dad in the universe!

I got a letter from Lindsay today. Finally. It's only been like two and a half months since I wrote to her. But nobody else has written back, so I guess I should be happy she answered at all. Except that her "letter" was barely more than a paragraph.

She thanked me for writing, told me she got her braces off, and said I should vid-vox her sometime.

Earth to Lindsay! I told you I'm not allowed to use vid-vox here!

Maybe she didn't really read my letter. Who knows? Who cares?

Well, me. I care. I care a lot, darn it.

Maybe Mom's right. Maybe I need to make new friends. But that's not easy, since I don't go to school.

I've been thinking more about making my own website. Maybe I can make friends online.

Webscape 5   *Mary's Corner of the Web*   *W*

www.webville.com/~merrymary

Welcome to
Mary's Corner of the Web

Hi! I'm Mary! Welcome to my site!

There's not much here, yet, but there will be in time.

You can read a little about me, <u>here</u>.

My lists of <u>favorites</u>.

Come again soon!

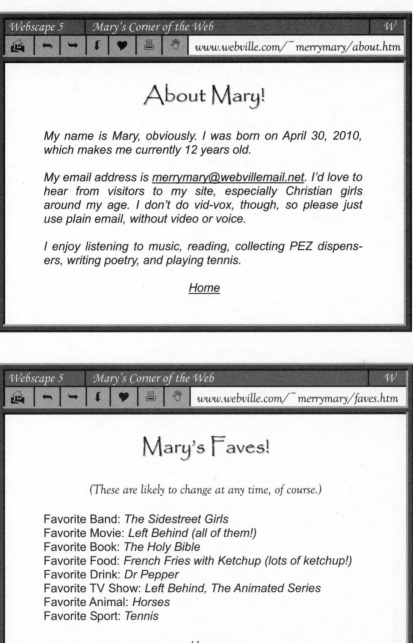

Webscape 5 — *Mary's Corner of the Web* — *W*

www.webville.com/~merrymary/about.htm

About Mary!

My name is Mary, obviously. I was born on April 30, 2010, which makes me currently 12 years old.

My email address is <u>merrymary@webvillemail.net</u>. I'd love to hear from visitors to my site, especially Christian girls around my age. I don't do vid-vox, though, so please just use plain email, without video or voice.

I enjoy listening to music, reading, collecting PEZ dispensers, writing poetry, and playing tennis.

Home

Webscape 5 — *Mary's Corner of the Web* — *W*

www.webville.com/~merrymary/faves.htm

Mary's Faves!

(These are likely to change at any time, of course.)

Favorite Band: *The Sidestreet Girls*
Favorite Movie: *Left Behind (all of them!)*
Favorite Book: *The Holy Bible*
Favorite Food: *French Fries with Ketchup (lots of ketchup!)*
Favorite Drink: *Dr Pepper*
Favorite TV Show: *Left Behind, The Animated Series*
Favorite Animal: *Horses*
Favorite Sport: *Tennis*

Home

May 24, 2022

I've been visiting that horrible Voice of Reason site some more. I hate the things he's saying about my dad. I wrote an email to him once, but never sent it. It was too mean and insulting, and I don't want to be that way, no matter what I think of his opinions.

Sometimes I wish I could tell people that President Christopher is my dad, and tell them how wonderful he is. If they only knew him, they'd see for themselves! But I can't. Mom and Dad went all freaky when I told them I put my own site online. But they looked at it, making sure I didn't have anything on there that would even hint at who I was, and then they calmed down.

Anyway, I thought about trying to bring this Jefferson Paine guy to Jesus, but maybe I should start with someone who's not quite so bad. I've been visiting chat rooms where atheists hang out. I always invite them to email privately with me so I can tell them about Jesus. But they never do. I can't figure that out. Why wouldn't anyone want to hear about something that'll give them eternal happiness and save them from hell?

Date: May 28, 2022
To: jefferson_paine@voice_of_reason.com
From: jec@anonymail.com
Subject: Re: Proposition

Mr. Paine:

I'm flattered at the offer of joining your little group, but I'm afraid I'm just swamped with my own activities. Certainly, I agree that your venture is a noble one, but my goals are more specific than your own. You know my work, after all. Sisco is my only concern right now. And I fear he'll eventually be yours, too.

By the way, did you catch his interview with MSNBC last night? He said, "I didn't get where I am today without a certain amount of sacrifice."

It's funny... When most people say that, they mean SELF-sacrifice. But he doesn't. Keep that in mind.

And keep up the great work, my friend.

Coop

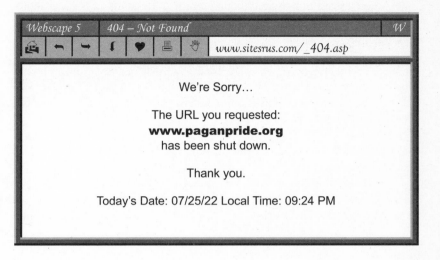

Date: July 26, 2022
To: jefferson_paine@voice_of_reason.com
From: autoresponder@sitemail9.com
Subject: Re: Are you still around?

THIS IS AN AUTORESPOND MESSAGE

The email address samhain@paganpride.org is no longer in service. We apologize for the inconvenience.

DO NOT REPLY TO THIS MESSAGE.
YOU WILL NOT RECEIVE A RESPONSE.

NPR: Eleanor Adams, thank you for being our guest today on National Public Radio. Now, you have a Doctorate in History from the University of Pennsylvania, is that correct?

Adams: Yes, that's right.

NPR: The infamous website, *The Voice of Reason*, is run by an individual going by the name of "Jefferson Paine." Are we correct in assuming the name is a combination of Thomas Jefferson, our third President, and Thomas Paine?

Adams: I think that's quite obvious, yes, and incredibly appropriate as a pseudonym for the person running this site. Jefferson gave us the terminology of "a wall of separation between church and state." He explained in a letter to the Danbury Baptists, who were concerned about the First Amendment, that its purpose was to keep government out of religion and religion out of government.

NPR: Jefferson also wrote the Declaration of Independence, of course.

Adams: He is credited with doing so, although there are some who believe the Declaration is actually the work of Thomas Paine. Or at least heavily influenced by him.

NPR: Interesting. So tell us about Thomas Paine.

Adams: Gladly, as he's one of my personal heroes. Paine was a contemporary of Jefferson's, and was greatly admired in his day by many, including Jefferson, Benjamin Franklin, and others. He gave our country its name, The United States of America. But due to his unkind criticism of the Bible, his name has not enjoyed the same recognition as his co-founders.

NPR: Didn't President Teddy Roosevelt refer to him as a "filthy little atheist?"

Adams: Sadly, yes. Paine was a truly great patriot and very influential in his time, if not exactly known for being the picture of personal hygiene. The ironic part of Roosevelt's condemnation of him, though, is that Paine wasn't an atheist, but a Deist.

NPR: And what is that, exactly?

Adams: A Deist believes in "nature's God," as opposed to the Biblical God. A Deist believes this deity created the earth and all natural laws, but does not believe anything can be known about it, and does not believe in any "holy" documents such as the Bible. Many of our country's founders were privately Deists, including our first four Presidents, though some, like Washington, put on an outward image of going to church in order to appease the masses.

NPR: Paine was a writer, as well.

Adams: Yes. He wrote and published many short pieces on liberty that were very well-received. His most popular work was titled "Common Sense." It sold over half a million copies, which was utterly remarkable for the time, considering the small population of our country. His was possibly the most audible voice in the fight for independence.

NPR: Pretty big names this fellow has adopted for himself. Pretentious?

Adams: Perhaps. But it'll be fun watching to see what he has to say. I know I'm looking forward to it!

NPR: And what of his role as recruiter for this "Freethought Underground?" Do you have any information on that?

Adams: Well, as I'm sure you've heard rumored, the Freethought Underground was, in fact, my idea. And I did ask this gentleman to act in the role of recruiter and "switchboard" for us.

NPR: Fascinating. And what do you see this Freethought Underground of yours doing?

Adams: Already we have reached thousands of people nationwide, explaining to them the dangers of the socio-political path our country is on. We're encouraging them to stand up for their rights, that's all.

NPR: Well. Best of luck to you on that front. And thank you for being our guest today.

Adams: Thank you for having me.

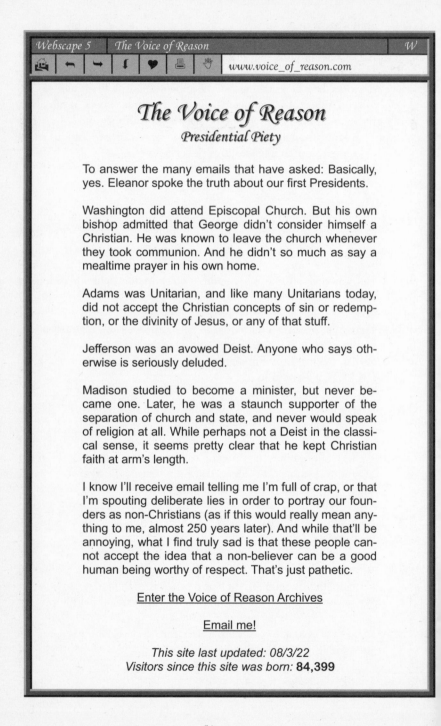

The Voice of Reason
Presidential Piety

To answer the many emails that have asked: Basically, yes. Eleanor spoke the truth about our first Presidents.

Washington did attend Episcopal Church. But his own bishop admitted that George didn't consider himself a Christian. He was known to leave the church whenever they took communion. And he didn't so much as say a mealtime prayer in his own home.

Adams was Unitarian, and like many Unitarians today, did not accept the Christian concepts of sin or redemption, or the divinity of Jesus, or any of that stuff.

Jefferson was an avowed Deist. Anyone who says otherwise is seriously deluded.

Madison studied to become a minister, but never became one. Later, he was a staunch supporter of the separation of church and state, and never would speak of religion at all. While perhaps not a Deist in the classical sense, it seems pretty clear that he kept Christian faith at arm's length.

I know I'll receive email telling me I'm full of crap, or that I'm spouting deliberate lies in order to portray our founders as non-Christians (as if this would really mean anything to me, almost 250 years later). And while that'll be annoying, what I find truly sad is that these people cannot accept the idea that a non-believer can be a good human being worthy of respect. That's just pathetic.

<u>Enter the Voice of Reason Archives</u>

<u>Email me!</u>

This site last updated: 08/3/22
Visitors since this site was born: **84,399**

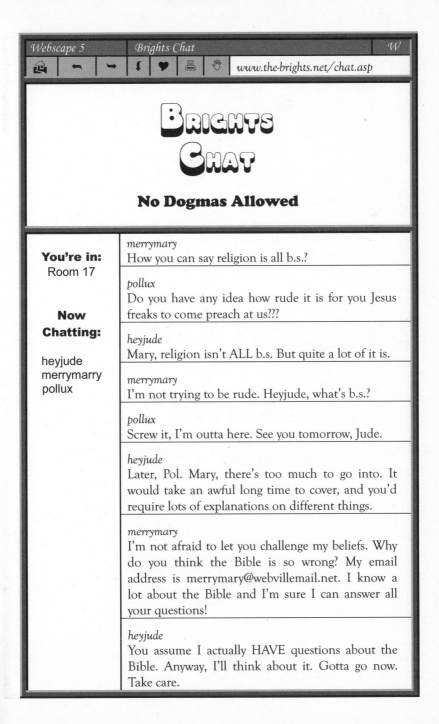

Date: August 4, 2022
To: jefferson_paine@voice_of_reason.com
From: ham@pigginpage.com
Subject: Your Page

Dude:

Your page rocks. Keep on keepin' on.

Your Friend,
Big Pig
http://www.pigginpage.com

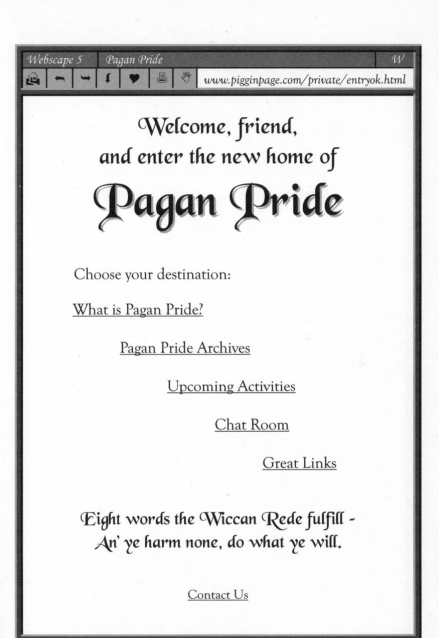

Webscape 5   Pagan Pride   W

www.pigginpage.com/private/entryok.html

Welcome, friend, and enter the new home of

Pagan Pride

Choose your destination:

What is Pagan Pride?

Pagan Pride Archives

Upcoming Activities

Chat Room

Great Links

Eight words the Wiccan Rede fulfill -
An' ye harm none, do what ye will.

Contact Us

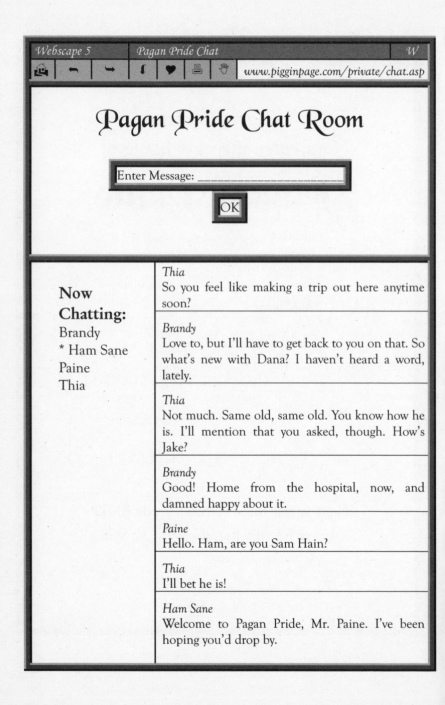

Webscape 5 — Pagan Pride Chat — W

www.pigginpage.com/private/chat.asp

Pagan Pride Chat Room

Enter Message: _____

OK

Now Chatting:
Brandy
* Ham Sane
Paine
Thia

Thia
So you feel like making a trip out here anytime soon?

Brandy
Love to, but I'll have to get back to you on that. So what's new with Dana? I haven't heard a word, lately.

Thia
Not much. Same old, same old. You know how he is. I'll mention that you asked, though. How's Jake?

Brandy
Good! Home from the hospital, now, and damned happy about it.

Paine
Hello. Ham, are you Sam Hain?

Thia
I'll bet he is!

Ham Sane
Welcome to Pagan Pride, Mr. Paine. I've been hoping you'd drop by.

Date: September 20, 2022
To: merrymary@webvillemail.net
From: heyjude@beatles4ever.ws
Subject: Re: I thought you were going to email me!

Mary:

Yes, you could say I'm a pretty big Beatles fan. Obviously, so are my parents. Good thing I like their music, or I might hate my name, huh?

Anyway, when we met online, I didn't really think you were serious in wanting me to "challenge your beliefs." So that's why I hadn't emailed you. But since you apparently do want me to, I will. (By the way, it's hard to believe you're only twelve! You sure don't sound it. I'm nineteen, incidentally.)

Okay. During our chat, I recall you saying that you consider the Bible to be literally true, free of errors or contradictions. My question is, "Why?"

Several hundred years ago, Church officials went through all the documents to be included in the Bible and decided which would stay and which would go. All were supposedly from authentic sources, so why not include them all? The answer is they simply didn't want some included.

NONE were regarded as the literal word of God, though. It's only been in the past couple centuries that some people got the notion that the Bible was literally true, every word of it. But why? If people a thousand years ago didn't think it was literally true, why do people today?

Not only is the Bible full of contradictions, it's full of questionable history, too. Take the story of the Jews being enslaved in Egypt. There's no archaeological evidence of a mass exodus from Egypt, no Egyptian historical accounts of it, and even more revealing, no intermingling of the Hebrew and Egyptian languages. If the Jews had been there for some time, their language would have some words of Egyptian origin, and vice versa. But neither is true. This is utterly unheard of. Whenever two societies are in close contact, it always happens. Always. Despite these serious flaws to the idea, Jews and Christians blindly believe the book of Exodus to be fact.

There is no record of a city called Nazareth during the first century, even by noted historians of that area. The modern Nazareth can't possibly be the city in the Bible, for many reasons.

Archaeology shows that the walls of Jericho did not come tumbling down all at once, but fell over many years, probably decades.

Show me a four-legged grasshopper. Show me a hare that chews its cud. Neither of these animals ever existed in nature, yet the Bible says they did. And these are just the tip of a very large iceberg, Mary.

You're putting absolute faith in a book undeserving of it.

Jude

Date: September 22, 2022
To: heyjude@beatles4ever.ws
From: merrymary@webvillemail.net
Subject: Literal Truth to the Bible

Jude:

Yes, I'm really twelve. And you're not the first to say I seem older. I guess it just has to do with the way I was raised. I'm an only child. I've gone to pretty strict private schools, where I was always expected to act a certain way. I think I've spent more time around adults than I have around kids my own age. I guess I'm one of those "sheltered" kids, but there's not a lot I can do about it. It's just how I am.

Anyway, about your email, I don't believe how naïve you are. The books that were not included in the Bible were thrown out because they weren't the word of God! Can't you see how obvious that is?

How do YOU know there has NEVER been a hare that chewed its cud, or a four-legged grasshopper? Just because we don't know of these things doesn't mean they didn't exist in the past. What are you basing your other statements on? One historian's ideas? One archaeologist's? Get real. Where's your proof? The Bible says it, so it's true. The Bible is an accurate historical document, and science backs it up 100%.

I've seen what some people say are contradictions in the Bible, but they're just people misunderstanding what the Bible says. The Bible is perfect. It doesn't have contradictions or mistakes.

And by the way, I've always considered it really arrogant that you atheists refer to yourselves as "Brights," as though only atheists can be smart. And you call Christians rude!

Mary

Date: September 30, 2022
To: merrymary@webvillemail.net
From: heyjude@beatles4ever.ws
Subject: Re: Literal Truth to the Bible

Mary:

Regarding Brights... First, we aren't just atheists. Anyone with a worldview based on reason without superstition may be considered a Bright. That would include lots more than just atheists.

The term was inspired by the period known as The Enlightenment, when reason made significant advances over superstition... as opposed to the Dark Ages, when it was pretty much the other way around.

As for arrogance, is it arrogant of conservatives to call themselves "the Right," implying that everyone else is "wrong"? No. It's understood that it has a different meaning. (Although certainly some conservatives do, in fact, view liberals as "wrong" on principle.) Ditto for "Bright." We're not saying everyone else is "dim." Lots of words have multiple meanings in our language, and you have to grasp the correct definition from the context. This is just another such case.

Regarding the Bible... It's clear to me that you have certain notions in your head that aren't going to change just because I say something contrary. And that's fine. I mean, you're still young, and at your age, I was in a non-questioning state of mind, too.

For that matter, I'm not especially trying to change your mind. All I'm trying to do, really, is make you see that you shouldn't accept things without questioning them.

We humans have a tendency to just accept as truth nearly anything our parents tell us. (Until we're teenagers, of course, when we suddenly know everything, and our parents have grown stupid beyond words. This reverses after a decade or so.)

My point is that you believe what you believe because it's the religion you were raised in, just as I did as a child, and countless others do, too. It could be years before you're to the point of saying to yourself, "Just because I've always believed this doesn't mean it's true."

Anyway, perhaps we'd better just slow down, okay?
Take care.

Jude

October 1, 2022

Is Jude making fun of me? Is that what he meant by his comments about being young, and thinking I know everything? (I'm almost a teenager.) I can't tell.

He's just wrong about my beliefs being only because I was raised that way. I'd believe in Jesus and God even if I'd been raised an atheist, like him.

I suppose he's right about one thing, though. Nothing he says will make any difference. My faith is strong, just like Uncle Gene's. Nothing will lead me astray.

Date: October 6, 2022
To: merrymary@webvillemail.net
From: heyjude@beatles4ever.ws
Subject: Re: You're wrong.

Mary:

You tell me that nothing could possibly change your mind, but I'm betting that if I were to say the same thing to you, you'd accuse me of being closed-minded.

Truth is, I CAN imagine certain things that could cause me to think my atheistic views might be mistaken. No one's ever been able to present me with any of these things, but still... they could one day show up.

But you tell me that nothing could ever convince you that there's no God. To me, that's being closed-minded... which is what we atheists are often accused of being.

Pretty ironic, huh?

By the way, I visited your website today. The Sidestreet Girls? Are you KIDDING???

You've definitely got to improve your musical tastes if we're going to talk about anything other than religion.

Jude

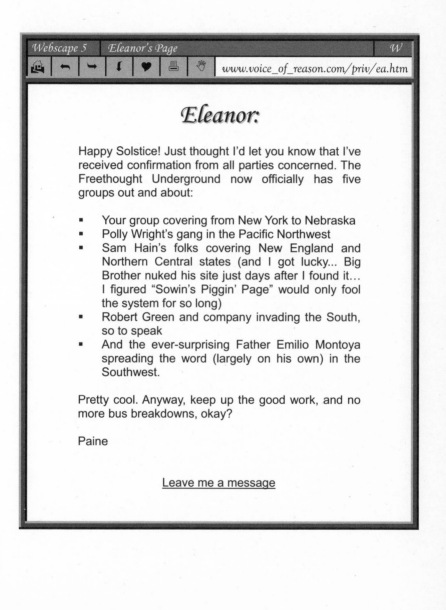

Eleanor:

Happy Solstice! Just thought I'd let you know that I've received confirmation from all parties concerned. The Freethought Underground now officially has five groups out and about:

- Your group covering from New York to Nebraska
- Polly Wright's gang in the Pacific Northwest
- Sam Hain's folks covering New England and Northern Central states (and I got lucky... Big Brother nuked his site just days after I found it... I figured "Sowin's Piggin' Page" would only fool the system for so long)
- Robert Green and company invading the South, so to speak
- And the ever-surprising Father Emilio Montoya spreading the word (largely on his own) in the Southwest.

Pretty cool. Anyway, keep up the good work, and no more bus breakdowns, okay?

Paine

<u>Leave me a message</u>

Year Three

2023

Little Rock—There was trouble in Liberty Park yesterday, as members of the Freethought Underground spoke out against government policies.

Eyewitnesses described a chilling scene. As the speaker, identified as former Atheists USA publicist Robert Green, spoke to the crowd, approximately a dozen members of the Ku Klux Klan arrived and circled the group.

One Klansman allegedly leveled a shotgun at Green as his cohorts forced Green's head into a noose and threw the loose end over a tree branch.

At this point, two as yet unidentified men in the crowd allegedly surprised the armed Klansman from behind, disarming him, and ordering the others to cease their actions.

Witnesses say one of the Klansmen continued in the attempt at lynching Green, at which point one of the men shot the Klansman in the leg.

As a firefight broke out, the crowd scattered in panic. Two more Klansmen were injured in the shooting. All three are scheduled to be released from Mercy Hospital tomorrow.

No one else was hurt.

As the Klansmen were driven off by the gunmen, the Freethought Underground, including Robert Green and his rescuers, escaped.

Little Rock Police warn that the two men are still at large, and are considered dangerous.

Further, they warn that the public should report to the police anyone claiming to be part of the Freethought Underground, for their own personal safety.

Washington—The House of Representatives will vote today on the controversial "Blasphemy Bill." The bill was introduced by New York Republican Bob Lackey, and would make blasphemy and heresy crimes punishable by law.

As written, the bill "Creates the crime of ridicule of religious beliefs or practices which is a class C felony; provides that a person is guilty of the crime when in a public place he/she holds up the deity or the religious beliefs of any religious class of people to ridicule or hatred or presents religious beliefs in an obscene, lewd, profane or lascivious manner." The definition of "ridicule" is defined in the bill thusly: "A person is guilty of ridicule of religious beliefs or practices when in a public place, he holds up the deity or the religious beliefs of any religious class of people, to ridicule or hatred. Furthermore, a person is guilty of religious ridicule when he presents the religious beliefs, practices, symbols, figures or objects of any religious class in an obscene, lewd, profane, or lascivious manner."

The above language is identical to another bill, originally put forth a quarter of a century ago by Senator Serphin R. Maltese of New York, with the only change being that Senator Maltese's bill labeled blasphemy a Class B misdemeanor. That bill was never passed.

House Democrats have voiced much opposition to the bill, as has the public, but if the expected partisan vote is received, the bill will pass.

The bill is also expected to pass the Republican dominated Senate, and the President has already voiced his support of the bill.

The Voice of Reason
Yes it Is! No it Isn't!

I know my readers appreciate irony as much as I do, so let me share some with you. The "Blasphemy Bill" is worded in such a way that it does not specify which religions may not be impugned.

And for as long as I can remember, lots of theists have been maintaining that atheism is a religion. Of course, it's not. But, they've insisted it is, in part, I think, because if they can get away with saying "Everyone is religious," they'll be more apt to get away with undermining the separation of govern-ment and religion. (Or at least, that was probably the reason at one time. Rather beside the point, now.)

Anyway, the irony here is that all those who've so adamantly proclaimed that atheism is a religion will now just as adamantly be proclaiming the contrary. For if atheism were considered a religion, it would be illegal for them to say derogatory things about it.

Of course, atheism isn't a religion, any more than agnosticism is, or secularism. Or science, for that matter, even though some loonies out there think it is. Nope. Any and all of these will still be prime tar-gets for the epithets of the closed-minded.

But at least I'll get to chuckle at the fact that so many of these boneheads will now have to choke down their own words.

Enter the Voice of Reason Archives

Email me!

This site last updated: 02/10/23
*Visitors since this site was born: **95,445***

13 February 2023

Hard to believe it's been more than two years since I took office. They've positively flown by. I had no idea it would be like this. We've accomplished a lot, but there is still so much to do. I hadn't honestly expected to run for a second term, but now I think it's a necessity. Four years. Who can accomplish everything they need to in such a short span of time?

I regret that my family life is suffering, though. Sarah keeps herself busy with various projects and groups. We hardly see each other. And Mary... well, she spends most of her time online. Were it not for the fact that it's a much safer place, now, I'd be very worried about that. Still... I do wish she would engage in less passive activities. I know she plays a lot of tennis, so she's getting enough exercise. But her online activities won't really make her use her brain. That's the tragedy.

February 21, 2023

I must not understand something. The "Blasphemy Bill" that Dad told me about... well, it just doesn't make sense to me.

I mean, people shouldn't be allowed to say bad things about God or Jesus. I get that part. But there are so many religions out there that are wrong. It seems to me that this law could apply to anyone speaking out against them!

Or even someone speaking out against Satanism! That's a religion! How could they pass a law that would make it illegal to condemn Satan worship?

I mentioned this to him, and he looked at me as though I were speaking in Japanese or something. It was like he'd never thought of that at all.

He told me not to worry about it, that everyone knew it only meant Christianity.

Well, obviously not, if I didn't know it.

Date: March 18, 2023
To: heyjude@beatles4ever.ws
From: merrymary@webvillemail.net
Subject: Re: The Greatest Band in the World!

Jude:

Okay, I give up! I'll listen to some Beatles songs, I promise. You've been bugging me about this since last fall! Quit it, already!

And you don't need to send me any sound files. My mom has one of their CDs, from like a hundred years ago or something. It's got a black and white cover. Like a drawing of their heads, I think. I'll listen to it. Now stop pestering me about them! But they're NOT "the greatest band in the world," I can guarantee you that.

Let's go back to something from our first emails. I promise to take you seriously this time.

You said one time that the Bible had other inaccuracies beyond the ones you mentioned then. So what are they? Give me something that really shows me that the Bible can't be literally true, word for word.

I don't think you can, but I'm willing to listen. So go for it.

Mary

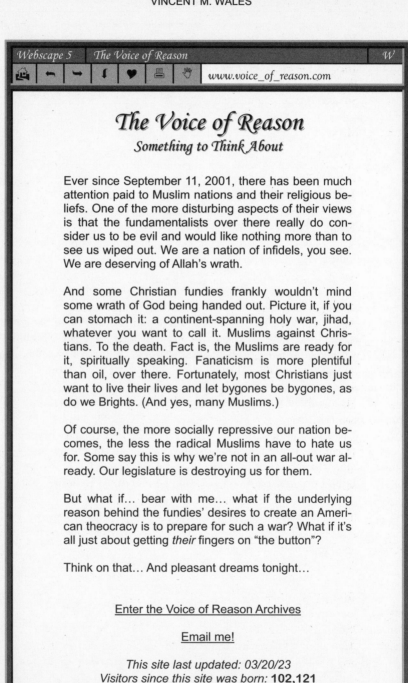

Date: March 20, 2023
To: merrymary@webvillemail.net
From: heyjude@beatles4ever.ws
Subject: Easter Challenge

Mary:

First of all, REVOLVER is an awesome album. If not their best, then darn close to it. You'll love it. And it's not a hundred years old. Well over fifty, but not a hundred.

Second, okay... I'm willing to dive back into the religion thing if you want to, though I've enjoyed just chatting with you about other things, too. As it happens, I do have something that fits what you're asking for. And it's timely, too.

Easter is approaching, and I'm sure you'll go to church and hear some sappy sermon about the sacrifice of Jesus. (Though if he was the son of God, or God incarnate, how is giving up life in human form any kind of real sacrifice at all?)

By the way, did you know that Easter was originally a pagan holiday? It was called "Oestre." Yet another holiday Christians "appropriated." I don't expect you to take my word for it. Look it up.

Anyway, here's a challenge for you. I want you to take your Bible and reference the story of the crucifixion and resurrection. All versions of it... the four Gospels, plus Acts and I Corinthians. The sum total is something like 165 verses. Not that much.

Then I want you to write your own chronological account of it, from start to finish, using details from the different texts. Here's the tricky part: You MUST use every bit of information given in the Bible, omitting nothing. Every detail given in these verses must be present in your account.

If you can put together a time line that makes sense, without contradiction or inconsistency, I will personally go to church with you on Easter Sunday. Good luck. You'll need it.

And just because you're soon to be a Beatlemaniac...

Today in Beatles history:
1969:   John and Yoko married in Gibraltar.
1967:   "Strawberry Fields Forever" awarded Gold status.
1964:   "Can't Buy Me Love" released as single in U.K., having already sold over two million copies in pre-orders, an instantaneous Gold disc.

Jude

March 23, 2023

I don't get it. I've been trying to answer Jude's challenge for two days, and I can't seem to put it together in an order that makes sense. The different books don't agree about a few things. Like who was at the cave when the women showed up, or even which women they were, or if the stone was in front of the doorway or not, or when or where certain things happened, plus lots of other stuff.

One book mentions earthquakes and dead saints rising and walking around, but the others don't. That's not a contradiction, but you'd think the other books would talk about it. That's pretty big stuff! Why wouldn't they include it?

I know Uncle Gene could figure this out, but he's not here. I asked Dad about it, but he said he was too busy to play with some stupid atheist's trivia. Mom's not much help, of course. I know the Bible better than she does.

As for that "Oestre" thing, I found lots of listings online about a pagan holiday called that, but it's just got to be a coincidence that it fell around the same time as Easter. Why he thinks this means early Christians stole the holiday is too weird for me to figure out.

And saying Jesus didn't really sacrifice anything is just totally stupid. He gave his life! What more can you give?

This guy is just so dumb! And weird! What's with this "Today in Beatles history" stuff? What a freak.

I hope Uncle Gene gets back soon.

6 April 2023

Today I actually heard one of the radio folks — I can't recall which one; I think it's the attractive blonde who sometimes is a guest on Gene's show — actually agree that we should have a holy war, just invade the Middle East and convert all the survivors to Christianity.

Sometimes I'm embarrassed to share the label "Christian" with such people. No true Christian would ever support such an idea.

The Voice of Reason
A True Victimless Crime

Another nail has been pounded into the coffin containing Freedom of Speech. The "Blasphemy Bill" passed the Senate yesterday, after a last-minute amendment, and St. Paul sure isn't going to veto it. Now anyone criticizing Judeo-Christianity can be nailed with a minor felony. (No crime to say nasty things about other religions, though.) It's funny… All this fuss being made about a being that doesn't even exist!

Hey, guys... THERE IS NO GOD! Ignorant, superstitious people invented gods, and religion was created by self-serving, power-hungry fools such as you. Jesus? Probably fictitious, but even if real, certainly not a deity. Just one of the dime-a-dozen "messiahs" of 2000 years ago. The God of the Bible is a malicious, capricious monster, and Jesus a hypocrite. Neither of them are the examples of love and morality that most people claim. The "good book" is one of the vilest tomes ever written.

There. That victimless "crime" would get me thrown in jail, if the powers that be had any idea of who I am. What a pity that they don't.

> *"One man's religion is another man's belly laugh."*
> –Robert A. Heinlein

<u>Enter the Voice of Reason Archives</u>

<u>Email me!</u>

This site last updated: 04/29/23
Visitors since this site was born: **132,678**

30 April 2023

So much controversy this new law has generated! And the loudest of it from outside the U.S.

Those Europeans... I swear I'll never understand them. Even the most conservative European government is to the left of the Democrats. Such a festering hole of sin it's become.

It's like they've gone communist. They have a socialist healthcare policy, socialist education policy (even through college), subsidized newspapers and other media, and they spend probably fifty percent more per capita than we do on social programs.

Of course, I'm not blind to the fact that they generally have lower unemployment rates than we do, and they positively spoil their workers. Five weeks of vacation to start. Huge retirement rewards. Et cetera and so on.

And they haven't been involved in any military actions since the last of them pulled out of the war in the Middle East.

I suppose that's what galls me more than anything about these liberal European nations. They left us holding the bag on that one. They don't see how important the ongoing War on Terror is.

Well, that's not quite true, either. They just disagree with our methods of fighting it. And to a degree, I understand their point of view. But I refuse to be the President who loses that particular war. It may have begun two decades ago, under someone else's watch, but I'll not be remembered for making twenty-two years of fighting in vain.

I just wish it were easier to lift the veil of ignorance from the eyes of so many in the world. How can they think it should be legal to ridicule God? Nothing should be more sacrosanct than His name, His image.

Returning America to righteousness has always been, and always will be, my foremost duty.

A close second is family duty. Tomorrow is Mary's birthday, and I nearly forgot! How could I do that? And she'll be a teenager, no less.

Running a country, I think I can handle. But raising a teenaged daughter? God help me.

Date: May 14, 2023
To: merrymary@webvillemail.net
From: heyjude@beatles4ever.ws
Subject: You still there?

Mary:

Gee... Almost two months, Mary. Easter came and went. And since I didn't get invited to church, I have to assume you're having some problems.

I figured you would, of course, because the challenge I gave you is an impossible one to win. I'm guessing that's what you've discovered.

I didn't figure you'd quit emailing, though. What's up? (Oh, and what did you think of REVOLVER?)

       Jude

Date: May 15, 2023
To: heyjude@beatles4ever.ws
From: merrymary@webvillemail.net
Subject: Re: You still there?

Jude:

I'm sorry I didn't reply before. I didn't mean to be rude. I am having trouble. I admit it. But I'm only thirteen. (Yes, I had a birthday since our last emails.) My uncle is the real Bible expert, and he'll be back in town this weekend, so if you don't mind, I'd like to get his help in this. I'm sure he'll be able to do it in no time, flat. So just hold on until then.

As for the Beatles... Well, they're better than I expected. Some of the stuff sounded like oldies, but some of it almost seemed fresh. I didn't expect that.

I know you like the trash Jefferson Paine puts on his site, but I think he should be put in jail for the rest of his life, once we find out who he is.

My dad was talking to me about something he said last month, about Christians wanting a holy war. It's stupid! It's not Christian! How can that dummy think we believe in such things?

And he said Jesus was probably fictitious! How can anyone think that? There's more proof that Jesus was real than there was that Napoleon was!

       Mary

SISCO: Thank you for the warm welcome, and for joining me once again on this final evening of my visit here at Penn State. It's heartening to see so many fine young souls concerned about the future of our nation and wanting to do something about the evils that threaten it.

Tonight's topic will be one of the most pernicious of evils... one that has been around for centuries, but never so flagrantly as in recent years. Until the liberal "free love" mentality of the sixties, it was considered a shameful thing, something you never allowed others to know.

I'm talking, of course, about homosexuality.

Homosexuality is a sin, as I'm sure you're all aware. But that hasn't stopped it. There is talk of a federal law making homosexuality illegal. And while I endorse this, I am not naïve enough to believe this will stop it, either. It is not enough to attach a penalty to something. We must educate. We must make our youngsters aware that homosexuality is not something to be "experimented" with. That is why I'm here. To help you understand.

(Unseen male): No, you're not.

[Sisco stops. He squints against the lights, peering at the audience.]

SISCO: Yes, I am. It is important to understand that homosexuality is the product of Satan, and will lead you straight to hell.

(Unseen male): Rubbish! You're here to justify your corrupt actions.

[Sisco pauses again. He motions to security guards, who move forward. The heckler from the crowd stands. Recognizing him, Sisco motions for the guards to stop. The man walks to the stage and climbs the stairs. He stands facing Sisco, who places the microphone in a stand and allows the man to join him.]

SISCO: Ladies and Gentlemen, it appears we have a... special guest. Father Emilio Montoya of the New Anglican Church.

MONTOYA: Thank you, but you neglected a more recent affiliation.

SISCO: Which is?

MONTOYA: The Freethought Underground.

[Sisco's eyes widen and he stammers for a moment.]

SISCO: So the rumors are true. You assist these atheists?

MONTOYA: While many of the Freethought Underground deny God's existence, they care deeply about their fellow man, and have no desire to see them persecuted. This pleases the Lord.

SISCO: The only persecution going on is against those who offend the Lord. *This* pleases Him, I would say!

MONTOYA: Yes, *you* would. But you're the one doing the persecuting.

SISCO: I am but one of many doing the Lord's work.

MONTOYA: So said Hitler. Do you think the millions of dead Jews, atheists, homosexuals, and others would agree with him?

SISCO: Hitler was not doing the Lord's work, Father. He was a vile atheist who murdered any who opposed him.

MONTOYA: In my less educated days, I agreed with you. But it is impossible to read Hitler's writings, to hear his speeches, and not realize he was a believer, however misguided, nor to admit the likelihood that he honestly felt he was doing Christ's will. It is a great shame to know that the churches of the time did little to stop such a madman, and indeed, some aided him. All Christian sects today therefore bear some guilt over the Holocaust. I would hate to see future generations of your denomination carrying another similar guilt, Reverend.

SISCO: What? Preposterous. And just why would they?

MONTOYA: Because you and your kind are driving this country toward another holocaust. You insist that yours are the only correct views. What of free will? If one chooses to disobey God, or deny His existence, you and I may grieve for them. But it is not our place to forbid them that God-given right.

SISCO: It is our God-given responsibility to save those misguided souls, Father. Or have you forgotten that?

MONTOYA: I have forgotten nothing. It is you who seem to have forgotten that you and I cannot "save" those souls. We can counsel, and we can guide. But we cannot save. That is up to the individual. You are not saving, Reverend. You are coercing.

SISCO: Is not a little coercion worthwhile, if a soul spends eternity in heaven instead of hell?

MONTOYA: It is a sad truth that unethical methods been regularly used by Christians since the apostle Paul, who endorsed the use of deception in converting people to Christianity. But why not answer the question yourself? Put yourself in the place of those you are perse... sorry... those you are "saving."

SISCO: I cannot, sir, for I am not a sinner.

MONTOYA: We are all sinners.

SISCO: Yes... of course. I meant to say that I am not committing any sins that are illegal.

MONTOYA: Then you cannot answer the question, and cannot know whether your efforts are worthwhile or not.

[Montoya faces the audience.]

           My friends, Reverend Sisco and I share some common beliefs, but differ in how we believe they should be applied. The New Anglican Church does not endorse laws against sins that harm only the sinner. While my faith tells me homosexuality is unnatural, I do not agree that it is evil, and certainly not sinful. No one should be forbidden the opportunity of making that personal choice.

SISCO: Then you betray the will of God.

MONTOYA: The will of God, as I understand it, is for His creations to be happy and treat each other nicely. Reverend, how many homosexuals do you think are present tonight?

SISCO: I would hope none. These appear to be *intelligent* young men and women.

MONTOYA: Then you are oblivious to the truth of human nature. Statistics dictate that one out of every eight of these students is not heterosexual, in one form or another. Your laws and damning rhetoric cannot change that. All you are doing is forcing these people back into the closet, back into a world of shame. Back into a prison-like existence.

SISCO: We are cleansing the nation of abominations in the eyes of God.

MONTOYA: Reverend Sisco, if I were to cleanse this nation of those I feel are abominations in the eyes of God, you would not be standing here.

[Sisco stammers again, while equal amounts of clapping and booing erupt from the audience. Montoya addresses the audience]

My friends, do not believe for a moment that there is only one way to heaven, or one way to properly live your lives. People like Reverend Sisco are interested only in their narrow-minded concepts of how the world should be, and have no true anchor in reality. If you value freedom of choice, freedom of will, you will not fall into the trap of fundamentalism. You will join those of us who oppose...

[Security ushers Montoya off the stage.]

Date: May 20, 2023
To: merrymary@webvillemail.net
From: heyjude@beatles4ever.ws
Subject: Question

Mary:

I hope your uncle has safely returned from his trip. While he ponders the question you couldn't handle, here's one just for you:

You go to a restaurant with two friends, both of whom smoke. You know that one of your friends doesn't smoke in the restaurant because it's illegal, and the other wouldn't do so even if it were allowed, because she knows it's inconsiderate of others. Which friend is more "moral" in this scenario? The first one, just because she obeys the law? Or the second one, because she takes her fellow humans into consideration? Which one shows more morality, in your opinion? Is it even "moral" to do "good" just because you're told to, out of fear of punishment?

As for Christians and holy wars, you really need to read your Bible. The Old Testament is full of wars against unbelievers, waged on God's express order. Those today who wish for the same are only going by what God has wanted in the past.

Believe it or not, there are many historians who do not feel that Jesus was actually a real person who walked the earth. The idea that there is more evidence of his existence than that of Napoleon is ridiculous. Outside of the New Testament, there is virtually zero corroborating evidence that he lived. First century historians who lived in that area and wrote about the region extensively do not mention him... except for a couple examples that are accepted by biblical historians to be later insertions by Christian apologists, or hearsay that only referenced the followers of Christ, rather than Jesus himself.

As for Jefferson Paine, while I may not agree with everything he says, I see no reason he should be imprisoned. Why do you think he should be?

Jude

Date: May 21, 2023
To: heyjude@beatles4ever.ws
From: merrymary@webvillemail.net
Subject: Re: Question

Jude:

Yes, my uncle is back, but he's in a really bad mood. I think something bad happened on his trip, but I don't know what. I guess I'll have to work on your Easter thing myself, but I really am confused by it.

About Jefferson Paine-in-the-Butt, I think he should be jailed because he's telling so many lies... about the President, about the Bible, about darn near everything. He even lied about science, saying evolution is a fact. What baloney. If evolution is so true, why isn't it being taught in schools anymore? Why didn't it stand up to creationism? Okay, so lying isn't a crime, but it is a sin. He'll burn in hell, and that's good enough for me.

As for the Old Testament, you're right, but you're forgetting something. Jesus changed the old laws. Now it's "turn the other cheek," instead of "an eye for an eye." The old laws, including death for unbelievers, don't apply anymore. Jesus said so.

And you're wrong about evidence outside of the Bible for the existence of Jesus. LOTS of historians wrote about him! Tacitus, Suetonius, and especially Josephus! We learned this in Sunday School, Jude. That's how common knowledge this is!

About your morality question, I think I see what you're getting at. You want me to say that the friend who doesn't smoke because it's inconsiderate to others is being more moral than the other. And it's true that we should put others before ourselves. The Bible says so. And now you want me to say, "Golly, I guess obeying the word of God isn't really moral behavior. People who are good 'just because' are more moral than those who blindly follow God's word."

But I'm not going to say that. The Bible also says that we are to put God first in our hearts, even before others. So obeying the word of God is totally different than obeying a regular human law. You can't compare the two. To obey the Lord is moral, honorable, and good. To obey human law isn't anything other than being a law-abiding citizen.

If the Supreme Court hadn't kicked God out of the classroom and made it illegal to pray in public schools, more people would understand this.

Mary

83

May 21, 2023

Tonight I prayed for God to help me. Jude's question about morality made me think of even more questions. Why is obeying the word of God "moral," when my understanding of the word would make me think the other smoker is truly the more moral? And if that's true, then why doesn't that apply to the word of God?

The Bible says to love our neighbors as ourselves. If we love someone, we treat them with respect. Smoking in front of them isn't respectful.

Uncle Gene's answer was pretty much the same as the one I emailed to Jude. It didn't sound any better coming from him.

I prayed to God for understanding about this. I hope He answers me soon. Jude's questions are just too hard! I can't answer them. I need God to tell me the answers.

Part of me wants to stop emailing with Jude. I wonder sometimes if he is not really a tool of Satan, tempting me to lose my faith. Mom is right... you never know who you're online with.

I'll pray to God for an answer to that, too.

Things here at home (and even after two years, it still feels weird to call the White House "home") aren't very fun. I almost never get to spend any kind of time with Dad. It's not like it used to be back in California, when we'd play games together and watch movies all the time. I can't remember when the last time we had a real conversation was.

Mom and I have never been as close as me and Dad, and that hasn't changed much. And even she doesn't have a lot of time, either. She's involved with different groups and is away from home almost as often as Dad.

I miss my friends, but I guess I really can't even call them that, anymore. I haven't heard from any of them in months. They don't email. They never call. They never return my calls, and only answer my emails with snippets.

I just want some friends! I just want someone to talk to! Is that too much to ask?

Date: May 22, 2023
To: merrymary@webvillemail.net
From: heyjude@beatles4ever.ws
Subject: Creation and Evolution

Mary:

I figured these topics would come up sooner or later. Let's start with why evolution isn't being taught in schools.

Fundamentalists have always been deeply offended at the entire notion of biological evolution, because evolution explains the existence of humans without the necessity of divine creation.

In earlier decades, they tried like crazy to get "scientific creationism" taught in public schools alongside evolution. Their argument consisted of saying, "Evolution is only a theory, so let's teach other theories, too."

The thing is, in science, "theory" means something entirely different than the word does in everyday usage. Gravity is a theory, too, but this doesn't mean that it's just a vague idea. In science, a theory is an explanation, supported by significant (sometimes overwhelming) evidence, of how and why things happen.

No one, for example, doubts that gravity exists. But the theory of how it works is constantly being refined. So it is with evolution. The evidence is monumental, and there is no question that it happens, but the explanation of exactly how it works is amended with every new bit of information that comes along. The same holds true for many, many scientific theories.

But it would be easier to sell sand to an Arab than to get creationists to accept this, since it ruins their whole "it's just a theory" argument.

On the other hand, the Supreme Court DID realize the truth about the definition and ruled, rightly, that creationism is a religious belief, not scientific in any way. As such, it had no place in public schools.

So then the creationists had to change their tactics. Since they couldn't get creationism taught in the schools, they decided to get evolution thrown out. And their method of accomplishing this rested on trying to poke holes in the theory of evolution in an attempt to prove it bogus.

One of their "points" was familiar: "evolution is only a theory." Only this time they weren't saying it to the Supreme Court, but to parents (who, generally, don't understand the distinction and certainly don't understand the science behind evolution). With this approach, they were much more successful.

The layperson hasn't really got a grasp of what evolution is, after all. It's a complex science, and can't really be understood properly without a basic understanding of other sciences, too, including biology and chemistry. And as you know, the U.S. doesn't have a good track record of scientific education.

Of course, scientists themselves are partly to blame for what happened. Scientists take evolution for granted. Only an idiot would not believe it, given the overwhelming evidence, they say. But they forget that the average citizen hasn't seen this overwhelming evidence. The average citizen, in fact, is lucky to understand that the earth revolves around the sun, and not vice versa. So when the shit hit the fan, scientists were caught totally unprepared, and their efforts to bring understanding to the public were too little, too late. The next thing we knew, it was back in the courts, and things went differently this time.

Before I even entered high school, evolution had been relegated to only being taught at the college level. Sure, some private high schools taught it, but they were few and far between. In public schools, not only was it not taught, it was ridiculed.

How can a scientific fact be ridiculed? Well, in addition to getting fundamentalists on school boards, they also urged many of their clan to enter the field of education. Specifically, to become science teachers. (With the horrible teacher shortage of recent decades, it was all too easy.) So now we have biology teachers telling their students about "created kinds" and "random macro-evolution," and other non-scientific terms. Never mind that no creationist can give a scientific explanation of what a "kind" is, or admit that "macro-evolution" and "micro-evolution" are fundamentally the same thing.

They talk of how there are "no transitional fossils" to be found. Archaeopteryx? It's not a transition between reptile and bird, they insist. It's fully formed, as anyone can see! It's just a bird with scales and teeth! Creationists evidently expect a transitional to be some sort of weird, half-formed creature. But evolution doesn't produce such things.

And when shown an animal that clearly was an intermediate, they'll often call it a hoax, even when multiple fossils of the same creature were found, over hundreds of years, and across several continents. Conspiracy theorists have nothing on creationists.

Or else they insist that there are still missing links. In a way, showing them transitional fossils only gives them more ammunition. For if you have animal "a" and animal "b" with animal "c" as a transitional, now you have two gaps instead of one! You have a gap between "a" and "c" as well as between "b" and "c" instead of just between "a" and "b." Nutty. Just nutty.

Creationists will say things like, "a kangaroo doesn't give birth to a chicken." They feel that if such an event would happen, it would prove evolution to be true, and nothing less ever would. This is ironic, since if such an event did happen, not only would it blow big, bloody holes in the theory of evolution, it would be good evidence that something miraculous might be afoot.

Evolution would never imply that a kangaroo could give birth to a chicken. Evolution simply doesn't work that way. But you can't tell this to a creationist. They have their own warped ideas of what the theory of evolution does and does not say, virtually none of which is grounded in fact.

In short, creationists never have understood, and probably never will understand, what evolution is and what it isn't. Because they don't want to.

But what about creationism, you ask? Well, I already mentioned that they can't explain exactly what a "kind" is, but the truly hilarious part is that they can't even offer up a working Theory of Creation. They can't do this because the entire "theory of creation" is summed up thusly: "God dunnit."

There is absolutely no science involved in the concept of creationism. None whatsoever. It is purely, 100%, religious conjecture.

Despite this, Creationists claim up and down that science supports the idea of creationism. Don't ask me how they can do this with a straight face, because it's a bald-faced lie. There is absolutely no scientific evidence to support the notion of the existence of a god, let alone the idea that this god created life on earth.

We could go on and on about how wrong creationism is and how much evidence there is to support evolution. In fact, there's no way I could even present to you all the evidence in support of evolution. Not in my entire lifetime. But this should at least illustrate how evolution came to be kicked out of the schools, and why creationism shouldn't be taught in its place.

Now to quickly address the whole Jesus thing...

You have to realize that neither Tacitus nor Suetonius actually wrote about Jesus. They wrote about CHRISTIANS. Big difference. In other words, they were only repeating the hearsay that Christians were spreading. Neither of them had any first-hand knowledge of Jesus.

And as for Josephus, biblical scholars are almost unanimous in agreeing that his passage about Jesus was an insertion by a later Christian apologist. The writing style isn't the same as the rest of the work, and (here's the real kicker) no version of his writings prior to the 4th century contain the passage about Jesus! Clearly, it was added later, just one of many deceptions committed in the name of spreading Christianity.

Regarding your assertion that Jesus wiped out the old laws... in the book of Matthew, Jesus says, "Think not that I am come to destroy the law or the prophets: I am not come to destroy, but to fulfill. For verily I say unto you, till heaven and earth pass, one jot or one tittle shall in no wise pass from the law till all be fulfilled."

So much for doing away with the edicts of the Old Testament.

Gotta sleep now, but tomorrow: the Supreme Court and Prayer.

Jude

Date: May 23, 2023
To: merrymary@webvillemail.net
From: heyjude@beatles4ever.ws
Subject: School Prayer

Mary:

Sorry I didn't tackle this yesterday, but I was up late doing the evolution email. I need my beauty sleep. Anyway, I hate to point out your errors, but the Supreme Court did NOT make it "illegal to pray in public schools." They simply ruled it unconstitutional to force or coerce students into hearing another's prayer. No "captive audience" scenario, in other words.

If prayers are done over the P.A. system or led by teachers or students at the front of the class, children have no choice but to hear them. They're required to be in school, so this is a captive audience. Children who objected were often given the option of leaving the room. But kids doing so would be subjected to stigmatization from his/her peers. (Kids can be mean, I'm sure you realize.) And since no kid should have to be subjected to that, this was not an acceptable solution.

Ironically, one of the events that helped the religious "right" more than anything in recent decades was a similar decision. More than 20 years ago, a California court ruled that the words "under God" in the Pledge of Allegiance were unconstitutional, because the words themselves effectively made the Pledge into a prayer, and when the Pledge was recited, school children were again captive audiences. The Pledge therefore was unquestionably in violation of the First Amendment. (By the way, the Pledge was written by a minister. And even he didn't deem it necessary to insert "under God" into it. So it's not like removing it would be hurting the Pledge at all.)

Naturally, the religious right practically foamed at the mouth in outrage. They, like so many people today, didn't care about the rights of anyone beyond themselves. They couldn't see that these words really did create a problem for the millions of Americans who don't believe in any gods.

Many of those who defended the Pledge thought they were defending patriotism. But in my mind, I can't see how forcing kids to pledge allegiance to a nation "under God" is at all patriotic.

Of course, atheist and other Bright organizations of the age stepped up to support the decision. But their voices were barely heard above the outrage of the politicians and the general public. The decision came less than a year after the terrorist attacks on the World Trade Center and the Pentagon, and the mixing of patriotism and religion was still strong. This just put things right over the top. The religious right went absolutely ballistic from then on in trying to make "religious freedom" a right only Christians could enjoy, despite the fact that the U.S. was, and is, the most religiously diverse nation on Earth.

The case went all the way to the U.S. Supreme Court., and after the case was heard, the Court took months to come to a decision. And the decision was to dismiss the case, thus overturning the California court's decision. But the very idea that such a case could make it to the highest court in the land served to galvanize the religious right even more.

When the plaintiff endeavored to get the case reopened, his opponents said he was attempting to foist his personal views on the nation. At the time, children weren't required to say "under God," or even to say the Pledge if they didn't want to. They claimed this was a balanced approach, which protected the rights of individuals and vast majority of the American public.

This, of course, utterly missed the point, completely ignored the whole peer pressure/stigmatization aspect. And it was bullcrap, anyway, for all the reasons I've been saying. The only balanced approach would've been to remove "under God" from the Pledge.

Anyway, getting back to the earlier Supreme Court decision... In the decades that followed, religious conservatives blamed nearly every evil in society on what they viewed as God having been "kicked out" of the schools. But in truth, children were able to pray quietly to themselves any time they wished! Before classes began, during lunch, study halls, between classes, and of course, during tests. But silent, private prayer wasn't what these people wanted. They wanted prayers to be spoken over the public address systems every morning, and for the students to recite it along with the loudspeakers.

So when the California court's decision was made, it gave them the chance to say, "This has gone far enough, and we're going to stop it!" Given the nation's emotional climate at the time, it wasn't difficult for religious organizations to convince schools and courts that concessions had to be made. They convinced them that it was okay for student-led religious activities to be allowed, even if school figures were really the ones directing their actions. If the students wanted it, who should deny them?

Students would gather around the flagpole before classes began, and pray together. Parents thought it was wonderful, religious politicians thought it was wonderful. Just about everyone thought it was wonderful, except those who worried about the separation of government and religion. And of course, those who weren't Christians. But the common attitude was "screw them." They didn't matter. The only ones who mattered were Christians, after all.

Meetings around flagpoles led to meetings in hallways (it was just too cold in the winter to be outside, after all), then to meetings in study halls, and so on. And little by little, actual prayer made it into the classroom, right alongside the Pledge to "one nation under God." This was, of course, to the detriment of many, and the advantage only of the control-hungry "religioso."

And that, my dear, is how it really happened.

Jude

Date: May 28, 2023
To: heyjude@beatles4ever.ws
From: merrymary@webvillemail.net
Subject: I know what you are

Jude:

It doesn't seem to matter what I say. You always have something right at your fingertips to throw back at me. For everything I say, you have an argument against it.

And everything you say makes sense, the way you say it. Except that it really DOESN'T make sense. Whenever I repeat your words to someone else, like my parents or my uncle, they just sound stupid.

So I'm convinced that you're a tool of the Devil. You're deceiving me with your words. You're trying to turn me away from God, but I'm telling you that it will never work!

And don't bother emailing me anymore, because I'm not going to answer. I was taught to avoid the temptation of the Devil, and that's what I'm going to do.

So tough luck. You can't win against a true Christian. My faith is as strong as ever.

Mary

Washington— Evidently, history does repeat itself. For the second time in two decades, Washington, D.C. area restaurants are staging a protest against France.

Almost exactly twenty years ago, D.C. restaurants renamed "French" foods on their menus after France protested the U.S.'s upcoming war against Iraq.

And today, in response to France's recent condemnation of the United States enacting laws against blasphemy, several eateries are doing the same thing. French fries, for example, are "potato strings." French toast is now called "Eggy toast." French bread? Not renamed, just replaced with Italian bread.

Date: June 1, 2023
To: merrymary@webvillemail.net
From: heyjude@beatles4ever.ws
Subject: Re: I know what you are

Mary:

Oh, give me a break! Pardon me for being rude for just a moment, but you religious freaks are so egotistical!

Even if there were a God and a Devil, why in the world would you think that you are significant enough to warrant direct temptation by Satan? You're thirteen! A kid! Why would Satan give a crap whether you have a strong faith or not? You put far too much importance on yourself, I think. You're one of eight billion people on this planet, Mary. And that's one very tiny fish in a very big pond.

The fact is, you came up with this asinine idea of me being a tool of Satan simply because I'm encouraging you to actually THINK about things, which you've probably never done before. You've gone through your whole life being force-fed religion, being taught to blindly accept whatever is poured into your impressionable little mind. Actual thought is foreign to you. I don't mean mulling over a Bible passage to see how you can apply it to your life. I'm talking about real THINKING, where you take a concept and explore it from all angles until you begin to see things you'd never see otherwise.

It's not the easiest thing to do, and sometimes it reveals things you'd rather not see. But the truth is always preferable to fantasy, no matter how much you like the fantasy.

Get over yourself, Mary. You're not that significant.

On the other hand, no one else in the world, in all these billions of people, is quite like you. Even if you had an identical twin sister, you'd still be different from her. You ARE unique, and you have gifts that no one else can give the world. But you'll never be able to express them if you don't free your thoughts from the prison they're in.

End of rant.

If you mean to never email me again, so be it. But I hope you do.

And today in Beatles history:
1981:   Harrison's SOMEWHERE IN ENGLAND released in U.S.
1969:   Lennon's "Give Peace a Chance" recorded in Montreal hotel room.

Jude

June 12, 2023

Well, here I am at Camp Sonlight again. I'm glad. It's good to get away from the craziness of the White House. (How can someplace so busy be so boring?) It's great to be camping again. I forgot how much I love being out in the woods, until I got my first deep breath of fresh air and whiff of pine tree.

Today I had a big long talk with Renée about Jude. She says I was right to stop emailing with him. She said I should just forget I ever started emailing with him, forget everything he said.

Thing is... I don't think I can do that. I mean, sure, I can stop emailing with him, but I can't just erase from my memory everything he said. Especially the things that actually made sense.

I've thought about talking with the counselors here, but I probably won't. When I mention Jude's arguments to someone else, they come out sounding really dumb. I'm not very good at repeating them.

It bothers me that Uncle Gene wasn't any more willing to talk about them than Mom or Dad. Isn't it his job to do that? When I mentioned it again before leaving for camp, he told me to shut up and quit bringing it up. He's never been that mean to me before. But I didn't say anything to Mom or Dad.

And why won't that "Yellow Submarine" song leave my head???

6/15/23

Mary phoned unexpectedly this evening. Most years, she goes to camp and that's the last we hear from her until the day she returns.

But she didn't sound herself. Or rather, she sounded like she so often does around here. I suppose I just expected her to be in better spirits, since that's usually the effect Camp Sonlight has on her.

I'm concerned, though. She asked me some questions that lead me to believe that she is headed down dangerous roads of inquiry about her faith. I placated her as best I could... it was something about morality and God's word. But tomorrow I'll phone her counselors and have them spend some extra time with her. This camp is supposed to prevent that sort of behavior in children, not bring it out.

June 20, 2023

I don't know why, but today I was thinking of something that happened one day in school back in California. Some kid in class refused to say the Pledge of Allegiance. And other kids made fun of him for weeks. Most were just goofing around, but some of the kids were really mean to him, calling him names and saying he wasn't a good American or a good Christian.

I didn't really know this boy, and at the time, I just thought it was something funny that happened. But now I feel bad for him.

Why didn't I feel bad for him then, though? I should have.

And speaking of feeling bad, I'm ashamed of myself for saying Jude was the tool of Satan. I don't know what I was thinking. I guess I wasn't really thinking, just reacting emotionally.

I know I should apologize, but for some reason, I can't. I don't mean just because I don't have computer access here at camp, either. I know my email gave him just one more reason to think Christians are rude, but the truth is I'm sort of afraid to face him again... even if it's only in email.

The thing is, though... Jude doesn't really seem to think all Christians are rude. Just some of them. And heck, I can't argue that. Some of them are.

I miss emailing with him. But why? I mean, when we first started emailing, I couldn't stand him. He was irritating and I hated the things he said. But why should I hate them? They're just his opinions.

He's never been anything but polite to me, except in his last email. And I guess I deserved that bit of rudeness.

For a long time, I thought he only wanted to convince me that I was wrong about my beliefs. But he's said he doesn't really care what I believe, and I think he means it. We spent all that time just after our first exchanges without talking about religion at all. But if he doesn't want to convince me, why does he actually seem to care about me? And why do I think I actually care about him? We've never met, probably never will, and even if we did, we could never...

What? We could never what? What am I thinking? Am I really that lonely???

The Voice of Reason
What a Wonderful World...

In the past three weeks, our wonderfully righteous American society has seen:

An outbreak of "bashings":
* ★ Six dead GLBs, seventy-one hospitalized
* ★ Two dead atheists, twenty hospitalized
* ★ One dead pagan, eight hospitalized

A rash of arrests:
* ★ Sixty-four (peaceful anti-Christopher rally)
* ★ One hundred ninety-two (for blasphemy)
* ★ Twelve (doctors, for illegal abortions)

And of course, these things are only what I've learned from the newspapers. And like rape, I'm guessing lots more have been unreported.

Tell me, Paul... Is this the America you envisioned?

> *"History affords us many instances of the ruin of states, by the prosecution of measures ill suited to the temper and genius of their people. The ordaining of laws in favor of one part of the nation, to the prejudice and oppression of another, is certainly the most erroneous and mistaken policy."*
> —Benjamin Franklin

<u>Enter the Voice of Reason Archives</u>

<u>Email me!</u>

This site last updated: 07/12/23
*Visitors since this site was born: **256,124***

Sounding OFF
By J. E. Cooper

Tracking Gene Sisco and Our Father's Family Since 2015.

Issue No. 16   **Summer, 2023**

"The Only Good Feminist...

...is a dead feminist."

So proclaimed our favorite bigot, Rev. Gene Sisco, on the July 16 broadcast of *The Family Hour*.

Even I was shocked. And I didn't think this guy had the ability to shock me, anymore.

Certainly, he shocked more than just me. Women's organizations around the entire world have been in a lather (and justifiably so) ever since his statement.

The Christopher Administration is catching some of the flak for this, of course. It's no secret to the public that Sisco is Christopher's close friend and confidante.

But I'm sure he's every bit as shocked as the rest of us. Well, okay, I'm not *sure*... but I can't imagine him actually agreeing with Sisco. I mean, Sarah Christopher may not be a feminist, but she is a very strong woman. And Paul has a daughter, too. I can't imagine him siding with his misogynist friend in a house full of women. Even if it's the White House.

I've particularly been enjoying the outcry from the public. Polly Wright was particularly scathing in a press release from the now pretty much defunct *American Queers*. She

(Continued on p. 3)

A Voice of Reason

This is almost certainly old news to you all, but I promised a pal I'd do a bit of promotion for him. So if you aren't already a frequent visitor of this site, please become one:

www.voice_of_reason.com

Trust me. You won't regret it.

Inside This Issue...

20 August 2023

Mary has returned from camp and has been pestering me for days with questions… disturbing questions about morality and faith and seemingly everything else under the sun. I asked her where all these questions have been coming from and she (rather impudently) reminded me about this atheist she emails with, named Judy, I think.

I confess I was angry, initially. That forsaken Internet. You can purge it of pornography and traitors, but not of atheists, apparently.

The very thought that my precious, innocent daughter is being led astray by the serpentine words of a non-believer just makes me want to…

Well, it makes me want to take her computer away, but I can't very well do that. She needs it for her studies. Besides, that would only be a bandage on the wound, rather than healing the disease. For that, she needs to have her faith bolstered.

Most all of us go through this at one point or another. Usually, it's at an age more advanced than Mary's however. Apparently, she's ahead of her age on a lot of fronts.

At any rate, tonight we had a long talk, and I think… I pray… that she benefited from it.

August 21, 2023

I told Dad, again, about Jude, and the questions I have about lots of things. I expected something wise and wonderful, some sort of simple, perceptive insight into how Jude is wrong. But what he said wasn't any more convincing than what my camp counselors had to say.

I mean, he told me the standard stuff. I need to study the Bible more. I need to pray more. I should talk to Uncle Gene. Blah, blah, blah.

But I _have_ studied the Bible. I _have_ prayed. And Uncle Gene doesn't seem to want to make time for me, so he's no help.

The thing that confuses me so much is that the answers to these questions shouldn't require a bunch of studying or a lot of praying. These questions should be able to be answered by anyone with real faith. My faith is apparently not solid enough. But I thought my dad's was.

Maybe I was wrong.

The Voice of Reason
The Non-Apology

Well, the outraged masses finally got to Sisco. He "apologized" for his nasty jab at feminists on his show the other night. But come on. Does anyone believe he meant it? I sure don't.

Gene Sisco undoubtedly was on the Christian Coalition's mailing list back in 1992, when Pat Robertson said:

"The feminist agenda is not about equal rights for women. It is about a socialist, anti-family political movement that encourages women to leave their husbands, kill their children, practice witchcraft, destroy capitalism and become lesbians."

See? There's nothing original in what Sisco said. He can't hold a candle to the kind of vitriolic slander spewed forth by Robertson, who is, of course, one of Sisco's personal heroes. In fact, I've heard Sisco actually has that quote tattooed on his left ass cheek.

Sisco never says anything he doesn't mean, and when he apologizes for saying something, you can be sure he only means that insofar as it'll get him out of the fire.

But don't worry. He'll be right back in it before too long. He hasn't learned to keep his big mouth shut.

Enter the Voice of Reason Archives

Email me!

This site last updated: 09/5/23
*Visitors since this site was born: **301,013***

September 9, 2023

I'm really shocked right now. I read on that Voice of Reason website about something said by Reverend Pat Robertson a long time ago. And it also said that Uncle Gene thought Rev. Robertson was a great man, and I know that's true. I've heard him say such things, myself.

But that quote was horrid! When Uncle Gene said what he did about feminists, I thought it was just a bad joke. Really bad taste. But what if he really meant it?

I mean, I don't consider myself a feminist, but the stuff in Rev. Robertson's quote is obviously just stupid. Feminism doesn't turn women into witches or lesbians. Why would he say such a thing? I don't understand.

Ever since I read this online, I've been wondering what Jude would have to say about it. But why? Why should I care what he has to say about it? What makes his opinion so important?

Well, I'm certainly not going to email and ask him. I'm never emailing him again.

10/10/23

Mary and I had a long talk last night about all sorts of things, including Gene's tirade a couple months ago against feminists. I'm ashamed to say that I didn't know what to tell her. So I told her I thought he just made a little joke that was blown out of proportion by the liberal media.

Lord knows, I sincerely hope that's what it was. But I fear he was quite serious. He despises feminists even more than I do. I may hate their work, but I would never wish harm to them. At least his apology seems to have silenced his critics.

Still, I do so hate stretching the truth when I talk to my daughter. She's a bright girl, and I know she sees through my words. Last night, she just looked at me, as though to say, "Mother. How dare you try to feed me such baloney?"

I'm afraid I'm losing her trust.

"Ladies and Gentlemen of the Press...

"The past few years have been difficult. I think we've made some excellent progress in restoring morality to America, but we're certainly not there, yet. I look forward to a day when I can rest from a job well done, and enjoy the new society we've created together. But that day is still a long way off. Therefore, I am listening to the public and running for re-election.

"Some of my opponents have said some harsh things about this administration, and I'd like to make a few comments, if I may.

"Democrat James Sherman points out that our economy isn't in the best of shape. And he's right. Times have been better. But I would remind Mr. Sherman that the cost of purifying America is high. I guarantee that in the next few years, America will rebound in a big way. Once all the poisons are washed from our society, you will see a healthier America than ever before. And this includes economic health. Hang in there. It'll be amazing.

"Gary Wayne urges citizens to 'vote Green.' What he really means is, 'Vote for Gary Wayne.' Now, that's what campaigning is about... raising votes for oneself. But if Mr. Wayne has to hide behind a party name, what else would you expect him to hide? I'm not sure I want to know.

"Libertarian Michael Lee has been my harshest critic. 'If there is a hell,' he says, 'there must surely be an especially horrible part of it reserved for those who take away liberty from those whose right to protest has already been removed.' Let me be honest. Mr. Lee's comments trouble me deeply. It pains me to know that any citizen has such a warped view of reality.

"And speaking of warped views, most Americans are aware that small towns across our great country are being harassed by a group of infidels calling themselves The Freethought Underground. I caution all citizens to be wary of these people, as they are notorious for spreading lies. But they are also gifted orators, many of them, as was the serpent in the garden.

"In addition, they promote a website called The Voice of Reason. Technical difficulties have prevented us from blocking its filth from the eyes of impressionable youngsters and sensible people of all ages, but this should soon be resolved. This site is evil, ladies and gentlemen. A better title for it would be The Voice of *Treason*, for that is exactly the nature of the statements to be found there. And once the author is identified, he will be dealt with.

"On the road to recovery, sick individuals often encounter setbacks and relapses. The Freethought Underground is definitely a sickness, a cancer, driving America into a relapse of immorality. The medicine against it is knowledge. Be aware of it. Forewarned is forearmed.

"In closing, I would like to thank all my supporters. I have tried to make America a better, more wholesome place, and I think that goal has been accomplished. And with your help, it can be even more of a reality.

"Thank you."

Year Four

2024

January 5, 2024

Uncle Gene is still upset. I hoped Christmas would take his mind off his fight with Father Montoya, but I guess it didn't. I swear... some people will just not let things go! And Uncle Gene is one of them.

I saw the video of their meeting at Penn State. That website, The Voice of Reason, had it posted online.

It was pretty bad. But I don't think it bothered me the way it did him. It bothered me because what Father Montoya said made sense to me. I mean, a little bit. But I know the things he said are against the Bible.

I guess that's the real problem. I'm doubting that the Bible really is the direct, accurate word of God. I can't see how it can be, given the things Jude showed me. And neither Uncle Gene nor Dad can or will show me how he's wrong. It's frustrating.

I sent an apology email to Jude. I'm not sure why. As the saying goes, it's too little, too late. I mean, I accused this guy of being a tool of Satan! There is no way he's going to forgive me for that. And he's an atheist, so he'll probably just use my rudeness as an excuse to hate Christians.

I just got so mad at him after he said I was egotistical. I knew I was being rude, but I never apologized before now. And that was wrong of me.

But what if he does forgive me being so rude, especially after I ignored him for six months? Would that mean I'm wrong in my views of atheists?

And what if Jude's been right all along? What if what Uncle Gene says is wrong? I don't mean about God, of course, but about God's will, or about Brights or other groups?

How do I know what to believe, or what to think? Was Jude right about that, too? Have I just accepted whatever I've been told without honestly thinking about it? I know I should pray for guidance on this... but for some reason, I can't bring myself to.

Date: January 10, 2024
To: merrymary@webvillemail.net
From: heyjude@beatles4ever.ws
Subject: Re: Apology

Mary:

Well, color me surprised. I thought I was never going to hear from you again. I'm glad I was wrong. You didn't really need to apologize. I was pretty harsh in my mail to you. Not that you didn't deserve some of what I said, but I suppose I could've said it more politely. So I'll accept your apology if you'll accept mine.

Besides, I understand how conflicted you were feeling because of our discussions. I know that's what caused your outburst and disappearance. Don't worry about it.

And yes, I did have a nice holiday season, thanks for asking. Hope you did, too.

Want to continue our talks?

Jude

Date: January 11, 2024
To: heyjude@beatles4ever.ws
From: merrymary@webvillemail.net
Subject: Yes, but...

Jude:

First, thank you for accepting my apology. It was very... I was going to say it was very "Christian" of you, but you'd probably think that was rude. So I'll just say it was very decent of you, probably more than I deserved.

And yes, I really do want to continue. But let's get right to the heart of it. You once said that your biggest problem with the whole "God thing" was God Himself.

So what, exactly, is it about God that is such a problem?

Mary

Date: January 12, 2024
To: merrymary@webvillemail.net
From: heyjude@beatles4ever.ws
Subject: Re: Yes, but...

Mary:

Okay. The biggest problem I have with your god is that he can't exist. Not as described, anyway. You're rolling your eyes right now, but bear with me.

The Judeo-Christian God is described as being all-powerful, including all-knowing, and all-everything-else. It is put forth as an absolute, with no qualifiers (a qualifier is a limitation, and God is without limit). I say such an absolute is impossible. To not put any constraints on the definitions applied to God is to say that God is capable of the impossible. Even that old cliché of whether God can create a boulder so heavy that he can't lift it. This seems lame, of course... if God CAN do so, he's not omnipotent because he can't lift it. And if he can lift it, he's not omnipotent because he can't create such a thing. This is a perfect example of the problem with absolutes without qualifiers. But many Christians adamantly refuse such qualifiers. They're perfectly okay with having God be able to do the logically impossible.

Then there's the problem created by omniscience: if God is omniscient, then you and I can't possibly have free will. Think about it. If God created everything, and knows everything (and has ALWAYS known everything), then he knew even before we were conceived exactly what you and I would do every moment of our lives. We haven't the ability to do anything that God didn't know a million years ago that we'd do. And since he created us, that means we were created with his knowledge of exactly what we'd be like, exactly what we'd do. So if God knew we'd do a certain thing, and he still created us, then obviously God wanted us to do that certain thing. Otherwise, he wouldn't have made us at all. We don't have free will. We were programmed, just like a computer is programmed.

As for the portrayal of God himself, let's be honest. Why would the (allegedly) omnipotent Creator of All That Exists REQUIRE his creations to worship him? Look at the Old Testament. He does require it. The First Commandment pretty much spells that out. And if you don't worship him? He acts like a spoiled child, throwing a tantrum, and if the New Testament is to be believed, he'll also send you to hell. This is a loving god? Please. I can only call that behavior immoral and incredibly egotistical. And that's not the type of being I'd ever have respect for, let alone worship.

And yes... I do consider it rude to say "that's very Christian of you." It's like saying "that's very white of you."

Jude

The Voice of Reason
Once Again, It's Xian vs. Xian

Don't you think it's pretty pathetic how Sisco is smearing Father Emilio Montoya at any given opportunity? I mean, I may be an atheist, but I certainly admire anyone willing to stand up to the bullshit of the Christopher Administration. Keep up the good work, sir!

Which brings me to this: I've received many emails asking why I hate Christians so much. Folks, I do *not* hate Christians. I've never claimed to. Most of my friends, not to mention everyone else in my family, are Christians. No, my vitriol is aimed only at those people (who just happen to be Christian in large numbers) who practice bigotry and prejudice as a way of life. I have no problem with "average" Christians (or "average" followers of any other faith), just with those who insist that everyone *must* believe what *they* believe, or behave in ways that THEY determine to be "right."

Like Sisco. Like Christopher. Like so darn many nutballs out there.

And boy, it must be nice to have a forum like *The Family Hour* in which to do your smearing. TV, radio, webcasts, etc. Sure beats the crap out of an internet site.

But hey! Since Christopher's condemnation of my site, I'm getting more hits than ever!

Thanks, Paul!

Enter the Voice of Reason Archives

Email me!

This site last updated: 01/15/24
Visitors since this site was born: **691,246**

The Voice of Reason
Asexual Fantasy

Sarah Christopher must be nuts. Her anti-choice zealots, The Saviors, apparently expect millions of teenagers with raging hormones *to abstain from sex.* Sure. That'll work. And Elvis will perform a concert from my bathroom, where he's lived for the past 46 years.

Fundies have this illusion that the world was so much different in the "good old days." Well, I've got news for them: there never *were* any "good old days." Times have always sucked. Sure, the suckage shifts from one thing to the next, but something always sucks, and some things always stay the same. One of these things is that unmarried people, including teenagers, will have sex. There have always been and always will be unplanned pregnancies. Even back in the first half of the twentieth century (which seems to be what people think of as the "good old days"), teenagers had sex! They had abortions, whether legal or not. They had babies out of wedlock. They certainly didn't practice the type of abstinence that S.C. and her Saviors are advocating.

The "good old days" weren't any better. They were just less honest. Anything unpleasant was hidden away, giving the false impression that everything was better than it was.

So get a clue, Mrs. Christopher. You and your "Saviors" are fighting a losing battle. Get used to it.

Enter the Voice of Reason Archives

Email me!

This site last updated: 01/19/24
Visitors since this site was born: **724,906**

1/20/24

Paul was practically foaming at the mouth today over that website he's been talking about lately. The author of the site had some choice things to say about me, calling me "nuts," apparently.

As long as I live, I don't think I'll ever understand the mentality of people like this man. They just don't understand what it's like to be a Christian in this increasingly secular society.

Though, to be fair, I also don't understand why Paul gets so worked up over the online ravings of some opinionated buffoon. It's not like this fellow has any real influence on society. Let him rant and rave. Let him label me crazy. I frankly have better things to do with my time than worry about what he says, or of what people think of what he says.

Still, it's not as though Jefferson Paine was telling an untruth. Teens in my Grandmother's day did, in fact, fornicate. Obviously, since she was an unmarried seventeen year old girl when she became pregnant with my mother.

But that doesn't matter. I'm proud of the work The Saviors are doing. Abstinence-only sex education is the only sex education we should be teaching. Children do not need to be burdened with knowledge of physical intimacy, or worse, urged into taking part in it by secular sex education, which only encourages promiscuity.

It makes me sick to my stomach to think of my dear Mary, at her tender age, being handed a condom by a teacher and shown how to put it on a rubber penis. Thank God she's not in public schools. If it were up to me, public schools would be abolished and churches would handle our children's education.

Date: January 21, 2024
To: heyjude@beatles4ever.ws
From: merrymary@webvillemail.net
Subject: I am NOT programmed!

Jude:

NO WAY can I accept that we're nothing more than computers. I know I have free will. Not just because the Bible tells me I do, but because I FEEL it! Don't you? I'm not being programmed. I have control over my actions.

And besides, just because someone knows something is going to happen ahead of time, it doesn't mean he or she CAUSED it to happen! If I see someone drop a rubber ball, I know before it hits the floor that it's going to bounce. But I don't MAKE it bounce. See how that makes you wrong?

I asked my father the old "boulder question," and his answer was, "Of course he can create a boulder so heavy he can't lift it. Until he decides he CAN lift it." That sounded good, at first. But when I thought about it, it seems like that's really about God CHOOSING to use his abilities, not about the abilities themselves. So that's no help. It only makes sense to say that God can do anything that isn't logically impossible... like creating a round square. Something that is impossible by definition is also impossible for God. But as you said, many Christians don't agree. And I've always been told God can do anything. There's never any talk of "anything that isn't logically impossible."

I'm so confused over things and I just don't know what to say. I don't know anymore whether to think the Bible is literally true, or even if some of it is accurate at all. But I KNOW there's a God, the same way I KNOW I have free will. I FEEL HIM! There's a warmth inside me whenever I think of Jesus. I wish you could feel it, too, and then you'd be just as sure as I am! In fact, I've prayed for you to feel that love, that presence of the Holy Spirit. And if God wants you to become a believer, then he'll answer that prayer.

Answer me a question. Do all Brights think abortion is okay? I ask because of what I read on Jefferson Paine's site. He was blasting The Saviors. How can you think abortion isn't murder?

And it's so hypocritical that you call God's behavior "immoral." What does an atheist know about morality, anyway? Morality comes from God.

Mary

"Ladies and Gentlemen of the Press...

"In keeping with this administration's solemn effort to return America to a righteous, God-fearing land, I am happy to inform you that a bill is currently before Congress, a bill that will continue our quest for morality, propelling it forward possibly more than any other act of legislation thus far. The bill is expected to pass, and I assure you I will not veto it. Once enacted, any public display of homosexuality will be considered a criminal offense, punishable by mandatory counseling to cure the condition. As an abomination in the eyes of God, it is heresy for us to accept it as 'natural' in any way.

"I see looks of astonishment on the faces of many of you, and believe me, I understand. This aberrant behavior has been tolerated for so long that many of you are possibly of the opinion that being gay or lesbian is okay, that it's accepted. But that is not the case, let me assure you.

"This announcement may seem to be a radical change in the *status quo*. But that's a good thing. The *status quo* needs to be challenged now and again.

"And lest there be any confusion, this law will include any unnatural sexual preferences, including lesbianism, bisexuality, polygamy, and so on. The only relationship approved by our almighty Lord is monogamous heterosexuality. And that's all America will tolerate, too.

"I wish it were possible for me to assure you that this legislation would be able to root out all such people and reform them, but that is simply not possible. Many are still "in the closet," and therefore somewhat safe from the law. But eventually, these people will be reported by friends or family, for their own good, and sent for rehabilitation.

"God help us in our mission to save them."

> *Ottawa*—Canada today issued a stinging rebuke of President Christopher's statements about homosexuality. Prime Minister Yulka said, "The condemnation of homosexuals by the United States is evidence of their backward-thinking mentality. Over twenty years ago, Canada came to its senses and allowed homosexuals to marry, no differently than heterosexuals. President Christopher should be ashamed of himself for his archaic views."

The Voice of Reason
What is Freedom?

"Freedom is the right to choose: the right to create for yourself the alternatives of choice. Without the possibility of choice and the exercise of choice a man is not a man but a member, an instrument, a thing."

—Archibald MacLeish

Our fascist leaders are now telling us who we may and may not sleep with, and have urged us all to spy on each other! But America was formed to have a government "of the people, by the people, and for the people." Not just for the radical right Christians, but for everyone. Can we allow our elected officials to bring the witch hunts into the 21st Century?

The root of the situation is ignorance. This is why the Freethought Underground is doing their thing. Join them, or at least learn from them how to take action. Many of you want to take action, but don't want to be arrested. There are things you can do without risking arrest! Print up fliers urging all to seek the truth. Put the URL for this website in the text. Distribute them far and wide, but secretly. And I, Jefferson Paine, will be the source of education. For the whole world, if I have to.

Enter the Voice of Reason Archives

Email me!

This site last updated: 01/28/24
Visitors since this site was born: **865,254**

REV. SISCO: Bless you all, and welcome to The Family Hour. Our guest today is someone special. I've spoken of him many times on this program, and consider him my closest friend. I am thrilled and honored that he has chosen to appear today. Ladies and Gentlemen, President Paul Christopher!

[The audience erupts into loud applause as Christopher enters from off-stage. He takes a seat next to Sisco.]

CHRISTOPHER: Thanks so much. It's delightful to be here.

REV. SISCO: Before we get to the main reason for your visit, I must ask you how you're handling the many criticisms that have come your way recently. Many have been outraged of your use of the term "unnatural" with regard to so-called "alternative" sexual lifestyles.

CHRISTOPHER: Yes, they certainly have. But Gene, the only opinion I care about is God's opinion. He makes it quite clear how he feels about these lifestyles. So the so-called "sex researchers," the psychologists and other doctors... frankly, they're going to have as much luck swaying me to their views as would an atheist.

REV. SISCO: Ha! Well spoken. Thank you for being so blunt about it. Now, let's move on. Your mission as President, if I may sum it up, has been to return America to its moral roots, to shake off the foulness that has pervaded our great nation for too many years. You've made some tremendous steps in that direction.

[The audience cheers. Christopher smiles and nods at them.]

REV. SISCO: But there is still much to do, I'm sure we all agree. And you're here today to announce exactly what that next step will be, correct?

CHRISTOPHER: Absolutely. Let me ask... If you were to name the top five problems facing America in the 21st century, what would they be?

REV. SISCO: Well, obviously the number one issue would be the exclusion of God from the lives of our children. But this issue has been addressed, and I congratulate you on your successes in bringing God back to public schools.

[More audience applause, at which Christopher smiles.]

REV. SISCO: Abortion... Homosexuality. Both tackled. The Internet. But you've rid it of pedophiles and other degenerates. So... I'd have to say pornography outside of the Internet.

CHRISTOPHER: My thoughts exactly, Gene. And I think we agree that pornography doesn't consist merely of shameful photographs and so-called "art" of human genitalia.

REV. SISCO: Absolutely! Pornography is anything that disgraces God. Writings on homosexuality, even when not graphic, are pornography.

CHRISTOPHER: Yes, as would be any writings considered to be pro-abortion, or anti-God. This smut is still in existence. Big Brother was enacted purely for the Internet. But bookstores around the country, not to mention libraries, are absolutely full of porn of all sorts.

REV. SISCO: And that is the next step?

CHRISTOPHER: It is. Ladies and Gentlemen, I would like to announce that anti-obscenity laws are soon to be expanded. Measures will be taken to remove this offensive material from circulation. Libraries will be purged. Publishing companies will be required to cease printing certain titles. In short order, you will not have to worry about your children reading these hurtful materials.

[The audience becomes frenetic with applause.]

REV. SISCO: More on this after these words from our sponsor.

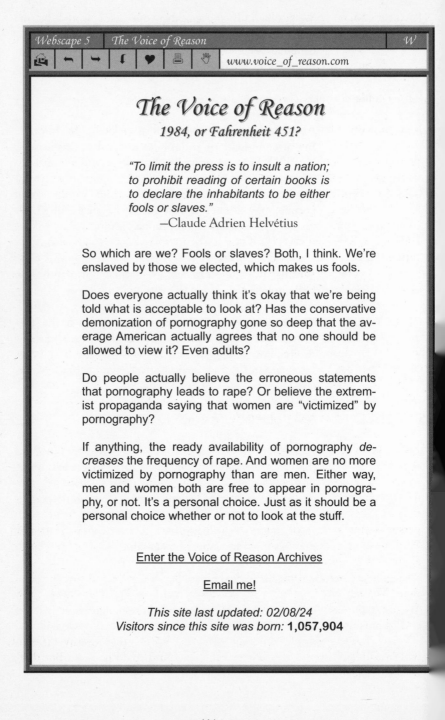

www.voice_of_reason.com

The Voice of Reason
1984, or Fahrenheit 451?

"To limit the press is to insult a nation; to prohibit reading of certain books is to declare the inhabitants to be either fools or slaves."
—Claude Adrien Helvétius

So which are we? Fools or slaves? Both, I think. We're enslaved by those we elected, which makes us fools.

Does everyone actually think it's okay that we're being told what is acceptable to look at? Has the conservative demonization of pornography gone so deep that the average American actually agrees that no one should be allowed to view it? Even adults?

Do people actually believe the erroneous statements that pornography leads to rape? Or believe the extremist propaganda saying that women are "victimized" by pornography?

If anything, the ready availability of pornography *decreases* the frequency of rape. And women are no more victimized by pornography than are men. Either way, men and women both are free to appear in pornography, or not. It's a personal choice. Just as it should be a personal choice whether or not to look at the stuff.

<u>Enter the Voice of Reason Archives</u>

<u>Email me!</u>

This site last updated: 02/08/24
Visitors since this site was born: **1,057,904**

Date: February 14, 2024
To: merrymary@webvillemail.net
From: heyjude@beatles4ever.ws
Subject: Abortion and Morality

Mary:

I don't know if you have a boyfriend, but Happy Valentine's Day!

So about this hypothetical rubber ball... Did you create it? Or the person who dropped it? Or gravity? Nope. So how could you be responsible? But you say God created gravity, the ball, and the one who drops it. He controls everything. Therefore, God caused the ball to fall and bounce.

So if God knows everything, AND CREATED EVERYTHING (that's the important part), then he created everything while knowing BEFORE CREATING ANYTHING exactly what would always happen in the future. Thus, it is designed. There's no other explanation.

Let me go off on a tangent about morality for a moment, since it's clear that we disagree about what it is and where it comes from.

There are basically three types of morality:

1.   Universal Morality, which is imposed upon us by a Creator, and therefore identical for everyone.

2.   External Morality, which is imposed upon us by an outside source, such as society, and identical to all within the affected group.

3.   Internal Morality, which is imposed upon us by ourselves, and is unique to a person.

You, of course, believe the first kind to be the only "real" morality. But in truth, the only type of morality that truly "works," in the long run, is the third. When morality is imposed upon us by an outside source, whether society, "the majority," or an alleged deity, there will always be those who don't feel it applies to them. We hate being told what to do, especially when the reason given is "because I said so." And it doesn't matter whether the person saying so is your parent, your president, or your priest. And God? Well, until you can get 100% of the populace to agree 100% on everything about that Creator, you're not going to have much success.

And morality imposed upon us by ourselves? We never question that, right? Wrong. We do question it. We constantly re-evaluate, constantly grow. We are free to improve it over time, because it is our own. It's the only moral code that is not static and lifeless. And this is the morality of atheists, Mary.

You're probably thinking that this means that twenty different people will have twenty different moral codes. And you'd be right. But that's not a terrible thing.

Some believe that this is why we have so many sickos and psychopaths. I disagree. If anything, we have fewer than we would otherwise. Why? Because of how independent humans are.

One of the things that allowed primitive society to survive from its infancy to the present day is our innate need to cooperate. If we hurt one another, we hurt the tribe. If the tribe shrinks, there may be fewer mouths to feed, but there are also fewer left to gather the food. Treating others well is simply a matter of self-preservation. And that holds just as true today, though it may not seem to. Treating others well, far from being a matter of "enlightenment," is actually a deep-seated instinct.

This instinct would lead to a society far more pleasant than our own, if left to flourish. But rather than allow humankind to evolve in a self-preserving fashion, we have instituted governments and religions to stifle us, to program us, to make us behave by external laws rather than self-imposed common-sense rules. That's a recipe for rebellion in its most basic form. And look around you. Does it appear the imposed morality, whether by society or religion, has worked? It doesn't to me.

Finally, regarding abortion: No, all Brights do not support abortion. But most support the right to choose. I wish no one ever had an abortion. But it's not for me to say that a woman can't have one.

You've heard the slogan, "It's a child, not a choice." But who's to say when a fertilized egg is a child? Obviously this isn't about LIFE, period. You never hear anti-choicers weeping about the millions of sperm that die in every ejaculation, or every egg that dies during regular menstruation. These things are undeniably alive. But at what point is the embryo more than a collection of cells entirely dependent upon the mother, like a parasite? No one knows. But the anti-choice people CLAIM they know. They say a "soul" enters the body at the moment of conception, but this is simply religious conjecture.

Personally, I think it's whenever the higher brainwaves can be detected, which is around the sixth month. And the vast majority of abortions are performed well before this point.

So, pretend you got pregnant tomorrow, and that your family would freak out if they knew. You'd be ostracized at school. And you're way too young to properly raise a child. Is it right for the government to forbid you the option of an abortion, whether or not you personally agree with it? Or should you have the right to decide based on your own views?

Let's extend this to another topic—the President's latest violation of the Constitution. Should the government have any say whatsoever in what we are or are not allowed to read? If anyone desires to read pornography, or anything subversive, should that person not have the right to do so? How can you possibly justify censorship?

Jude

Date: February 15, 2024
To: heyjude@beatles4ever.ws
From: merrymary@webvillemail.net
Subject: Re: Abortion and Morality

Jude:

No, I don't have a boyfriend. But thank you for the Valentine's Day wish. I hope yours was nice. Do you have a girlfriend?

I'll have to give some thought to your ideas on morality. As usual, what you say makes sense, but also as usual, I'm suspicious of it. Something always just seems basically WRONG about what you say, even though I can't always put my finger on what it is. I KNOW you're wrong about God-given morality. But I can't prove it.

As for abortion, you're not far from the truth. No, I'm not pregnant, but if I got pregnant, my family WOULD freak. It's not something I could EVER tell them. Not until I'm married, anyway.

I don't know if I agree with you about abortion and pornography. Maybe the Bible doesn't say anything about them, but my gut feeling is that they're wrong. My mother says that porn causes sex crimes. And abortion DOES kill, whether scientists think of an embryo as "human" life or not. If the soul doesn't enter the body at conception, when would it? And why wouldn't it do it then? I know you don't believe in a soul, so you're not going to give me any answers.

Tell me something. Why do you Brights always point to the Constitution? You seem to rely on it like it was the Bible (if you'll pardon the expression). What's the big deal? It's just something some old guys wrote more than two hundred years ago.

I hope you understand it's hard for me to admit that you make me doubt things. It's like there's a part of me that hates you for putting these ideas in my head. I resent it. But at the same time, I don't know... it's exciting. I can't explain why.

But believe me that you haven't changed my mind about God one little tiny bit. I still believe in Him as much as ever. Even if it could be shown that the Bible was false in many places, you still can't prove there's no God. God is the source of all that is good in the world, and I can feel Him in my heart. And I hope one day you'll feel Him, too.

Mary

Date: February 21, 2024
To: merrymary@webvillemail.net
From: heyjude@beatles4ever.ws
Subject: I FEEL IT!!!

Mary!

That feeling you mentioned! I feel it! A warm, fuzzy feeling inside... like I know there's something bigger than myself, something so wonderful that it makes you just ache! It's glorious! It's...
Oh, wait.
I was thinking of a hot fudge sundae with nuts. Sorry.
No, no girlfriend. Haven't found one who'll put up with me, yet.
Anyway, as for your mother's comments, there are quite a number of studies out there that say she's wrong. Pornography doesn't lead to sex crimes, but in fact, lowers such rates. If smut is accessible, why would anyone have the "urge" to commit a sex crime? Admittedly, there are addictions to pornography, but that's no different than addiction to anything else. It's a personal problem, not something the government should be addressing. You have to understand that the government has no place doing certain things. The government can't legislate morality. Not only CAN'T it, it shouldn't even try.
As for the Constitution, I think you're selling it short. Though it's far from a perfect document, it is the document upon which our country is founded. Yes, it has its faults, but it has some amazingly good things in there. Rather like the Bible, in that respect. The thing is, whether we like it or not, our country's highest laws are contained in that document. And if we don't like parts of it, we have a process of amending it. But ignoring it is out of the question. You wouldn't think of disregarding the Ten Commandments, would you? Well, the Constitution is the secular equivalent, or the closest there is, anyway.
You're right, too. I can't prove there's no God. Then again, why should I have to? You're the one claiming that God exists. The responsibility rests with you to prove it.
Don't agree? Well, let's say I tell you that I've just discovered a race of invisible pygmies living in my back yard. Not only are they invisible, but they're totally insubstantial. They can't be detected by any known means. But I know they're there. They're pygmies, they're invisible, and they have long beards. Even the women.
Would you have any reason to simply believe me, or would you demand that I prove it? If you're smart, you'll want proof. Or solid evidence, anyway. Proof is for mathematics and alcohol. And if I say I can provide none, and that you'll just have to take my claims on faith, what would you think? Again, if you're smart, you'll think I'm trying to con you.

Claims require evidence to be believed. Compelling evidence. The more extraordinary the claim, the more extraordinary the evidence must be. The existence of an omnipotent god is the most extraordinary claim of all. And yet, there's not a scrap of evidence to support that claim.

So you think God is the source of all that's good, huh? Well, what about evil? According to the Bible, God is also the source of all evil. But even if it didn't say that, this would be the natural conclusion. God created everything... evil exists... so God created evil.

Why did he do that? Why did he create the devil?

He must have. He created everything. He knows everything, too, so he must've known that Lucifer would fall from grace and become Satan. (Remember our talk on free will?) This means God meant for there to be a Satan, for there to be evil, long before he ever created Adam and Eve. Hell was all ready and waiting before that tree ever bore fruit in Eden.

Funny, though, how the Old Testament mentions not a word about hell. Only the New Testament brings that into the picture. If one didn't know better, it might be assumed that it was the creation of whoever wrote the books of the New Testament, wouldn't one? It sounds to me like your God has had the game fixed from the very beginning.

You know, it's strange that you said that you sometimes hate me for putting ideas in your head. Because I've often thought that this is the root of society's hatred of atheists. Not that we're putting ideas in others' heads... teachers do that all the time, but they're not hated. Rather, it's the particular ideas we espouse.

It's like when a kid finds out that there's no Santa Claus. They sometimes feel a literal sense of loss, as though something wonderful had just been taken from them. They may feel betrayed, too, when they realize they'd been fed a fairy tale from the start. And eventually, many feel a bit stupid, not wanting to admit that they'd believed in flying reindeer and all that stuff.

This is a bit like what happens to many Brights during their conversion process. We go through the same steps. And it's rarely a pleasant thing. Yes, most of us find it very liberating to be free of the mythology. But it's often a painful road to that liberation.

And I think that's why so many people hate us. They don't want to go down that painful road. They don't even like the very idea of questioning their beliefs, because they're afraid of that road. In voicing our views, we are pushing them toward that road, and they're not at all happy about it.

And today in Beatles history:
1966:   "Nowhere Man" released as single.

Jude

Date: March 1, 2024
To: heyjude@beatles4ever.ws
From: merrymary@webvillemail.net
Subject: Very funny

Jude:

Y'know, a year ago, I would've gotten mad at you making fun of my faith by comparing it to your love of ice cream. But not today. Oh, I still think you'll be amazed when you finally feel God's love, but I can understand you making fun of it. You can't understand it if you've never felt it, and I can't do a good job of explaining it.

Your comments about me being the one to have to "prove" the existence of God really bothered me. As usual, you made sense, but it has to work the other way around. Atheists are the ones claiming God doesn't exist. Why shouldn't they have to provide the "extraordinary evidence" to support such an extraordinary claim? After all, something like ninety percent of the world's population believes in a God of some sort. They can't all be wrong!

As for your question about God "fixing" the game, well you're right. God did create evil. But he did it because he knew Adam and Eve would sin. He knew because of that, evil would have a place in the world.

Of course, I know what you're going to say. You're going to mention God's omniscience, and the lack of free will, and everything you said before, and I just don't have an answer!

Darn it, Jude! Why do you have to make things so hard? Why can't you just accept God? Why can't you just have faith?

Mary

Washington—The DHS has issued arrest warrants for the leaders of the Freethought Underground, complete with rewards for their safe capture.

The government is willing to pay $20,000 each for the arrests of Robert Green, Polly Wright, and Sam Hain. For leader Eleanor Adams, the price is $100,000.

Father Emilio Montoya, however, has escaped the DHS's wrath. No warrant for his arrest has been issued, although they warn that future subversive actions on his part will find him in the same situation.

3 March 2024

I wish I could say I was happy about this situation. Gene feels we're doing the right thing by offering rewards for the safe capture of the Freethought Underground leaders. In fact, it was his idea. But I am not so sure.

Offering a reward is something I never would have considered. We are suggesting that citizens become vigilantes. And while I favor individuals taking control, of making a difference, this is pushing it to an extreme. And of course, my biggest fear is that some of these people may be hurt in the process, especially the Freethought Underground people. I may despise their agenda and beliefs, but I have no wish to see them harmed.

Oh, I tried to talk Gene out of it, but he convinced me that this action would, beyond a doubt, clinch my re-election. I suppose it is weak and vain of me to desire re-election so badly, but how else will America be restored to its previous glory? How else will God's will be done?

If left to its own devices, America will wallow happily in its own excrement, poisoning itself more with each passing day. God help me, but sometimes I actually agree with the militant Muslims who decry our American ways. It's no wonder they still hate us in Iraq. We're working on establishing democracy there (and what an arduous job it is), which they perceive as making them more like us, the ones they hate. They're not much warmer to the idea now than they were twenty years ago, as evidenced by the occasional violence against our soldiers there. The attacks are of little consequence. We hold the upper hand there, unquestionably. The Iraqis are little more than nuisance guerilla fighters now.

I digress.

I entered the political arena with a promise to clean up the filth Americans are wallowing in, and by God, that's what I aim to do. It's rewarding work, though difficult. And it's not a task I'll finish in four short years. Only by winning re-election can I carry out that promise.

Topeka—Eleanor Adams was captured yesterday by a lone citizen armed with a handgun while giving a speech in Liberal, Kansas.

The former president of AtheistsUSA is in protective custody pending a hearing.

5/3/24

Paul and I have been discussing this whole "reward" tactic the Department of Homeland Security has instigated. Neither of us is thrilled with it. And though it's nice to know that this horrid Adams woman is not out there perverting the minds of everyone she runs into, a part of me finds even that to be cause for concern. Eleanor and I have never agreed on anything, it seems, and perhaps she's deserving of imprisonment. But where will this go? At what point will it stop?

I can't help but think that these ideas Gene is putting into Paul's head are not really the best ones. I fear we could be on a slippery slope toward social disaster.

I don't know how to explain it, but over the past few years, my trust in Gene Sisco has waned. He seems to act less and less like Paul's friend of so many years. Yesterday I even wondered if he ever truly considered Paul his friend, or just a charismatic person to plant in the White House... a person he could influence under the guise of friendship.

But even if that is true, what of it? Gene's vision of America is one that Paul and I both would love to see become reality. And Paul is certainly not a politician.

They're a team, I suppose. And if they seem not to be the friends they once were, surely it is only because of the stresses of that partnership.

Date: May 16, 2024
To: merrymary@webvillemail.net
From: heyjude@beatles4ever.ws
Subject: Sorry...

Mary:

I'm sorry it's taken me so long to respond. Life kinda got in the way. And I missed your birthday, too. Sorry about that. Hope it was happy!

Anyway, I've been thinking about your last email, and have to say first off that denying someone else's claim is NOT the same as MAKING a claim. Theists have been pulling that one on us for centuries. It's faulty logic. Besides, the burden of proof lies on the one making the POSITIVE claim. In this case, theists. To get back to my previous example, is it your responsibility to provide proof that my invisible pygmies DON'T exist? Of course not. And so it is with the assertion that God exists.

Mary... my goal has never been to aggravate you or piss you off or make you hate me. All along, it has only been to make you think. I mean REALLY think... to think critically about your beliefs and how they affect your life. But maybe my tactics aren't the best. I know I can come across as abrasive, defensive, arrogant, and a host of other colorful adjectives.

But believe me when I say that I'm not trying to make fun of what you believe, and I'm not saying that I think you're a bad person for believing it. Just understand that many people, including myself, CAN'T take things on faith. And we CAN'T simply accept things without REALLY looking at them.

We are that ten percent of the population without a god belief, and YES... the other ninety percent CAN be wrong. Once upon a time, virtually everyone thought the world was flat, after all. Or that the sun went around the earth, rather than vice-versa. That "fact" was plain for anyone to see! And yet, still dead wrong.

Look, it's obvious that our emails are causing you a lot of grief. Maybe this is too much for you. Maybe we need to take a break. I don't know.

But I do know that I think you're a sweet girl. I've enjoyed emailing with you, especially when we've gone off on tangents totally unrelated to the religious discussion. Most assuredly, I don't want to drive you nuts. So maybe we shouldn't talk about this.

Think it over and let me know what you want to do.

Jude

Date: May 20, 2024
To: heyjude@beatles4ever.ws
From: merrymary@webvillemail.net
Subject: I've thought it over

Jude:

Thanks for the late birthday wishes. Yes, it was pretty nice. Thank you for remembering.

Okay. Here's what I suggest.

I think I do need a break from this. Right now you've got me so confused that I don't know which end is up. I'm leaving in a couple weeks for summer camp. (Camp Sonlight. I've been going there since I was little.) I won't have email, so we'd be stopping for a while, anyway.

I'll be thinking things over while I'm away. And when I come back, maybe I'll have some answers for you. Or maybe just more questions. Who knows? I'll email you when I get back, around the middle of August.

Thanks for the compliment, by the way. I think you're sweet, too, in your own way. And I want you to know that I have a lot of respect for you, much as my family would be appalled to hear such a thing. I'll be thinking of you while I'm away.

Have a great summer!

Mary

Washington—Hundreds of protesters are expected to participate in the fourth annual "Rights for Brights" march on the Capitol, scheduled for tomorrow.

As they have for the past three years, the protesters are crusading under the banner of the First Amendment, which they insist demands total separation of church and state.

June 18, 2024

Less than a week and I'm ready to go home. I've got well over a month, yet, and feeling like this will sure make it drag.

I mean, it's nice seeing familiar faces. But I don't feel close to them, anymore. It's weird, but I feel left out. I mean, they're not shunning me or anything. It feels more like it's me, not them.

When I stop to think about it, I know what it is. It's the doubts I've been having ever since I started emailing with Jude. It's not his fault, though. All he did was take me up on my invitation to be challenged. He's asked me questions that I'd never asked myself before. And what I've been wondering a lot lately is why I never did. Some of the things are so obvious that I feel almost stupid that I didn't think of them myself.

I look at my friends here, and at the leaders and counselors, and I see something on their faces that I don't think is on mine. So many of them seem... I don't know how to describe it. The only words I can think of sound insulting.

I mean, everything with them is "God this, Jesus that." And that's great. I love Jesus as much as the next person. But don't these people ever question the things I'm questioning? They quote scripture and everything, and never seem to even think that... just maybe... the book is less than 100% true and perfect.

But I can't seem to think that way anymore. A year ago, I was mad at Jude for making me doubt. But now... Now I'm almost glad. I'm actually <u>thinking</u> about things. I'm using my brain to take information and examine it. These people around me seem only to accept what's fed to them without really doing that. It's like... It's like I'm actually <u>eating</u>, but they're being fed through their veins. They don't taste anything. They get the nutrition, but there's no work involved, and maybe... I don't know... Maybe they're not even getting the nutrition.

Am I nuts to think this way? It seems to me that our brains are meant for analyzing things. God gave us that ability. Why wouldn't he want us to use it? To have such an ability and not use it seems to me like it would be an insult to our Creator.

Or maybe I'm just babbling.

This is a strange thing for me to admit, but I miss emailing with Jude. He's really nice, aside from his religious and political views, and his love of really old music. I wonder if he's cute. I wonder if he'd think I'm cute.

6/20/24

Mary phoned today from camp, absolutely miserable. Apparently, she's not enjoying her experience there as she has in the past. Poor girl.

I can't say I'm surprised. Ever since Rev. Sisco took a more active role in Paul's campaigning and Presidency, he hasn't had his usual active hand in his camp. Doubtless, it is his absence that makes Mary feel so dejected there.

Mary asked if she could come home early. Much as I wanted to say yes, I urged her to keep a stiff upper lip and before she knew it, it would be time to come home.

But was that the right reply? Is there a good reason to keep her there if she's unhappy? I do miss having her around.

But no. Camp is where she needs to be. With the questions she's been asking lately about the Bible and abortion and so on, this is definitely what she needs. Even without Gene's direct hand, surely her camp counselors will be able to help her.

I just feel so guilty that her childhood has been so disruptive, so unlike what a childhood should be. But she'll be stronger for staying there. I just know it.

This is, I guess, just another of the many times a woman feels as though she's not being a good mother. It's so hard, sometimes. I'd thought the earliest years would be the most difficult, what with all the things necessary in caring for an infant. But those were, in retrospect, merely physical demands. Nothing that rest couldn't cure.

But the older Mary grows, the more complicated become the demands of raising her. Now they are far more psychological than physical. They are more emotionally turbulent.

I envy how easy it is for Paul. He never seems to be at a loss on how to approach her or handle her moods. But since becoming President, I haven't been able to rely upon him so often for help.

For better or worse, Mary and I are going to have to have a more dependent relationship than ever before.

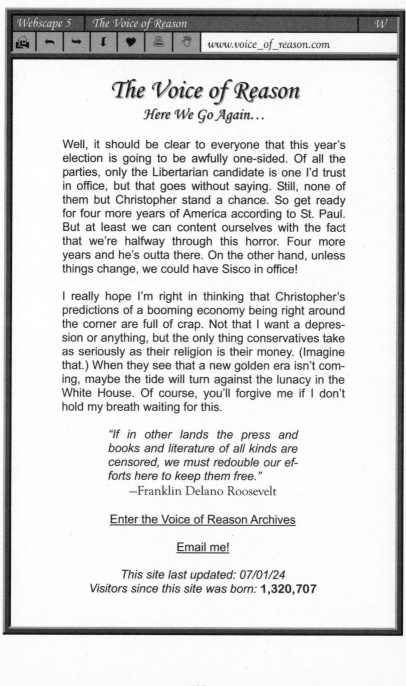

Webscape 5 · The Voice of Reason · W

www.voice_of_reason.com

The Voice of Reason
Here We Go Again...

Well, it should be clear to everyone that this year's election is going to be awfully one-sided. Of all the parties, only the Libertarian candidate is one I'd trust in office, but that goes without saying. Still, none of them but Christopher stand a chance. So get ready for four more years of America according to St. Paul. But at least we can content ourselves with the fact that we're halfway through this horror. Four more years and he's outta there. On the other hand, unless things change, we could have Sisco in office!

I really hope I'm right in thinking that Christopher's predictions of a booming economy being right around the corner are full of crap. Not that I want a depression or anything, but the only thing conservatives take as seriously as their religion is their money. (Imagine that.) When they see that a new golden era isn't coming, maybe the tide will turn against the lunacy in the White House. Of course, you'll forgive me if I don't hold my breath waiting for this.

> *"If in other lands the press and books and literature of all kinds are censored, we must redouble our efforts here to keep them free."*
> —Franklin Delano Roosevelt

Enter the Voice of Reason Archives

Email me!

This site last updated: 07/01/24
Visitors since this site was born: **1,320,707**

July 12, 2024

I can't stop thinking about things Jude has pointed out. I was thinking of that whole morality issue while reading scripture this week. And I came up with my own questions, like are the commandments really moral? I mean, what if parents abuse their children? Should the children continue to honor them? And if so, why? Is it a sin to steal food to prevent a baby from starving?

Why does God so often break his own commandment? He kills people all throughout the Old Testament, and even orders his followers to kill in his name. Where's the morality of that? I mean, the victims may have been sinners, but how much clearer than "Thou shalt not kill" can you get? Even if the translation should be "murder" instead of "kill," as some say, it's still murder.

And what about slavery? The Bible seems perfectly okay with the idea. I <u>really</u> don't get that.

I want answers to these questions, but I guess I want answers that no one here is willing to give me. I asked one of the counselors these questions after dinner tonight. She looked at me like I had two heads. Then she said, "Yes. The children should still honor their parents, and pray that God forgives them. Yes, stealing in that situation would still be a sin, but God may forgive." As for God breaking the commandment, she insists that if God orders it, it can override anything, even his own word. When I asked about slavery, she got all bent out of shape and told me she had to go make a phone call or something.

Her focus seemed to be on forgiveness. It seemed that there was nothing a person could do that would be too awful for God to forgive. And if that's the case, what's the point of having laws at all? I just don't get it.

I didn't like her answers, but I can't think of anything better without having doubts about my whole belief system. And while I'm becoming more and more convinced that the Bible isn't literally true, word-for-word, I can't possibly say it's baloney, as Jude seems to.

Should I pray for answers? The obvious answer is that I should. But it seems to me that praying to God about something like this would be almost blasphemous.

Date: July 26, 2024
To: jefferson_paine@voice_of_reason.com
From: ingersoll@anon-e-mail.com
Subject: Re: What to do?

My dear Mr. Paine:

I understand your concern. Many in the Underground are distressed, certainly including me. I haven't stopped worrying since I heard the news.

But we mustn't despair. There is still much to be done, and we're entirely capable of continuing without her direct guidance. She taught us well. We need, as Eleanor would say, to "keep on keepin' on." Or something archaic like that.

So change nothing. What you've been doing is excellent. The website is fantastic, and your assistance to the Underground has been invaluable.

Thanks to you, we have been able to contact people in virtually every town we visit, people who were once affiliated with organizations like the ACLU, or freethought groups, and so on. These folks are continuing to spread the word long after we're gone, including traveling to other towns to do so.

In short, we're accomplishing exactly what we wanted to: bringing awareness to the masses. And of course, we're still circulating your URL, so please continue to keep The Voice of Reason as great as it's always been.

A suggestion—in order to keep the public aware of Eleanor's plight, how about a sub-page of the site that will do exactly that? Explain what's really going on, and just maybe it'll offend some people. Public outrage can be our ally just as much as Christopher's.

I eagerly await the day when this is all over. Eleanor speaks very highly of you, and I look forward to meeting you one day soon.

Robert Green

July 27, 2024

There's a new girl at camp this year. Her name's Vicki something. She's really pretty (not that I'm envious, of course) and is in the same bunkhouse as Renée. I really don't know what to think of her. She keeps to herself, not really participating in many of the activities. Anyway, she was in her cot, next to Renée's, as we were talking.

I was telling Renée about my questions. And she wasn't being very understanding. She gave me funny looks a lot. Anyway, after I'd gone over my list, ending with the thing about slavery, Vicki looked up from her magazine and said that if I thought that was shocking, I should take a look at how the Bible treats women.

I had no idea what she meant by that, but when I asked, Renée changed the subject and Vicki turned back to her magazine.

But in the end, Renée was no help. Truth is, she didn't even seem interested in talking about it. She asked me why I was thinking all this stuff. I started to tell her about Jude, but she cut me off, telling me that I was flirting with Satan by talking to an atheist.

I was offended. How dare she? Jude isn't like Satan at all! (Yes, I can see the irony, since I accused him of the same thing.) In fact, he's nicer to me than Renée has been this year. And I pretty much told her that.

And then Vicki said that Jude was nicer to me because Brights generally aren't arrogant bigots. And she said this right to Renée's face! Then she said she couldn't listen to Renée's B.S. anymore and left the cabin.

Renée didn't feel like talking after that, so I left, too.

I wonder about Jude a lot. Nobody here is as interesting as he is, to be honest. I wish the counselors would let us use the computer they have in the office. I'm dying to ask him my questions. But am I ready to hear the answers?

That's a good question, but I think I'm ready. There's nothing that Jude can say to me that will shock me any more than what he's said to me already.

July 29,2024

Okay, so I <u>can</u> be shocked more. I spent about an hour talking to Vicki. She's really interesting. But boy, has she had a harsh home life!

Her parents are really religious, and really strict, too. On holidays, she had to go to church at least twice a day. Sometimes three times, morning, noon, and night. They had Bible readings in their home, and Vicki stopped inviting friends over when she was about ten, because her father would force her friends to take part in the Bible readings. And one time, when she was at school, her father took all of her music and threw it away. He said that any music that doesn't glorify God is music of the Devil. She finally stood up to them, and was sent here as punishment. Well, she said there was another reason, but wouldn't say what it was.

I just can't even imagine having to deal with that kind of zealotry! My mom thinks the Sidestreet Girls are a bunch of sluts, but at least she lets me listen to them. What causes people to be like her parents?

Anyway, I asked Vicki what she'd meant about women in the Bible. She just smiled and started rattling off a bunch of different things.

I looked up the ones I could remember, and I can't believe what I read! There are passages that show horrible treatment of women! They're practically treated as property, in some cases, even in the commandments. Even Jesus speaks rudely to Mary! This is unbelievable! I've read the Bible cover to cover three times in my life. Why did I never see this before?

This is some scary stuff. Not because women were treated so poorly in those days… everyone knows that… but because neither God nor Jesus seems to think anything was wrong with this, and in some cases, even urged such treatment.

There's got to be an explanation. There's just got to be. Between all that Jude has told me, and all I'm reading in the Bible itself, I just don't know what to think! What I'm learning now goes against so much of what I've been taught all my life.

I think I'm beginning to understand why there are so many different Christian sects out there, and I don't feel good about that. I'd always been told that all those other ones were misguided, that they didn't really understand the word of God. But now I'm not so sure. How do I know my understanding of the Bible is any better than theirs?

July 30, 2024

I tried to find Vicki today to talk more about Bible stuff, but evidently, she's being punished. Renée says she mouthed off to one of the counselors and has been confined to one of the solitary cabins for a week. A week! That's unheard of! I wonder what she could have said to deserve that.

The funny thing is, from what I think I know of Vicki's personality, I'll bet she doesn't mind this kind of punishment at all.

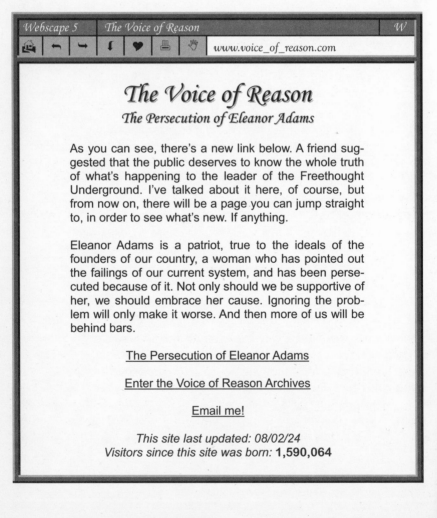

Webscape 5 · *The Voice of Reason* · *W*

www.voice_of_reason.com

The Voice of Reason
The Persecution of Eleanor Adams

As you can see, there's a new link below. A friend suggested that the public deserves to know the whole truth of what's happening to the leader of the Freethought Underground. I've talked about it here, of course, but from now on, there will be a page you can jump straight to, in order to see what's new. If anything.

Eleanor Adams is a patriot, true to the ideals of the founders of our country, a woman who has pointed out the failings of our current system, and has been persecuted because of it. Not only should we be supportive of her, we should embrace her cause. Ignoring the problem will only make it worse. And then more of us will be behind bars.

The Persecution of Eleanor Adams

Enter the Voice of Reason Archives

Email me!

This site last updated: 08/02/24
Visitors since this site was born: **1,590,064**

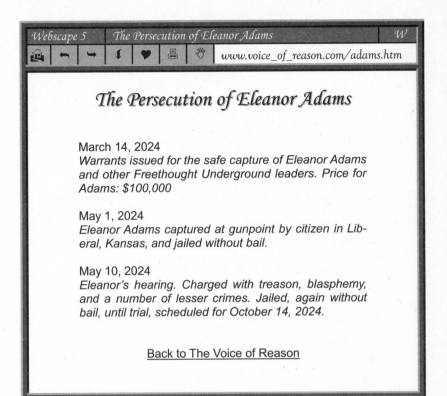

The Persecution of Eleanor Adams

March 14, 2024
Warrants issued for the safe capture of Eleanor Adams and other Freethought Underground leaders. Price for Adams: $100,000

May 1, 2024
Eleanor Adams captured at gunpoint by citizen in Liberal, Kansas, and jailed without bail.

May 10, 2024
Eleanor's hearing. Charged with treason, blasphemy, and a number of lesser crimes. Jailed, again without bail, until trial, scheduled for October 14, 2024.

<u>Back to The Voice of Reason</u>

8/14/24

Mary is apparently none the worse for wear, having survived Camp Sonlight one more summer. And I think she's glad she stayed. She seems to have made a new friend. Mary was evidently quite impressed by her knowledge of the Bible.

It's gratifying. One of our hopes in sending her to camp was that she would make friends. And only at a place such as Camp Sonlight could we be certain that she would make friends of the right sort.

Date: August 15, 2024
To: heyjude@beatles4ever.ws
From: merrymary@webvillemail.net
Subject: I'm back!

Hey, Jude!

I heard that song at camp! Someone else there likes old fogy music, too! Anyway, I'm home from the wilderness and back in cyberspace! Hope you've been well while I was gone.

Camp was... frustrating. I don't know if you know it or not, but Camp Sonlight is a religious camp started by Reverend Sisco. And the thing is... I wasn't buying all the stuff they were telling me. There were so many things going on in my head, things I wanted to ask you. Actually, I wanted to ask my uncle, too, but he's away, darn it.

I've decided the Bible can't be literally true. I still believe in God and love Jesus, but the Bible itself seems to have stuff that isn't pure. Okay. Honestly, there's a lot of stuff about the Bible that freaks me out, and I can't see how these things could possibly be considered holy. I mean... slavery? What's up with that? And women as property? And God telling his armies to destroy entire cities, including babies, except for virgin girls, who became the property of the conquering soldiers?

I must not be interpreting these things correctly.

Mary

Date: August 19, 2024
To: merrymary@webvillemail.net
From: heyjude@beatles4ever.ws
Subject: Welcome home!

Mary:

Hey... good to hear from you. You might not believe this, but I really missed our conversations. Go figure.

Sorry about camp. Hope you at least enjoyed seeing your friends.

As for your questions... Let me ask you one before I answer them: Why would the "word of God" even NEED to be "interpreted"?

Jude

August 20, 2024

He missed our conversations! He said so! This is so cool! And I thought he was only emailing with me in order to "break" a Christian. But he really likes me!

I like him, too. It's funny, but I guess Jude is really my best friend. Since moving to D.C., I haven't really stayed friends with the gang back home. And the girls at Camp Sonlight... well, I don't really consider them close friends.

Jude has been my most frequent contact outside of my family. We have fun emailing, particularly when we're not discussing religion. And yet, we'll probably never meet. And he doesn't even know I'm the President's kid. I keep wanting to tell him, but I guess I have to keep it secret.

Best friend or not, Jude's still confusing me. He's right. Why would the word of God need any interpretation at all? Shouldn't it be perfectly clear? So what does he expect me to think about that? That the Bible isn't the word of God at all, I suppose.

And the thing is... I can almost believe that's true, for some of the Bible. The kinds of things I read are certainly not the kinds of things the God I love would ever say. I'm sure a lot of it is right on the money, but obviously not all of it.

Still... how can I tell which is true and which isn't? Do I pick and choose to suit my own ideas? And what if my ideas are different than someone else's? Which one of us is right?

What if things I think are true turn out to be false? What if the Ten Commandments are just something someone made up? And why don't they say things you'd think should be there? Like, instead of mothers and fathers, why not honor the children? Or "Thou shalt not rape"? That's more important than not coveting.

Good grief, what if Jesus never even lived? What if he's just a character someone made up? Or maybe real, but the stuff written about him is mostly fictional, sort of like King Arthur?

How do I know what to believe, anymore? I feel so confused, I'm about to throw up.

Date: August 24, 2024
To: merrymary@webvillemail.net
From: heyjude@beatles4ever.ws
Subject: Re: I think I'm going to scream!

Mary:

Hey, if screaming helps, go for it. The conflict you're feeling right now is known as "cognitive dissonance." In a nutshell, cognitive dissonance is that weird, unsettling feeling you get when you see something that apparently contradicts something you've held as true. You can't deny what you're seeing, but find it almost impossible to question your previous truth. But don't worry. In time, it'll stop.

And yes, I do consider the Bible to be entirely the work of man. Much of it was adapted from older sources. The Ten Commandments bear a striking resemblance to the Code of Hammurabi, which predates the Ten C's by a thousand years. Try comparing the life of Jesus to the life of Krishna, for example. Or Mithra. Or Zoroaster. Compare the similarities between Christianity and the religions of these other savior figures. Lots of so-called saviors were similar to Jesus, including many who predated him. It's like the old saying goes, "Every god has its day."

And then there are your holidays. I told you about Easter, but even Christmas is stolen from an old Babylonian holiday. Holidays were adapted by the Church in order to draw pagans to Christianity. Obviously, it worked.

But yes, there are some nice things in the Bible. I won't deny that. As to what you should believe, well... Believe whatever works for you. Clearly, believing the book to be literally true didn't work out. And that's not surprising. The Bible was written by men, in male-dominated cultures where women were not considered equal to men, and slavery was common. This is why the Bible reflects those things you find so distasteful. So decide what parts DO work for you. It could be quite a lot. It could be none. Most likely, it'll be somewhere in between.

I also suggest you not limit your reading to the Bible. There are many other "sacred" texts out there, and I'd suggest you check them out. Many are online. Meet other people, too, of different beliefs. Certainly don't limit yourself to conversing with one atheist, dear.

Eventually, I think you'll see that many religions have certain elements in common, both good and bad. My rule of thumb is to ignore the bad ones and give some thought to the good ones. But it all comes down, in my opinion, to being a very personal decision.

Let me know how you're progressing.

Jude

Date: August 25, 2024
To: heyjude@beatles4ever.ws
From: merrymary@webvillemail.net
Subject: Wait a minute...

Jude:

I'm not sure I like the tone of your email. It almost sounds like you're going to stop our conversations. Please tell me I'm reading that wrong. God knows why, but I've become pretty fond of you.

Your idea is a good one. I won't talk to just you. But I also won't STOP talking to you, unless I've just been a little experiment for you, and now you're done with me.

Please tell me I'm just being paranoid.

Mary

August 26, 2024

The more I read of the Bible, the more I find that disturbs me. I want to talk to Dad or Uncle Gene about it, but I can already hear what they'd say to me. And it's not helpful.

I could talk to Jude, of course, but that's assuming I misunderstood what he said in his last email. What I really wish is that I could talk to Vicki. But I don't know how to contact her. It bothers me that I never saw her again before camp ended. She seemed so cool. And so pretty! I'd love to have her as a friend.

I've also been reading old diary entries, and tonight I found one that disturbed me. Back in early 2021, I accused Jefferson Paine of judging my father without knowing him. But now I realize that he wasn't judging my father. He was judging his actions. Paine said what he did because he disagrees with my father's policies. And I suppose I can understand some of the complaints he has.

I'm embarrassed about how I judged Paine himself. I don't agree with most of what he says, either, but I do respect him for standing up for his beliefs the way he does.

26 August 2024

If I've learned anything over the years, I've learned that life isn't simple. I know I should be optimistic. It's certain as can be that I'll be re-elected. But I can't sit back and ignore my campaigning, even though that's what I should do,

Between my duties and Sarah's involvement with The Saviors, I've barely seen her or Mary.

Ah, Mary. Such a precocious child, very intelligent and inquisitive. I love her more than life itself, but I suppose I should've seen certain things coming. Tonight she confronted me with a long list of questions about the Bible. I wish Gene had been here to handle it, but I guess this is one of my fatherly responsibilities.

I must say, some of her questions were difficult to answer. And when I asked who put these ideas in her head, she became huffy and accused me of not giving her credit enough to be able to think of them on her own.

Teenagers. I suppose I was one, once.

Still… Perhaps the questions are original to her. Some of them. But I know she's been influenced by that blasted Internet. Despite our efforts, it's still a haven for the dregs of morality. I remember her mentioning an email friend of hers who is an atheist. Perhaps this is his doing.

That blasphemous, treasonous "Voice of Reason" site is a prime example of the type of immoral garbage to be found on the Internet. Yesterday, it had an animated game that visitors could play: "Pie for Paul." The visitor uses the mouse to aim crosshairs at a caricature of myself that goes back and forth across the screen. Clicking the mouse button hurls a cream pie at the caricature's face. When the pie splats on the face, the expression changes to one of indignation and a stern warning of "You'll go to hell for that!" flashes on the screen.

What kind of message is this sending? Our children should respect public figures, and certainly not be amused by threats of damnation.

I suppose, however, that I should be thankful. This site is unique in its resistance to Big Brother's abilities. If there were other such sites out there, it would only be worse.

I just wish the Lord would show me how to best bring America to his grace.

8/26/24

Poor Paul. He is so certain that Mary's questions are the result of outside forces. Did he not go through a similar period of questioning as a boy? Perhaps not. But I certainly did during my college years, and know that it's perfectly natural.

Mary will find her path to Christ. Paul just needs to be patient and help it to happen, rather than trying to figure out why she's suddenly wondering about things.

Still, it's not hard to see why he becomes so upset. I don't suppose I'd be very happy about a "Pie for Sarah" game on an atheist's website.

Date: August 26, 2024
To: merrymary@webvillemail.net
From: heyjude@beatles4ever.ws
Subject: Don't worry

Mary:

No, I have no intention of stopping our correspondence. But I do think you need to broaden your horizons beyond just me. I could give you suggestions of things I think would help you, but I'm not going to do that.

You need to find your own path in life, Mary. I'm not going to force feed things to you the way your parents obviously did when they indoctrinated you to Christian fundamentalism.

I'll be here whenever you want. My responses may not be immediate, but they'll always come.

Take care.

And today in Beatles history:

1968: "Hey Jude" released as single in U.S., the debut release of Apple Records. (Yay!)

Jude

Welcome to

Mary's Corner of the Web

Fellow Christians, I need your help. If you can, please answer these for me. I'm stumped!

Question Number One:
   What did God do with His time before He created us? God has always existed, but our world has been around for a much shorter period of time. So He would have had a lot of time on His hands before creating the world. Why'd He wait so long?

Question Number Two:
   Why did He create us? What possible use could it have accomplished? I mean, if humans had the ability to merely think life into existence, do you think we'd be thrilled to create microbes? Do you think we'd love the microbes? Realize that the difference between God and us is much greater than between us and microbes.

Question Number Three:
   Why does God want us to worship Him? Would you demand that the microbes worship you? Or would you allow them to just live their lives, and be happy that you were the reason they had lives at all? Would you create hell? Would you send the microbes there if they didn't worship you?

These are just a few of the questions that really bother me. I don't have answers, and the answers I've gotten from others just don't even come close to satisfying me. If you can help, please drop me a line at: merry-mary@webvillemail.net

<u>About Mary</u>   <u>Mary's Faves</u>

Date: September 5, 2024
To: merrymary@webvillemail.net
From: saints_alive@catholictown.com
Subject: Your questions

Mary, I think the answer to your first question is obvious. Before creating the world, God planned it. Only later did He create us.

And I think you're selling God a little short. Humans may not love microbes, but we're not perfect. God is, as is His love for all.

The creation of Hell may seem inexplicable to us, but it has a purpose in God's great plan. How could it be otherwise?

I will pray that you begin to understand God a little better and are no longer plagued by such questions.

Sister Mary Josephina

Date: September 7, 2024
To: merrymary@webvillemail.net
From: bigjimmyjohn@truckinforjesus.com
Subject: questions

I ask the same questions sometimes. I don't have no answers neither. If you ever find answers, let me know.

J.J.

Date: September 9, 2024
To: merrymary@webvillemail.net
From: praisehim@mysweetlord.net
Subject: Your "questions"

Nice try, you filthy atheist whore!

It's bad enough that you people put down us believers, but you don't have to pretend you're a Christian in order to make fun of us. Is that the only way you can get your Satanic message out there, now? I'm surprised Big Brother hasn't shut you down.

I'm so happy you're going to burn in hell. Those who doubt the Lord are lower than snail shit.

Quit posing as a Christian, bitch.

Date: September 12, 2024
To: heyjude@beatles4ever.ws
From: merrymary@webvillemail.net
Subject: Can you believe this?

Jude:

What's up with some of these people? The email from "praisehim" wasn't even the worst of what I've received, and all from people claiming to be Christians! How can they claim that? They're not abiding by the words of Jesus, who brought a message of peace and love to mankind.

Mary

Date: September 19, 2024
To: merrymary@webvillemail.net
From: heyjude@beatles4ever.ws
Subject: Re: Can you believe this?

Mary:

Your messages weren't so bad. I've had some so nasty I had to use eye drops to wash some of the filth away. And every last one was from a Christian.

And remember there's more to the Bible than the words of Jesus. The Old Testament clearly says that certain things are punishable by death. In fact, I should be stoned to death, according to Leviticus. Go pick out your rocks, hon.

Any way you slice it, religion causes divisiveness and gives people reasons to hate others. Worse, it gives them an excuse to act upon that hatred, no matter how warped that excuse might be.

Most hatred in the world is the result of religion, from the killings of gays to the bombings of abortion clinics. Look at just about anything nasty, and you're likely to find some kind of religious outrage at the heart of it. Or at the very least, fanning the flames so they leap nice and high.

On the other hand, I've never heard of anyone being killed in the name of atheism. Even those who happen to be non-believers and commit horrible deeds do not do so to further the non-belief in God. They do it because of a lust for power or control or wealth or whatever. Not because atheism "tells" them to do it. The same cannot be said for religious atrocities.

Jude

Columbus—Libertarian Presidential candidate Michael Lee has been arrested and charged with blasphemy. The arrest came the day after Lee spoke here at a fundraising rally, during which he said, "We must return to the public the rights taken away from them by an administration that serves mythology rather than mankind."

The White House declined to comment.

Dear Mary:

After our talks at camp this summer, I knew I had to write. I was quite disturbed by the questions you asked me. I'm in fear for your soul, dear friend, and have felt guilty ever since returning home. You were crying out for help, and I didn't pay attention. We have been friends since we were little, even though we only see each other once a year. I can't bear to think that I may have let you down.

I know you have access to a biblical scholar far beyond my abilities, but perhaps Reverend Sisco has not had time for you, considering his schedule. Either way, I want you to know I'm here for you, and Jesus is there for you. He'll help you see the light again, if only you ask.

If you continue associating with atheists, you're likely to end up like that horrible Vicki Law. Bad enough that she blasphemed, but she even said some things that I think were homosexual in nature! I'm not sure, but she might be a lesbian! Except that she talked about boys, too. Of course, she might be one of those bisexuals. I swear, if any one class of person deserves hell, it's bisexuals. I hear they'll go to bed with absolutely anyone! It's sinful! But then, she's from San Francisco, so it shouldn't surprise me.

Anyway, I'm so glad I won't have to put up with her next year.

But now let me help you, old friend. Please write back to me and let me know how I may help. Perhaps you can come visit me in Denver. That would be wonderful! Do you ski? I don't think I've ever asked. Let's plan a winter trip!

I pray for you daily.

Yours in Christ,

Renée

Date: October 20, 2024
To: merrymary@webvillemail.net
From: biwitched1@sf.ca.home.net
Subject: Re: Remember me?

Mary:

Of course I remember you! I'm impressed. I didn't think you even knew my last name, let alone where I lived. Should I be flattered?

Goddess... Camp Sonlight... I remember telling you one reason I was sent to that barf-inducing place. The other was because my parents found out I was Wiccan. They freaked. Guess the staff at camp wasn't too thrilled, either. (That's why I was put in lock-down, in case you didn't know, and banned from returning.) Anyway, my folks sent me there in an attempt to brainwash it out of me, I suppose. It's funny, really. They think I only recently became Wiccan, but I have been for years. They'd REALLY flip if I told them it was my mother's sister who got me into it! I'm glad I won't have to go back there again.

I gotta dash, but email me again, soon!

Vicki

October 21, 2024

Vicki's not even Christian! How'd she even get into Camp Sonlight? I've heard of Wicca, but I thought it was a type of Satanism. I can't believe Vicki would worship the devil! I need to do some research.

Things are pretty crazy, right now, so I might not get back online to talk with her for a while. Election Day is almost here, and Dad will most likely need family support, even though he doesn't need to worry about being re-elected. The polls are showing him well in the lead of whatever his name is... the Democrat running against him.

And his approval rating is something like 80% or so. I thought that wasn't too great, but they tell me it's pretty darn good. Well, it should be! It's my dad!

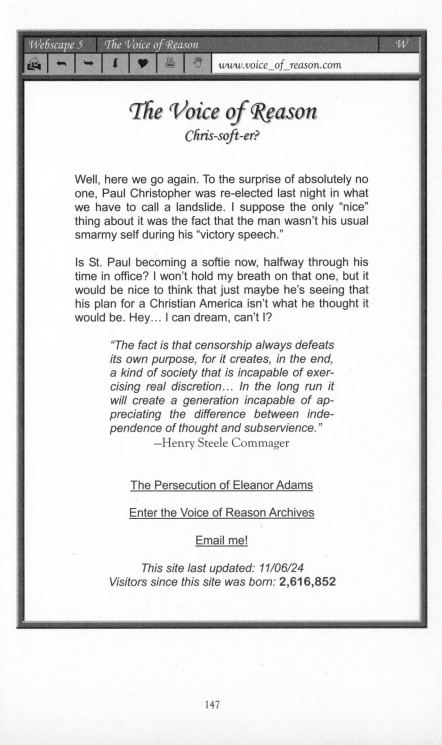

The Voice of Reason
Chris-soft-er?

Well, here we go again. To the surprise of absolutely no one, Paul Christopher was re-elected last night in what we have to call a landslide. I suppose the only "nice" thing about it was the fact that the man wasn't his usual smarmy self during his "victory speech."

Is St. Paul becoming a softie now, halfway through his time in office? I won't hold my breath on that one, but it would be nice to think that just maybe he's seeing that his plan for a Christian America isn't what he thought it would be. Hey... I can dream, can't I?

> *"The fact is that censorship always defeats its own purpose, for it creates, in the end, a kind of society that is incapable of exercising real discretion... In the long run it will create a generation incapable of appreciating the difference between independence of thought and subservience."*
> —Henry Steele Commager

The Persecution of Eleanor Adams

Enter the Voice of Reason Archives

Email me!

This site last updated: 11/06/24
Visitors since this site was born: **2,616,852**

Date: November 10, 2024
To: heyjude@beatles4ever.ws
From: merrymary@webvillemail.net
Subject: Hi!

Jude:

Hey, stranger. Sorry I haven't written in a while, but the truth is, I've found another email friend! Actually, it's a girl I met at camp. I think I mentioned Vicki to you before. She is so amazingly cool!

And it turns out she's Wiccan! Do you know anything about Wicca? It sounds kind of weird, but sort of interesting. Vicki also seems to know as much about Christianity as you do. She and I have been talking about how the Judeo-Christian faith has oppressed women for centuries. It's been hard for me, but I have to agree with what she says. All a person has to do is open their eyes and look at how things are and why they are. Then you can't help but realize that religion (a man-made thing, after all) has caused problems.

But I still believe in God and Jesus, so don't go thinking the two of you have converted me or anything. True, I'm having problems with what the Bible says about women, but I'm leaning toward the idea that these were simply the words of men, not God.

Hey, would you mind if I gave her your email address? I've mentioned you to her, and she says you sound like a fun guy to talk to.

Gotta run. Write back soon.

Mary

Date: November 20, 2024
To: merrymary@webvillemail.net
From: heyjude@beatles4ever.ws
Subject: Sorry...

Mary:

That's great that you and Vicki are becoming friends. I hope you find it to be a learning experience.

Yes, I know a bit about Wicca. And I agree with you. It is pretty interesting. I like their cyclical view of things. Very naturalistic. I've even heard of some people who consider themselves to be "secular pagans." I haven't decided, yet, whether that's an oxymoron or not.

Either way, I don't buy into the mystical aspect of it, with all the gods and goddesses, and whatnot. But overall I find it a lot more innocuous than most religions.

Sure, you can give Vicki my email address, but warn her that I'm not the best correspondent, these days.

So let me ask you something. You seem to agree that the Bible isn't really the literal word of god. If that's the case, then what causes you to still believe so fervently in a deity? Especially that particular deity. And what about Jesus? I mean, there's no evidence at all for the one, and not a whole lot for the other.

Just curious.

Jude

Date: November 24, 2024
To: heyjude@beatles4ever.ws
From: merrymary@webvillemail.net
Subject: Evidence aplenty!

Jude:

I swear, sometimes you really make my jaw drop. I can't believe you. Okay, I admit there's no solid "evidence" for God. He must be taken on faith, after all. The Bible even says as much, so trying to prove his existence is almost sinful, I suppose.

But as for Jesus, I thought we'd already been through this! There's TONS of evidence, and I think it's just silly of you to deny it.

The gospels, of course, are the biggest source of evidence. Lots of biographers of that time wrote about him. There are a bunch of letters in the Vatican written by those who knew Jesus. And then there's that bonebox thing they found that has his name on it! It says, "James, son of Joseph, brother of Jesus." Seems like pretty solid evidence to me!

Come on, Jude! Being an atheist is one thing, but you just sound stupid when you deny that Christ even lived.

I'll go ahead and pass your email address on to Vicki. But I'll warn her how pig-headed you can be.

Mary

Date: November 29, 2024
To: merrymary@webvillemail.net
From: heyjude@beatles4ever.ws
Subject: Wrong again

Mary:

I'm sure you must realize that the gospels were written decades after the alleged death of Jesus. No one knows who wrote them. The names by which you know them (Matthew, Mark, Luke, and John) are not necessarily the names of those who wrote them. There is nothing outside of these books to confirm their veracity. And they don't even confirm each other's, since they contradict one another. (Remember the Easter challenge?)

I don't know what biographers you're talking about. I already explained to you how the passage in Josephus was fake. More significantly, his earlier work, "The Jewish War," doesn't mention him at all, even though it would make perfect sense for it to have done so. And probably the most renowned Jewish historian of the period was Philo, who lived during the alleged time of Jesus, and in the same area. Philo never once mentions Jesus.

The Vatican letters you're probably referring to are known as the Archko Volume. Hon, they're fake, dated to the nineteenth century.

Now, the ossuary (your "bonebox") has been dated to about AD 63. But the inscription, which you so accurately quoted, is not any kind of solid evidence for Jesus. First, the names James, Joseph, and Jesus were, at that time and place, quite common. But more importantly, the part of the inscription referring to Jesus is almost certainly a fraud. Experts on inscriptions will tell you that the first half meets all the criteria for such historical inscriptions. But the second half was added probably much later and not by the same person who did the first half. It's just like the Josephus entry: later Christians attempting to manufacture a history for their Christ figure. It's likely that someone found this ossuary, saw the common names of James and Joseph, and added the rest. And didn't even do it well, apparently, if the inscription experts are to be believed. And why wouldn't they be believed? Oh, yes... because what they have to say isn't what Christians want to hear. In short, the ossuary is not even close to being reliable evidence. And in case you weren't aware, the owner of the box was arrested on suspicion of forgery. Not just of the ossuary, but lots of other historical objects, too.

The Jesus of the gospels is almost undeniably mythological. The stories of his life, as told in the NT, are blatantly lifted from stories of other, older "messiahs." I gave you examples before. And I could list a dozen "saviors," all of whom were crucified in some manner, most of whom "returned" to life, and many of those were after three days. Just like Jesus. And many of these predate Jesus. I can name several who were, it's said, born of a virgin, too.

The Jesus you claim to know and love was thrown together from older sources, many of which were familiar to people of that time period. This was done deliberately, as I've said before, to make the pagans more amenable to converting to the church, just as the church adopted many pagan holidays.

I suggested earlier that you should look into Mithraism and other cults that existed before the alleged time of Christ. Did you? If not, you should. You'll be stunned at how many similarities you find between them and Christianity.

Now, if you think I'm full of it, here's another challenge for you. The oldest books of the Bible that mention Jesus are the writings of Paul. Read through his writings in the New Testament. As you read them, pretend you've never read Matthew, Mark, Luke, or John (after all, Paul had never read them, since they were written later). And if you read an accurate translation of the Greek, guess what you'll find? Or rather, what you won't find. You'll find no clear reference to Jesus as a living, historical figure. How do you explain that?

That being said, it's still entirely possible that there could have been a real Jesus, around whom these stories grew. But we wouldn't know anything about him, aside from the idea that he was a self-proclaimed messiah executed for sedition (rather like what President Christopher would like to do to me). Beyond that, it's just myth and speculation, and a lot of hype.

And today in Beatles history:

2001:   George Harrison dies of cancer at the age of 58.

    Jude

Newark—The Newark campus of Rutgers University erupted in violence yesterday between members of the Campus Crusade for Christ and the Campus Freethought Alliance. Eyewitnesses claim that CCC members heckled attendees of a CFA recruitment drive. The heckling escalated to harassment and eventually to a brawl ultimately quelled by campus security. Four individuals were hospitalized with minor injuries. This is the fourth such conflict between these groups on campuses around the country in the past year.

Date: December 1, 2024
To: merrymary@webvillemail.net
From: biwitched1@sf.ca.home.net
Subject: Jude's email

Mary:

Y'know, the thing is, it really doesn't matter whether I agree or not with Jude. It doesn't matter whether I think Jesus was a real person or not. And not just because I'm not a Christian.

Truthfully, I don't know why it really matters to you whether Jesus was real. It shouldn't matter. Isn't the message what's important?

Even if Jesus proves to be 100% myth, he's credited with saying some really great stuff. You can live your life by his words even if those words weren't from a god in human form, right?

I know that the words of the Wiccan Rede were made by "mere" humans. But what's wrong with that?

Stop stressing so much over this, hon. It's not worth getting upset over!

Vicki

Vicki's right. It shouldn't matter whether Jesus was real or not. The message really is the most important thing. But I can't help it. The very idea that Jesus might not have even existed just freaks me out.

I know that most everything Jude has told me has been difficult to disprove. But this… this is much bigger than anything he's hit me with.

Am I being stupid? I mean, I've been told "the truth" by my parents, Uncle Gene, and others for years. But what if it's not really true at all? What if Jesus did have myths spring up about his life?

I had to look up "sedition." I found reference to a Sedition Act from 1798. It made it illegal to criticize the government. I think that's kind of weird. I mean, I learned in social studies that we're supposed to be able to criticize the government. That's what's meant by a government "of the people," or something. And as Jude pointed out, that's pretty much why Jesus was killed, because he criticized those in charge.

And that's just wrong. Any citizen should be free to point out the problems with that government. He shouldn't have to keep quiet because he's afraid of going to jail. Or worse.

But would that apply to Jefferson Paine, who complains about problems that aren't really problems? Should he be allowed to say nasty things about my father just because he doesn't like the laws he's passed?

I guess he should be.

But something that's been bothering for a while is that I'm not entirely sure Dad's doing the right thing. I mean, I love him with all my heart. I think he's the best dad in the world. And my heart tells me he wouldn't do anything that wasn't right. But things like this blasphemy law make me have doubts. Heck, I get offended when someone says something bad about my religion, but I don't think they should go to jail for it. Aren't people allowed to say whatever they want? Isn't that what Freedom of Speech is?

If Dad agrees with that, why did he pass that law? He tells me politics is very complicated and there are things I can't understand and that I have to trust him. Well, I may not understand politics, but I do understand the difference between right and wrong.

I've been thinking of Vicki a lot, lately, too. Remembering her from camp… how she looked. On some level, I think all girls look at other girls that they find pretty. We look at each other and think, "Oh, I wish I had hair like hers," or, "I wonder if my boobs will ever be like hers," or, "Why can't I have gorgeous green eyes like she does?"

We girls always check each other out, making comparisons, and admiring each other (or being envious), whether we admit it to ourselves or not.

Do guys do that? Do they wonder if their cheekbones are as handsome as the next guy's? Do they want their hair to be as silky as so-and-so's? Do they evaluate other guys' butts? (I've heard they compare the sizes of their things, but that's so gay.)

Whatever they might do, I doubt it's as common as between girls.

So I think Vicki is beautiful. So what? I'm not blind. She's got the look. I admit it.

But I still feel "wrong" about admitting it. Because the truth is that I'm not just admitting that she's pretty. I'm admitting that I'm actually attracted to her. And no, I don't really know what I mean by that. It's just when I think of her, it feels different than when I think of a girl that I just think is pretty. I don't feel anything when I look at magazine models, no matter how beautiful they are. But with Vicki...

This goes beyond what is expected or accepted. It's bordering on sinful.

And I don't know if this is the result of talking with Jude or not, but I'm not even sure what is really meant by "sin." I've heard it said that a sin is anything that offends God. But... what really could offend God? I mean, if God's perfect, it makes sense to me that it would be impossible to offend Him.

It seems to me that a better definition of sin would be anything that deliberately harms another person. So it wouldn't be sinful to accidentally hurt someone, but to do it on purpose would be. Anyway, that's a definition that makes sense to me, but I doubt it would go over very well with Mom or Dad or Uncle Gene.

So do I really believe this? Or is it just my way of trying to tell myself that it's okay to be attracted to Vicki without feeling guilty? I mean, it's just attraction to one girl. So what? It's not like she's attracted to me, and even if she were, it's not like I'm gay or anything. It's not that kind of attraction. That definitely is sinful.

Isn't it?

Year Five

2025

20 January 2025

At last, I can relax. The pressures of campaigning are behind me, and the holidays are past. That proverbial huge weight has been lifted from my shoulders. I'm busy, of course, since there is still so much to do for my country. But campaigning is so draining a task. I'm glad it's over.

Sarah and I spent a romantic weekend in the Poconos earlier this month. It was nice to "reconnect." I just don't see enough of her. Or Mary, for that matter.

Last night she asked me if the religious freedom guaranteed by the Constitution applies to all religions. When I assured her it did, she asked me why so many faiths are not accepted. She didn't specify any, but didn't need to. It's common for children her age to become curious about things, and where religion is concerned, those pagan "religions" seem to have a tremendous amount of interest to them.

Sarah saved me the effort of a reply, and it seemed to dampen the fire in Mary's eyes. But for how long?

I've long been deeply troubled by the popularity of witchcraft and other false religions over the past decades. Something should be done about them.

I suspect my allies in Congress could be convinced to introduce another bit of legislation. That may be the only answer. It would be a nice way to begin my second term, but it will be tricky. We must determine a way to justify taking action. Freedom of religion has too often stretched the definition of "religion" beyond what is acceptable. That's a high hurdle we'll have to leap.

Another thing bothering me is the continual barrage of criticism coming from the Christian camp. Not just Montoya and his New Anglican Church, but many of the more liberal Christian groups insist that our policies are too harsh. Gene tells me to disregard them. He says they're not "real" Christians. I suppose he's right. But still, it is troublesome.

Date: January 22, 2025
To: biwitched1@sf.ca.home.net
From: merrymary@webvillemail.net
Subject: Salvation

Vicki:

My mother said something to me at dinner the other night that has me all confused. We were talking about religions in general and she said that a lot of the persecution other religions suffer is because Christians are so concerned about the salvation of others. That's why they push Christianity on them so much.

I know you Wiccans don't believe in the whole missionary thing, or proselytizing, but how can you argue against that? I mean, salvation is the ultimate, isn't it? Nobody wants to go to hell! Of course, you don't believe in hell, either, so that's not much of an argument to you.

If I'd bring up salvation and proselytizing to Jude, he'd just say that the desire to save souls doesn't make up for all those who were tortured and killed in the name of religion. Or that people have done perfectly well without Christianity up to now, and can do fine without having it forced down their throats. Or that hell is just a threat used to scare people into being good.

The things I imagine he'd say to me are at least partially right. But from the Christian point of view, my mother's point is good, too.

How are people supposed to know what's what on this subject???

I'm still trying to do research on the historical Jesus, to see if Jude was off base in that last tirade I forwarded to you. But I'm not having much luck. I mean, most scholars (but not all) seem to think he was a real person, but there's not much actual evidence out there to back up the idea. But I'm still looking.

I'm glad you had a nice Thanksgiving with your Aunt Margot visiting. I know how important family is. Sometimes I don't see my mother for a week at a time, and I haven't been able to spend much quality time with my dad for years. They're both so busy.

But that's something else completely. I won't bore you with it.

Mary

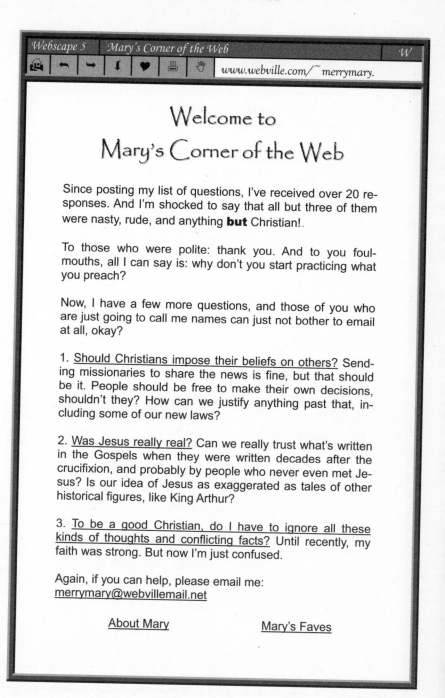

www.webville.com/~merrymary.

Welcome to
Mary's Corner of the Web

Since posting my list of questions, I've received over 20 responses. And I'm shocked to say that all but three of them were nasty, rude, and anything **but** Christian!

To those who were polite: thank you. And to you foul-mouths, all I can say is: why don't you start practicing what you preach?

Now, I have a few more questions, and those of you who are just going to call me names can just not bother to email at all, okay?

1. <u>Should Christians impose their beliefs on others?</u> Sending missionaries to share the news is fine, but that should be it. People should be free to make their own decisions, shouldn't they? How can we justify anything past that, including some of our new laws?

2. <u>Was Jesus really real?</u> Can we really trust what's written in the Gospels when they were written decades after the crucifixion, and probably by people who never even met Jesus? Is our idea of Jesus as exaggerated as tales of other historical figures, like King Arthur?

3. <u>To be a good Christian, do I have to ignore all these kinds of thoughts and conflicting facts?</u> Until recently, my faith was strong. But now I'm just confused.

Again, if you can help, please email me:
<u>merrymary@webvillemail.net</u>

<u>About Mary</u>   <u>Mary's Faves</u>

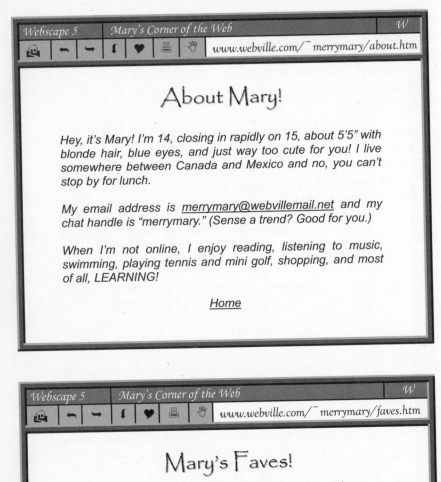

Webscape 5 — *Mary's Corner of the Web* — *W*

www.webville.com/~merrymary/about.htm

About Mary!

Hey, it's Mary! I'm 14, closing in rapidly on 15, about 5'5" with blonde hair, blue eyes, and just way too cute for you! I live somewhere between Canada and Mexico and no, you can't stop by for lunch.

My email address is merrymary@webvillemail.net and my chat handle is "merrymary." (Sense a trend? Good for you.)

When I'm not online, I enjoy reading, listening to music, swimming, playing tennis and mini golf, shopping, and most of all, LEARNING!

Home

Webscape 5 — *Mary's Corner of the Web* — *W*

www.webville.com/~merrymary/faves.htm

Mary's Faves!

(These are likely to change at any time, of course.)

Favorite Band: *Grey Eye Glances (thanks, Jude!)*
Favorite Movie: *The Lord of the Rings (all three!)*
Favorite Book: *Jonathan Livingston Seagull (thanks, Vicki!)*
Favorite Food: *Pizza!*
Favorite Drink: *Dr Pepper (some things never change)*
Favorite TV Show: *Saturday Night Live*
Favorite Animal: *Horses, especially Arabians*
Favorite Sport: *Tennis (unless you count miniature golf)*

Home

2/20/25

After looking at Mary's website today, I'm now not so sure about the nature of her questioning. I never thought she would post such questions on the Internet.

I'm probably just paranoid, but I keep fearing that someone will learn she is the President's daughter and make that knowledge widely known online. I don't think many Americans would be happy to know that the youngest Christopher is questioning her faith. It would certainly not cast a pleasant light on Paul or me. We are the ones professing that faith will save our nation, after all, and for our own daughter to appear in disagreement with us...

No. That is unacceptable. She cannot have such a forum any longer.

Date: February 12, 2025
To: merrymary@webvillemail.net
From: administrator@webville-inc.com
Subject: Site deletion

This message is to officially notify you that your website, www.webville.com/~merrymary, has been deleted from the Webville servers, upon instructions from the United States Government.

Your site contained content found to be unlawful by the government's Big Brother Internet Monitoring System. Such content may not be hosted by Webville.

Although your account with us is still open, it will be terminated if you should post such material again in the future. Such action will also render you liable for any fines imposed by the government for a repeat violation.

We trust you understand why this measure was taken.

Thank you.

Webville Administration Staff

Date: February 18, 2025
To: merrymary@webvillemail.net
From: biwitched1@sf.ca.home.net
Subject: Re: Can you believe this!?

Mary:

Hey, bummer about your site being nuked. That sucks. But I don't think there's anything you can do about it, unless you want to drop an email to that Jefferson Paine guy and see how he manages to keep his site alive.

So are you going to be going to Camp Sonlight again this year? My folks are still pissed that I was kicked out last year and banned from returning. I'm thrilled, of course. I'd vomit if I had to listen to one more round of Christian campfire songs.

Vicki

Date: February 20, 2025
To: merrymary@webvillemail.net
From: jefferson_paine@voice_of_reason.com
Subject: Re: Question

Thank you for emailing, Mary. And please thank your friend for her kind words about my site.

It probably will not surprise you to know that yours is a question I hear frequently. Naturally, everyone wants to keep his or her websites online. But I'm afraid I don't really have the answer you're looking for.

Today, Big Brother could easily penetrate the programming I used a year ago, so I constantly am updating the software. And I can't make the program publicly available to everyone because that would make it easy for the government folks to intercept it, analyze it, and beat it.

I'm sorry to hear yours was taken down, but there's nothing I can suggest to help you. What happened to you is what has happened to thousands of others in our country. This is why my site exists, after all – to protest the unconstitutional actions of President Christopher and his cohorts.

If you want to join the protest, I'd be happy to have a member of the Freethought Underground in your area contact you.

Take care, and good luck.

Jefferson Paine

March 19, 2025

Dear Renée,

I know I should have written long ago, and I apologize for not. As you can imagine, things were crazy during my father's re-election campaign. Then came Thanksgiving and Christmas, and so on.

Still, those aren't good reasons, and I hope you forgive me. But there's one other reason, and you may not be able to forgive me for this one. You see, I haven't really known what to say to you.

I want you to know, first of all, that you have not let me down in any way. Yes, it's true that you did not answer the questions I asked at camp last year. But remember, I have my parents, as well as Reverend Sisco himself to ask. And none of them have had answers that satisfy me, either.

The fact is, I don't know what to call myself anymore. I really can't call myself a fundamentalist. Too much of the Bible can't be taken literally and have it make sense. I still consider myself a Christian, but I have too many questions that can't be answered. Not by you, or by anyone, it seems.

Oh, and I have you to thank for something, though it probably won't make you happy. Your letter gave me enough information so I was able to track down Vicki, from camp. She and I have been emailing a lot (you really must join the 21st Century, dear), and she is the coolest girl! I wish I'd gotten to spend more time with her at camp! Vicki is opening my eyes to lots of things. Between her and Jude, I'm really a very different person than you've been friends with for so long.

And yes, that's the same Jude I mentioned at camp. The atheist I email with. I know you don't approve, but he's very nice, very smart, and I love talking with him.

Anyway, I think I'll end this letter now. Feel free to write back, but I'll understand if you don't want to. I'd normally say, "See you at camp," but honestly, I'm not sure I'll be there this year.

I wish you the best.

Always,

Mary

4/22/25

Mary asked us tonight if she could invite a friend to spend the summer with her. I was pleased to hear that it was a friend from camp. I remember her saying how knowledgeable the girl was about the Bible. This could be just the thing to help her through her questioning period. After all, a teenager will often not listen to parents, but will heed a peer.

I would be much happier, though, if we knew more about this girl. After all, there are those who are sent to Camp Sonlight not because they are filled with the Holy Spirit, but because they're lacking it completely.

22 April 2025

I'm such a pushover. Perhaps I just love Mary too much, and will do anything she asks. I can't say "no" to her.

I didn't even hesitate before agreeing to allow a camp friend of hers to visit for the summer. And I would have granted it even if Sarah hadn't expressed her approval.

We've both been concerned about Mary's lack of a social life ever since I took office. Camp can be wonderful, but this is the first time she's ever mentioned wanting to see one of her camp friends outside of there. I think close friends are important for children her age, and the fact is she has none.

Sarah shares my feeling that we should have asked more questions about this girl. Still, we must have faith in our daughter's judgment. She's never disappointed us, yet.

Date: April 24, 2025
To: heyjude@beatles4ever.ws
From: merrymary@webvillemail.net
Subject: Sorry!

Jude:

I was going through some old emails and discovered that you'd asked me a question that I never replied to. I'm really sorry about that.

You asked why I still believed in God at all. Well, basically, because I don't have any reason not to. I mean, even though I can't prove there was a real Jesus, there still must have been something that caused all those people to write about him, don't you think? The original apostles were martyred for their beliefs. Why would they risk their lives if there hadn't been a Jesus? And millions of people KNOW they've had personal encounters with Jesus and God! You can't just dismiss that!

Also, there's too much in the world that can't be explained, that MUST be the result of God's miracles. How can you explain it when a plane crashes and one person survives? Surely he was blessed by God.

Also, the universe is just too darn orderly for it not to have been designed by a Creator. Think of the millions of things that had to be JUST RIGHT in order for life to develop. It can't be just chance. And it had to begin SOMEWHERE. It couldn't just "happen." It REQUIRES a Creator!

Besides, I think it only makes sense to believe in God. I mean, if I go through my life believing, and there really is a God, I'll go to heaven. (Well, there's more to it than that, but you get the idea.) And if there isn't one, I've lost nothing. On the other hand, if I don't believe and there is a God, then I'll go to hell. And that's not something I'd want. Would you?

So my question to you is: with your immortal soul at stake, why not just have faith?

By the way, have you emailed with Vicki, yet? My parents actually consented to having her spend the summer here with me! I can't believe it!

Mary

Date: May 1, 2025
To: merrymary@webvillemail.net
From: heyjude@beatles4ever.ws
Subject: Re: Sorry!

Mary:

That's great that Vicki's coming to visit you! Yes, we've emailed, but it's been mostly introductions. I look forward to hearing all about her visit. She sounds nice. I'm glad your parents are being cool about it. (I'm assuming they know nothing about her.)

Anyway, allow me to comment on your response to me.

First of all, let's look at your religion. Can you tell me who benefits the most from it? It certainly isn't God. He's omnipotent. He certainly can't NEED the worship of his creations. Is it the common person? Well, not really. I've compared religion to a crutch before. And while a crutch can be useful for a time, the real benefit comes from healing the lame limb. Religion doesn't heal anything. It keeps the religious dependent upon it forever. But there is one group of people who benefit from religion greatly. And that's the clergy.

I don't need to tell you how wealthy the Vatican is, do I? Do you see the Pope funding centers to train welfare recipients and helping them find jobs, or financing ANY charity that does not promote his religion? Of course not. The money's for the church, and no one else.

In biblical times, sacrifices were demanded... animals to be "given" to God. Well, who do you think feasted on that roasted flesh after it was sacrificed? The priests did, that's who.

And today we've got multi-millionaire televangelists like Gene Sisco and others. Do you think their fortunes are being used to fund cancer research? Not a chance. To find a cure for AIDS? To hear some of them talk, AIDS is a curse from God to begin with. No... all that money goes only to pad their own pockets and to generate even more money. (Yes, some religious charities really do help people, but even St. Teresa's Missionaries of Charity didn't do the good they're believed to have done. They could have done a LOT of good, with the amount of funding they received every year. Instead, they did less than the average free clinic.)

So writing about God, around which a religion could be maintained, benefited the writers (not to mention millions of people who promoted the religion in years thereafter). Stories of Jesus could be 100% fiction and they'd still benefit the clergy, wouldn't they? (Just look at Scientology if you have any doubts about the lucrative nature of man-made religions.)

So I don't think your first argument holds up. There did not "have" to be real things around which the stories were told.

Nor did there need to be a real Jesus. Yes, early Christians were persecuted for their beliefs. But so were early Mormons. So were Zoroastrians. Many religions have "martyrs." I'll bet you don't believe that the gods they followed were real, do you? But they did.

As for the "miracles" we see every day, why do you think they're miracles? The example you gave would leave me with a different question in my head. I wouldn't wonder at how blessed the survivor was. I'd wonder what the dead people did to piss God off so much that he made their plane crash. Or is that a question that I shouldn't ask?

Thousands of years ago, no one knew what caused lightning and thunder. It was eventually attributed to one god or another. But in time, we came to understand it. The same can be said for a million other things that were, at one time, regarded as "miracles," but today are understood. And a thousand years from now, we'll understand things we're baffled over today. So unless you want to produce some actual miracles today, I don't think we can use that argument.

Yes, there are people who claim that they've spoken with God or seen Jesus or angels, and so on. They're utterly convinced of this, and you couldn't possibly convince them otherwise. But I'd like to point out that there are also people who are just as convinced that they've been taken aboard spaceships and experimented upon by sexually perverse alien creatures. Nothing you can say would convince them that they've only imagined such things. So we obviously cannot take someone at their word, no matter how convinced they themselves are, without some sort of evidence.

As for your assertion that the universe is orderly... well, yes and no. There is an apparent order to things, but order does not imply much of anything, least of all a Creator who designed. There are things that form orderly patterns all by themselves. Crystals, for example. Like snowflakes, or salt, or diamonds. Nice, orderly shape, without anyone making them that way. Or try this. Pour a bunch of ball bearings into an empty box. The spherical objects form nice, neat little rows in the rectangular container, all by themselves. Did you force that to happen? Nope. No "intelligent design" behind that pattern.

Is the "purpose" of the universe to support life? Most fundamentalists you meet will insist we're alone in the universe. If that's the case, then it's an awfully big universe just to support life on this itsy bitsy planet. Even if there is life elsewhere, why so much empty space in between stars, or galaxies? Why would God be so wasteful?

The truth is, you only THINK all these things had to be perfect for life to exist because you think human life is the purpose of the world. That's very species-centric. The purpose of the world could just as easily have been to provide a place for cockroaches to live, not humans.

Why, exactly, do you think the universe "had to begin SOME-WHERE?" I understand that the idea of an infinite regression of causes makes your stomach turn. I'm not to keen on it, either. But there are plenty (mostly those of Eastern religions) who have no problem whatsoever with it.

Beyond that, if you're saying everything must have a cause, then what caused God? If you say God is the exception, then you're violating your own rule. If nothing had to cause God, then it is NOT true that "everything must have a cause." Therefore, you can save yourself a step and say that the universe itself is the "first cause."

Your last argument is known as Pascal's Wager, named after the French philosopher and mathematician who made this argument famous, almost 400 years ago. But I'm afraid it's not logical, either. (And that's very strange. You'd think a mathematician would know logic when he saw it.)

First of all, I base my beliefs on reason. To me, "faith" is contrary to my nature. So, believing in God on faith would be being untrue to myself. I would lose a bit of my integrity. And I think one's personal integrity is very important.

Aside from that, is this the sort of thing you think God would want? You've said it yourself—you have the ability to use reason. And if you believe this is a gift of God's, why wouldn't he want you to use it? Why would he insist on "faith," which is CONTRARY to reason?

But possibly the biggest problem with this argument is that it isn't an either/or proposition. If I'm wrong in stating that there's no God, does that automatically mean that you're correct, that the God you worship exists? No, it doesn't. It might be any of the other thousands of deities worshiped throughout history, any combination thereof, or something else entirely that no one's even thought of yet.

In other words, even if I'm wrong, that doesn't make you, Pascal, or anyone else, right.

Well, enough for now. (Gee, this is getting to be like our old days of emailing. I refuse to stop making you think!) Take care.

Oh, and I hope you had a happy birthday!

And today in Beatles history:

1965:   BEATLES FOR SALE debuts at #1 in U.K.

Jude

The Voice of Reason
Is the Press Free Again?

TIME magazine asks this week, "Is the Christopher Administration in Trouble?" Maybe our Press is finally getting over said administration's intimidation tactics.

Or not. The article got off to a good start by mentioning all sorts of dirt (like the idea that Sisco is really the man in charge), but then got all wishy-washy. By the end of the article, I was left with a feeling of buttkissing-as-usual. If people would stop reading after the fifth paragraph, it might be enough to start the public thinking, and questioning what's going on in our country.

Or maybe not. I'm probably expecting too much of Mr. & Mrs. Average American. But that's why The Freethought Underground exists: to educate them. Every day, I'm happy to say, I receive emails from people wanting to know what they can do, how they can help turn this country around.

Remember, if you don't know how to find the Underground, let them find you. Email me, and I'll see that your message gets passed along.

> *"No government ought to be without censors; and where the press is free, no one ever will."*
> —Thomas Jefferson

The Persecution of Eleanor Adams

Enter the Voice of Reason Archives

Email me!

This site last updated: 05/10/25
*Visitors since this site was born: **3,101,628***

Date: May 25, 2025
To: heyjude@beatles4ever.ws
From: merrymary@webvillemail.net
Subject: Excited!

Jude:

I can't wait! Vicki will be arriving here on the 9th. She'll be staying for four weeks! I'm so excited! I have no idea what all we'll be doing, but it'll just be so cool to spend so much time with a new friend. And you know what? I'm not even going to miss Camp Sonlight. Yeah, I like camping and doing things outdoors, but nothing ever really changed, there. The activities last year weren't much different from the activities there when I was little. It just got boring.

I've been thinking a lot about your last anti-religion rant. And, as usual, I don't have much to say about it. I guess the thing that keeps coming back to me is that even if you're right, and it's all based on things that never happened and people who didn't exist, millions of people around the world still get comfort from their faith. Religion does do some good! Whether you want to think of it as a crutch or not, what difference does that make? Just because you think human beings are better off standing on their own two feet, without the crutch of religion, who are you to demand that everyone abandon their faith?

If I, or a billion other people, want to go through life with this religious crutch, what difference should that make to you? It doesn't harm you at all! Why can't you just let people live their lives the way they want?

Mary

Date: May 30, 2025
To: merrymary@webvillemail.net
From: heyjude@beatles4ever.ws
Subject: Good point

Mary:

Okay, I'll concede that many people DO benefit from their faith, and that some people are, in fact, utterly incapable of functioning without it. Yes, I think that makes them weaker people, but I don't insist that they get rid of their crutches. I've never insisted that, and never would!

As I've said before, I don't care what anyone thinks about religion. I DO believe that people should live their lives the way they want, including believing whatever they like, no matter how silly I may think that belief is. Heck, you once thought the Sidestreet Girls were the greatest gift to music in the history of the world. I found that ridiculous, but it was entirely your right to believe it. I didn't insist that you consider The Beatles to be the best.

I commend you on being outraged. I think anyone who's not outraged isn't paying attention. But I'm afraid your outrage is aimed in the wrong direction. It is not ME who is trying to take the freedom to believe silly things away from anyone else. It is people like Sisco who seek to force others to THEIR way of thinking and living!

Can you not see this? In all the time we've been emailing, in all the examples I've given you of the atrocities of religion, how can you think it is Brights who are out to control the rest of society?

Mary, open your eyes! Religion can only thrive if it has adherents. Remember our talks, and your postings on your web site, about missionaries? For that matter, take a look at the history of the Christian church.

The majority of the church's history is positively rife with atrocity after bloody atrocity. It's enough to make you sick. Take the Crusades... essentially a widespread "convert or die" mentality that killed millions of people over hundreds of years. The Inquisition was an extension of this, and the "witch hunts" that followed were an extension of the Inquisition. Century after century of people being killed for no other reason than because they didn't believe the same things the killers believed. That's all it was about, Mary! Belief. The ones killed hadn't done a damn thing to harm the killers. They just refused to believe in the same god as the killers. Some crime, huh?

And then there's the Dark Ages, when superstition largely replaced science, leading to untold misery. The church forbade such things as the use of medicine to combat disease, leading to untold deaths. I'm sure you've heard of the Black Plague. The church discouraged bathing, and rats love filth, so the fleas that carried the plague had easy access to people.

The plague wasn't the fault of the church, but the church was undeniably a major reason that so many millions died. Simple sanitary measures, such as those common in pre-Christian times, would have minimized the damage done by disease. Maybe kept it from reaching epidemic proportions.

And how about cats? Cats kill rats. But the church felt that cats were evil, the familiars of witches, and were killed with abandon. Just one more religious superstition to blame for staggering numbers of deaths.

Truth is, fundies like Sisco and others want to reinstate this kind of church control over everything. There has NEVER been a theocracy in history that has been concerned with individual liberty, or the welfare of the masses. Not one! Why on earth do you think a theocracy under today's Christianity would be different than one under the Christianity of 1000 years ago?

Look what's been done in this country in just the past few years. We've got widespread censorship of all media (and you, yourself, have been a victim of it). We've got creationism being taught in schools, which is nothing but a religious idea without a shred of scientific support. We've got abortion outlawed again, and doctors being imprisoned or put to death for performing them! We've got BLASPHEMY being a crime! Blasphemy! A victimless crime!

Is this the America you think we deserve? I guarantee this is but a hint of the kind of America the fundies WANT to have. I'd rather not live to see the day such a theocracy exists here, thanks very much.

Again, it's not the individual belief I'm against, sweetie, it's the mandatory adherence to religious policies. I believe every human being has the right to believe whatever he or she wants, no matter how idiotic I may personally find it. But religious zealots DON'T believe this. They're saying that everyone must live by a certain set of rules. THEIR rules.

Vicki's Wiccan. I'm an atheist. And we most certainly don't care for their rules. Have no doubt, we would be punished for that by those in charge, if they could possibly get away with it. And that could be just a matter of time.

So tell me... who's the bad guy here? Is it me? Vicki? Jefferson Paine? J. E. Cooper? The Freethought Underground? Or is it Sisco, Christopher, and all those who would force their personal beliefs onto the rest of society?

And today in Beatles history:

1973:   Harrison's LIVING IN THE MATERIAL WORLD album released.
1969:   "The Ballad of John & Yoko" released as single in U.K.
1968:   Recording of the "White Album" begins.
1966:   Capitol Records releases "Paperback Writer" as a single.
1964:   "Love Me Do" hits #1 on the U.S. Billboard charts.

Jude

9 June 2025

Mary's friend Vicki arrived this evening. She's... Well, she's not quite what Sarah and I were expecting. She's maybe a year older than Mary, but quite obviously far more worldly.

She also has a quality about her that I found difficult to label. But Sarah said it perfectly, later this evening. "Unwholesome" was the word she used. And she's right. Though she doesn't actively do anything to convey this, Vicki exudes an aura of sexuality. But she's from San Francisco, so this should hardly surprise me.

What does surprise me, frankly, is the fact that our daughter is friends with this girl. Vicki is practically Mary's polar opposite. But then, perhaps that's the appeal.

Either way, Sarah and I have some trepidation, I'm afraid. I suspect Sarah will be keeping a close watch over the two of them during Vicki's visit.

June 9, 2025

Vicki arrived tonight, and we are having an absolutely fantastic time already! I don't think my folks are all that thrilled with her, though. They can be so judgmental at times. So she showed up at the White House wearing jeans and a T-shirt. She's a teenager! That's what we're supposed to wear. And it's not like she was coming here to meet the President, after all.

Okay, maybe it shouldn't have been a shirt with an anarchy symbol on it...

Anyway, we talked for hours until we got too tired to talk. I'm exhausted, but wanted to write this entry first.

I'm so glad she's here. I've never known anyone like her. She's different than my friends back in California, and definitely different than my camp friends. She's so much more... <u>real</u> than they are.

I wish I could be more like her.

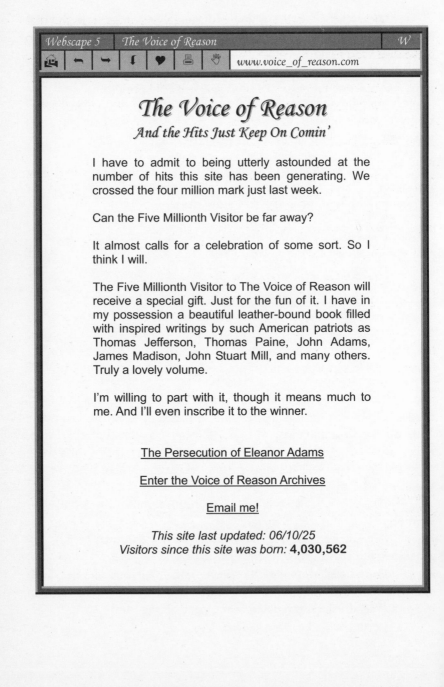

www.voice_of_reason.com

The Voice of Reason
And the Hits Just Keep On Comin'

I have to admit to being utterly astounded at the number of hits this site has been generating. We crossed the four million mark just last week.

Can the Five Millionth Visitor be far away?

It almost calls for a celebration of some sort. So I think I will.

The Five Millionth Visitor to The Voice of Reason will receive a special gift. Just for the fun of it. I have in my possession a beautiful leather-bound book filled with inspired writings by such American patriots as Thomas Jefferson, Thomas Paine, John Adams, James Madison, John Stuart Mill, and many others. Truly a lovely volume.

I'm willing to part with it, though it means much to me. And I'll even inscribe it to the winner.

The Persecution of Eleanor Adams

Enter the Voice of Reason Archives

Email me!

This site last updated: 06/10/25
Visitors since this site was born: **4,030,562**

June 11, 2025

Vicki and I chatted online with Jude! He doesn't really chat much, but we convinced him to. And it was super! Of course, I had to make sure Vicki never mentioned anything about the White House. Jude still doesn't know I'm the President's daughter, though I'm starting to think my father's a little paranoid. I should just tell him.

We talked about a lot of things. And of course, Jude had to mention how he's been making me re-think my religious beliefs. He joked about making an atheist out of me, yet.

Then Vicki said that even if I decided Christianity was bogus, it wouldn't mean that I'd think atheism was the right answer. She said she'd make a Wiccan out of me first. I laughed, since neither one will happen!

Later we watched movies in my room, stuffing ourselves on popcorn and chips. Vicki loves James Bond movies, too!

Tomorrow we'll do the grand tour of D.C. Vicki especially wants to see the Vietnam Wall. I'm not looking forward to that. I was there once and got so depressed looking at all those names. It's even worse than looking at all those white rows of markers over at Arlington.

Vicki stayed in a private room the first night, but now she's in mine. We might as well, since we stay up until all hours gabbing, anyway. It's strange, though, sharing a bed with her. I haven't done that with a friend since I lived back in California. Seems forever ago.

6/13/25

Vicki is most certainly not what I envisioned. I don't care if she has extensive Biblical familiarity or not. I have bad feelings about her.

Last night at dinner, I asked her to say grace. And while she readily did so, there was no mention of God or Jesus. She spoke of being grateful for the bounty of the earth, or something like that.

I did not question her about it, as I did not want to seem rude, but Paul and I exchanged glances after she finished.

She is the model of consideration. She treats both of us with respect, speaks without half as much slang as Mary does, and does not in any way misbehave.

Why, then, do I not trust her?

June 19, 2025

Today Vicki and I had a long talk in the Rose Garden about Wicca. I brought it up, since I've been really curious about it. But now I'm really confused. Because everything Vicki's telling me about her religion is so different from what I've been told about it by others. Vicki says that's not surprising, though. She says Christians have been badmouthing the earth religions for two thousand years. Why should they stop now?

One thing that really surprised me was that there's no devil figure in Wicca. This is especially funny, since I'd been told that Wiccans were Satan worshipers.

Here's the weird thing I don't quite get. Vicki calls Wicca her religion. But I always thought you needed a god to have a religion. Vicki doesn't worship a god. Oh, she'll talk about "the goddess," but when I asked about this, Vicki said she thinks of it as more of a metaphor than anything else. "Mother Nature" is the closest analogy she can think of. She doesn't view her "goddess" as being real in the same sense as I believe God to be real.

I told her that sounded more like being an atheist, but she explained that she does believe in "something," just nothing that can be easily defined. So that would make her a Deist, I suppose. And she mentioned that her form of Wicca is as a "solitary," not really following a specific form of Wicca. But she does have a set of beliefs and rituals she engages in, which is why she's comfortable with calling it her religion.

Vicki is, essentially, a person who worships the earth. And by "worship," I don't mean that she prays to it, expecting some sort of answer, like I do when I pray. Rather, she honors the earth by caring for it, treating it with respect, and never forgetting for a moment that all we have, all we are, is from the earth. I think that's really beautiful.

She also said it made more sense to her to celebrate life itself, rather than go to a church where people just listen to boring old sermons condemning others, or sitting and praying all day. If religion is a joyful thing, you should express it! That's interesting, because I've never seen my mom or dad express any sort of religious joy. Come to think of it, I haven't exactly experienced religious ecstasy, either.

Anyway, Saturday is the Summer Solstice, which is apparently a Wiccan holy day called Litha, or Midsummer. Vicki plans to perform a ritual on that day. I'm excited, to be honest. I can't wait to see what it's like.

June 21, 2025

I am so totally freaked out right now. It's late. Or rather, it's early. I put Saturday's date on the top of the page, but it's technically the twenty-second, since it's about three in the morning on Sunday.

Something happened a couple hours ago that I just don't know how to handle. Maybe writing about it will help me think more clearly about it.

Vicki and I got up really early on Saturday. Around 5:30, I think. She wanted to celebrate the first ritual of Litha, which is the greeting of the sunrise on the solstice. So we grabbed one of my yoga mats and off we went to the Truman balcony's eastern side.

While we waited for it to come closer to sunrise, Vicki explained that she usually celebrates Litha in three rituals...one at sunrise, one at mid-day, and one in the evening, ending at sunset. I told her it was okay with me if she wanted to do all three, but she said one would be enough this year.

Then she said that she needed to get ready, and (much to my shock) proceeded to take her clothes off! And I mean every stitch! Right there on the balcony! I mean, it was still dark outside and the chances of anyone being able to see us was pretty slim. But still... one of the Secret Service guys could have strolled on by and had himself an eyeful! Vicki didn't seem to care.

But it made me really uncomfortable. Vicki noticed, and even seemed amused by it. She told me it was okay, that she didn't mind if I saw her naked.

Then she invited me to take part in the ritual with her. I shook my head. I wasn't Wiccan, I reminded her. But she smiled and said, "Now you know what it's like to be invited to a Christian church when you're not Christian." It was like being punched in the stomach. I'd never thought of it that way, of how inappropriate such an offer could be.

So I said, "Would you go to church with me tomorrow if I do this?" And she said yes! I was kinda hoping she'd say no, because the idea being nude in front of her made me even more uncomfortable than seeing her naked. But she said I didn't have to. Only if I wanted to.

I don't know if it was because I wanted to experience the full ritual or what, but I convinced myself that it wasn't really that big a deal. Other girls saw me naked at camp, when we'd be getting dressed. Of course, that was usually just a glimpse of butt and maybe a flash of boob. Not the full deal. And not for so long.

But I did it. I took off everything, feeling her eyes on me the whole time. She watched me without any shame or anything. It made me feel... Well, it made me feel weird... but at the same time, I didn't mind it. I can't explain why, and I feel pretty weird about that, too.

We sat next to each other on the mat, stark naked, and watched for a glimmer of sun toward the east. Of course, I was also looking out for Secret Service or others, too! Vicki sat in lotus position and relaxed. I tried to do the same. Our knees were touching, and it made me feel all queasy inside. I know it was just our knees, but still... we were naked, after all.

We sat there until we felt the rays of the sun on our bodies. Then, when the sun was fully above the horizon, we stood up. I copied Vicki's motions as she raised her arms above her head, toward the sun. She was chanting something quietly. I didn't catch it all, but it sounded like a poem, with lots of summer imagery. It was pretty.

I did some deep yoga breathing and enjoyed the warmth of the sun on me. Then she finished with her ritual. She smiled and thanked me for joining her in it. Then she gave me a big hug.

I was just totally unprepared for that. I had no idea what to do, but automatically hugged back. I mean, that's what you do when you get hugged, right? You hug back. But I felt dirty doing it. I mean, we were still naked! Our boobs were touching! But as dirty as it made me feel, I liked it. Hugging her felt really... comfortable, I guess is the word.

It seemed to last forever, but we finally let go. And this is where it gets really weird. Because even though I was relieved, I was also a little bit disappointed. I'm ashamed to admit it, but I liked how it felt, embracing her, feeling her skin against mine... no matter how wrong it was. It may have been a sin, but it was really, really nice. Almost beautiful. And feeling that way freaks me out.

For the rest of the day, Vicki seemed to think nothing of the whole experience, and never mentioned it at all. I kept wondering why she didn't think it was wrong, or at least... I don't know... strange.

Anyway, around midnight we went to bed and, as usual, just talked and talked. I'd tried to put the whole thing out of my head by this point, but then something else happened.

When we were both exhausted and talked out, I said goodnight to Vicki, and she rolled over to hug me. Then before I knew it, she kissed me! Right on the lips! And it wasn't just a quick peck, either, but a soft, almost lingering kiss. Then she smiled, said goodnight, and snuggled up next to me. Her head was on my shoulder, and her arm around my waist.

I didn't know what to do. So I just laid there, my heart going like a jackhammer, and hardly breathing. And I prayed.

I prayed because I felt sinful and guilty again. And after an hour of this, which didn't help even a little bit, I got up and started writing this.

Why was I praying? Because of how I felt. Even writing about it makes me feel all funny inside, especially down in my...

Look at that. I can't even write it. Even in my own diary, I can't write about my own private parts. Am I just a prude, or is it because of my mother's anti-sex crusades?

Whatever. It doesn't matter. What matters is the truth: when Vicki kissed me, I was turned on.

There. I said it.

She kissed me, and it literally took my breath away. And when she snuggled next to me, in such a familiar and intimate way, it felt so wrong... and yet... so right.

Writing this all down hasn't really helped me come to grips with it all. I'm just as confused as ever.

But if I'm honest with myself, I have to admit that all I've been able to think about all day is hugging her naked body, and how it felt... and now, of how the kiss felt...

I liked it.

And God help me... I want to do it again.

Date: June 22, 2025
To: merrymary@webvillemail.net
From: heyjude@beatles4ever.ws
Subject: Re: Please Help!!!

Mary:

Wow. Where do I start? That's some heavy news you just laid on me.

Don't let it totally freak you out. And especially don't treat Vicki any differently because of it.

You know as well as I do that your feelings of guilt are entirely because of your upbringing. I know you've been... shall we say "re-evaluating" your belief system. Let me just say something regarding personal views for a moment.

As you know, I'm an atheist. But I often refer to myself as a "freethinker." Most people apply this term only to matters of religion, but I don't. I think that being a true freethinker means that you refuse to allow dogmatic thinking to affect ANY area of your life, that you base your views and opinions about everything upon reason and logic, rather than emotion and dogma.

This is why most Brights, who are used to thinking without dogma, have no problems with the subject of alternative sexuality. They realize there's really no good reason to condemn it. No one's hurt by it. And you'll notice that most of those who are rabidly against such things are religious zealots, so blinded by dogma that they can't even see that other peoples' sexual lives are none of their damn business.

Vicki has probably already shared with you a core tenet of Wicca, which is: "If it harms none, do what you will." That's a very sound philosophy in my book, hon.

Now, as for what you're feeling toward Vicki. I don't think you should try to repress it. Of course, you're obviously not emotionally prepared to act on it, either. You're attracted to her. And you're of an age when most people start to become heavily influenced by raging hormones.

I'm sure Vicki isn't the first person to stir up excitement within you. She's just the first female. It could be just a passing phase for you. It could also be that you're just misunderstanding your own feelings. Maybe you're not really sexually attracted to her, but are feeling a deep friendship bond, and your hormones are putting a different spin on it.

I just don't know, Mary. Only you can make that determination, I'm sorry to say. Good luck on figuring things out, and of course, I'll always be here to listen if you need to talk.

Jude

June 23, 2025

Today Vicki asked me point blank why I've been acting weird around her. And so I told her how strange I'd felt when she kissed me. She apologized, saying she just did it without thinking, because she was grateful that I was so understanding about her Wiccan ritual thing, because we'd had a great day together, and because she liked me.

I told her that was fine, but why not a kiss on the cheek? She looked at me funny, repeated that she liked me, then said, "Wait. You really didn't know I'm bisexual?" And at that point, I couldn't live in denial about it anymore. It was true.

"Bisexual." Without thinking, I said that sounded even worse than being gay or lesbian. Weren't bisexuals just sex fiends who'd sleep with anyone? Weren't they just people who couldn't make up their minds whether they wanted to be straight or gay?

As soon as the words were out of my mouth, I regretted saying them. When anyone else said these things around me, I didn't think much of them. I even agreed. But now they sounded hurtful and narrow-minded. I wanted to take them back, but the words were already out there, already hurting her.

But she didn't yell at me. I saw anger and pain in her eyes, but she calmly explained that bisexuals are no more sex fiends than anyone else. They aren't "undecided." They just don't think love should be based on gender. She said love is about what's inside a person, not what's outside. You fall in love with personalities, not with bodies.

I felt terrible, because what she said made sense. We always say that we fall in love with the "person inside." If we're not supposed to let things like physical appearance matter, why should gender? I know what the Bible says, but it doesn't help. Besides, I'm not the biggest Bible supporter, these days. Anyhow, I felt ashamed of the stereotype I'd slapped on her. I'm sure Jude would say Vicki is more of a freethinker than I am.

When she asked if I wanted her to leave, my heart about burst. I apologized a lot and explained that I was pretty ignorant about different lifestyles. And we were okay after that.

I've been thinking all day about what she said. And I still feel weird inside. But I'm glad she didn't decide to leave. I feel happy when we're together. The thought of being apart from her makes me feel awful. And when I think about being with her... all I can think about is the kiss.

What am I feeling? I'm almost afraid to know.

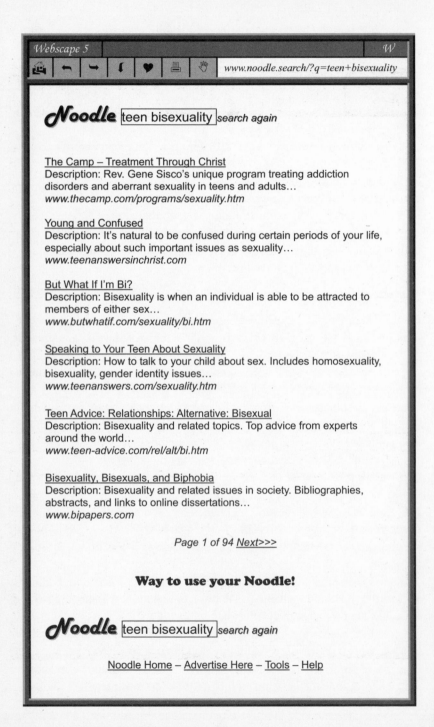

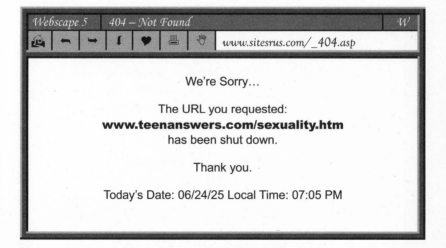

Date: June 25, 2025
To: merrymary@webvillemail.net
From: heyjude@beatles4ever.ws
Subject: Re: Why???

Mary:

I'm sorry... have you been living in a box for the past few years? Of course you can't find useful information about bisexuality online. The Christopher Administration has deemed such behavior immoral, and Big Brother has shut down all sites that would hint otherwise. Any sort of alternative sexuality is effectively a crime.

Would these sites have been informative to you, and millions of others? Of course. But the government thinks the only useful information about it is religious crap about how sinful it is and where you can be sent to be cured of it, as you saw on the links that did work.

Sorry, hon. I don't know what to tell you. Just thank your President, Congress, and anyone who voted for them.

Jude

June 26, 2025

Vicki and I had a long talk today about bisexuality. I wish I could say it was all polite and informative, but it wasn't. I was raised to believe that anything other than monogamous heterosexuality was a sin, condemned by God. And even though there's no reason given in the Bible other than "God said so," I still can't get past that.

Vicki had no answer, other than to say that not everyone believes the Bible to be true, including her. She told me again how she feels about me. And even though I'm morally ashamed of it, I'm pretty sure I blushed. I told her I was uncomfortable to hear her say that, and then she asked me if it was because I thought it was "wrong" for her to like me, or if I was uncomfortable because I felt the same way about her.

I swear I about died! And I said I get a knot in my stomach whenever I think about such things. But I didn't tell her it's because I'm afraid it just might be true.

27 June 2025

I am deeply troubled by questions Mary asked me this evening. As her friend was bathing, Mary came to me and asked me why homosexuality was considered wrong.

My first reaction was one of surprise. Mary knows her Bible, far better than most people in this country do. When I mentioned the Bible, she became almost irritated. She said she knew what the Bible said, could quote me chapter and verse of every passage mentioning it. But then she asked me why God would find any sort of love between two people to be sinful.

I told her that homosexual "love" isn't love, but lust. She actually rolled her eyes at me. Then I explained that God's plan is only for one man and one woman. His command to Adam and Eve was to go forth and multiply, to populate the earth. Homosexuals cannot breed, thus they are disobeying God's wishes.

Her response was that we've already populated the planet nearly to capacity. And if breeding were a requirement, then why did God say nothing about infertile couples, or those who choose to remain childless just because we have such a high population? Is this wrong in God's eyes? If breeding is God's plan, should not those who marry with no intention of producing children be considered sinners? Should those unable to conceive be forbidden from marrying?

The Catholic Church still officially condemns contraception for this very reason, considering sexual relations to be for the purpose of procreation only. But Mary said if it's not sinful for a man and woman to engage in copulation using birth control, why is it for two men or two women to have sex?

I insisted there was more to it than that, but ultimately I had no real answer for her, beyond saying, "God said so."

At the time, my mind ignored this embarrassing situation by focusing on the fact that Mary was asking these questions while her friend Vicki was visiting. Vicki, who is from San Francisco, the Queer Capitol of the world.

Is something going on between her and my daughter? The thought nauseates me, but I now think it to be true. I have no proof, just my instinct.

I must speak with Sarah about this. Her maternal intuition will guide us better than my paternal urges.

I hate my parents!

Vicki is gone! She was kicked out!

This afternoon, we returned from playing some tennis and my mother was in my bedroom reading my diary! She looked at Vicki and said, "Pack your bags. You're no longer welcome here."

Then she threw my diary on my bed and walked out of the room, saying, "You and I will be having a long talk, young lady."

I couldn't believe what was happening. Naturally, Vicki wanted to know what she'd read in the diary that caused this. I told her I'd written about the Litha ritual, and could only assume it was the Wicca thing that got her so mad. I couldn't bring myself to mention the other stuff. About how I might feel about her.

So she packed, and my heart ached more with every item she stuffed into her bags. Then one of the staff came and escorted her out. She was taken to the airport and I wasn't even allowed to go along.

As soon as she was out the door, Mother raked me over the coals. I was accused of being under Satan's spell, of being a lesbian and a witch, and a bunch of other things. She never even gave me any chance to defend myself.

She said my father had come to her with concerns after I'd asked him those questions about homosexuality. And she saw no reason whatsoever not to invade my privacy by reading my diary to find out what was going on in my head.

I still can't believe she could do such a thing. I mean, she was the one who bought me my first diary. She was the one who told me how important it was to capture my private thoughts that I shared with no one else. What a hypocrite.

And here's something Jude would get a kick out of: Every condemnation that came from her mouth made me want to vomit. Not because I was the target, but because I kept hearing the same sort of thing in my own voice… things I used to say back when I was…

I was about to write "when I was a Christian." Instead, I'll just say, "when I was closed-minded."

And I was treated to two more punishments after the tongue-lashing was done. First, I was commanded never to have contact with either her or Jude again. They took away my computer, cell phone, even the telephone in my room. And second, tomorrow I'm being flown to Camp Sonlight for the rest of the summer.

I'm so angry and upset right now that I really can't even think straight. I've been crying for the past half-hour.

I ask myself over and over why this had to happen. Why did my mother make these assumptions? Why didn't she let me explain? But I keep coming up with the same answers. And they come to me in a voice I think of as Jude's. It's like he's answering me, telling me that I only have religion to thank for her behavior. Her narrow concept of God and His will is responsible for her narrow views of what is okay and what isn't, and she thinks it gives her the right to inflict it on others. This is what religion can do to people, my Jude voice tells me.

But why it happened is less important now than what I'm going to do about it. And I just don't have an answer to that. I can't bear not seeing Vicki again. Or hearing from Jude again, for that matter.

Yes, there are other computers in the White House, and I'm sure I can get access to one of them without being observed. But that'll have to wait until my return from the prison camp. Oh, and Mother told me that I can't even mail a letter to Vicki from there. Camp staff has been instructed not to allow any letters to go out from me unless they're to the White House.

I'll even have to take special pains to hide this diary so she can't read it again.

I can't believe all this has happened!

6/30/25

I cannot believe how blind I was. Mary's doubts about religion were apparently no passing phase. Instead, she is corrupted. The proof is all there on the computer. Every email to and from Vicki, and the absolutely unspeakable correspondence with that atheist, Jude.

He has been turning her away from God, while Vicki has been turning her to Satan. And she imagines that she has feelings for this corrupt witch… Vicki is turning her gay, igniting her lust. Unnatural lust. Perverted, sick lust.

Much as I'd like, I cannot lay all the blame on Vicki and Jude. It is just as much my own fault. I have been far too lenient with her.

The Voice of Reason
Hold Your Cards, We Have a Bingo!

At 2:15 A.M., July 4, 2025, The Voice of Reason received its Five Millionth hit.

I tracked the IP address of the visitor's computer and have discovered her name and address. In less than a week, she'll be the recipient of the previously mentioned book of writings by early American patriots.

Over the years, I have found many passages of this book inspirational to the point of taking my breath away. I sincerely hope she appreciates their words as much as I have.

> "These are the times that try men's souls. The summer soldier and the sunshine patriot will, in this crisis, shrink from the service of their country, but he that stands now, deserves the love and thanks of man and woman. Tyranny, like hell, is not easily conquered; yet we have this consolation with us, that the harder the conflict, the more glorious the triumph."
> –Thomas Paine

The Persecution of Eleanor Adams

Enter the Voice of Reason Archives

Email me!

This site last updated: 07/04/25
Visitors since this site was born: **5,001,776**

"Ladies and Gentlemen of the Press...

"We have received a tremendous amount of approval from the public concerning the dissolution of anti-religious organizations. But there has also been some criticism. Many Americans feel we haven't yet taken it far enough. They feel certain "religions" should not be acceptable, either. So-called "new age" religions, or "earth religions," when one looks at them more than superficially, are clearly Satanic in nature. And as such, they do not belong in America. I agree with these astute citizens. Such practices have no place in a country founded upon the word of Christ.

"Some would challenge us on this issue, citing freedom of religion as guaranteed in our Constitution. But our Founders clearly meant the Christian religion. These cults clearly do not qualify. And in fact, practice of these religions is a form of blasphemy, as they hold themselves, not Christianity, to be the truth.

"I address you today to put you at ease. A bill is currently in the House that says, effectively, that since America is a Christian nation, any non-Christian faith will no longer have the protection of the First Amendment. This includes not just Islam and other major religions, but all forms of paganism, Humanism, Satanism (naturally), and of course, atheism. Atheism is a faith, too, and obviously anti-Christian. Further, public practice of the rituals of these belief systems, including preaching, will be considered a form of blasphemy, subject to current law.

"Those of Jewish persuasion need not be concerned. We Christians acknowledge you as cousins in our faith, though we will maintain our prayers that you will eventually accept Jesus as your savior. We do worship the same God, and we are sure that when He is ready, He will lead you to the Truth.

"Let me assure everyone that we are making every effort to end the spread of anti-Christian sentiment. But we ask your assistance. If you know of a practicing anti-Christian, do not take it upon yourselves to save these misguided individuals, especially friends or relatives. Instead, call upon those who can best help them. The professionals are much better able to help bring these souls to the light. We need to save them quickly, and that's the purpose of Reverend Sisco's camps.

"And there is also the risk of being tainted by the rants of atheists or others. Many of them have an impressive command of language and give the illusion of being well-read in history. Satan's tongue is smooth as silk.

"Budgetary changes have been made in order to allocate significant funds for the rehabilitation of these heathens. These camps have been a decades-old dream of Reverend Sisco's. With your help, his dream is becoming a reality in every state. But without your assistance, the dream will die, and the heathen lifestyle will continue to flourish.

"So please... Help your neighbors see the Truth. Help save your friends. Help save America."

New York—Rabbi Ira Friedman, current head of the Jewish Anti-Defamation League, today protested the President's recent speech. "If history has shown us anything," Rabbi Freidman said in a press release issued this morning, "it is that the Jewish people are almost always justified in being 'concerned' about any laws which inhibit the religious freedoms of any group. For such discrimination always gets out of hand. Therefore, we respectfully suggest that our President reconsider both his words and his actions."

Tucson—Vice-President Daniel Goodwin has been hospitalized after suffering an apparent heart attack after presenting the keynote speech at the annual meeting of the Western States Oil Coalition. The White House has issued no statement beyond describing the Vice-President's condition as stable.

July 30, 2025

I am faced now with the very real possibility that I will one day have to appoint a new Vice-President. This is a task I would prefer to avoid for several reasons, not the least of which is that I would hate to lose Dan. Though we are far from the best of friends, I do genuinely like the man and pray daily for him to have a full recovery.

Still, even if he were to be cured by Jesus Himself, there's no telling what tomorrow may bring. Having a replacement in mind for him is simply a wise idea.

But who would it be? My inclination would be to nominate Gene for the position. It's no secret that he is one of my closest counselors. Why not put him in a position of importance in name as well as fact?

The Voice of Reason
The Wrong War

1964: Johnson declares War on Poverty.
1972: Nixon declares War on Drugs.
2001: Bush declares War on Terrorism.

Johnson thought throwing money at the poor would eradicate poverty. Nixon thought outlawing drugs and imprisoning users would stop drug abuse. And Bush thought violence against countries out of which terrorists operated would somehow put an end to terrorism.

Talk about superficial thinking! Answers to complex social phenomena are never so simple. Poverty cannot be reduced without eliminating the causes of poverty, which would require an overhaul of employment, commerce, tax, and other laws. The solution to the drug problem cannot be solved without the decriminalization of drugs and the education of the public about them. We learned this perfectly during Prohibition. And terrorism cannot be lessened without revamping the oppressive policies that cause nations to view us as evil. These steps are just the beginning, of course. As I said, it's not simple.

These facts illustrate our nation's long-standing tendency to address the wrong issues, to avoid looking at the real problems, and to think the wrong things will solve these problems. We think welfare and minimum wage laws will help reduce poverty. We think "Just Say No" will prevent kids from taking drugs. And we think bombing a country will stop them from hating us.

And today?

This site last updated: 08/02/25
*Visitors since this site was born: **5,303,468***

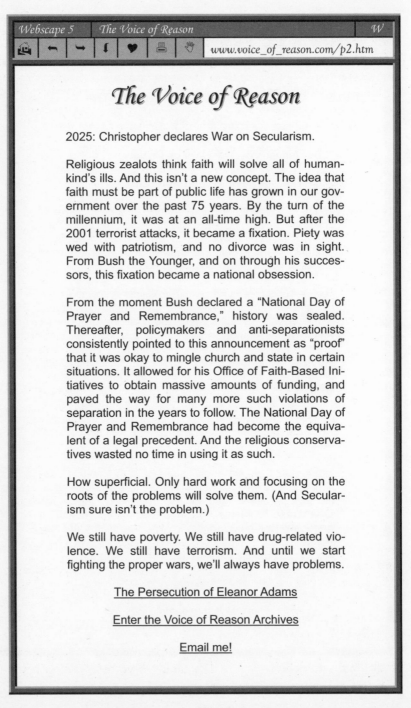

The Voice of Reason

2025: Christopher declares War on Secularism.

Religious zealots think faith will solve all of human-kind's ills. And this isn't a new concept. The idea that faith must be part of public life has grown in our government over the past 75 years. By the turn of the millennium, it was at an all-time high. But after the 2001 terrorist attacks, it became a fixation. Piety was wed with patriotism, and no divorce was in sight. From Bush the Younger, and on through his successors, this fixation became a national obsession.

From the moment Bush declared a "National Day of Prayer and Remembrance," history was sealed. Thereafter, policymakers and anti-separationists consistently pointed to this announcement as "proof" that it was okay to mingle church and state in certain situations. It allowed for his Office of Faith-Based Initiatives to obtain massive amounts of funding, and paved the way for many more such violations of separation in the years to follow. The National Day of Prayer and Remembrance had become the equivalent of a legal precedent. And the religious conservatives wasted no time in using it as such.

How superficial. Only hard work and focusing on the roots of the problems will solve them. (And Secularism sure isn't the problem.)

We still have poverty. We still have drug-related violence. We still have terrorism. And until we start fighting the proper wars, we'll always have problems.

The Persecution of Eleanor Adams

Enter the Voice of Reason Archives

Email me!

August 3, 2025

I am sick to death of this place! I've only been here a week and I'm ready to scream. Renée is trying her best to save my soul. I swear I just want to slap her. Does she have no idea how idiotic she sounds? We got into a huge fight about homosexuality and other alternative lifestyles. She kept trotting out the same old stupid arguments. I pointed out that these lifestyles don't hurt anyone, so what's the big hairy deal? And I feel some guilt every time she condemns gays and lesbians. She never mentions bisexuals, of course. I know she thinks they're even worse. And, God help me, I'm afraid I might really be one.

I'm still angry and don't know how I'll be able to forgive my mother. Ha! Forgiveness – a cornerstone of Christian teachings. And yet, will she forgive me for the sins she thinks I'm committing? No. Will she forgive Vicki for her "transgressions" last week? Of course not. Forgiveness isn't a Christian belief that Mother practices much. But of course, I will forgive her, in time. She's my mother, after all, and I love her. Even if I don't particularly like her much sometimes.

And what about Daddy? I can't believe he had a part in sending me here. There's no way he'd have been okay with the idea. I'll bet she didn't even consult him. I'd call and ask, but he's got enough on his mind with Mr. Goodwin still recovering from his heart attack.

Oh, who am I kidding? I can't say anything to him about it. I've never been able to stand up to him, or Mom, either. Not that I've ever had much cause to, but it's like I just can't protest at all. Even after Vicki was kicked out, I never said a word. I just accepted it, accepted my punishment of being sent here.

Still, I do wish I could let them see how horrible it is here, how everyone walks around with a look on their faces like they think the Rapture will happen any minute. They're getting on my last nerve.

Mother wasn't kidding about me not being able to send letters to Vicki. I was read a list of special rules, applying only to me, when I arrived. It was mortifying. I am also forbidden from making outside phone calls. I have my own cabin, too. Apparently, Mother doesn't want to run the risk of me seeing other girls undress. I guess she thinks it'll encourage me toward lesbianism. And I'm not allowed to go off without a camp buddy. She's afraid I'll run away, it seems.

In short, I spend most of my time alone in my cabin. And frankly, that's fine with me. The less time I have to spend with these empty-headed camp brats, the better.

The Voice of Reason
Some Senators See the Light?

Given a clean bill of health by the medical wizards on the Presidential payroll, the Veep will live to spread his own special bigotry for another day.

Please don't think I have any desire to see Goodwin among the ranks of the recently deceased. Not at all. There are very few people in this world I'd actually wish dead, and Danny-boy isn't one of them.

And it's not looking good for those of us who aren't Jews or Christians. The Senate passed the bill that makes the practice of other faiths illegal, including atheism (which isn't a faith). At least it was close. It passed by only two votes. Since Republicans outnumber Democrats and others by a margin of fifteen, apparently there are some Republicans who think this legislation is too over-the-top for our country.

You'll pardon this Bright for saying so, but we really need a miracle now.

> *"We are now at the point where we must decide whether we are to honor the concept of a plural society which gains strength through diversity or whether we are to have bitter fragmentation that will result in perpetual tension and strife."*
> —Justice Earl Warren

The Persecution of Eleanor Adams

Enter the Voice of Reason Archives

Email me!

This site last updated: 08/17/25
Visitors since this site was born: **5,602,535**

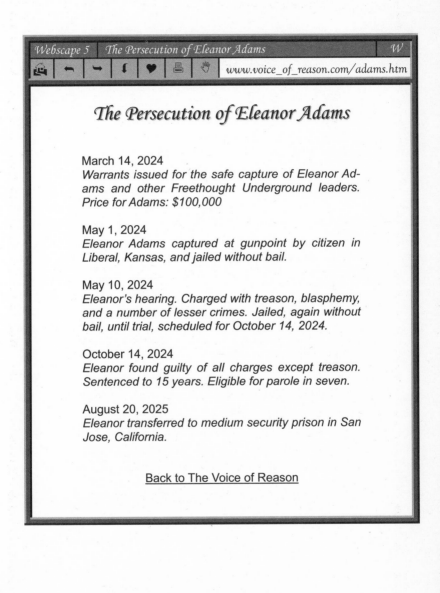

August 19, 2025

I wish I could say that life since camp has been better. But it hasn't been. In fact, it's been pretty awful. Mother wasn't done heaping indignities upon me. When I got back, I was told that I had to see a psychiatrist! Dr. Goodhead (I'm <u>not</u> kidding) considers homosexuality a disease, and is out to cure me. And while I'm still uncomfortable with the things I'm feeling, I do know I'm not diseased.

I've had five sessions so far, and I've decided the only way to get this quack off my back is to pretend to be cured. I'll just tell him I've been reading the Bible and praying a lot and I've seen the error of my ways, and with God's help, I'll be fine. That'll shut him up. It's just what everyone wants to hear, anyway, so I'll let them hear it.

Frankly, all the constant religious pressure being put on me is having the exact opposite effect they're intending it to have. Instead of bringing me closer to God, it's pushing me away. I just resent it all so much! Can't they see that?

Anyway, I hope playing this game will be enough to get me to be treated like a daughter again, instead of a prisoner of war. I'm fifteen, but you'd think I was five, from the way they're behaving.

But the worst thing is this wall between me and Dad. I can tell he's very disappointed in me. It's all over his face. I just want to make him understand, but he won't let me. It's like he's shut me out. And again, I can't say anything.

I've been thinking a lot, lately, about my inability to confront my parents about anything really important. I'm just afraid of them considering me to be a bad daughter, of not respecting them. I don't want to disappoint them, but I know I have. What Mom read in my diary sure wasn't something they'd want to tell their friends. "Oh, yes, Mary is flirting with witchcraft and recently she had her first same-sex kiss! We're so proud!" Nope. Can't see that happening.

And Dad went and approved that horrible bill! I can't believe it! How could he do such a thing? Could Uncle Gene be as manipulative as some people say? I could almost see him wanting this legislation passed, but not my father.

What if Vicki or Jude is thrown in jail? Or sent to one of those camps to be "rehabilitated"? This is just so... so wrong!

I think I'm going to be sick.

9/3/25

Mary is still quite angry with me. But that's fine. In time, she'll realize I'm only doing these things out of love. When she has allowed God back into her heart again, she'll understand.

Paul, of course, fairly bleeds with sympathy for her. He's not very good with tough love. That's why he's letting me handle this.

Even so, he didn't react well when I told him I didn't like the bill recently passed. Perhaps, as he says, it's for the best. But it doesn't seem right, somehow. Isn't this the same sort of persecution the Pilgrims came to America to escape?

September 5, 2025

Mother had to add insult to injury. Now she's taken back her promise of letting me go to school, rather than being tutored here privately. I was supposed to start at Holy Trinity next week, but she withdrew me.

She has absolutely no regard for my feelings. But when I said so, she turned the tables, as she always does. According to her, I'm the one who has no regard for the feelings of anyone else.

Apparently, she is convinced that I'm a lesbian witch. And she went on and on about the damage I could do to my father's Presidency, if anyone got wind of this, and of how bad it would make her look.

I know her words are selfish, but I do feel guilty of those things. I don't want to hurt either of them. But can't she see how I feel?

I'll try to be optimistic. I keep telling myself that I probably wouldn't have been very comfortable at Holy Trinity, anyway. A year ago, I thought it would be great. But these days I'm not sure I could stand the kind of education I'd get at a Christian school.

Let's face it. Mom and Dad are right, to a point. Jude definitely did affect me. He made me start to really think about things. And I like it.

My parents, on the other hand, don't like what I'm thinking.

Dear Vicki,

Surprise! I'll bet you weren't expecting a letter from me, were you? Well, frankly, I wasn't expecting to be able to write to you, either. See, the mail staff has been instructed to watch for any incoming or outgoing mail of mine, and if it's to or from you, it's to be destroyed. I'm not allowed out without supervision (not that I ever am, really, but now it's <u>close</u> supervision), or I'd have written to you long ago.

I'm pretty much a prisoner in the White House, when it comes right down to it.

But Mom and Dad are both away for a time, and I'm pretty sure I can sneak out using the "Marilyn entrance." (It's a secret passage that leads underground into the Treasury Building.) If you're reading this, then obviously I had a lot of luck and good timing, and actually pulled it off.

Anyway, I need to say some things to you, and hope you'll understand how difficult it is for me to say them.

Ever since your visit here, I've been feeling some things that are very strange to me. I think you know what I mean. I'm talking about feelings for you. Feelings that my upbringing tells me are wrong, but that my heart tells me are anything but. And yet, I have fifteen years of upbringing to fight against. It isn't easy, believe me.

Sometimes I wish I'd never met you, because then I wouldn't be feeling these things, let alone feel guilty for feeling them. But whenever I think of not knowing you, I feel a horrible emptiness inside. It's like a part of myself is gone. I miss you terribly and want more than anything to be with you. But I don't know how to make that happen.

I wish there were some way I could talk to you. But I don't know how much time I'll have on my temporary escape. Besides, I don't want to run the risk of your parents answering. I wish I could hear back from you, but don't know how that can happen, either. I guess we'll just have to play it by ear and hope my folks ease up.

I should go, now, and prepare to make my "escape." You'll get this before Halloween, if you get it at all. So have a happy Samhain, even though it's illegal to celebrate it. Sorry about that, by the way. My dad's a butt-head.

Anyway, take care! I love you!

Mary

Date: October 20, 2025
To: heyjude@beatles4ever.ws
From: merrymary@freewebmailer.net
Subject: Message from Mary

Jude:

Hey! How's it going?

I only have a minute to type this to you, and don't have time to explain. I'm going to assume you've heard from Vicki. I'm sure she's filled you in on what happened while she was here.

Oh, it was terrible, Jude. I still can't believe everything that's happened since then. And sometimes I think the worst part is the fact that my mother invaded my privacy by reading my diary. I can't believe she'd do such a thing!

After Vicki was given the boot, Mom turned into a total Nazi. No computer, no phone, monitored mail, etc. Enough to make me puke.

Normally, these restrictions would only be a minor setback. But I've essentially been placed under house arrest. It's only a result of lots of planning on my part that I've been able to get out of the house right now.

Still, I have to get back soon. I set up this free web-based email account, so you can reply to this. I just wish there were some way to make sure these things would be private, you know? I mean, I'm using a computer at a coffee shop and just don't know how reliable these places are.

Anyway, I wanted to let you know that you probably won't be hearing from me for a while. But know that I think of you often and wish like crazy that things were different.

Take care of yourself.

I love you!

Mary

Date: October 24, 2025
To: merrymary@freewebmailer.net
From: heyjude@beatles4ever.ws
Subject: Re: Message from Mary

Mary:

Hey there! Man, I was beginning to think you fell off the face of the earth! I hope you're okay.

As for your concern about email privacy, there are certainly ways to ensure as much privacy as you can expect in this day and age. Check out http://ultracryptforfree.com. This is an encryption program that you can set up yourself. When you install it, you'll generate a pair of keys (long strings of coded letters and numbers). One is a "public" key; the other is a "private" key. The private one is used to "unlock" messages sent to you. The "public" key is what others use to "lock" the email to you. And since no one but you has the "private" key, only you can "unlock" the message.

It works pretty well! The whole thing is highly mathematical, which means I don't understand a lick of it. But I've used it in the past and it's easy to do. Maybe it's what you're looking for. In case you want to try it on me, first download the program from the above site. Then go to http://cryptkeys.org/ and do a search on my email address. You'll be able to grab my public key and use it to send me an encrypted message.

I have to admit, I was taken aback when I read "I love you" in your email. I'm glad you consider me a friend. I love you, too.

And because I know you've missed these...

Today in Beatles history:
1980:   Lennon's "(Just Like) Starting Over" released as single in U.K.
1979:   McCartney issued Rhodium Record by the Guinness Book of World Records (most successful musician of the century).
1976:   Lennon's "Imagine" re-released as single in U.K.
1975:   Lennon's "greatest hits" SHAVED FISH album released.
1969:   Lennon's "Cold Turkey" released as single in U.K.

Jude

> *Omaha*—Thousands of bonfires dotted the American countryside last night as lawbreakers celebrated the ancient pagan festival now known as Halloween. The Freethought Underground is thought to be responsible for the unlawful celebrations. The former leader of Pagan Pride, a man who calls himself Sam Hain (a name taken from this celebration, called Samhain by the ancient heathens), is a member of the Freethought Underground. Several arrests were made. There were no reports of violence.

11/20/25

    The Satanic Halloween events a few weeks ago got me to thinking about Mary's diary again. I'm concerned that she may be engaging in these horrible rituals right here under our own roof.

    As I understand it, these heathens celebrate something other than Christmas. Well, I will certainly not stand for any witchcraft taking place here on the day of our Lord's birth.

    Gene suggested something rather unusual, and I may take him up on it. It would mean not having Mary here for Christmas, but that's a sacrifice we may have to make.

    I'm rather annoyed with Gene, however. He seems very unconcerned about Mary, as though he's willing to just let her burn in hell.

    I swear I will never understand this man.

December 12, 2025

I'd hoped all the punishments since Vicki was kicked out were over. But they're not. And this latest is the worst of the bunch. I leave in a week for something called "Christmas Camp." I'll spend a week in some town in Texas made up to imitate Bethlehem at the time of Christ's birth. I'll spend a week experiencing the Nativity from different points of view, like Mary & Joseph, the Wise Men, etc. It all ends on Christmas Day with some re-enactment of the birth of Jesus.

It seems very, very weird to me. I honestly don't understand the point. But more than that, who would want to send their kid to spend Christmas away from home? That's just cruel! I was so stunned when Mom told me about it that I didn't even know what to say. She handed me this brochure about the place and said, "Here's where you'll be going this year," and I just stood there with my mouth hanging open.

I've never spent Christmas apart from my parents! Why do they want me to? I just don't get it!

Maybe I'm wrong. Maybe I'm not being punished. Maybe they're so ashamed of what I've done that they just don't want me around.

14 December 2025

I wish I could say that I'm pleased with the way Sarah is handling Mary, but I am not. Her decision to send Mary off to that camp is not sitting well with me.

Yes, it may be the best thing for her, but she is our daughter, and she should be with us for Christmas.

Sarah says it was Gene's idea and that she therefore assumed that I was in agreement with it. This bothers me, as well. For while I certainly admire Gene and consider him a great friend, we do not see eye-to-eye on everything. And where our daughter is concerned, it is none of Gene's business.

I'm afraid we had quite the argument over this after Mary left. I've half a mind to send someone to bring her home, but Sarah thinks she should stay for the duration.

I consented to that, but when she does return, I am going to have more of a say in how we're handling her situation.

San Antonio—Fifteen-year old First Daughter Mary Christopher is missing. Mary was last seen yesterday evening, December 23, at Carson's Christmas Camp, outside of San Antonio. Mary was attending the camp as part of her observance of the holiday.

Orville Carson, owner of the camp, was interviewed by police after his frantic 911 call was placed. "We'd all had dinner around a campfire," Carson said, "and had just begun singing carols. Mary excused herself to go lie down. She'd been complaining of a headache or stomachache all day. And that was the last anyone saw of her."

Carson estimates the time of her disappearance to approximately 8:00 P.M.

Police have not ruled out the possibility that Mary could have run away from camp, even though a full suitcase was found in her cabin.

No one has claimed responsibility thus far, and there was no sign of a struggle.

The AMBER Alert system has been initiated, and the FBI is working diligently on the case, but no leads have been reported as of this time.

The President has offered a reward of half a million dollars to anyone with information leading to the safe return of his daughter.

Those with information on the disappearance are urged to contact the nearest FBI office immediately.

Year Six

2026

Washington— Prime Minister Hiro Akatani announced today that the nation of Japan would cease all trade with the United States, effective January 31, if recent laws making several non-Christian religions illegal in America were not rescinded. Japan's primary religions are Shinto and Buddhism. The Prime Minister called the laws "unspeakable."

White House Press Secretary Walter Admundsen stated, "The White House finds it very disappointing that Japan has chosen this path. But we have no intention of caving in to threats. We consider such embargoes to be little better than financial terrorism."

Japan's announcement was also met with derision from several members of Congress, but also with some support by many civil rights and liberal Christian organizations here in the U.S. The White House has reportedly been besieged with email from these groups, protesting the passage of the laws and urging Congress to reconsider. Japan, however, is the first country to act on threats made during these past few months.

Prime Minister Akatani stated, "Americans wishing to escape this blatant religious persecution would be welcomed with open arms here in Japan."

Japan is now the ninth nation condemning U.S. legislation and extending such open invitations to American citizens. The others are The Netherlands, Sweden, Denmark, Holland, Norway, Switzerland, Germany, and Russia.

4 January 2026

Japan's embargo is causing a tremendous uproar, but all I can think about is Mary. Sarah has been a wreck since she disappeared, and I haven't fared much better. I received word today from my friend Wes Noonan in the Bureau that they have a lead. It seems a taxi driver claims to have given a ride to a lone girl fitting Mary's description. A team has been dispatched to comb the area of her drop-off. Sarah took the news with some relief. She said little, but it was written in her face.

This confirms our belief that Mary did run away. This is such an embarrassment. Word of this must never get out. The cabbie has taken an oath of silence, but who knows if he intends to stay quiet?

Sarah and I have talked a bit about why Mary would choose to run away. Can we simply chalk this up to teenage rebellion? That would be the easy way out. But in my heart I think we both know it to be false.

We drove her away, Sarah and I. What does this say about us as parents? I know most would forgive us for not being perfect role models. We have a country to run, after all. And yet, Mary is our own daughter. How could we not see what was going on with her?

Sarah blames Vicki, a I chastise myself for allowing the girl to visit. But if Satan was bent on corrupting our daughter, he could easily have chosen another agent besides Vicki.

I have spoken to Gene about this, but he seems ambivalent about her welfare. He points out that I have a country to save, and this matter is taking my attention away from that. But how can I save a nation if I can't save my own daughter?

Gene is so obsessed with his little vendetta against Father Montoya and the Freethought Underground that he doesn't care about much else, either. Nearly every episode of his television show contains indictments against either or both of them for the corruption of America. And while I agree that the Freethought Underground is a reprehensible group of people, I do think Gene's gone over the line now and again. He's taking it personally, especially Montoya's occasional commentaries.

We simply must find Mary. For her sake. For our sake. For the country's sake.

Date: *January 5, 2026*
To: *biwitched1@sf.ca.home.net*
From: *merrymary@freewebmailer.net*
Subject: *What have I done???*

BEGIN ULTRA-CRYPTED TEXT

Vicki:

I'm SO glad you have an encryption key! I just took a chance and looked up your email address on the CryptKeys site, hoping you'd have one. But I do wish you'd get an anonymous email address, too.

I'd call you, but your phone was probably tapped within an hour of my disappearance being reported. I'm thinking of getting a pre-paid cell phone, the next chance I get. They're fairly anonymous. But still, if your line is tapped, what's the point?

I didn't think this through very well. I don't even know what made me do it! I've just been feeling so devastated by Mother's constant punishments since you were sent home. And it's hard to accept that my parents are too ashamed of me to keep me around. I guess I figured I might as well strike out on my own.

Did I do the right thing? Should I have stayed? Am I being selfish? Should I have considered what this would do to my dad? The last thing in the world that I want to do is hurt him. This is all my mother's doing, I just know it. She's always been a pain in my neck.

But what do I do now? Part of me wants to go home. But a bigger part wants to be with you. I don't know what that really means, with regard to my feelings, you know? Anyway, I'm not even sure you'd want to see me.

I'm in Castle Hills, north of San Antonio. I'm staying at a YWCA, but spend most of my time here in the library on the computer. Even with electronic billboards flashing my face every fifteen minutes, I haven't been recognized. I dyed and cut my hair (close to your color, in fact), and got some fake eyewear. Everyone's looking for a long-haired blonde, so a short-haired brunette with glasses isn't going to flip many switches. Besides, everyone thinks I was kidnapped, so they're looking for this blonde kid in the company of someone else, not by herself.

I don't have much money, and aside from the clothes on my back, all I've got is my journal. And I don't know what to do. Please help me!

Mary

END ULTRA-CRYPTED TEXT

Date: *January 9, 2026*
To: *merrymary@freewebmailer.net*
From: *biwitched1@anon-e-mail.com*
Subject: *Are you kidding???*

BEGIN ULTRA-CRYPTED TEXT

Mary:

Goddess! How could you think I wouldn't want to see you??? Of course I do!

I'm sorry you're so torn over this. I've often wanted to run away from my fundie folks, but I can't imagine what it's like for you. You've got balls, girl!

So what can I do? Should I take my parents' car and come get you?

That probably won't work, though. Our home has been under constant surveillance since you "disappeared." Both the FBI and the DHS have been here to question us. My folks are freaked, by the way, and I'm pretty sure they think I had a part in this. If I tried to meet you, I'm sure I'd be followed.

As for the confusion you're feeling, I'm not sure what to tell you. I'm thrilled that you're attracted to me. You know I like you. A lot.

But I can't make peace with the dogma demons for you. Only you can do that. I'll help in any way I can... by answering your questions or just offering myself as a sounding board. Hell, if you're in a library most days, you might be able to find books on sexuality issues. Unless your dad hasn't had them all purged and burnt, that is. (Sorry. That was probably uncalled for.)

But it's not like you need to decide what you are today, you know. If all we ever are is friends, that's fine, too. I hope for more than that, but I'll be happy having you in my life in whatever way you're comfortable with.

Let's just get you out here, okay?

You might want to consider letting your folks know you're okay, at least.

As for the cell phone idea, though they wouldn't know who you are, they can still monitor the calls. And it's a no-brainer that they'll be monitoring calls around San Antonio right now. It's probably safer to stick with encrypted email. Oh, and speaking of email, I took your suggestion. New address!

Vicki

END ULTRA-CRYPTED TEXT

January 11, 2026

Should I let them know I'm okay? Probably. Am I going to? No. Maybe it's petty of me. Maybe it's even sinful. But they put me through hell for six months. I can put them through a bit of it for a while, too.

But Vicki's right about a cell phone. I don't know what to do. Should I try to get out of here? Hitchhike my way to California? Should I just buy a bus ticket? They wouldn't ask for I.D. if I'm paying cash, would they? I don't know. Well, they're probably watching the bus and train stations, anyway.

I need to be careful with the little money I've got. I can't risk using an ATM to get more, and sure can't use any of the FingerFund scanners to buy anything. I don't believe it when they say the fingerprint database isn't tied into any law enforcement agencies. One scan to buy a Slurpee at 7-11 and that would be it for me.

And what do I do when Vicki and I are together? I never had time to accept or understand what I'm feeling before all this happened. Am I in love with her? And would that make me bisexual? I guess so. Assuming I'm still attracted to guys, which I'm pretty sure is still true.

I still feel guilty whenever I think about it, and honestly, I try not to. I know it's because of how I was raised. But what if homosexuality really is a sin? In my heart, I don't believe a loving God could send someone to hell just because they chose to love someone of the same sex. But what if I'm wrong?

And what about Jude? I'll let him think I meant "I love you" only as a friend. Maybe that's all I really did mean. But could I honestly have feelings for him? I've never even met him, and probably never will. But he's so honest and forthright and caring. Even if he does hold opinions I don't agree with.

I'm not even sixteen, yet! Am I supposed to be feeling or thinking these things? Even about guys?

I feel like a butthead for not telling Jude who I am. I mean, he's not stupid. There's all the fuss in the papers about Mary Christopher disappearing, and at the same time, he learns that his friend Mary is suddenly using a different email address. I'm sure he knows. But I still have to confess.

And on top of that, there's a woman at the library that looks at me suspiciously every single day! Does she know who I am?

Too many things to think about! I just want to scream!

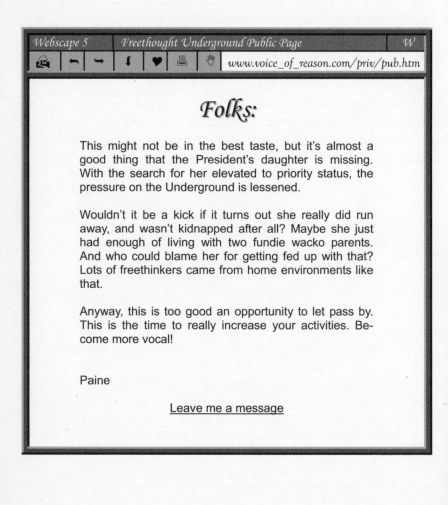

January 12, 2026

I know I shouldn't have risked going back to the library, but I did. And now I'm even more confused. I was reading the news when the woman who's been eyeing me every day walked by and dropped a piece of paper in my lap!

It says, "Mary – I'm a friend. I imagine you could use one right now." It was signed "Cat, Freethought Underground." And there's a phone number with it.

If she'd been an agent of the FBI or DHS, she would've just apprehended me, right? Or would she? Maybe not, since it would cause a scene in the library. Maybe this is just a trick to get me to trust her, making her job just that much easier.

This is driving me nuts! I'd scream, if I didn't think it would get me caught.

> *Washington*—The White House issued a statement today reporting that little progress has been made in the search for fifteen-year-old Mary Christopher, who was abducted from a Christmas Camp near San Antonio just a few days before the holiday. Though there have been leads, none have been productive. No ransom notices have yet been received, perplexing investigators and worrying the President and First Lady.
>
> Also mentioned were the announcements by the seven nations who have chosen to cease all trade with the U.S. until "gross civil rights violations come to an end." The President said he regretted the decisions of these nations, but that the public should look at this as all the more reason to "buy American."

Folks:

Okay. We've made contact. An Underground operative in the San Antonio area has confirmed that Mary Christopher did run away. She's safe, and our operatives in the southwest will be assisting her over the coming days.

When the time is right, we'll divulge the truth of her situation. But in the meantime, we'll see how the Christophers handle things.

Good work, Cat! And thanks also to everyone in the Underground who took part in trying to locate Mary. It really paid off.

Paine

Leave me a message

February 7, 2026

Dad must have every government agent in the country here in Texas! I'd like to think it's because he's worried about me and wants me back home. But I suspect it's mostly out of anger, and just to save himself from looking bad. Either way, getting out of the city was really tough! Cat is great, though! And she should've been an actress! We were stopped by agents on our way north at a checkpoint they'd set up on the road, and Cat pretended to be my mother. The agent asked for our identification. She gave hers, but refused to give mine. She really raked the guy over the coals, demanding to know why she, a "good Christian Texan," was being harassed by government agents when all she was doing was taking a drive with her daughter. She really lit into him! And he got so flustered, he let us pass.

Of course, it probably helped that before we left, she performed a little cosmetic magic on me. I swear I must've looked twenty-five! She styled my hair, put makeup on me… We even padded my bra to give me big ones! She gave me an outfit that made me look almost like a professional of some sort, rather than a teenager. My real mother wouldn't have recognized me.

And speaking of that, I asked her how she recognized me at the library. She said that Freethought Underground members began looking all around San Antonio for me as soon as my disappearance was announced, and that she just got lucky.

I find that hard to believe. I mean, I've been very careful. Why would she be in that library? And my disguise is pretty good, if I do say so myself. I think she's not telling me everything.

Anyway, this is scary and exciting at the same time. I wish Cat could take me the whole way to San Francisco, but it seems I'm to be transferred along like a baton in a relay race. She's got Freethought Underground members from here to California lined up to ferry me along. It'll probably be time consuming, but I'll get there.

We left in the late afternoon and arrived here in Sweetwater around ten o'clock. Tomorrow we'll drive up to Amarillo, where I'm to meet my next "friend."

I've been so scared since leaving the camp. And I still don't know if I'm doing the right thing. But at least now I have the feeling that everything will be okay.

2/9/26

Only six weeks since Mary's disappearance, but it seems like six months.

I have been blaming myself ever since I heard the news. I was too rough on her. What was I thinking? Mary had never before given us cause enough to even ground her for a week. She's been as good a daughter as any mother could hope for.

I've always attributed that to the fact that Paul and I raised her right, in a good Christian environment. She knows right from wrong and has always acted accordingly.

I'm still not sure how Satan's guile was so easily able to wrest her away from us. We raised her to be stronger than that!

Perhaps that was the problem, though. Just as a child must be exposed to germs to build up biological defenses, perhaps so should a child be exposed to some degree of temptation, some hint of evil, in order to recognize it and build up immunity to it. Did Paul and I shelter her too much? It seems difficult to accept, but it could well be true.

Whatever the case is, I want her safely back here with us. I pray that she has the sense I believe she does, enough to steer clear of temptation, to avoid the darker side of the world out there.

But I still ache inside, remembering the horrid things I read in her diary. I suppose that's why I punished her so harshly. I couldn't believe my eyes. The very thought that my own daughter could be a lesbian is just too much to stomach. I could never show my face to any of The Saviors again. My activist career would be destroyed, to say nothing of Paul's political career.

Can't she see that? What is wrong with her?

February 14, 2026

I'm a happy girl! It's Valentine's Day, and I got to email with Vicki! I stopped at a coffee shop with a 'net connection a couple hours ago. And she sent me an online Valentine! She signed it "S.W.A.K."!!!

It makes being stuck here in Gallup, New Mexico, more bearable. Cat took me as far as Amarillo. We stayed overnight in a humongous Holiday Inn where the rooms were set up in a big square. In the middle was a recreation area. They had a pool, a spa, senso-games, pinball, pool tables, ping pong... even shuffleboard! It was pretty neat. Cat and I played a lot of pinball. She's really good!

Back in our room, we talked most of the night away. Cat's a Bright, but was raised Baptist. She told me how she left the faith. It was pretty similar to Jude's story, in fact. (I really need to email him.)

I'm going to miss her. I wish my mother was more like her.

Anyway, the next day, a man named Black Eagle met us. Cat drove back to San Antonio, and Black Eagle and I set off for New Mexico. We talked a lot on the trip. He's a sort of religious humanist. He's also a Libertarian, like that Michael Lee guy that Dad always complained about. His "cause of choice" is our country's marriage laws. He feels they are discriminatory and wrong. There's a bumper sticker on his car that reads, "MARRY THE ONE YOU LOVE, GO TO JAIL."

I know it's a slam at my dad and his policies, but I agree that it's wrong to forbid people from marrying just because they don't fall into certain "approved" groups. Anyway, I'd assumed the bumper sticker was referring to same-sex marriages, but it turns out he was talking about group marriages or something like that. I had no idea what to think about that, but he talked about poly-something-or-other. I don't know. Group marriages. Seems pretty weird, to me.

Anyway, Black Eagle has an amazing amount of information in that head of his. Seems every subject I'd bring up, he knew something about! He thinks women are stronger than men, more connected with Deity, and should be honored. Definitely not your typical male mind-set!

At any rate, we stopped in Gallup, which is as far as he was supposed to take me. But the next person who was supposed to meet me had a death in the family. So now we're waiting for, I guess, a substitute driver. Neither of us knows who it'll be.

February 19, 2026

Well, Black Eagle went out of his way and drove me as far as Flagstaff, where we met his replacement. When we parted, B.E. gave me a huge hug. He said he needs lots of hugs. I said, "Don't we all?" What a great guy. I really enjoyed talking with him.

So my new "cabbie" is Father Montoya! We didn't get off to a quick start, though. Today's Sunday, and he was guest speaker at a New Anglican church in Flagstaff. I sat in on the service. It was interesting. He spoke about the Freethought Underground. I thought for a minute he was going to mention me, because he looked right at me. But he didn't. Good thing. Who knows what would've happened?

We're in Fredonia, now, and on the trip here, I spoke to Father Montoya about my feelings for Vicki, how half the time I'm just fine with it (just a tad confused), but the other half of the time, I feel guilty. I told him about my belief that God wouldn't really consider any kind of love to be wrong.

And he agreed! He said God would never punish anyone for loving another, for God is love, and our entire purpose here on Earth is to love one another, no matter what. I don't know if he's right. But it sure made me feel better.

2/20/26

Paul told me last night that he's not happy with Gene's behavior over Mary's disappearance, either. This comes as a great relief to me. I was beginning to think my husband was holding Gene in such high regard that he couldn't see the man's faults. Still, I don't think Paul sees as many faults with the man as I do.

He's unhappy now because it involves our daughter, and his love for her is second only to his love for Jesus. But the idea that his best friend doesn't care what happens to Mary... that's not something he can tolerate. Nor should he.

Nevertheless, I stopped short of telling Paul that I don't trust Gene anymore. I'm not sure how well he'd take that.

February 20, 2026

So Father Montoya and I talked about my whole religious questioning thing. It left me feeling very weird. He honestly shocked me.

He said that he finds most Christian clergy to be hypocrites. He said that they essentially lie in order to keep their jobs.

I asked what he meant, and he said that in seminary, they learned that the Bible is full of common mythological themes, from the creation and flood story to the virgin birth and resurrected hero. They learned that the stories of the Old Testament patriarchs are known as "temple legends." He said their purpose was to enhance the history of the Hebrew people and are mostly fictional. And, as Jude so often would say, that the gospels were not written by anyone who knew Jesus personally. He also said that the Christ myths and formulas are direct copies of Zoroastrian myths adopted by the Jesus sect. I think Jude may have told me that, too.

He said that these clergy, through the sin of omission, continue to promote superstition. He said he couldn't even count how many times he was told by his colleagues to just "Shut up and play the game."

He even told me of how a guy in his church met him in the parking lot one day and said: "I don't care about where the Bible stories came from. I'm the biggest financial patron of this church, and if you don't start talking more about Jesus, I'm taking my money and my family to a different church." Montoya said, "Well, goodbye, then." And then the guy punched him in the stomach!

No wonder Father Montoya sides with the Freethought Underground!

I talked to him about running away, too, and he urged me to contact my folks. He said that it was wrong of me to keep them worrying for so long. No matter how badly they treated me, they're still my parents, and they deserve to have their minds put at ease.

He's probably right. I should've sent an email long ago. That's just another example of me not being a good daughter.

I'm working on a letter to him, which I'll send off in a few days. That'll have to be good enough.

February 21, 2026

Well, I'm in northern Utah, now. Father Montoya and I arrived yesterday, after a grueling drive. It's a long ride from Fredonia!

One of the towns we passed through on the way was called Hurricane. Father Montoya told me the locals pronounce it like "hur-riken," for some bizarre reason. He also told me it's not a place friendly to the Freethought Underground. Apparently, there are a lot of White Supremacists there.

How can you think someone is inferior because of skin color? That's just stupid! I know that racists often use the Bible to defend their views the same way sexists do. It's pretty scary how easy it is to use the Bible that way.

Anyway, it's beautiful here. I can't get over how amazing the mountains are! This is the closest I've ever been to them. They're so huge, and the snow on them just takes your breath away!

Father Montoya left this morning, but I'm staying for another day or so with my next "cabbie," a woman named Lorelei. She's really great. She lives in a cute little house near the base of one of the mountains. I've just been resting today. Even though I'm anxious to get to California, I'm sick of traveling.

Lorelei says the next leg of the journey will not be so scenic, so I'm enjoying the beautiful country here while I can.

We talked most of the day and drank fantastic coffee drinks she made. She has probably fifty bottles of flavor syrups! And she made us other drinks, too, like Italian sodas and something she called an "egg cream." Didn't have any eggs in it, though. Or cream, for that matter. But everything she whipped up was delicious!

We watched some movies on satellite and ordered in Chinese food. It was a great day!

Date: *February 22, 2026*
To: *merrymary@freewebmailer.net*
From: *biwitched1@anon-e-mail.com*
Subject: *Re: Greetings from Mormonland!*

BEGIN ULTRA-CRYPTED TEXT

Mary:

I can't wait to see you, too! But hon, I think we've got problems. I heard through the grapevine that there are patrols stopping traffic into California on all the major routes.

If you're coming from the Salt Lake area, you're coming in on I-80. Don't do it! You're sure to be checked. Find an alternate route, and the smaller a road you can take to get into California, the better!

Things here at home are bad. The feds keep harassing us, and my parents are starting to interrogate me, too. Imagine that.

There's no way you can come here. We'll have to come up with another idea.

Just keep checking email every chance you get. I'll let you know what to do.

Love,
        Vicki

END ULTRA-CRYPTED TEXT

The Voice of Reason
Sarah's Back in the Saddle

I admit my heart goes out to President and Mrs. Christopher. I sincerely hope their daughter shows up safe and sound in the near future. And I understand that some people, when faced with a crisis such as this, will throw themselves into their work. That's what Sarah Christopher seems to be doing right now. Unfortunately, her work happens to be as head of The Saviors, that fun and feisty group of anti-choice, anti-gay, anti-freedom freaks responsible for any number of protest rallies across the country in the past five years.

Not long ago, Sarah seemed to lose interest in being the public face of this group, but now she's back in action. Of course, now that both abortion and homosexuality have been outlawed, the "protests" of The Saviors are really more like public lynchings. Take last week's "protest" in Boise, Idaho. The mayor of Boise was publicly "outed" as gay by these thugs. The man was arrested on the spot. Scuttlebutt says he was one of the best mayors the city has ever had. So tell me, what's been gained by doing this? Huh, Sarah?

> *"This country will not be a good place for any of us to live in unless we make it a good place for all of us to live in."*
> —Theodore Roosevelt

The Persecution of Eleanor Adams

Enter the Voice of Reason Archives

Email me!

This site last updated: 02/22/26
Visitors since this site was born: **6,163,015**

Dear Dad,

I apologize for not writing sooner, but frankly, I haven't been in the mood to say anything to you until now.

You know very well that I was not kidnapped. I think it's shameful of you to allow the public to continue to think I was. Face up to the truth, Dad—I ran away because you and Mother made life unbearable for me. I know I'm a disappointment to you as a daughter, but that's something we both have to live with, now.

I love you both dearly, but the truth is, I've lost a tremendous amount of respect for you. Your actions... Okay, Mom's actions combined with your inaction... have made me realize that however much the two of you love me, you don't respect me. Maybe I don't deserve your respect, but even so, I can't live like that.

I'll be sixteen, soon. And I think that's old enough to know what I want out of life. If at sixteen I'm mature enough to decide on a college major, or sit behind the wheel of a car, then I can decide other things, too. Though, in truth, there's still a lot I'm unsure of.

Am I a lesbian? I don't think so. I'm still attracted to boys, so I guess I'm bisexual. And though I still feel some guilt over it, I'm beginning to come to terms with it.

As for the "witchcraft" thing... I don't know if I consider myself Wiccan or not, but I'd be lying if I said it didn't intrigue me. It's still a confusing time for me. But I'll work it out. Either way, it's a religion, Dad. It's not Satanic. It doesn't even have a devil figure! I expect you to take it seriously, because I sure do.

What the two of you did to me is inexcusable. I know you're my parents and have the right to raise me and punish me however you like. But how can you expect me to work things out on my own if you're basically imprisoning me? The truth is that you don't want me to work things out. You want me to fit into the little mold you've made for me.

Well, I can't do that. I have to live my own life. I'm sorry if it's not one you approve of, but it's my life, not yours. It's harder than you can know for me to say all this, but I have to. I have to be my own person.

I am so sorry for disappointing you, Dad. I think you're the greatest guy in the world, and I look up to you so much. If you have any love left for me, I ask a favor of you. Call off your goons. Stop harassing Vicki and her family. And stop lying to the public about me.

Your loving, if wayward, daughter,

Mary

February 23, 2026

Well, Lorelei was right. The journey was pretty boring. The salt flats were kinda cool, but after that it was just ugly old desert.

We're in Winnemucca, Nevada, right now. We waited a few days more in Utah before leaving, while Lorelei worked out an alternate travel plan. Taking Vicki's advice, we'll be sneaking into California via a very small road that's barely on the map. That will be tomorrow, I guess.

It'll be a while before we get to California, anyway. We'll be staying a day or two at different stops along the way. That's good, since I still haven't heard from Vicki. I have no idea what our final destination is going to be. But if her family is acting the way she says, and the FBI and DHS are constantly watching, what's she going to come up with?

Lorelei and I talked about bisexuality today. And it turns out she's bi, too. She was so great, telling me how she came to grips with it. For her, though, it was probably easier. She hadn't been religious for some time before accepting her sexuality, and didn't feel nearly the amount of guilt I've been feeling. But listening to her story really helped me feel better about myself and my feelings for Vicki.

Dad should have received my letter by now, if Cat got it in the mail for me right away. I'm probably hoping in vain that he'll actually call off the search for me, though.

We'll just have to wait and see.

24 February 2026

The letter was postmarked San Antonio and came in an envelope addressed only with my private zip code. Could she still really be in Texas? I find that hard to believe. She simply must be on her way to San Francisco.

Her words hurt, and deeply. How can she think we do not respect her? It is because we respect her, because we love her, that we did what we did. Only an unloving parent would allow their child to hightail it down the road to hell.

Mary thinks calling off the search is a way to show her I love her. But in reality, I can only intensify the search. That, as she will one day understand, is the true loving response.

Washington—The President today announced that he received a letter stating that his daughter Mary is alive and unharmed. The letter came from San Antonio, the city in which the girl was last seen. No mention of ransom was made.

The letter is now in the hands of the FBI, whose forensics experts are searching it for clues to the identity of the kidnappers.

The President has stated that search measures will be increased. He insists that any ransom demand that might occur in the future will be ignored. He maintains that Mary will be found and returned, safe and sound, no matter what.

February 25, 2026

What a relief! There was no checkpoint on the road into California. We're now in the town of Cedarville, in a nice little Bed & Breakfast. We'll probably be here a couple more days.

I need to hear from Vicki! We only have one more stop before San Francisco, if that's really where we're heading.

But I can't believe how Dad is maintaining the false story that I was kidnapped! Not only maintaining it, but expanding. The FBI looking for clues? What is with him? When did he become such a <u>politician</u>???

Date: *February 28, 2026*
To: *merrymary@freewebmailer.net*
From: *biwitched1@anon-e-mail.com*
Subject: *I've got it!!!*

BEGIN ULTRA-CRYPTED TEXT

Mary:

I'm a genius! This is perfect! Don't come to San Francisco! Instead, go to the town of Guerneville, to my Aunt Margot's house! (I've attached a map with directions to this email.) I have no idea how I'm going to get there, myself, but Margot knows you're coming. She's entirely trustworthy, so don't worry about that.

Tell me I'm brilliant!

XOXO
        Vicki

END ULTRA-CRYPTED TEXT

March 1, 2026

We've stopped in Fortuna for a night or two. What a spectacular trip! Northern California is absolutely stunning. So different than where I grew up.

Lorelei is concerned about taking me to Vicki's aunt's house. She's afraid Margot might be under surveillance, too.

I can't really blame her, especially after what my dad's done. Maybe Margot's house is being watched. I'm concerned, too. How will we know if it is?

Still, there's no sense worrying about things we can't affect, right?

March 4, 2026

If the drive from Cedarville to Fortuna was beautiful, the drive down to Guerneville was beyond belief.

Lorelei took me on the Avenue of the Giants. It's a road right through these humongous redwoods, and is the most incredible thing I've ever experienced. We pulled over a couple times to walk into the groves.

It's weird, but I can only think of one word to describe how I felt, walking among these thousand-year old giants, with what looked like blankets of shamrocks at my feet (Lorelei said it was Redwood sorrel) and the smell of woods in my nose. And that word is "spiritual."

I really thought I knew what it meant to feel spiritual. But what I felt when I still considered myself a devout Christian just can't compare to what I felt in the redwood grove. I felt closer to God (or Mother Nature, or whatever) in that grove than I ever did in church. Even just writing about it now, hours later, makes my heart feel all full.

Can this be what Vicki feels, being Wiccan? Is this the feeling that inspired earth-based religions in the first place? I can imagine so! I've never felt anything like it before. And I really, really didn't want to get back in the car and continue our trip.

We arrived in Guerneville in the mid-afternoon. It's a cute little town, right along a river. It's very pretty here. Lorelei will stay the night, then be back on her way to Utah tomorrow. I'll really miss her.

I can't believe how much I've enjoyed meeting all these people from the freethought underground. They're all so nice, and not one of them even said anything negative about my father. I'm rather surprised, considering that they've been oppressed by his policies for as long as he's been in office. I imagine they just didn't want to hurt my feelings.

Then again, I feel bad enough about him right now without them saying anything.

Vicki's aunt Margot is nice enough, though a trifle on the quirky side. We'll get along fine. She's set me up in my own room. And since she has a computer, I can email and chat with Vicki. With vid-vox! Yay!

Date: *March 5, 2026*
To: *merrymary@freewebmailer.net*
From: *biwitched1@anon-e-mail.com*
Subject: *Re: I'm here!*

BEGIN ULTRA-CRYPTED TEXT

Sweetie:

Yay! You made it! I'm so glad!

Yeah, Auntie Margot is a bit on the wacky side, but delightfully so. A few words of warning, though. Don't let her get started talking about her rhododendrons. Good grief, she will bore you to tears talking about them! You let her start, she'll never stop.

Also, I hope you like Mediterranean food, because that's about all she cooks.

As I mentioned before, Margot is Wiccan, and she'll be more than happy to answer any of your questions. Most of her friends are pagan of one variety or another, too.

I've explained your entire situation to her, so she knows all about your home situation, so you don't need to feel awkward about talking to her about that. She's totally trustworthy and not exactly a fan of your father's politics, if I can be blunt.

I'm looking forward to emailing with you, too, but vid-vox might not be a good idea. Remember how suspicious my folks are of me? Well, I think they listen at my door sometimes. If they heard me talking to someone, especially a girl, they'd walk right in, I just know it. So, as much as it sucks, we'll still have to limit this to regular text. Sorry.

I think you'll like Guerneville, though. I always enjoy visiting. It doesn't have anywhere near as much to do as San Francisco, but it's quieter.

Have fun getting settled in!

Vicki

END ULTRA-CRYPTED TEXT

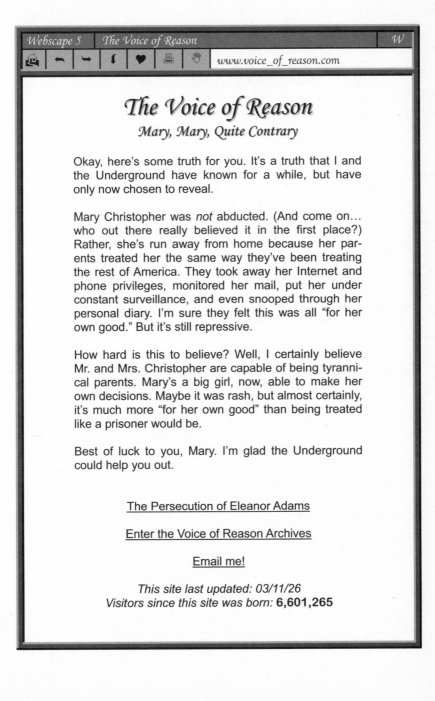

The Voice of Reason
Mary, Mary, Quite Contrary

Okay, here's some truth for you. It's a truth that I and the Underground have known for a while, but have only now chosen to reveal.

Mary Christopher was *not* abducted. (And come on… who out there really believed it in the first place?) Rather, she's run away from home because her parents treated her the same way they've been treating the rest of America. They took away her Internet and phone privileges, monitored her mail, put her under constant surveillance, and even snooped through her personal diary. I'm sure they felt this was all "for her own good." But it's still repressive.

How hard is this to believe? Well, I certainly believe Mr. and Mrs. Christopher are capable of being tyrannical parents. Mary's a big girl, now, able to make her own decisions. Maybe it was rash, but almost certainly, it's much more "for her own good" than being treated like a prisoner would be.

Best of luck to you, Mary. I'm glad the Underground could help you out.

Enter the Voice of Reason Archives

Email me!

This site last updated: 03/11/26
Visitors since this site was born: **6,601,265**

Date: *March 12, 2026*
To: *biwitched1@anon-e-mail.com*
From: *merrymary@freewebmailer.net*
Subject: *Guerneville*

BEGIN ULTRA-CRYPTED TEXT

Vicki:

Margot and I went shopping, today. Well, mostly just browsing, since I'm running pretty low on money. It was fun!

I really like this town. It's very friendly. I've seen stickers on cars that say "The Hate Stops Here." And signs and things that say, "Guerneville is a Hate-Free Community." That's so cool! Why can't every town be like that?

There's something else I find a bit unusual. Keep in mind that I've lived in the White House through all my teen years so far, and that I might simply have not noticed this elsewhere when I was young, but... Guerneville seems to have a lot of gay people.

Seems like every other shop we went into made it known that they catered to gays, lesbians, bisexuals... Transgendered, even, which is something I just DON'T understand, thank you. (Do people really feel THAT uncomfortable being the sex they were born?)

Oh, Vicki, what kind of world have you dragged me into? *lol*

Seriously, though, I think it's terrific that an entire community can be so accepting of a person's freedom of choice, no matter what that choice happens to be.

Wouldn't it be amazing if the whole world could be like that?

Please write soon!

Mary

END ULTRA-CRYPTED TEXT

13 March 2026

I have done something terribly foolish. Lord knows I don't often partake of alcohol, but after yet another telephone argument about Gene with Sarah, last night I had a few. And then came the call.

In response, I visited that vile site. And I saw his words, his evil words, broadcasting to all visitors that my daughter had run away. The fact that the God-forsaken Freethought Underground has been helping her makes it all even more abhorrent.

Something possessed me, then, and I sent him an email. I know I shouldn't have, and I'm certain he'll post it on the website, making me look even more like an ogre.

Oh, what have I done? What have I done?

March 14, 2026

Margot runs a really cool bookstore downtown called The River Reader. I hung out with her this afternoon. It's fantastic!

Her store has an entire section of books on Wicca and other pagan stuff! I asked her how she could sell them, since my father's administration made it illegal to publish them. Margot rightly pointed out that it wasn't illegal to sell remaining stock. She says her pagan section used to be much larger than it is now.

And of course, she's got her own personal books, which I'm now reading. The more I read, the more fascinating it becomes. Today I read about the different Wiccan holidays, or Sabbats. They call Halloween "Samhain," which isn't pronounced anything like it's spelled. It's pronounced "SOW-in." Weird. Now I understand why Margot calls her cat that. I just thought it was a bizarre name for a cat.

Her store also has some books on alternative sexuality. I wonder if any of them can help me deal with the confusion I'm feeling. Maybe I should talk to Margot about it. Vicki thinks I should.

Speaking of Vicki, in her latest email, she said the surveillance on her is really bad. They even follow her bus to and from school. She says she's got to figure out a way to get up here without being followed. I don't know what to tell her.

Date: *March 16, 2026*
To: *merrymary@freewebmailer.net*
From: *jefferson_paine@voice_of_reason.com*
Subject: *FWD: I know you know where she is*

BEGIN ULTRA-CRYPTED TEXT

Miss Christopher:

Several days ago, I received the following email via the link on my website. I think you'll recognize the return address. Through contacts in the Freethought Underground, I was able to locate your public key and private email address.

Good luck with your situation. And by the way, I'm relieved to hear that you're okay.

Jefferson Paine

—Begin Forwarded Message—

Date: *March 12, 2026*
To: *jefferson_paine@voice_of_reason.com*
From: *The_Prez@whitehouse.gov*
Subject: *I know you know where she is*

Listen, you Goddamned son of a bitch. I know you know where my daughter is. I know you know how to contact her. You MUST tell me. You MUST give me this information.

If you don't, I swear if it's the last thing I do, I'll see you executed for treason.

For once in your life, do something decent. Please help me. Mary's disappearance is a knife in my heart.

I have no choice but to continually increase the efforts to find her. She's probably on her way to meet with that little witch dyke Vicki. It's all HER FAULT, you know. The slut.

Please help me. She's just a child.

—End Forwarded Message—

END ULTRA-CRYPTED TEXT

March 18, 2026

I've read my father's email to Jefferson Paine probably a hundred times since he forwarded it to me. And I'm still torn. On the one hand, I'm embarrassed that he actually stooped to emailing Paine, and that he threatened him and acted so badly. On the other hand, I keep focusing on where he said my disappearance is like a knife in his heart. It just kills me to read that. I love him so much. And I miss him. But lately, he hasn't been himself.

I knew that him being President would change our relationship, but I never imagined it would cause such a rift between us. Since his first year in office, things have been so different between us.

Margot and I had a long talk about this, and she pretty much agrees with the conclusion I came to, myself – that I need to do what I feel is right for me, no matter what my mom or dad think.

But that doesn't tell me what I should do. What really is the right thing for me? I'm not quite sixteen. Does anyone this age really know what's best for them?

I can't help but put myself in the shoes of other people. Like it or not, I now belong to certain outcast minorities. Because of my sexual confusion (if not outright preference) and my interest in a "forbidden" religion, I am now an outsider.

I feel guilty for not having been thinking of what these outsiders thought and felt all along. Why did I have to become one to have sympathy for their situation?

I guess my path is clear. I'm not at all comfortable with it, but my heart won't allow me to stand idly by. I have to stand up to my father, to what he's doing not only to me but to so many in our society. It makes my stomach do flip-flops just thinking about it. But what else can I do?

I was about to write that I guess that makes Vicki and Margot wrong, because I do not need to do what's best for me, but what's best for everyone else, too.

But then I realized something: what's best for those others _is_ what's best for me.

Date: March 20, 2026
To: The_Prez@whitehouse.gov
From: merrymary@freewebmailer.net
Subject: Ultimatum

Dad:

Jefferson Paine forwarded your incredibly rude email to me. You're wrong, by the way. He doesn't know where I am, and had to get my email address from someone else.

I really hate that it has come to this. You have no idea how badly I just want things to be normal between us. But I've had to accept that they'll never be normal, even if one day they might be better than they are now.

This is very hard for me, but I have to say it. You've driven me to it. So here you go:

1.   I want emancipation. You can either give me your consent, or at least call off the hunt for me.
2.   I want all surveillance of my friends to stop immediately.
3.   I want you to cancel the ongoing "hunt" for leaders of the Free-thought Underground, and release Eleanor Adams and Michael Lee from prison.

If you do not agree to these things, I will contact the press. I will state publicly that I'm bisexual and a witch. Yes, I much prefer the term "Wiccan," but "witch" is the word that would hurt you the most. (No, I haven't embraced Wicca completely, yet, but I'm closer to that than Christian.) And I'll denounce every policy your administration has put in place. In other words, I will do everything I can to ruin your political career.

Don't think for a minute that I won't. You may be the most popular President this country's ever seen, but you can't afford the negative press of your only child turning against you in a very, very public fashion.

I'm sure you know that I do not want to do these things. But I cannot allow you to wreck my life, the lives of my friends, and the lives of millions of other Americans.

Honestly, I wouldn't even regard these actions as something I'd be doing to my father. I love my father more than he could know. But the President... the guy my father turned into five years ago... that's a guy I don't particularly like, and won't hesitate to hurt.

You have one week to decide.

Mary

3/22/26

Paul came to me this evening asking my advice. I was shocked, as he rarely does so when the question involves matters of state. But as it was about Mary's demands, I suppose that made it an exception.

I confessed that I do, in fact, believe she would try to carry out her threats, with some degree of success. I'm certain of it, in fact. I'm only now beginning to understand just how headstrong our girl is.

I don't know if he asked Gene his advice. But I'm sure I can imagine his reaction if Paul does what I think he's going to do.

However things ultimately work out, I'm glad the charade of the kidnapping is soon to be behind us. I never felt good about that pretense.

26 March 2026

I have made my bed, and now I am forced to lie in it. Mary certainly has me over a barrel right now. I honestly have no idea if she's bluffing or not, but I have to assume not.

Certainly there are publishers out there who would think nothing of ignoring any gag order we'd implement. And certainly many of those would leap at the chance to undermine me in any way. Do I have any idea how the public would react to Mary's announcements? I could talk to the analysts. I'm sure they'd break it down conveniently into "points" for me. My popularity is strong. I could survive it, I'm sure.

Or rather, the Presidency could. But could Paul Christopher, the father?

I'm not handling the whole situation well at all. Nor is Sarah. I can't speak for my wife, but I dwell on this, every minute of the day. The fact that my only child, my lovely, precocious daughter, is a lesbian... I can't deal with it. And worse, she's succumbed to Satan's witchcraft.

Her soul is in limbo. I'm sure it could be saved, but not by me. The fate of the nation is more important than the fate of even my own daughter's soul.

Lord have mercy on mine.

March 27, 2026

It's been a week since I emailed Dad, and I still haven't heard back from him. I don't know whether to be disappointed or not. For all I know, he's not even in Washington, or not accessing his email. I haven't been very good about keeping up on his comings and goings.

I suppose it's possible that he's just ignoring me, figuring that I'm just bluffing. And really, I'm not so sure there's much I can do. It was mostly hot air, I suppose.

Or maybe he's angry with me for issuing an ultimatum in the first place. Can't blame him, if he is. It was probably wrong of me to do that. I can't help thinking I'm a bad daughter.

I feel awful whenever I stop and think about it. I know they were treating me like a prisoner, but does that really justify what I've done? How could I have been so disrespectful? Running away like that... it must have been torture for them.

Maybe I should just apologize and tell him to forget the whole thing. Maybe we can try to mend the rift between us. I'd really like that. I miss him so much. Mom, too.

I'm happy that I'm going to be with Vicki, of course, but she's not my family. Half the time, I'm scared. I wasn't ready to become as independent as my actions required of me. I'm not a grown-up, and I certainly haven't been behaving like one.

So why, then, do I expect my folks to treat me like one?

I'm so stupid.

"Ladies and Gentlemen of the Press...

"It is with great relief that I confirm reports that my daughter has been located. She is safe and sound. But I regret that I cannot tell you where she is. No reason to have a media circus following her.

"I also need to address a rumor that has been circulating. Some of you may have heard that Mary ran away from camp, and was not abducted at all. In fact, this is true. I apologize for maintaining the façade of a kidnapping. The ruse was suggested by my advisors, who felt that the public would not take the truth very well. I disagreed. I think the truth is always received better than a lie, no matter how well-intentioned.

"It turns out... surprise... that Mary is very much like her parents. Sarah and I are both exceedingly headstrong, and our daughter is no different. Like many teenagers, Mary didn't always see eye to eye with her parents. And like many parents, we didn't make a tremendous effort to see things from our child's perspective.

"Mary didn't like living in the White House. And who can blame her? People her age need social interaction with peers, and the freedom to live a life out of the public eye.

"Sarah and I are very proud of our daughter. We're so proud of her, so certain of her intelligence and maturity, that we are acceding to her wishes.

"We will consent to her request for emancipation. She'll be sixteen in a month, and is perfectly capable of managing her own life, independently.

"I want to make one thing perfectly clear. Mary wants her privacy, and I want her to have it. I do not want to see one paparazzi photo of her in any newspaper. I do not want her tracked down by reporters and interviewed. I don't care if she calls you up and asks for one. Don't do it.

"Please humor the wishes of your President. No... I ask you now as a loving father, not as the President. Allow my daughter to have the privacy she desires.

"Thank you. No questions, please."

The Voice of Reason
They Put the Fun in Dysfunctional!

Wow. Who would have expected this kind of development? The President's daughter runs away, and the Prez *lets her!* Maybe there's more at work than meets the eye, here, though. I mean, think about it. This is the same President (latest in a series, collect 'em all) who preaches "family values" at any opportunity. What does this say about his own family?

Of course, he's expecting his sheep... er, his followers... to praise him for treating his daughter like an adult, rather than focusing on the fact that he drove her away in the first place.

And did my ears deceive me, or did St. Paul actually tell the Press to butt out of the lives of his family? In the name of *privacy?* Does anyone besides me detect a teensy bit of irony, here?

Mr. Christopher, I've said it before, and I'll say it again: You're a Grade-A hypocrite. No wonder your kid ran away.

> "The only freedom deserving the name is that of pursuing our own good in our own way, so long as we do not attempt to deprive others of theirs."
> —John Stuart Mill

The Persecution of Eleanor Adams

Enter the Voice of Reason Archives

Email me!

This site last updated: 03/31/26
Visitors since this site was born: **7,751,639**

Washington—The bounty offered to the public for capture of Freethought Underground leaders has been lifted, according to the White House.

"We can no longer ask the public to put itself at risk," President Christopher said in a press conference late yesterday afternoon. "The Freethought Underground is a dangerous group, and there's no telling what efforts they may make to protect themselves."

When asked if the hunt for the remaining leaders at large was being cancelled completely, the President made it quite clear that this was not the case. "These people are still breaking the law, and should be brought to justice. The FBI and the DHS are still under orders to safely capture them. Our hope is that they will soon join Eleanor Adams behind bars. By all means, citizens are urged to do their civic duty and contact the authorities whenever they run across these felons. But no reward will be given for this information, beginning today. We do not condone any vigilante-style justice. It was an error in judgment to involve the public at all."

March 31, 2026

Well, I guess I'm in no danger of being abducted in my sleep, anymore. And I'm happy the Freethought Underground leaders don't have to worry about being shot by trigger-happy citizens. But I'm upset that Dad's not calling off the hunt completely, even though I understand his reasons.

I'm amazed at how easily he gave in. I know he did it because he cares so much about his image as President. It was to avoid looking like a fool, not out of love for me. If anything, I'm more upset now than I was a week ago.

Anyway, I guess it won't be a problem for Vicki to come up here, now. I'm really nervous about seeing her. The last time we were together, I was only just beginning to have "those" thoughts about her. But now...

Will it be the same? Will I still feel this way when I see her again? I hope so. I like this feeling.

Date: *April 1, 2026*
To: *biwitched1@anon-e-mail.com*
From: *merrymary@freewebmailer.net*
Subject: *My feelings*

BEGIN ULTRA-CRYPTED TEXT

Vicki:

As you know, I've been thinking a lot about my feelings for you. I've even talked to others about them, including Lorelei, Father Montoya, and your Aunt Margot. Sometimes I think I've got a good handle on how I feel, and am okay with it. Other times, I'm not so sure.

It's possible that I might be confusing friendship with feelings of love. I honestly don't know. In fact, sometimes I wonder if lots of people don't do that. I mean, I see some couples who seem to be little more than friends. They don't act like you expect a couple in love to act.

On the other hand, sometimes I wonder what the real difference is. I know we're taught to expect "true love" to be this amazing thing. Being swept off our feet, and all that. But I think that's mostly just Hollywood. Maybe I'm just cynical from all I've seen in the past couple years, but sometimes I just wonder.

All I can say for 100% certain is this: I do love you. Maybe it's just as a really dear friend who's teaching me a lot about the world. Or maybe it's something else. I honestly don't know.

But I do know that I want to be with you. I want to be your best friend in the world. I want to learn from you. I also feel tingly inside when I think of certain moments that we shared. And that excites and scares me at the same time.

So. Is that friendship? Or something more?

The way I figure it, we can just let time decide for us. Because I sure can't figure it out without having you here beside me.

Mary

END ULTRA-CRYPTED MESSAGE

Date: *April 1, 2026*
To: *merrymary@freewebmailer.net*
From: *biwitched1@anon-e-mail.com*
Subject: *Re: My feelings*

BEGIN ULTRA-CRYPTED TEXT

Mary:

Sweetie, I'm not expecting you to know exactly how you feel, yet. Goddess, I'm not even sure that I know, either! I don't have any expectations for "us" beyond what you described so well. Now stop stressing over it. There's no need.

However, there might be something you do need to stress over. Nothing has changed with regard to us being watched. They still follow me to school. I think they're waiting to see if I try to leave town, to come to you. Then they'll know where you are.

I think I can fool them long enough to get out of town, after which I can hitch my way up to Guerneville. It involves cutting out from school around lunchtime, a Druid friend who's given me his oath of secrecy, and a good bit of luck from the Goddess.

Probably best if you don't tell Margot my plans. She may be the coolest Aunt a little witch could wish for, but she is my mother's sister. She'd never allow Mom to worry about a missing daughter.

I've written a letter to my parents and will mail it tomorrow. I'm not telling them anything specific, just that I'm safe and that they shouldn't worry. Who knows? Maybe they'll be glad to be rid of me.

Anyway, I'll save the hitching for Friday, and with luck will make it to Guerneville by that evening, if I'm lucky enough not to be picked up by any rapists or serial killers. Or the FBI.

Calm down. That was a joke.

I'll see you soon!

Vicki

END ULTRA-CRYPTED MESSAGE

April 2, 2026

I can't believe she's going to hitch-hike to Guerneville! That's just so insane! I'm going to be a bundle of worry until she gets here. And I can't let Margot know why I'm so stressed, either!

Speaking of Margot, she's going to help me with the emancipation. I'll need to be able to show some income, so she's offered me a job in her store.

We talked a lot about Wicca, and I find myself more drawn than ever to it. I like the sense of balance Wicca gives, focusing on a god and goddess, rather than just a god. I know some people say the Christian God is without gender, but I was raised to believe God was 100% male, through and through.

And reading the Bible, especially the Old Testament, certainly portrays God with masculine qualities. Only in the New Testament do we hear of any nurturing, feminine qualities of God, and really, they're just descriptions of Jesus.

I've about given up on the Bible, though. It's not the book I thought it was. Despite Jesus' message of love, most of the Bible is just a series of atrocities and condemnations. I don't like it.

Wouldn't Jude be pleased?

I feel like a total ass about him. I think about him every day, but haven't emailed him once since I escaped that idiotic camp. I'm such a coward. I haven't emailed because I'm not looking forward to the conversation. I know he'll be upset with me for not telling him who I am. And I can't blame him.

April 4, 2026

Vicki's still not here. I'm really worried.

It shouldn't take two whole days to hitch a ride to Guerneville! It's only 75 miles.

Something's happened to her. I just know it.

April 6, 2026

Vicki's mother finally called here today. Margot was really put out by it, because she effectively had to lie to her sister. It's no lie that Vicki's not here, and it's not a lie that Margot hadn't heard from her. Both those things are true, unfortunately.

But she's not stupid. As soon as she heard Vicki was gone, Margot knew she was coming here.

She promised she'd let her sister know if Vicki showed up here. But how can she? If she does, then they'll know I'm here, too.

Have I put too many people at risk with all of this? Should I just let it be known that I'm here?

And where is she???

6 April 2026

I suppose we should simply stop underestimating the resourcefulness of teenagers. Somehow, Vicki has also disappeared, despite the surveillance I've had placed on her and her family.

Evidently, she vanished a few days ago, but I was only told about it today. Doubtless, they felt they'd find her in short order and I'd never have to be told at all.

It seems that Vicki departed Abraham Lincoln High School at lunchtime in a friend's car. Our agents lost them briefly in Golden Gate Park, and when they finally caught sight of the boy's vehicle again, it was headed back toward the school. But when they reached the school, only he got out. Vicki obviously got out somewhere in the park and, my observant agents think, probably got into another friend's vehicle.

She has not returned home, and her parents have begun to bristle under the constant surveillance. They're not speaking to my agents.

I'll allow them another week to find her, to try to redeem themselves.

Sounding OFF
By J. E. Cooper

Tracking Gene Sisco and Our Father's Family Since 2015.

Issue No. 22 **Summer, 2026**

Twenty-Five Years of Bigotry

This issue is early, I'm sure you've noticed. It's a rare thing, so don't get used to it.

But the truth is, this issue's lead story is easier than most to write, because it's been building up for so long.

This year is, in case you haven't been paying attention, the 25th anniversary of Sisco's television show, *The Family Hour.*

Sometime this year (it hasn't been announced exactly when), Sisco will be airing a special episode of the show, in which he'll go over all the heinous activities he and his "Family" have been involved in over the past two and a half decades.

Doubtless, he'll also "modestly" mention his part in getting Paul Christopher elected President. And why shouldn't he? Everyone with half a brain realizes Christopher never would've been a contender had not millions of Christians under Sisco's spell been hypnotized into voting for him.

Nevertheless, I think everyone out there who actually cares about the things Sisco would have eradicated from the world... like a woman's right to choose, the freedom of gays to be "out" (let alone anything further than that), and the freedom of non-Christians to worship (or not) as they please in society... these people should do something to commemorate this anniversary.

We need to let Sisco... no, not just Sisco... we need to let the whole world know exactly how we feel about the man and his organization (and, by proxy, his powerful puppet in the White House).

So I'm suggesting a bit of an activist campaign, like my friends in the Freethought Underground are always urging us to do.

So on the day when this broadcast occurs, I want all of you to contact the media... whether by email or fax or whatever... and bombard them with messages saying

(Continued on p. 3)

Inside This Issue...

April 10, 2026

Vicki arrived in Guerneville yesterday, finally! Safe and sound, no bad experiences on the way. And even more importantly, she wasn't followed by government agents.

Turns out she <u>walked</u> the whole way! Well, most of it. A friend dropped her off in Golden Gate Park. Then she took a cab to Sausalito and walked from there. No wonder it took her so long!

I wish she'd called, though! She says she didn't want to risk being traced electronically when she used pay phones. Guess it never occurred to her to just get change and use cash.

Anyway, I'm really relieved that she finally got here safely. I was so afraid something had happened to her.

We stayed up until the wee hours, just talking. I expected things to be awkward between us, but it wasn't. Well, maybe a little. I'm just so unsure of what I'm feeling. I've never been in love, so I'm not sure if this is love I'm feeling. But it feels like what I've always imagined it's supposed to feel like. It's exciting and scary all at once.

One of the things we talked about was my fear of being discovered. My face has been on so many magazine covers and newspapers over the past few months that I'm bound to be recognized eventually. I don't want to be hounded by the press. Then again, maybe they'll obey my dad's not-so-subtle request.

And then there's Vicki's parents. Naturally, Margot called Vicki's mom not long after she walked through the door. Neither of us can blame her for doing so. I mean, Vicki and her mother don't even get along, but she talked to her on the phone.

What will they do? That's anybody's guess. But Margot spoke with her sister for a long time, and told us she doesn't think we'll be in any danger of being tracked down. I guess Vicki's mom gave her word or something.

Let's hope she keeps it.

May 1, 2026

Yesterday was my birthday. Sweet Sixteen, finally. We had a small celebration here at Margot's house. She made a cake and there were presents. One of these, from Vicki, was a book. It's very nice. It's got the writings of Jefferson, Madison, and a bunch of others. And inside is an inscription. It reads: "On the occasion of the five millionth visit to The Voice of Reason. Thank you. Jefferson Paine." How about that?

After the gift giving, we went out to dinner and had an absolutely fantastic meal. Vicki had told the staff it was my birthday, and they treated me like royalty. It was really nice, though it made me think a lot of Mom and Dad. My birthdays were always something special.

Yesterday was also a major Wiccan Sabbat – Beltane. As I understand it, Beltane is sort of about fertility, love and desire. It honors the union of the god and the goddess, as well as the beginning of summer.

But last night was a Wiccan double-dip, because it was also a full moon. Esbats are held on full moons. Our celebration was sort of a combination of the two.

Several of Margot's friends came over, all of them pagan, I presume. There were lots of kids, too. I was introduced simply as Vicki's friend Mary. No one seemed to recognize me. Around sundown, we went into Margot's huge back yard and built a big bonfire. It was fantastic! Many of the guests brought instruments… drums, flutes, and so on. We danced around the fire and had a really fun time.

A young oak tree in Margot's back yard served as a maypole. Huge red and white ribbons were attached to the trunk, and the kids all grabbed one and circled the pole, weaving in and around each other so the ribbons sort of braided around the pole. They sang a song, too. I didn't really catch everything they sang, but it was obvious they'd done this before.

Vicki embarrassed me by explaining that the maypole represents a phallus, thrust into Mother Earth. The red and white represent menstrual blood and sperm! I wonder if the little kids know that.

This went on for hours! Dancing, singing, laughing and drinking. Someone brought mead, which is a drink made from fermented honey. I tried some, but it was really strong. I wasn't too crazy about it. I had "virgin" Wassail, a punch made from apple juice, citrus, and spices. Margot made some wonderful little crescent shaped cookies. I'll have to get the recipe.

As the night wore on, some of the guests started dancing around the fire in various states of undress, from topless to fully nude, which they refer to as "skyclad." At first I was very uncomfortable with this, since my old and judgmental Christian influences said, "They're going to have sex! It'll be an orgy!"

Nothing of the sort happened, of course. Although at one point one of the men did develop an erection. At first, I giggled when I saw it. But I have to admit I was fascinated, too. I've never seen one before. Not in real life, anyway. But he wasn't ashamed or embarrassed. He didn't even bother hiding it, just kept dancing. And since it's a fertility holiday, I guess it was appropriate. No one else acted like it was unusual, anyway.

There may have been no sex, but there certainly were some erotically charged moments. Sometimes the dancing was positively lewd. At one point, Vicki and I danced together, and I was very aware that she was dancing in a seductive way. Or so it seemed to me, anyway. It crossed my mind at the time that it could've just been wishful thinking.

Sometime after midnight, things started to wind down. Some of the guests left. It was, after all, a Thursday night. I'm sure some had to work the next day. Others hung around until the bonfire burnt down. It became pretty relaxed, which I found bizarre, after all that had gone on. I was still pretty up, in fact. Then Vicki grabbed a blanket and a lantern and we headed off into the woods. She said she wanted to celebrate the esbat.

As we walked through the trees, I asked her if it would be the same sort of ritual that we did together back in Washington. We reached a clearing and she put down the blanket and said, "Who said anything about a ritual?"

And then she kissed me. I was too startled to do anything, but when she started to slowly undress me, my heart began beating so hard I thought it would explode.

And we did it. Right there in the trees, we made love. It was absolutely dreamy. I felt like I was in another world. The feeling of her lips on mine... how could I have wondered whether I'd really enjoy it or not? I was nervous and self-conscious, but it was so relaxed and unpressured.

That was almost twenty hours ago, and I can still feel the chills up my spine when she touched me in certain places. How on earth can anyone say this is wrong, or "sinful" or whatever? It was the most beautiful thing I've ever experienced.

I'm so in love with her!

Backpage: Eleanor, it's been two years, to the day, since you were appre-
             hended. A lot has gone on in our country in those two years.

Adams: [laughs] That's an understatement.

Backpage: Atheists USA was a very vocal group in its time, and helped
             prevent or reverse many social injustices over the last fifteen
             years. Do you think you and your organization would have been
             able to stop some of the legislation the Christopher administra-
             tion has passed?

Adams: Thank you. We certainly did our best. But to answer your
             question, I honestly can't say. The truth is that the Freethought
             Underground is still carrying on the mission of Atheists USA,
             albeit in a different fashion. They're out there, spreading the
             word, enlightening the people.

Backpage: Well... Eleanor... I understand what the Underground is doing,
             but you can't really think it's going to have much effect, can you?
             Atheists USA had a large membership, published a monthly
             magazine, and had the ability to reach and motivate many thou-
             sands of people easily. The Underground doesn't have that kind
             of ability, no matter how well-intentioned their motives.

Adams: That's true, but you're forgetting one thing, Lisa. The Free-
             thought Underground is going out there *in person*, reaching out
             to people on a one-to-one basis. They may not have the slick lit-
             erature available to Atheists USA or other high-profile organiza-
             tions, but they have something better: faces. When one of the
             Underground groups visits a town, the citizens can meet with
             them, ask questions, have discussions. This is the way the con-
             servatives played it when they started their exceedingly effective
             grass roots campaigns. They knew people responded better to a
             personal appearance than a letter in their mailboxes.

Backpage: Okay. So what have they accomplished? What do you see them
             doing in the future? Will they be responsible for big changes in
             our country's policies?

Adams: Indirectly, I think yes. The purpose of the Underground isn't to
             make change so much as it's to educate others, empowering the
             people to make the changes they want to have.

Backpage: Do you have any idea what they've been up to? I understand you used the Internet to communicate with other members, but your access here is restricted.

Adams: My access here is *not* restricted, but it is *monitored*. I cannot communicate with other members via the 'net without putting them in jeopardy. But I still receive word from visitors who are not so closely monitored. And I hear some pretty impressive things.

Backpage: Which you obviously can't share with us.

Adams: Obviously.

Backpage: If you had the chance to do it all over again, is there anything you'd do differently?

Adams: Not get caught? [laughs] Well, no, I don't think so. I did what I felt we needed to do. I was very fortunate, I think, to have accomplished so much between Christopher's election and my arrest.

Backpage: Such as?

Adams: Getting the Underground organized. I certainly didn't do it alone, of course. We have some very fine, highly motivated people involved.

Backpage: Including the mysterious Jefferson Paine?

Adams: An inspiring fellow. He has been a great assistance to us, though he was never a member of Atheists USA. Through his kindness and computer wizardry, the Underground has been able to do far more than we would have otherwise.

Backpage: You are aware, of course, that our government has issued a warrant for this man's arrest, on charges of high treason.

Adams: Yes. I've been questioned about him, but the simple truth is that I do not know his real name, or where he lives, or any other specific information about him.

Backpage: Is there anything at all you can tell us about him?

Adams: [laughs] Well, he's handsome! A bit young for me, though. Beyond that, no.

Backpage: Speaking of attractive men, rumor has it that you're engaged to Robert Green, the Freethought Underground leader who was nearly lynched by Klansmen in Arkansas a few years ago.

Adams: [clears throat] Yes. I'd thought it a bad idea for him to take his Underground group to the South. Atheists aren't generally welcome in the South, especially black atheists. After his close call, I met him at their next stop, in Conway, Arkansas. I proposed. He accepted.

Backpage: *You* proposed?

Adams: It's the twenty-first century, Lisa.

Backpage: Many people find it hypocritical that atheists get married, since they believe marriage to be a holy, religious institution.

Adams: And when performed in a religious ceremony, it is. But people have been forming marriages for longer than there has been organized religion. Civil ceremonies are just as meaningful as religions ones.

Backpage: You're eligible for parole in 2039. Do you think you'll qualify?

Adams: I'm being used as an example. I am the symbol of atheism in America, and as long as we have fundamentalism running rampant in this country, I'll remain behind bars. Only a massive social revolt will change that. Of course, that's exactly what the Freethought Underground is trying to effect. And I think it'll happen.

5/3/26

Adams is one smooth operator. So blasé about her imprison-ment, even joking about it. She wants so much for the world to see her as the stoic martyr, even happy to be behind bars, so long as her minions are out carrying on her evil work.

Is she partly responsible for Mary's fall from faith? Yes. She and that horrid Jefferson Paine. I was wrong, so wrong, to treat Paul's outrage over the website with such a cavalier attitude. Mary visited that site regularly. We had one of the computer technicians pull a detailed history from her computer.

Her online activities weren't limited to this, though. They found searches for information on bisexuality, lesbianism, witchcraft, pagan-ism, and more.

Between these things and her emails to and from that vile atheist with the Beatles fixation… I just want to scream.

I haven't shared most of this information with Paul. He has too much on his mind as it is, but beyond that, I don't want Mary to fall even further in his eyes. I see every day how much she has hurt him with her actions and would not add to it.

It shames me to admit that I have long envied their closeness. Yet despite that, I would see it restored.

But that cannot happen until Mary accepts the Lord back into her heart. And I'm afraid I don't see that happening without some sort of miracle.

I will, of course, continue to pray daily that this miracle presents itself. But the Lord must be invited. He will not force himself. And Mary does not at this point seem inclined toward issuing an invitation.

The Voice of Reason
The Perpetual President

The 22nd Amendment to the Constitution reads, in part: "No person shall be elected to the office of the President more than twice…"

A new Amendment proposal has been submitted this week. It reads, in part, "The Twenty-Second Article of Amendment to the Constitution of the United States is hereby repealed."

That's right, folks. St. Paul wants another term.

This, of course, has to be approved by Congress, then ratified by a whole slew of states before it's official. But it's looking like that won't be much of a problem.

If this passes, we might be subjected to Christopher's Theocracy until the day he dies.

If this thought scares the snot out of you the way it does me, drop me an email. I'll make sure you are contacted by a member of the Freethought Underground, who will tell you how you can help stop this travesty of justice.

The Persecution of Eleanor Adams

Enter the Voice of Reason Archives

Email me!

This site last updated: 05/23/26
Visitors since this site was born: **8,189,290**

"Ladies and Gentlemen of the United States of America...

"Two hundred fifty years ago today, our nation was born. Twenty-five decades ago, a handful of good Christian men banded together here in Philadelphia to give birth to the greatest nation the world has ever seen. Two and a half centuries ago, we celebrated our independence.

"We honor that celebration, and those men, on this day. A quarter of a millennium later, we are stronger than ever, more righteous than ever. And the credit for that goes to you—the American public.

"It is you who have shed blood, sweat and tears to make this country what it is. Your leaders have stood by, watching with pride, as American Christians spread goodness throughout the lands, using the word of the Lord as their guide. I cannot speak for other Presidents before me, but I have never been more proud of my country than in these recent years. It touches me to know that so many of my fellow citizens share my dreams of preserving America's greatness for another two hundred fifty years.

"On this very, very special day, please pray with me. Pray for an even better tomorrow. Pray for an America the likes of which our forefathers only dreamed. Pray for a true Heaven on Earth.

"Bow your head, as our forefathers did, and ask Jesus to enter the hearts of each and every American, for only with his help can we ever hope to purge the final sins from our lands.

"Our Father, who art in heaven, hallowed be thy name..."

Date: July 14, 2026
To: heyjude@beatles4ever.ws
From: merrymary@freewebmailer.net
Subject: Re: Where the heck are you???

Jude:

I am so, so sorry for not staying in touch with you. It's unforgivable of me, but you seem to be a very forgiving person so maybe you'll understand.

Okay, I can't keep secrets from you any more. In fact, I have a strong suspicion that what I'm about to tell you isn't really a secret from you, anyway.

You know why I needed the email encryption (and why I don't anymore). You know why I was offline for so long. And you know why questioning my faith was so difficult for me. And of course, you know who I was talking about when I referred to my "uncle."

I'm in California with Vicki, living with her aunt. I'm working in her aunt's bookstore and will soon have my official emancipation. Come fall, Vicki and I will be moving to the Sacramento area, where I'll be enrolling in the Sacramento Valley School. Even though I would only have one year of school left, I like the idea of going to SVS. Are you familiar with schools based on the Sudbury Valley School in Massachusetts? You probably are. Anyway, that's what Sac-Valley is. It sounds fantastic.

I could, of course, just go for my GED. I'd probably pass whatever test they give even now. But I've realized lately just how sheltered of a life I've led. SVS, I think, will give me some independence and freedom to grow in ways I never would have before.

I do miss my parents. For all their faults, I do still love them. I don't respect them much, right now, but I love them. I don't regret leaving, though. It was something I just had to do.

In general, life right now is... well, it's very, very nice. Vicki and I are crazy about each other (yes, I got over my hang-ups) and we live in a town now that is very accepting of our relationship. I hope Sacramento is like that.

Listen, if you ever have the chance to come out to California, let me know. I'd love to meet you in person after all this time.

I hope you can forgive the unfortunately necessary deception I had to put you through. Please write soon.

Your friend,

Mary Christopher

Date: *July 17, 2026*
To: *merrymary@freewebmailer.net*
From: *heyjude@beatles4ever.ws*
Subject: *Not a good idea*

BEGIN ULTRA-CRYPTED TEXT

Mary:

I thank you for finally telling me your "secret." Truth is, though, I've known who you are since fairly early in our correspondence. I never said anything because I didn't want to upset you. I figured you'd tell me when you were ready.

I'm absolutely thrilled that you're having such an idyllic life right now, but please, please, PLEASE... do NOT become complacent. Sending me an unencrypted email, especially one containing specific information about where you are and where you're going to be, wasn't a good idea.

Don't assume that you're "safe" just because you're getting emancipated. Y'know, you had those Secret Service guys around you for a reason. There are plenty of people out there who'd be more than happy to kidnap you for real this time and hold you for ransom.

Don't give them the opportunity. Keep a low profile.

You've got my public key, so use it whenever you email me. Assuming you're going to.

I've missed our chats, but I know you've got other things to be doing with your time now. Again, I'm really happy for you and Vicki.

Thanks for the invitation to visit you. I've never been further west than Ohio, believe it or not. It would certainly be an experience. Someday.

Anyway, give my best to Vicki. I'll talk to you later.

And today in Beatles history:

1968:   The film YELLOW SUBMARINE premieres in London.
1967:   "All You Need is Love" released as single in U.S. (Okay, actually, when it was first released, "Baby You're a Rich Man" was the "A" side, and it was reversed not long thereafter. Not that you really care at all. Just thought I'd share.)

Jude

END ULTRA-CRYPTED TEXT

July 21, 2026

Jude claims he's known almost all along who I am! I was pretty floored by this, but I guess it wasn't that hard to figure out. Good old "merrymary" wasn't really much of a disguise to hide behind.

For a minute, I was mad that he hadn't told me before. But the more I think about it, the more I respect him for not doing so. And I'm amazed, too, that he never took advantage of that knowledge. I could trust this man with my life. And in a way, that's exactly what I'm doing. He's really something.

It really makes me ache inside to think of how low an opinion I had of Brights before I met Jude. Not that I think every Bright is as good as he is, of course. They're no different from anyone else, coming in all varieties.

I would have assumed (due to the brainwashing done to me all my life) that any Bright who knew "merrymary" was Mary Christopher would have announced it to the world. And even Jefferson Paine... He didn't post my dad's email on his site, even though it would've been in his interests to do so. That really surprises me.

But maybe it shouldn't. I was taught that Brights have no regard for anyone but themselves. Obviously, that's not true. I find the very idea offensive now.

Sometimes it just boggles my mind when I think of how many lies were fed to me by my parents and other Christians. All the bad-mouthing of Brights, pagans, and anyone who wasn't heterosexual and monogamous... I get sick when I think of it.

Then there's things having to do with the beliefs of the founders of our country. I've been reading the book that Vicki gave me, and it is just so clear that they really did mean that government and religion should be separate. Uncle Gene and others are wrong.

And science! Geez. Margot's shop has a ton of science books, and I've been reading about evolution and stuff. Jude was absolutely correct... creationists don't understand what evolution is and isn't, and most wouldn't know real science if it bit them on the behind.

It's like a whole new world has been opened up to me, a world seen without blinders on. A world not seen through stained glass spectacles.

This is the real world. And I love it.

Folks:

Okay, it seems we're in agreement, then. It's time to change tactics. The prospect of Christopher being elected to a third term is not one any of us like, so we've got to determine a way to prevent it.

Father Montoya has suggested going public. At least the "leaders" of the Underground. With all due respect, Father, I think the only one of us who can get away with that is you. You're the only one without a price on your head. Maybe it would be helpful if you did, but I certainly don't recommend it.

Sam has suggested a series of organized, public revolts (for lack of a better word), like the bonfire thing last year. I do like this idea. We'll probably lose some to arrests, though, so you'd better make the risks clear to all participants.

This might be a good way for all of you to reconnect with those you're most familiar with. Sam, I'm sure you've got ways to contact lots of folks in the pagan community. Polly, ditto for the alternative lifestyle crowd. And so on.

Keep me abreast of your activities, as always, and we'll see what happens. And be careful out there.

Paine

Leave me a message

August 1, 2026

Well, it's final! My emancipation was approved. I'm surprised it went so quickly. Now Vicki and I are free to move to Sacramento.

She has a cousin who's trying to get us into where she lives, and will also help us with job hunting. Vicki will find something full-time and I'll probably get a part-time job.

It'll be kind of a bummer, though, moving there. Sacramento seems nice… we went up there for a trip last weekend. But it's so pretty here along the Russian River. I've really developed a connection with nature, here. There are lots of trees, and we're only about half an hour from the shore. Sacramento won't be as scenic, and that'll be hard to get used to.

But there'll be lots to do, though. We had a great time last weekend. We went to Old Sac, a section of town with all kinds of cool little shops and old-time stuff. I bought a T-shirt that says, "I LIKE GIRLS." I have no problem wearing it here in Guerneville (or "Gooneyville" as some of the locals call it), but I'm not sure how it'll go over in Sacramento. With my luck, I'll be arrested.

8/1/26

And so it's done. Our daughter is now legally on her own.

I'm of mixed feelings about it. Certainly, there is the pain of how it all happened. There is the bitterness that comes with the knowledge that your child has been corrupted.

And yet, there is a part of me… admittedly a small part… that is proud of her. She's so independent, so strong. I guess I never saw these qualities in her before.

I have come to the conclusion, after much prayer and many tears, that I forgive her for her sins. It is up to God to offer final judgment, of course, but if He's willing, that won't be for many, many years, yet.

In the meantime, I want her to be happy. I don't think I could bring myself to tell her so to her face. But here in my private pages, I can say it: I love my gay daughter.

August 20, 2026

We've got a place to live! I found out, to my surprise, that my folks had started a trust fund for me. With my emancipation, I got access to it. I've got fifteen thousand bucks! Woo hoo!

But that money won't last long. I'll have at least a year of tuition at SVS, plus having to pay for housing and groceries and utilities and who knows what else. Bus fare, for crying out loud. Man, there's a lot involved with living on your own.

We'll be living at Southside Park Cohousing. It's a group of several homes on a lot, sharing community space. We'll have a one-bedroom apartment. Not very big. But it doesn't have to be. There are common areas, including one building entirely, common yard area, even a woodworking shop. They have common meals two or three times every week. Everyone is on a cooking team, and has cooking duties about once a month. A lot of people would hate this kind of environment, but I'm really looking forward to it.

Vicki has sworn her cousin to secrecy, and we'll arrange something with the folks in charge, to keep my identity hidden.

Tallahassee—The offices of Reverend Gene Sisco's religious empire, Our Father's Family, have been receiving thousands of faxes and other correspondence for the past several days. Each page reads only, in uncensored fashion, "F - - K O.F.F."

Letters, faxes and emails began flooding O.F.F. offices, as well as media outlets, during the airing of their recent 25th Anniversary broadcast. In the broadcast, O.F.F. presented a career retrospective, and boasted that the organization was responsible for much of the legislation passed by the Christopher Administration, including that which outlawed any and all forms of non-heterosexual relationships.

Many of the letters were stamped with pink triangles, rainbow flags, and other symbols of alternative sexuality.

September 11, 2026

I have to say, I feel like I'm living in some sort of alternate universe. My life today is so radically different than my life a year ago.

I'd gone to a religious private school before we moved to Washington, then was privately tutored. But now at Sacramento Valley... It's almost like not being in school. The fact that there are no established classes really blows my mind.

But it's an amazing place. You just never know what to expect from one day to the next. For example, today we had a guest at the school and he talked about terrorism. It was an optional attendance kind of thing, but almost all the kids were there. Today is the twenty-fifth anniversary of the terrorist attacks on New York and the Pentagon. Mr. Wolfe was a police officer who survived the collapse of the World Trade Center. It was chilling, hearing his account. He even had a disc of video shot that day.

By the time he was done with his talk, and we'd watched the vids, half the students were in tears. It was totally outside our ability to conceive of so many people dying like that. I think I'll have nightmares for weeks, thinking of the footage of the airplane plowing into the building.

But it's things like this that make SVS a great school.

I've spent a good deal of time talking with the staff members (I can't call them teachers, since they aren't) about what I want to get out of my time there. The thing is, I honestly have no idea what I want to do with my life.

I've been doing a lot of thinking about this, lately, and have realized that I've missed out on quite a bit. Science is really interesting to me, and frankly, my education in science has been virtually non-existent. The school has a lot of science books, and I'm planning to read as many as I can.

But my education was lacking in a lot of other ways. I guess the best way to sum it up is that I was sheltered from reality. I was fed everything from a certain perspective, namely a conservative Christian perspective. And that's just not how the world is. That's how my dad and lots of others want the world to be, apparently. And that's starting to scare me.

Yesterday I spent almost all day at school reading every column on Jefferson Paine's website. The guy is frequently harsh, but I find myself agreeing with him more often than not.

I can't honestly say, yet, what I want to pursue as a career. I'm drawn in many directions. Part of me wants to be a scientist. Part of me wants to be an activist for alternative lifestyles. Part of me, maybe because of my dad, is drawn to politics.

Not that there's any hurry to decide. I'm free to stay at SVS until I feel I'm ready to graduate, I guess. And when they think I am.

There's an incredible feeling of freedom at this school. I can't understand why more people don't send their kids to schools like this.

For that matter, I can't understand why more people don't live in places like Southside Park. This is really cool. It's like this little, tight-knit community. I suppose folks in retirement communities have the closest idea to what this is like. But most people have no clue how rewarding it can be. I mean, I know we haven't lived here long, but so far, we both love it. The people are all very friendly. It's fun having the community dinners and getting together for Monopoly games or to play pinochle.

Vicki has been attending regular meetings of one of the covens here in Sacramento (and there are probably half a dozen). She's taken me to a couple, too, and it's a great bunch of people.

I'm finding myself connecting more and more with paganism in general. No question, there's been a hole inside me since I left my parents' religion behind.

I've discovered the beauty of the river area in Sacramento! It's very nice. I plan to spend lots of time there. I really miss the redwoods, though, and the feeling of being surrounded by those ancient trees.

We're about two hours or so from Margot's place. Hopefully we can go visit soon. Vicki's thinking about buying a car. That would be nice. We're so limited, transportation-wise. The bus schedule is pretty good, I guess, but it would be nice to be able to go on little trips on weekends. We're within a few hours of lots of neat places... Lake Tahoe, San Francisco, Monterey, Yosemite... a nature worshiper's dream!

I don't know, though. We don't really have the money to do these kinds of things. She's working full-time, and I've got my trust fund. But after paying all our bills, we don't have much left.

I feel a bit guilty about not having a job. I could work part-time and go to school part-time, but Vicki doesn't want me to. She says it's bad enough that we don't see each other during the day. She's not going to be without me at night, too.

She's sweet. I love her.

Wow, it feels good to write that without feeling guilty!

New Anglican Review

Guest Editorial by Fr. Emilio Montoya

There are many words to describe what President Christopher and Reverend Sisco are doing to America. They are not kind words.

In this "land of the free, and the home of the brave," I see much less freedom than when I was younger. I see bravery, but too little, and mostly in those who speak out against this theft of freedom.

Let me rephrase. It's not "theft." It's an *abandonment* of freedom. We tend to forget that we had to earn our freedom in the first place.

And through the generations since the American Revolution, there have continually been battles for freedom within our own lands. These were social battles, not military battles. I speak of the freedoms gained by people of color, such as my friend Robert Green. I speak of the freedoms of those who do not conform to "standard" sexual roles, such as my friend Polly Wright. I speak of the freedoms of those who don't believe in the same gods as the majority, such as my friend Sam Hain. And I speak of the freedoms of those who believe in no gods whatsoever, such as my friend Eleanor Adams.

It sickens me to know that there are still those in America, well into the twenty-first century, who would call Robert a "nigger" and attempt to hang him from a tree. It offends me to know that there are those who would label Polly as "mentally ill" and condemn her to a brainwashing camp. It angers me that there are those who would accuse Sam of worshiping the devil, and spread lies about his faith. And it shames me endlessly to know that there are those who consider Eleanor so much of a threat that she is behind bars.

The words to describe these views are also not kind words.

But these things didn't just happen by themselves. We allowed them to happen, in fact, *helped* them to happen. We embraced freedom-limiting conservatism for years and years. We allowed the Supreme Court... that institution created to guard our freedoms... to be taken over by this ultra-conservatism. We elected Paul Christopher.

And if we did all this, we can *undo* it, too. But it won't be easy. And it will take more bravery than is being displayed today. It will take conviction. It will take commitment to our ideals.

I urge New Anglicans everywhere to simply remember what it was like before the Schism. Remember why we broke from the Old Episcopal Church.

This is no different. So stand up. Speak out. Become involved in your local government. Write letters, make phone calls, and most importantly, speak in a way your representatives cannot misunderstand. At the ballot box.

October 2, 2026

Tonight was just awful.

Vicki and I were out for dinner and as we were waiting for our food, we noticed these two guys at another booth staring at us. They apparently found it weird that we were sitting on the same side of our booth.

They kept looking at us as we ate. And at one point, one of them muttered, "Fucking dykes." Vicki and I both tensed up. We just aren't used to hearing that kind of thing.

I must've been staring at them, because the next thing I know, the other guy is saying, "What're you looking at, lesbo?"

I looked away, and could feel my face turning red. Vicki squeezed my hand. Someone at another table basically told them to mind their own business. And at this point, the jerk gets up and starts giving the other guy a hard time for defending us.

Then the manager showed up and asked the two buttheads to leave. But they wouldn't go! The one actually started shoving the manager around, like he was picking a fight with him! But the next time the guy went to touch him, the manager twisted the guy's arm up behind his back fast as anything! He tossed both of them out.

Unfortunately, that's not the end of the story. After dinner, we decided to go have a cappuccino. We got our drinks and went to carry them to the outside area, since it was so nice out. And naturally, the two homophobes were there.

I literally stopped in my tracks as soon as I saw them. In fact, I started to turn right around to go back inside, but Vicki put her hand on my arm and said, "No. We're not going to let them think we're afraid of them."

Who was she kidding? I _was_ afraid of them! And I told her so. But she pulled me to a table near the sidewalk gate and we sat down.

It took all of about two seconds for them to recognize us from the restaurant. "This doesn't look like San Francisco, does it?" one said to the other.

That was when Vicki decided to open her mouth. She said, "What is it about us that frightens you so much?" Or something to that effect. I was too shocked that she was speaking at all to really focus on her words.

Now, I know the term is homophobia, but I don't honestly think these guys are afraid of gays and lesbians. Or bisexuals, as the case may be. It's just a nicer way to say they hate us.

Certainly, these two didn't seem afraid of us, or of anything. And to prove it, they both got up and walked over to our table.

I was literally afraid for my life at this point. I mean, I'd heard stories of gay-bashing, and these two sure seemed the type.

They pulled a couple chairs over and turned them backwards, then straddled them, resting their arms on top of the backs. And they just stared at us. "Well, come on," one of them said. "Let's see something."

I just shook my head, totally baffled.

"Give us a show! Suck some face!" one said.

"Or some titty!" the other said, and they both laughed.

I couldn't believe it. I just sat there with my jaw hanging open. What is it about men like this? They'll condemn us at any given opportunity, but secretly, they're totally turned on by the very thought of two girls getting it on. I was totally disgusted. My stomach felt like it had just gone on a rollercoaster ride without me.

I looked at Vicki and we both decided it was time to go. There was certainly nothing to be gained by talking to these dorks. So we stood up to go. The guys weren't happy about this. They both reached out as if to stop us, and that's when we realized just how much our minds think alike, because as soon as they touched us, Vicki and I each threw our coffees into their faces.

But instead of just letting go of us when their faces were scalded, they <u>threw</u> us! I mean, they pushed us backward. We both fell over the table and onto the ground.

I hit my head against the wrought iron fence, and got really scared. The guys were absolutely pissed. I really thought we were about to get the crap kicked out of us.

Luckily, their screams had drawn the attention of the manager, who now stood in the doorway. He yelled at the guys to leave, but they barely hesitated, until he held up a phone and threatened to call the cops. At this, the guys backed off and moved toward the gate. But not before calling us "dyke bitches."

That was a couple hours ago, and I'm still not over it. I swear, I've never been that scared in my life. I guess because I've never been scared <u>for</u> my life before tonight. And I hope I never am again!

Date: *October 4, 2026*
To: *merrymary@freewebmailer.net*
From: *heyjude@beatles4ever.ws*
Subject: *Re: Homophobia*

BEGIN ULTRA-CRYPTED TEXT

Mary:

Hon, I have to agree with Vicki. At its heart, homophobia really is about fear. Yeah, you're right about the hatred being the most visible aspect of it, but take a closer look.

Quite some time ago, there was a study done where a group of heterosexual men were shown a variety of pornography, some of which was homoerotic in nature. The guys were all wired to devices that measured their level of sexual excitement. And guess what the results showed?

Those who showed the most sexual excitement when viewing the homoerotic porn were men who had the strongest homophobic traits. You could say, then, that these men were afraid of being gay, on some level.

Now think of other phobias, such as one I sort of have: arachnophobia. Spiders give me the friggin' willies! I see one, I kill it. No two ways about it. They creep me right out and I don't want them around!

Is this rational? No. Where I live, there aren't very many spiders that can really harm me. Intellectually, I know this. But phobias aren't rational.

I'm afraid the spider will do something to me. I'm afraid it will bite me, or lay eggs in my ears while I'm asleep, or whatever. And I SO don't want that to happen that I get all bent out of shape every time I see one of those little eight-legged bastards. It has to die, and it has to die quickly.

Homophobes are afraid that gays are going to turn them gay. Not like they're gonna sprinkle some fairy dust on them and POOF, they're queer. No, they're afraid (often on a completely subconscious level) that they'll be turned on by homoerotic behavior and will effectively "turn" gay.

It's not rational, of course. But that doesn't negate the fear. It's not an excuse for gay-bashing, any more than my fear of spiders is an excuse to kill any of them. Like gay people, the spiders are just going about their normal lives, doing what they do. They don't understand my fear or hatred of them any more than gays understand homophobes.

Of course, I do think there are those who hate gays for purely religious reasons, but I suspect they're very much a minority.

Jude

END ULTRA-CRYPTED TEXT

Corvallis—In a repeat of a similar action a year ago, lawbreakers last night lit bonfires all over the country and openly celebrated Halloween. This time, however, there was no question that it was being done as a political statement.

In hundreds of towns, police moved in to arrest the pagan troublemakers, only to find themselves pelted with rotting apples and other refuse.

Local news reporters filmed impassioned protests by pagan leaders before they were carted off to jail.

The Freethought Underground is apparently behind these actions. The notorious website, *The Voice of Reason*, has posted copies of several of these speeches.

November 1, 2026

Margot and some friends spent Samhain with us. We took part in the Freethought Underground's bonfire protest, right here in Sacramento. I really thought we'd all be arrested.

Sam Hain himself was there! What a hunk! He looks like something from Celtic mythology, with black hair down to his shoulders and dark, intense eyes. And big! He must be six-three, and mostly muscle.

Anyway, someone had somehow appropriated the proper permits. Well, maybe not "proper." There was a permit for a large gathering in the park. The paperwork said it was for a "family reunion."

I'm guessing probably a thousand or more were there. And of course, the cops did show up, but didn't really do anything. It was peaceful, if noisy. Lots of drumming. A TV crew was there, but Vicki and I kept mostly away from the action.

It was fantastic, though, having so many people voicing support. Lots of folks mentioned that they thought it was horrible that the government had outlawed pagan religious celebrations. It was always followed with, "I'm not pagan, of course, but still..."

Part of me is upset that they felt they needed to add "of course" to the disclaimer, but another part is pleased that non-pagans would say such a thing at all.

Anyway, the evening went without incident. And just maybe we showed some folks that we're not as bad as we've been painted.

Date: *November 27, 2026*
To: *merrymary@freewebmailer.net*
From: *heyjude@beatles4ever.ws*
Subject: *Re: Bummed*

BEGIN ULTRA-CRYPTED TEXT

Mary:

I'm happy that so many things are going well for you. SVS sounds great. And I'm glad you and Vicki are doing so well.

But I can understand you being depressed. With Thanksgiving just passed and Christmas still to come, missing your family is perfectly natural. Have you spoken to them at all lately?

I remember when my father passed away. It was a week or so before Christmas, and it really put a damper on things. Every year since then, the holidays have been a little less enjoyable.

I know your parents aren't dead, but the separation you've gone through is plenty traumatic. You're not part of each others' lives anymore, and being bummed out is totally normal.

Despite what you think, I'm guessing they'd love to hear from you. You're their only child, after all.

Hey, it's depressing when I don't hear from you for months at a time. Imagine how it must feel for them.

Anyway, that's my two cents. You do what feels right for you. And drop a line when you can.

And today in Beatles history:
1970:   Harrison's ALL THINGS MUST PASS released in U.S.
1967:   MAGICAL MYSTERY TOUR released in U.S., as well as the single "Hello Goodbye"
1964:   "I Feel Fine" single released in U.K.
1963:   WITH THE BEATLES debuted in the U.K. at #1, replacing PLEASE PLEASE ME. The combined #1 ranking of these two albums was 50 straight weeks by the same artist, an accomplishment still unmatched today. (Let's see your Sidestreet Girls accomplish that!)

Jude

END ULTRA-CRYPTED TEXT

11 December 2026

Mary phoned this evening, to my great surprise. I was delighted to hear from her, and regret that Sarah isn't here presently. She'll be upset to know she missed her call.

Things appear to be going well for her. At least, from her perspective. From mine... Let's just say I'm saddened by the path she's currently walking in life, but am relieved that she's not come to any physical harm.

I admit the conversation was not as pleasant as it could have been. Frankly, neither of us really knew how to talk to the other.

But I was overjoyed to hear her voice. I miss her so much. I hope she realizes this, even though I can't recall if I said it or not.

I spoke with Gene after hanging up with Mary, and he was decidedly indifferent to her welfare. I've never felt anger toward Gene before in all my years of knowing him, but tonight I wanted to slap him.

Mary may have rejected darn near every teaching we'd ever presented, but she is still my daughter. How dare he reject her so utterly?

Washington—The Thirtieth Amendment to the U.S. Constitution was formally ratified today, repealing the Twenty-Second Amendment, which limited the Presidential term limit.

President Christopher has been quite public about his intention to seek a third term should the Amendment survive. Rumors that he will seek a new Vice-Presidential running mate have not been verified.

Year Seven

2027

January 6, 2027

Yesterday at school I got into a conversation about global warming with three other students and one of the staff. I had no idea it was such a critical problem! We did research on the 'net and there were some books about it, too, in the school's library. Yes, we've made a lot of improvements on things like the increasingly common use of electric vehicles, but why haven't we totally eliminated the burning of fossil fuels? This is so scary!

People can be so stupid.

I learned a surprising lesson yesterday, too. I guess I assumed that because the school's format is so... well, I guess "liberal" is the word... I'd assumed that the students would be, too. But another discussion revolved around some of the laws my dad passed. There was actually an argument, with a couple students clearly taking Dad's side. They said some things that frankly made them sound like grade-A bigots. Homosexuality was brought up, and not in a nice way. I just sort of shut my mouth, though I felt guilty for not saying anything.

It honestly shocks me when otherwise intelligent people say such closed-minded things. Evidently, it shocks me into silence.

Speaking of closed minds, I got a letter from Mom today. It was polite, but not exactly overflowing with love. She said she loved me, of course, and that she wanted me to be happy. But then she talked of how hurt she and Dad are over my choices and hopes that I'll invite Jesus back into my heart, since that's the only way I'll ever find true happiness, or some such crap.

It made me sad. But then, that was probably her intention.

I hate that I've disappointed them so much. But I have to be true to who I am. And this whole series of choices I've been making is nothing but defining who I am. Before, I was just The President's Daughter. Now I'm Mary Christopher, a person in her own right.

It's too bad my folks can't appreciate that.

2 February 2027

I am highly concerned right now. The latest numbers show a significant drop in my popularity. My advisors agree that it is due to two major factors. The first is my "abandonment" of Mary. The conservative faction doesn't believe in emancipation of minors, apparently. Nor do I, frankly, but they don't know what sort of barrel she had me over.

The second is, of course, the actions of that damned "free-thought underground" group. They have been spreading their propaganda incessantly over the past months, and it seems that people are actually listening to it. Especially that speech by Montoya. It's really touching a nerve with people. The Underground has been sending it around the 'net as an e-mail chain letter. Seems everyone is talking about it.

And speaking of nerve, the media are getting theirs back, printing letters to the editor that agree with these atheists. And with Montoya, of course. A tremendous number of letters are calling for having that Adams woman released from prison, and all sorts of other ridiculous notions.

Gene insists that his group will turn the tide, that he'll get America swung back around to the right. He swears in a few months my numbers will be higher than ever, barring any unforeseen disasters.

God willing, he'll be able to do so.

Washington—Vice-President Daniel Goodwin is dead of a heart attack at age 67. Goodwin's attack came peacefully last night, in his sleep. He is survived by his wife Sandra, and two sons, William and Daniel, Jr. A memorial service will be held Saturday, February 13.

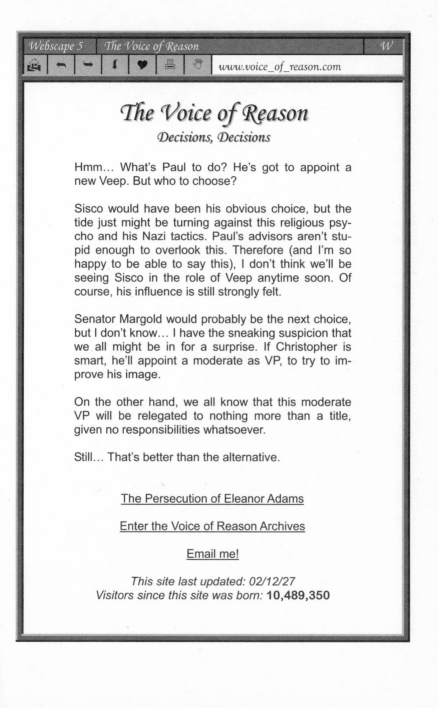

The Voice of Reason
Decisions, Decisions

Hmm… What's Paul to do? He's got to appoint a new Veep. But who to choose?

Sisco would have been his obvious choice, but the tide just might be turning against this religious psycho and his Nazi tactics. Paul's advisors aren't stupid enough to overlook this. Therefore (and I'm so happy to be able to say this), I don't think we'll be seeing Sisco in the role of Veep anytime soon. Of course, his influence is still strongly felt.

Senator Margold would probably be the next choice, but I don't know… I have the sneaking suspicion that we all might be in for a surprise. If Christopher is smart, he'll appoint a moderate as VP, to try to improve his image.

On the other hand, we all know that this moderate VP will be relegated to nothing more than a title, given no responsibilities whatsoever.

Still… That's better than the alternative.

The Persecution of Eleanor Adams

Enter the Voice of Reason Archives

Email me!

This site last updated: 02/12/27
Visitors since this site was born: **10,489,350**

277

15 February 2027

Gene has dropped unsubtle hints that he would like to be Goodwin's replacement. But my instincts say I shouldn't give it to him. The public is still under the sway of propaganda. They might not accept Gene as Vice-President, even though Congress probably would. And I can't risk alienating the public.

Margold is similarly too conservative. He'd do a decent job, I have no doubt, but his record is too well known.

Some other member of Congress, perhaps one not so much in the public eye? Yes. But which one?

Again, my instincts tell me I must please the public. This calls for someone not "conservative." But not too moderate. We can't have that, after all.

Or can we? What difference will it make? Even a flaming liberal as Vice-President wouldn't harm the country, provided I don't die like Goodwin. I keep him busy with trivialities, then name someone else as my running mate come election time.

By that time, the public will have forgotten all the vile things spewed by Jefferson Paine and his band of malcontents. They'll be ready to continue the purification of America.

2/17/27

Gene Sisco is not a happy man these days. He has been in a foul mood ever since learning that he is not going to be the new Vice President.

I must admit that man frightens me when he is angry. He seems almost to be a different person. I mentioned it to Paul, but he brushed it aside with a comment to the effect of, "What do you expect? Wouldn't you be upset, too, in his position?"

Frankly, no, I wouldn't. His calling, his duty, is to God. That was the role he accepted when he became a minister. Why does he covet the role of Vice President?

And why does Paul not wonder this, as well?

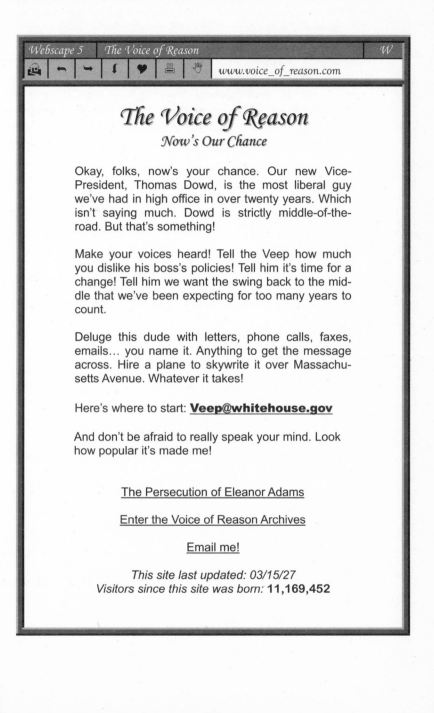

April 4, 2027

We talked at school today about how the rights of so many groups are unequal. Someone brought up same-sex marriage. (The bigots I encountered before didn't participate, happily.) We talked about the movement nearly 25 years ago, where actual marriages were being performed illegally in several states, and then legally (sort of) in Massachusetts.

For a while, it seemed like sanity would prevail and gays would be allowed to legally marry everywhere, but then the conservatives pushed hard for legislators to get things back to "normal," and they did. Eventually, the Constitution was amended to forbid same-sex marriage.

I never used to understand why they wanted "official" marriage so badly. But that's because I never understood how much favoritism was given to married couples. And it's not just the lack of inheritance rights or things like that. There are almost two thousand different protections given to married couples that aren't available to anyone else.

Even unmarried het couples are denied them, unless they go through a lot of expensive mumbo-jumbo to form some sort of legal domestic partnership. Even then, they still can't get everything.

And it's getting worse. Like it's illegal now for unmarried couples to adopt! Even unmarried het couples! Now what's the sense of that? The government is basically saying that married couples are the only ones who should raise kids? Come on!

And to think my own father is responsible for much of this makes me just want to scream! Except that whenever I think of it, I cry instead. How could he do this? He's a good man! I just can't believe he's responsible for all this!

4/29/27

> *Tomorrow is Mary's birthday. I have debated calling her, but am not sure she would welcome hearing from me, all things considered.*
> *I miss her so much sometimes it hurts. I wish I could erase so much of what's gone on between us.*
> *I should call her. I will call her.*
> *I will.*

Date: *April 30, 2027*
To: *merrymary@freewebmailer.net*
From: *heyjude@beatles4ever.ws*
Subject: *Birthday Wishes*

BEGIN ULTRA-CRYPTED TEXT

Mary:

Happy Birthday! How's it feel to be seventeen? Not much different than sixteen, if I remember correctly.

By any chance is that invitation still open to visit you and Vicki? As it happens, I've got some free time this summer, around the 4th of July. Let me know if that's good for you.

And today in Beatles history:
1973:   McCartney's RED ROSE SPEEDWAY released in U.S.
1970:   McCARTNEY, Paul's first solo album, achieves Gold status in U.S.

Jude

END ULTRA-CRYPTED TEXT

May 1, 2027

I'm stunned. I figured Jude would always be just this mysterious atheist I corresponded with, but would never meet in person. And now that I have the chance to do so, I'm almost scared! I don't know what to think. Vicki and I talked a long time tonight about it, and she doesn't quite understand my feelings. Not that I can blame her. Neither do I.

But I did have a nice Beltane/birthday bash. They threw me a big surprise party here at Southside. I got a card from Mom and Dad, with a check for a thousand bucks. Sure wasn't expecting that. Would have been nice if they'd called, though. I miss hearing their voices.

2 May 2027

Dowd is such an idiot. Yesterday he confronted me, thrusting fistfuls of letters and faxes in my face. He spoke of the hundreds of emails he's received from the public, complaining about our policies and demanding a shift back toward center.

I explained, rather impatiently, that these bits of fluff are the product of Jefferson Paine's tirade several weeks ago, in which he prodded his sheep into action. The complaints are from a small band of his "freethinkers." Now that's rich. They can't even think for themselves, just blindly do whatever he tells them. Hardly "free thinking," in my book.

I told him the whining of a couple dozen atheists isn't worthy of concern, let alone action. But he still doesn't get it. Dowd believes these emails and faxes are from actual citizens. Why he believes this is beyond my imagination.

Date: *May 3, 2027*
To: *heyjude@beatles4ever.ws *
From: *merrymary@freewebmailer.net *
Subject: *Why?*

BEGIN ULTRA-CRYPTED TEXT

Jude:

Thanks for the birthday wishes. And it does feel a bit different than sixteen. My life has changed so much over the past few years (thanks to people like you), and this past year has been a period of much personal growth. Living here in Sacramento is doing wonders for me, to be honest.

Regarding you visiting us here, I have to say you caught me totally off guard. I guess I never thought you'd take me up on the offer. I don't think I've ever truly expected to meet you face-to-face. Certainly, you're welcome here. But I have to ask you, why do you want to come?

I don't mean to be dense, but what would cause you to fly the whole way across the country for a week to be with people you've never met before?

I'm not trying to talk you out of it. I'm just curious.

Mary

END ULTRA-CRYPTED TEXT

Date: *May 5, 2027*
To: *merrymary@freewebmailer.net*
From: *heyjude@beatles4ever.ws*
Subject: *Re: Why?*

BEGIN ULTRA-CRYPTED TEXT

Mary:

Gee, that wasn't the excitement I'd hoped to hear from you. And if you don't want me to come, I won't. But as to why I'd like to, I should think that's obvious. Maybe I've never come right out and said it, but I admire the heck out of you. You're one of my personal heroes.

It took a tremendous amount of guts for you to do the things you've done. Most people never allow themselves to honestly question the religion in which they are raised. But you did. Most kids who take a stand against their parents do so only out of rebellion. But you did so because of your principles. And standing up to your father, ostensibly the most powerful man in the world, demanding your emancipation... Hon, that's nothing short of phenomenal.

Besides... I've grown rather fond of you over the past several years. I just thought it would be nice to spend time with you in real life, not just on the computer.

But again, if you'd rather I not come, just say so. I won't be offended.

Oh, and to reply to your other email... I can certainly understand your pain. There's an old quote – I can't remember it exactly, but it says that there's no more tragic a moment in the life of a child than the moment it is discovered that one's father is only human.

We do tend to idolize our parents when we're younger. And then one day, we realize they don't deserve to be on pedestals. We all see it happen. It's just that sometimes, the fall off the pedestal is a bit farther than others.

But if you truly believe your father to be a good man, perhaps his failings (whatever they are... you didn't say) aren't as bad as you might think.

Either way, if you need to talk, you know how to reach me.

And today in Beatles history:
1969:   "Get Back" released as single in U.S.

Jude

END ULTRA-CRYPTED TEXT

May 10, 2027

Jude will arrive on July 1st and go back on the 12th. He has a strange definition of "week."

I'm nervous. And stunned. He said I'm one of his heroes. I would have thought only folks like Jefferson Paine were his heroes.

It's kind of weird, though. I mean, I'm seventeen. Jude's twenty-five. I never paid much attention to the difference in our age when we were just communicating online. But now that we're going to be meeting in person, it seems more significant.

I got in a long talk with a couple girls at school today about it. It wasn't much help. One said age doesn't matter. The other said it does, and furthermore, you just never know who you're going to meet on the 'net. She sounded like my mother, who would be beside herself, knowing Jude was coming.

I miss her.

Date: *May 15, 2027*
To: *merrymary@freewebmailer.net*
From: *heyjude@beatles4ever.ws*
Subject: *Re: Jefferson Paine*

BEGIN ULTRA-CRYPTED TEXT

Mary:

I might count his namesakes among my heroes, but Jefferson Paine himself seems a bit of a coward to me. Oh, I agree with him, but let's face it... He hides behind his virtual wall. He's not really at risk, is he?

That's not my idea of a hero. A hero is someone who carries on with what he/she knows is right, despite the risk of dire consequences. (Like you do.) If he's kept his site online this long without Big Brother shutting it down, he's not really putting much on the line, is he?

I'm not putting the guy down. He's doing a hell of a lot more than most people. I admire anyone who speaks his or her mind, especially when it flies contrary to conventional "wisdom." But I'm sure not going to elevate him to "hero" status.

Jude

END ULTRA-CRYPTED TEXT

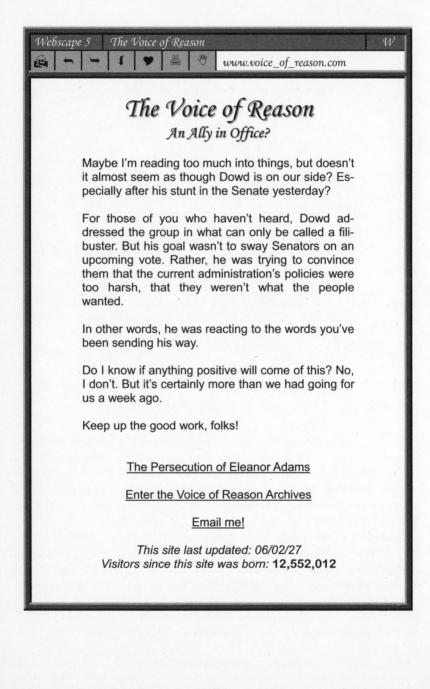

The Voice of Reason
An Ally in Office?

Maybe I'm reading too much into things, but doesn't it almost seem as though Dowd is on our side? Especially after his stunt in the Senate yesterday?

For those of you who haven't heard, Dowd addressed the group in what can only be called a filibuster. But his goal wasn't to sway Senators on an upcoming vote. Rather, he was trying to convince them that the current administration's policies were too harsh, that they weren't what the people wanted.

In other words, he was reacting to the words you've been sending his way.

Do I know if anything positive will come of this? No, I don't. But it's certainly more than we had going for us a week ago.

Keep up the good work, folks!

The Persecution of Eleanor Adams

Enter the Voice of Reason Archives

Email me!

This site last updated: 06/02/27
Visitors since this site was born: **12,552,012**

7 June 2027

Dowd isn't the idiot. I am.

Why did I choose him as Goodwin's replacement? Why did I think a moderate would be a good thing?

I thought it would placate the people, but never thought he'd actually listen to what the people had to say.

Last week he had his four-hour sermon to the Senate. And ever since, he's been meeting with individual Senators, those who are most likely to be pushed toward the middle, rather than the right.

And he just might be successful. He's counting on the fact that most politicians at some point in the past actually thought of themselves as representatives of the people. His pleas may cause some of them to weaken.

But the people are sheep, not intelligent enough to know what's best for them. That's what government is for. We're the shepherds.

Dowd has got to go. And though I can't get rid of him as Vice-President, I can get him out of the country, away from the sheep, away from the shepherds he's trying to corrupt.

He leaves tomorrow for South America on a "goodwill mission." I don't know why I didn't do this a month ago.

7/9/27

Paul has been virtually unapproachable ever since Dowd started becoming so outspoken. I'm very upset by this, since I've wanted to speak to him about so many things, including our estrangement from Mary.

But it's as though he's closed her off from his heart, since she was granted her emancipation. This is so unlike Paul. Mary was always his precious little girl. If anyone had been guilty in the past of shutting her out, it was me. We've never been as close as they were.

It pains me to see this rift between them, and I would do anything to seal it. But what hurts even more is seeing Paul behaving toward her like... I admit it... like I used to.

July 1, 2027

Well, the anticipation is over! After two months of anxiety, Jude is finally here!

We took the Vickmobile to the airport to pick him up. Both of us were curious to see what he looked like. He claims he didn't have any recent pictures of himself, but I think he just wanted to remain mysterious.

Anyway, his flight finally came in. Vicki and I stood back and watched all the people file into the baggage claim area, pointing out all lone males and hoping all the good looking ones were him. (Not that it would've made any difference if he wasn't, but still…)

I can't speak for Vicki, but I about stopped breathing when this tall, blond guy comes in and starts walking right toward us!

And it was him! Goddess, Jude is so cute! If there was any lingering doubt about me still being attracted to boys, it's gone now! I nearly stopped breathing when he hugged me.

Now that he was here, I was even more nervous! But he and Vicki started joking about my nervousness, and that made me get over it pretty quickly.

Anyway, we went out for a bite to eat before heading back to our place. I'm amazed at how comfortable I feel around him.

We didn't talk about anything of substance, really. He told me I look a lot different in person than in newspaper photos. Goddess, I hope I do! I look awful in newsprint pics.

Anyway, by the time we finished eating, it was nearly three in the morning by his internal clock. So we headed home.

Jude's asleep on the sofa right now. Vicki's taking a bubble bath, so I thought I'd write my initial impressions.

Geez, even writing about him has my heart racing! To think this is the guy I've been emailing with for half a decade! Wow.

Washington—Nearly half a million emails flooded the White House today as members and supporters of the Freethought Underground declared a new "Independence Day" geared, as they phrased it, "toward liberating America from the shackles of intolerance and ignorance." The messages condemned the Christopher Administration for many of its policies, and voiced support for Vice-President Dowd, who (it was claimed) had been sent out of the country in order to silence him.

A senior White House staff member, who remains anonymous, said, "Half a million sounds like a lot, but it's still only a fraction of one percent of the American population."

4 July 2027

Perhaps I've wasted too much thought on this "freethought underground" issue. As we told the reporters, the numbers simply aren't there to warrant any concern.

I've foolishly expected my presidency to be untarnished. But that's impossible. Even Reagan had the Iran-Contra scandal. I should have known better than to think something wouldn't jump up during my time in office.

But by focusing so much energy on it, I may be causing it to be more of an issue than it truly is. So what if we received over a million emails this week from these atheists? That's a drop in the bucket.

I shouldn't let them worry me a bit. If I appear worried, the damned media will sensationalize it, despite any threat of censure. I need to put on the face of a man utterly unconcerned by the rumblings of a few malcontents. No, not even rumblings. More like "mumblings."

They are insignificant. It's time I started treating them accordingly.

July 5, 2027

The past few days have been fantastic! Vicki worked Friday, so Jude and I spent the day in Old Sac, checking out the stores and eating ice cream. We hit it off really well, and I could swear there were some actual "sparks" there, too. But maybe that was just wishful thinking.

Saturday morning, the three of us went to Guerneville, Margot having invited us for the holiday. We took Jude to Armstrong Reserve. He was as overwhelmed by the redwoods as I was, the first time. While we strolled through the trees, I had some very strange feelings. It was almost as though something magical was going on, like something was guiding us along the paths in the forest. Literally.

I didn't know what it was, honestly, but I was suddenly moved to talk to Jude about Wicca. I told him how it makes me feel, the power I seem to get from the earth. And he (the atheist!) even said that being among those trees is the closest he's ever been to feeling spiritual. (Maybe he was feeling it, too?)

I mentioned all this to Vicki, later. She smiled, hugged me, and said, "Congratulations. You've just met your first goddess." I don't know about that, but it did feel like what you'd imagine that should feel like.

Anyway, Jude said he thought it was great that I'm identifying so much with Wicca. That surprised me, since I figured he'd prefer to hear that I'd become an atheist. I guess I haven't really figured him out.

Saturday night at dinner, Jude couldn't take his eyes off our extremely cute waitress. It made me jealous. I get jealous when Vicki looks at him, sometimes, too.

Why am I feeling this way? It's not like he's my boyfriend. It's not like I expect Vicki to ditch me for him, either. Sometimes I just want to kick myself for being so stupid about things.

Sunday was the 4th, and we had a lot of fun. We had a bonfire in Margot's yard, and lots of guests. Jude seemed a bit shy, though, and stuck pretty close to me and Vicki. There was a parade in town, fireworks down in Sebastopol, and all sorts of activities during the day. It was a blast.

Today we drove back to Sacramento. Vicki has the day off from work. We went out for coffee and talked for hours. After five years of emailing, you wouldn't think we could find much to talk about that we haven't, already. But we sure gabbed enough!

Now we can truly say we're all good friends. Vicki and I both really connected with him. And vice versa, I think.

July 9, 2027

Last night we went shopping downtown. In one store, Jude was looking over a selection of old lapel pins, and he pointed to two in particular. One was a heart with an infinity symbol inside. The other was a ribbon pin, like the pink breast cancer awareness pin, but this one was blue, red, and black, with a gold "pi" symbol in the center.

Jude called them "poly" pins. I remember when Black Eagle told me about polyamory, but I never quite understood it, really. So Jude explained (after buying both pins) that polyamory is the philosophy of romantically loving more than one person at a time. I made a joke about "wife swapping" and he got testy. He stressed that it's about love, not lust.

Seeing how seriously he took this, I listened. He explained that society has us conditioned to think there's something inherently "wrong" about so many things. Being gay, or bi, for example. And he said that people who choose to have multiple "spice" (plural for "spouse," evidently) are also frowned upon by society.

Jude brought his laptop with him, and this morning, he showed me a lot of articles he has on the subject. They're from magazines and books he's read. And after listening to him, and reading the articles, I can say that I can logically understand and agree with it in principle. I mean, I love Vicki. Nothing's likely to change that. But I'm finding myself also very attracted to Jude, and certainly not just on a physical level. I've known him online for years. Certainly, I do love him on some level. And if I were to allow myself to "fall in love" with him, it wouldn't change my feelings for Vicki in the least.

But could I do that? It sounds so hard! And yet, the more I think about it (and I've been thinking about it a lot since our talk), the more sense it seems to make. The more "natural" it sounds.

I mean, why should we limit ourselves to one love? Lots of people, upon losing a spouse, get remarried. These people always say they love their new spouse just as much as their deceased spouse, just that they love them "differently." My question would be, if they'd met both these people simultaneously, would they have been able to choose between them? And why should they have to? If they loved both of them, why not accept that?

But more importantly, what is Jude trying to say? Is he interested in me? Romantically? Is he interested in Vicki? Could I handle that? I'm only seventeen, after all. This is just too much to think about right now.

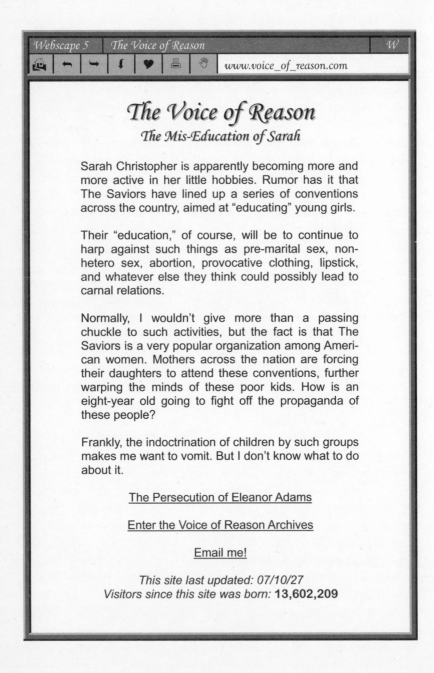

The Voice of Reason
The Mis-Education of Sarah

Sarah Christopher is apparently becoming more and more active in her little hobbies. Rumor has it that The Saviors have lined up a series of conventions across the country, aimed at "educating" young girls.

Their "education," of course, will be to continue to harp against such things as pre-marital sex, non-hetero sex, abortion, provocative clothing, lipstick, and whatever else they think could possibly lead to carnal relations.

Normally, I wouldn't give more than a passing chuckle to such activities, but the fact is that The Saviors is a very popular organization among American women. Mothers across the nation are forcing their daughters to attend these conventions, further warping the minds of these poor kids. How is an eight-year old going to fight off the propaganda of these people?

Frankly, the indoctrination of children by such groups makes me want to vomit. But I don't know what to do about it.

The Persecution of Eleanor Adams

Enter the Voice of Reason Archives

Email me!

This site last updated: 07/10/27
Visitors since this site was born: **13,602,209**

July 11, 2027

So last night I asked Vicki if she'd ever heard of polyamory. To my surprise (though maybe it shouldn't have been), she said, "Sure. Lots of pagans are poly." I guess this is something the whole world knows about, except for me. Then she asked if I wanted Jude to join us! In a poly relationship! She said she's known for a long time how I feel about Jude.

I didn't challenge it. She's right. And she knows me better than I know myself, sometimes. So what if I'm only coming to realize right now how I feel about him? Doesn't mean she couldn't see it.

I told her that it's a tempting thought, but that I was a bit taken aback that she mentioned it so casually. She put me at ease by assuring me that she knew it didn't meant my feelings about her had changed.

I guess I just have a lot to learn about what I'm capable of on an emotional level. I love Vicki a lot. And I'm attracted to Jude as more than a friend, too. I think I've actually felt that way about him for years, but never seriously thought about it.

A part of me says a poly relationship isn't possible, that it's an either/or scenario. But there's another part of me that isn't so sure.

11 July 2027

Apparently, some of the delegates at the U.N. have raised a fuss about our nation's attitude toward sin. They seem to see nothing wrong in rampant homosexuality and atheism, since they're condemning our control of such things.

How dare they criticize America? If it weren't for us, most of the world would be speaking German. Or Russian.

I'm glad my predecessor had the sense to extricate us from this organization. The Book of Revelations speaks of a world government existing before the coming of the anti-Christ, and to many people, the U.N. is that government.

Gene and I spoke about this today. It's the first he and I have really spoken in some time. I confess I had a difficult time in forgiving him for his callousness toward Mary. But he has apologized, and God has helped me get over my hardened heart.

He's a good man, and I wouldn't be here without his help; I know that. And I've decided that when I run for a third term, I'll replace Dowd. Gene will be my running mate.

July 12, 2027

Well, Jude's probably home by now. It's almost midnight. His flight left around five this evening.

I tried all last night and today to work up the courage to tell him how I was feeling about him. But I just couldn't. I was too nervous. Finally, at the airport, he and Vicki hugged goodbye. Then he turned to me. And he must have seen something in my eye, because after hugging me, he leaned in for a kiss. At first it was just a polite little thing, as friends would do. But apparently that wasn't enough for me. I pulled him in and kissed him for real. It shocked him, I think. Heck, it shocked me!

I promised him more, next time, and made him promise to visit again soon. He smiled and agreed. Then he took the "infinite heart" pin from his shirt and pinned it on mine.

Vicki teased me all the way home. But it must've turned her on, too, because as soon as we were home, she pounced on me.

What would it be like, really, to have Jude join us both? Maybe one day I'll have the guts to ask him.

8/20/27

I've been so busy with The Saviors, lately. I have an interview tomorrow with Christian World Radio, and hope I can muddle through.

The truth is, I fear my heart isn't truly in it. I think I've jumped back into this in order to get out of the funk I've been in for the past several months.

Still, the work the Saviors are doing is good work, the Lord's work, and I know if I only open my heart to it, I'll be able to do it the justice it deserves.

On the other hand, being around all these young girls makes me miss Mary all the more.

CWR: Sarah, thank you for joining us on Christian World Radio. You've done some fantastic things with The Saviors over the years, even before your husband's administration made such advances for the cause of morality in our country. So how does it feel to be the most powerful woman in America?

SC: Oh, George, you know I don't look at it that way. This isn't about anyone's power except God's.

CWR: Amen. So tell us, what's going on right now?

SC: A lot of people think that the work of The Saviors is over, that my husband's advances, as you called them, have done all our work for us. But that's simply not true. Laws are not the effective deterrents we'd like them to be. The real solution to the problem is education and faith.

CWR: Hence your group's nationwide tours.

SC: Exactly. We've found that by speaking to kids in schools, we're able to reach them on a level that actually makes a difference. All the laws in the world won't matter if a child doesn't honestly know better.

CWR: And what are you telling the kids, exactly?

SC: Without giving you the entire presentation, we promote abstinence as the only option for unmarried couples. We know, of course, that many do engage in pre-marital sex, so we offer Christian counseling for these troubled souls. The same goes for homosexuality. Though it's illegal, we know people still engage in it. We offer counseling for these offenders, as well, without threat of legal prosecution, I might add.

CWR: That's very Christian of you.

SC: Of course. We have no desire to see children behind bars. We exist, George, as a kind of warning to kids. Because if they're found guilty of these sins as adults, it's out of our hands.

CWR: What about abortion? It, too, is illegal, but we've been seeing evidence of a huge number of abortions being performed by people outside the medical profession. What do you tell kids about this?

SC: Naturally, the way to avoid this is to stress abstinence, which we do. But we don't avoid talking about pregnancy. We again do not focus on our nation's laws, but on God's law. Abortion is an abomination in his eyes, and we make this perfectly clear. We tell the girls flat-out that abortion is a mortal sin. It is murder, pure and simple.

CWR: But God can forgive.

SC: Oh, yes, George. God can and will forgive the remorseful. And that is our real message. That's why we're called The Saviors, after all, because we can show these kids how to save their souls. It's all about being saved.

CWR: Fantastic, Sarah. Now, your present tour has been underway for about three weeks. How long will you go? And how often will these tours be done?

SC: This current tour ends just prior to Thanksgiving. We'll be doing a similar tour, slightly longer, next year and in '29. By 2030, however, we intend to have members of The Saviors visiting schools year-round, since so many schools these days go the whole year. We've got the funding for such a large-scale project. We're just in the process of training the right people for the job.

CWR: The money, of course, comes from the government.

SC: Exactly. The Office of Faith-Based Initiatives has long been a friend to the Christian Right, and we're very happy to know that our funding has been approved for many years to come.

CWR: As are we, Sarah. Thank you for being with us.

West Chester—Dr. Flora Nussbaum, noted radio personality and speaker for The Saviors, was injured yesterday during a presentation at Henderson High School in West Chester. During the segment of her presentation dealing with witchcraft, a student hurled an object at the stage, striking Nussbaum above her left eye. She was taken to Chester County Hospital where she was treated and released. The thrown object was identified as a stale dinner roll from the school's cafeteria. The name of the student has not been released, pending criminal investigation. School officials stated that expulsion was likely. Nussbaum did not deny the possibility of pressing charges.

November 3, 2027

So many things in my life are wonderful. Things with Vicki are just... well, maybe not perfect, but close enough. And the whole Jude thing, while confusing, gives me the warm fuzzies, too.

But when I look outside my little bubble of happiness, I don't feel so good. The truth of just how bad things are in this country has been building and building within me. I've been in denial, but the truth is that so much of the awful stuff is my father's fault. Whenever I think of him, I don't think of the President. I think of the man who raised me. I don't think of him in Washington, but back home in L.A. I don't think of him as a cold and calculating politician, but as a fun and loving dad. It's no surprise I can't stand up to him.

But I have to. I can't think of him only in those terms anymore. Yes, he's my father, but he's also President. Yes, he's the man who raised me, but he's also the man who's passed legislation that directly affects me in a negative way.

It hurts, it really hurts, to think of him this way. But I have to. If I expect to be taken seriously, I have to treat him as exactly what he is. The enemy.

The Voice of Reason
Or Maybe I Just Have a Fever

Okay, I'm going to say something I never expected would come from my keyboard: I wouldn't mind having a Republican for President. Well, one particular Republican. And I'm sure you know I'm talking about Thomas Dowd.

Yes, I think the Republican party has done more harm to America than good in the last hundred years. But that has usually been the result of politicians pandering to the special interest groups who bankroll their campaigns.

Dowd, though, appears to be above all that. I admit I knew virtually nothing about the man before Christopher chose him as Goodwin's replacement. But the more I learn of him, the more I respect him. Yeah, he's still a Republican, and therefore holds some core beliefs about our government that I disagree with. But he seems to be a man of principle and integrity. So I'd like very much to see him in the Oval Office, rather than our current butthead-in-chief.

The Persecution of Eleanor Adams

Enter the Voice of Reason Archives

Email me!

This site last updated: 12/15/27
Visitors since this site was born: **14,526,049**

Dear Mom & Dad,

Thanks so much for calling, yesterday. It was good to you're your voices. I'm sorry you couldn't stay on the phone longer.

And I'm sorry for how I reacted when you wished me a Merry Christmas. I may not celebrate that particular holiday, anymore, but I shouldn't have thrown it in your faces like that. I guess I just want so much for you both to take me and my beliefs seriously. But being rude isn't the way to accomplish that, I know. So please forgive me.

But that brings me to the purpose of this letter: being taken seriously. Dad, you used to tell me when I was little that true happiness can be found by following your heart. And I've lived my life by that adage, I think you realize. I've followed my heart in many ways, and though it's brought much happiness to me, it's also brought much pain, specifically because my actions weren't ones you and Mom approved of.

Ever since becoming comfortable with my sexuality and spirituality, I've been noticing just how awful things are in this country with regard to so many minorities. And frankly, Dad, you're responsible for much of it. Oh, not the attitudes, but the legislation that gives sanction to the attitudes. And Mom, you're certainly doing your part to inflame the attitudes themselves.

It seems unbelievable to me that you both can be unaware that these actions of yours hurt many people in our country, including me. These groups you're persecuting, such as non-Christians and non-heterosexuals, aren't just groups, not just names. They're human beings, just like you. They have families. They have dreams. And they have feelings that can be hurt.

And I can't stand it anymore. I know I said I would stay silent. I'm terribly sorry, but I can't hold up my end of that agreement. I have to speak out.

Not long ago, one of my neighbors here asked me to speak to a group of former Christian fundamentalists at The Open Book, a local gay bookstore. These are people who found they couldn't remain true to themselves and true to their faiths simultaneously.

It was an amazing experience. Oh, I was nervous the whole time, and afraid I was just babbling, but after my little speech, we sat around drinking coffee and talking about our experiences and so on.

One of the questions asked of me was whether I went through a period of self-loathing for being bisexual. Many of them told me that their religious minds automatically labeled them as deviants or abominations or sinners, because they weren't straight. But the funny thing is, I really didn't go through anything like that.

Maybe it's because I led a much more independent life than most people. Your professional lives pretty much required me to do that, as you know. But perhaps the real reason is that I stopped being a fundamentalist Christian before I realized I was bi. That made it much easier for me to accept myself as I am, rather than blame myself for not being who the Bible said I should be.

Many of them talked of the negative reactions from their families when they came out to them. This only added to their guilt, for they felt they'd disappointed their loved ones.

But again, that's not how it happened for me. In fact, I never came out to you, but was outed when my personal diary was read. I'm still hurt over that invasion of privacy, but at the time, I was furious. So perhaps I embraced my bisexuality, even reveled in it, out of spite toward you both for your actions.

Whatever the reasons, I simply couldn't identify with what many of these people had gone through. But I was, for some reason, still able to touch their lives a little bit. Maybe only as far as reinforcing their beliefs. Or giving them inspiration. I don't know. All I do know is that they really seemed to need to hear what I had to say.

So what I'm saying to you, dear parents, is that I believe I have a "calling." Dad, yours was to become President. Mom, yours was to be active with groups like The Saviors. Mine is to become a civil rights activist. Other people might need to hear what I have to say, too. Or need me to be their voice.

For a while, I couldn't decide whether to address spiritual or sexual repression. Now I realize I don't need to choose. Jude once told me that a true freethinker is one who avoids dogmatic thinking in all areas. So I suppose I'm going to be a freethought activist in the broadest sense.

By virtue of being your daughter, I will have an audience. The media will want to carry my message. Your threats against them cannot defeat the all-powerful desire for ratings.

I know neither of you will be too happy about this. But I'm following my heart, Dad. You of all people should appreciate that.

Thanks for understanding. Assuming you do.

Mary

Year Eight

2028

"Ladies and Gentlemen of the Press, thank you for joining us here on such short notice. I will make this as brief as possible.

"It is no secret that President Christopher's most trusted advisor is Reverend Gene Sisco. It was a surprise to many people, myself included, that Reverend Sisco was not the President's choice for a replacement for the late Daniel Goodwin. No one was more astounded than I when he chose me, instead.

"This is because—and again, this is no secret—President Christopher and I do not see eye-to-eye on very many issues. I think the President was counting on my benign acquiescence to his decisions while in office. But I could not do that. And when I voiced my own opinion, I was sent away on a tour to press the flesh with foreign dignitaries.

"During my time abroad, I learned many things, but first and foremost is that many other nations do not like what's going on, here. They criticize the way we are treating our minority religions, our homosexuals, and more. It was, at times, a humbling experience.

"And during this trip, I came to a decision. I have decided to run against President Christopher in this year's election.

"I see the questions on your faces. The President has the Republican nomination again for this election. But that's okay. Because I am terminating my affiliation with the Republican Party. I will be joining the Libertarian Party, and hope to win their nomination.

"This is not in any way a compromise for me. I've become quite disillusioned with the Republican Party over the past eight years. It's time for a change. In more ways than one.

"Thank you for coming."

The Voice of Reason
Can't Tell the Players Without a Scorecard

No, I am not psychic. I had no idea Dowd was going to pull the old switcheroo.

Dowd may not be an ideal candidate for us, but he's a damn sight better than Christopher. We need to rally behind this man. Those of you who haven't been voting should get off your butts and do so.

Start up a support campaign for the guy! He'll need all the help he can get. (No offense, Mr. Vice-President.)

<u>The Persecution of Eleanor Adams</u>

<u>Enter the Voice of Reason Archives</u>

<u>Email me!</u>

This site last updated: 01/06/28
*Visitors since this site was born: **15,468,439***

January 7, 2028

I figured the press would be itching to talk to me, to hear what I had to say about things. But of the half dozen inquiries I sent out, the only sorts of responses I've been getting have been, "Thanks, we'll let you know if we need some filler."

<u>Filler</u>! One paper actually used that word. I can't believe it.

How am I going to be taken seriously by anyone, if not even the press wants to hear what I've got to say?

"Ladies and Gentlemen of the Press...

"I've been asked probably a hundred times, so let's make these answers official.

"No, I do not begrudge my Vice-President for choosing to run against me this fall. It is his right, and apparently, his desire.

"No, I am not worried about him taking votes away from me. In America, we allow the public to choose who they want for President. I cannot fault anyone for voting for their candidate of choice.

"No, I hold no ill will toward him, or against Senator Colgan for running for Vice-President with him on the Libertarian ticket.

"Yes, I do think my future opponent has betrayed the public somewhat. Certainly it is not as if he switched to the Democratic Party, but the people who elected him to the Senate elected a Republican, a man ostensibly loyal to Republican ideals. How can those people expect him to represent them accurately anymore?

"Finally, I can honestly say I do not expect this turn of events to affect our professional relationship in the slightest. We are both of us above that sort of thing."

1/9/28

Paul is so much more convincing of a liar than I could ever be. He puts on a good show for the press and the public, but in truth, he's absolutely livid over Dowd's defection. And who could blame him? If one were prone to being somewhat paranoid, it would not be difficult to see Dowd's actions as a premeditated effort to undermine Paul's Presidency.

Even without such conspiratorial thoughts, though, I can't imagine how anyone could have any respect for the man. Does no one understand the concept of loyalty, anymore? Does party affiliation mean nothing?

... I have re-read the above lines a dozen times since writing them, and a little voice in my head is crying, "Hypocrite!" The voice is telling me that I should substitute the word "family" for "party," and question my loyalty to my daughter.

What kind of mother have I become?

Date: *February 14, 2028*
To: *merrymary@freewebmailer.net
From: *heyjude@beatles4ever.ws*
Subject: *Re: Thank You & An Idea*

BEGIN ULTRA-CRYPTED TEXT

Mary:

Happy Valentine's Day! Give yourself a big hug from me. Vicki, too. Aw, hell, get yourselves some chocolates while you're at it. And you're quite welcome for the flowers. Glad you liked them.

I agree with you, by the way. I can't think of any reason the press wouldn't want to talk to you. I think your father must've said something to make them stay away from you. More threats of shutting them down, maybe.

Anyway, I think your idea is fantastic! Go for it! I can't think of a reason why he'd turn you down. I know you don't like him much, but I wouldn't judge Jefferson Paine solely based on his website. I've known lots of Brights in my day, and one thing that can be said for the vast majority of them is that they're very decent people. But, like most people, they tend to get a bit nasty when they're being rubbed the wrong way. And Brights today are being rubbed the wrong way by our government more than they ever have been before.

Paine has his forum in which he can speak out. He's chosen to speak out in an abrasive and pointed fashion, I'd guess, because he doesn't think being Mr. Nice Guy will really work. It doesn't seem to be working for anyone else. Not even your friend Fr. Montoya.

Clearly, this snubbing you're getting from the traditional press is your father's doing. There can't be any other reason for it, since (as you say) why wouldn't they want to talk to you? It makes no sense.

Anyway, that's my point of view, for what it's worth.

Jude

END ULTRA-CRYPTED TEXT

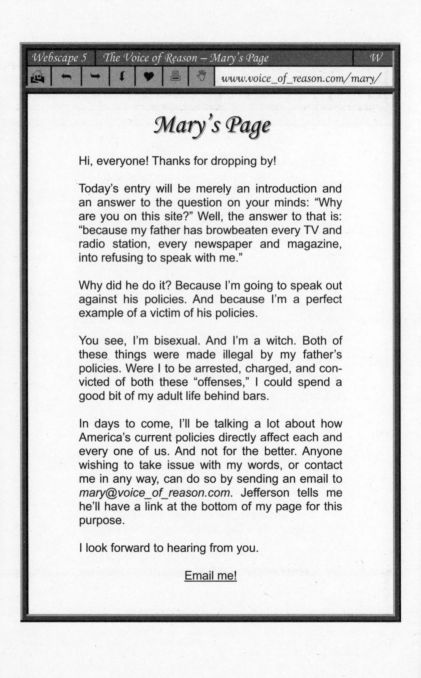

Mary's Page

Hi, everyone! Thanks for dropping by!

Today's entry will be merely an introduction and an answer to the question on your minds: "Why are you on this site?" Well, the answer to that is: "because my father has browbeaten every TV and radio station, every newspaper and magazine, into refusing to speak with me."

Why did he do it? Because I'm going to speak out against his policies. And because I'm a perfect example of a victim of his policies.

You see, I'm bisexual. And I'm a witch. Both of these things were made illegal by my father's policies. Were I to be arrested, charged, and convicted of both these "offenses," I could spend a good bit of my adult life behind bars.

In days to come, I'll be talking a lot about how America's current policies directly affect each and every one of us. And not for the better. Anyone wishing to take issue with my words, or contact me in any way, can do so by sending an email to *mary@voice_of_reason.com*. Jefferson tells me he'll have a link at the bottom of my page for this purpose.

I look forward to hearing from you.

Email me!

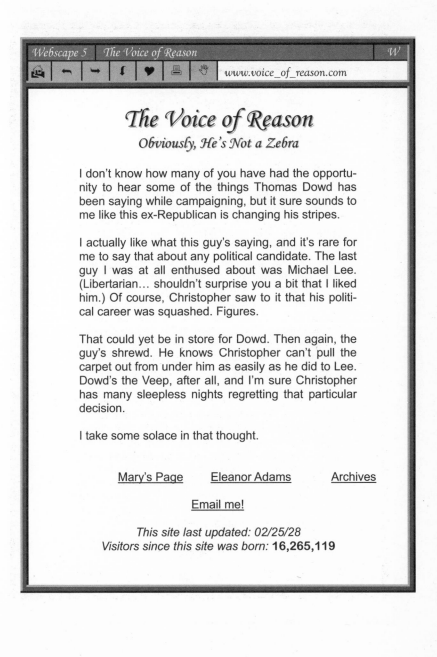

www.voice_of_reason.com

The Voice of Reason
Obviously, He's Not a Zebra

I don't know how many of you have had the opportunity to hear some of the things Thomas Dowd has been saying while campaigning, but it sure sounds to me like this ex-Republican is changing his stripes.

I actually like what this guy's saying, and it's rare for me to say that about any political candidate. The last guy I was at all enthused about was Michael Lee. (Libertarian... shouldn't surprise you a bit that I liked him.) Of course, Christopher saw to it that his political career was squashed. Figures.

That could yet be in store for Dowd. Then again, the guy's shrewd. He knows Christopher can't pull the carpet out from under him as easily as he did to Lee. Dowd's the Veep, after all, and I'm sure Christopher has many sleepless nights regretting that particular decision.

I take some solace in that thought.

Mary's Page   Eleanor Adams   Archives

Email me!

This site last updated: 02/25/28
Visitors since this site was born: **16,265,119**

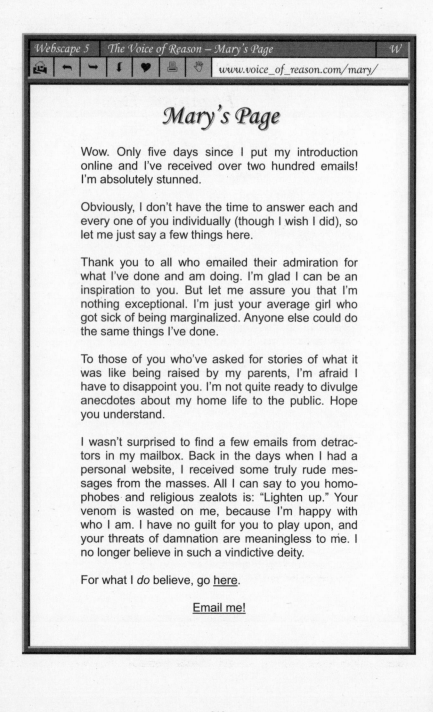

Mary's Page

Wow. Only five days since I put my introduction online and I've received over two hundred emails! I'm absolutely stunned.

Obviously, I don't have the time to answer each and every one of you individually (though I wish I did), so let me just say a few things here.

Thank you to all who emailed their admiration for what I've done and am doing. I'm glad I can be an inspiration to you. But let me assure you that I'm nothing exceptional. I'm just your average girl who got sick of being marginalized. Anyone else could do the same things I've done.

To those of you who've asked for stories of what it was like being raised by my parents, I'm afraid I have to disappoint you. I'm not quite ready to divulge anecdotes about my home life to the public. Hope you understand.

I wasn't surprised to find a few emails from detractors in my mailbox. Back in the days when I had a personal website, I received some truly rude messages from the masses. All I can say to you homophobes and religious zealots is: "Lighten up." Your venom is wasted on me, because I'm happy with who I am. I have no guilt for you to play upon, and your threats of damnation are meaningless to me. I no longer believe in such a vindictive deity.

For what I *do* believe, go here.

Email me!

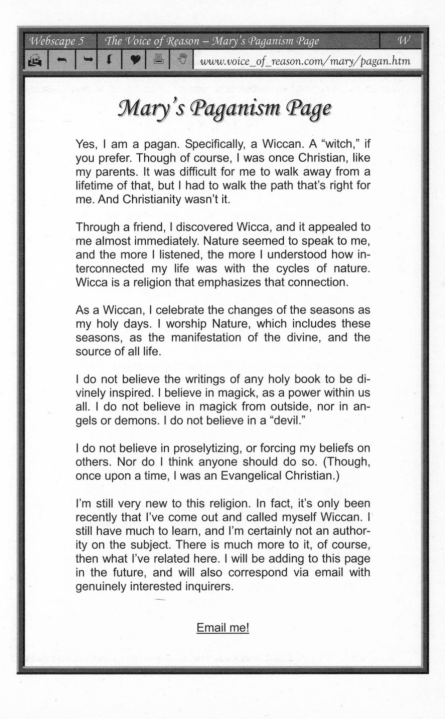

www.voice_of_reason.com/mary/pagan.htm

Mary's Paganism Page

Yes, I am a pagan. Specifically, a Wiccan. A "witch," if you prefer. Though of course, I was once Christian, like my parents. It was difficult for me to walk away from a lifetime of that, but I had to walk the path that's right for me. And Christianity wasn't it.

Through a friend, I discovered Wicca, and it appealed to me almost immediately. Nature seemed to speak to me, and the more I listened, the more I understood how interconnected my life was with the cycles of nature. Wicca is a religion that emphasizes that connection.

As a Wiccan, I celebrate the changes of the seasons as my holy days. I worship Nature, which includes these seasons, as the manifestation of the divine, and the source of all life.

I do not believe the writings of any holy book to be divinely inspired. I believe in magick, as a power within us all. I do not believe in magick from outside, nor in angels or demons. I do not believe in a "devil."

I do not believe in proselytizing, or forcing my beliefs on others. Nor do I think anyone should do so. (Though, once upon a time, I was an Evangelical Christian.)

I'm still very new to this religion. In fact, it's only been recently that I've come out and called myself Wiccan. I still have much to learn, and I'm certainly not an authority on the subject. There is much more to it, of course, then what I've related here. I will be adding to this page in the future, and will also correspond via email with genuinely interested inquirers.

Email me!

Sounding OFF
By J. E. Cooper

Tracking Gene Sisco and Our Father's Family Since 2015.

Issue No. 25   Winter, 2028

V.P. – Vocal Psychopath?

Vice-President Gene Sisco. The very thought should scare the snot out of each and every one of us. Sisco is, as I've said for years, a megalomaniac. But he's also a psychopath.

I'm not exaggerating. And I'm not in fear of any lawsuit for libel. I'm not professionally qualified to make the diagnosis, but my layman's assessment tells me he fits the definition.

There are twenty traits common to psychopaths. I'm going to list them and show how they apply to the "good" Reverend, too.

There are four main types of psychopaths, and Sisco fits the one called a "Charismatic" psychopath. Such a psychopath is usually gifted at something and uses this talent to manipulate others. Typically fast-talkers, they have the ability to persuade others out of or into damn near anything. They are often irresistible.

Sound like someone we know?

The following is adapted from Dr. Robert Hare's Psychopath Checklist.

Hare's Psychopath Checklist

Persuasive With Insincere Charm – Sisco is charming and convincing, all right, but he's totally superficial. Little that he says can be taken at face value.

Inflated Sense of Self-Worth – Sisco is self-assured, opinionated, and a braggart. He is arrogant and believes himself superior.

Easily Bored – Being a simple man of the cloth wasn't enough for him. He had to form Our Father's Family, have his own radio and television shows, then make his way into the White House!

Habitual Liar – We all know he spews lies about atheists, homosexuals, and others, though I'll concede that he may actually be twisted enough to believe them.

Manipulative – Sisco manipulates his followers like the sheep they are, to serve his own ends, which revolve around money and power.

(Continued on p. 2)

Hare's Psychological Checklist (cont'd.)

Lacks Regret or Guilt – Did Sisco seem at all remorseful when talking about the riots in Pocatello?

Emotionally Barren – Sisco is a cold bastard, despite his seeming gregariousness.

Lacks Empathy – His attitude toward people in general is cold and inconsiderate.

Parasitic Lifestyle – He lives off of the money and support of others, giving nothing back.

Poor Behavioral Controls – Sisco shows increasing irritability, annoyance, and impatience toward anyone who criticizes him.

Promiscuous – I have no desire to have info about his sex life. Ick.

Behavior Problems as a Child – Again, I don't know enough to say, but it wouldn't surprise me a bit.

Irrational Goals – Ten years ago, his goals might have seemed unrealistic. But more and more, they might just come to pass. I wonder if people thought Hitler's plans were unrealistic, too.

Impulsive – Sisco seems to be anything but impulsive. But I suspect there's a lot he does without planning that we don't know about.

Irresponsible – Let's see: "abstinence only sex education," "homosexual reorientation." Do I have to say more?

Denies Responsibilities for Actions – Sisco blames anyone but himself, whether atheists or Satan.

Numerous Short Intimate Relationships – Sisco's doesn't appear to have had any!

Juvenile Delinquent – Again, I don't know. But not unlikely.

Revoked Condition Release – This would pertain to people who've actually been convicted of a crime, so it doesn't apply. Yet.

Criminal Flexibility – This means showing a wide variety of criminal offenses, whether or not he's been caught. Again... wouldn't surprise me.

Gene Sisco hits 50% of these dead on. Of those remaining, half refer to things not commonly known about the guy, so we can't really say. And half of the ones remaining after that pertain only to people with criminal records.

I feel safe in saying that Sisco qualifies as a dangerous psychopath. But even if I'm wrong, is this the kind of guy we want as the Vice-President? Or, as I'm certain his goal is, President?

J.E.C.

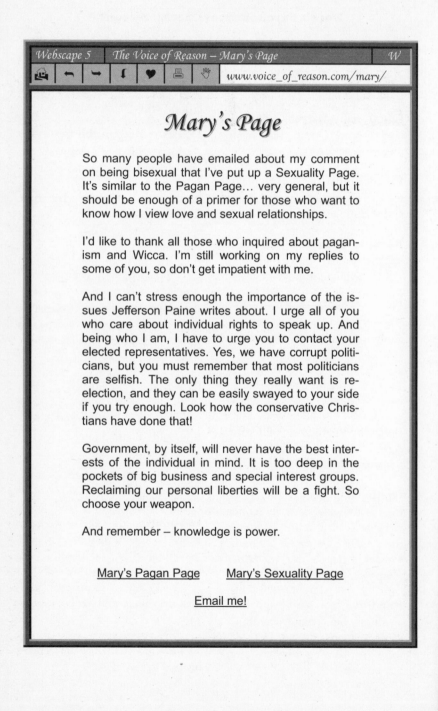

Mary's Page

So many people have emailed about my comment on being bisexual that I've put up a Sexuality Page. It's similar to the Pagan Page... very general, but it should be enough of a primer for those who want to know how I view love and sexual relationships.

I'd like to thank all those who inquired about paganism and Wicca. I'm still working on my replies to some of you, so don't get impatient with me.

And I can't stress enough the importance of the issues Jefferson Paine writes about. I urge all of you who care about individual rights to speak up. And being who I am, I have to urge you to contact your elected representatives. Yes, we have corrupt politicians, but you must remember that most politicians are selfish. The only thing they really want is re-election, and they can be easily swayed to your side if you try enough. Look how the conservative Christians have done that!

Government, by itself, will never have the best interests of the individual in mind. It is too deep in the pockets of big business and special interest groups. Reclaiming our personal liberties will be a fight. So choose your weapon.

And remember – knowledge is power.

Mary's Pagan Page   Mary's Sexuality Page

Email me!

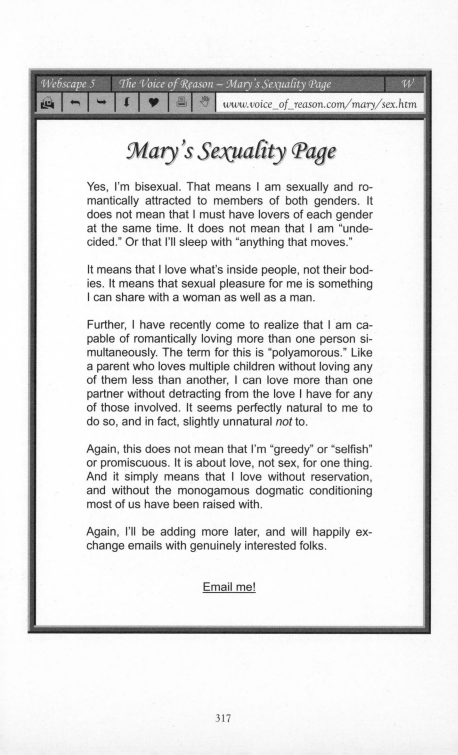

www.voice_of_reason.com/mary/sex.htm

Mary's Sexuality Page

Yes, I'm bisexual. That means I am sexually and romantically attracted to members of both genders. It does not mean that I must have lovers of each gender at the same time. It does not mean that I am "undecided." Or that I'll sleep with "anything that moves."

It means that I love what's inside people, not their bodies. It means that sexual pleasure for me is something I can share with a woman as well as a man.

Further, I have recently come to realize that I am capable of romantically loving more than one person simultaneously. The term for this is "polyamorous." Like a parent who loves multiple children without loving any of them less than another, I can love more than one partner without detracting from the love I have for any of those involved. It seems perfectly natural to me to do so, and in fact, slightly unnatural *not* to.

Again, this does not mean that I'm "greedy" or "selfish" or promiscuous. It is about love, not sex, for one thing. And it simply means that I love without reservation, and without the monogamous dogmatic conditioning most of us have been raised with.

Again, I'll be adding more later, and will happily exchange emails with genuinely interested folks.

<u>Email me!</u>

Date: March 4, 2028
To: mary@voice_of_reason.com
From: 1stLady@whitehouse.gov
Subject: How dare you?

Mary:

I have never been so mortified in my life! How dare you put this filth online for the world to see? What have your father and I ever done to you to deserve being humiliated like this? Or do you simply not consider us in your hedonistic mind?

For the longest time, I've deeply regretted the collapse of our relationship. I even berated myself for not trying to salvage it. But now, it makes my stomach churn, just thinking about you being my daughter.

You flaunt your devil-worshiping and sexual abominations like the whore of Babylon, and you are no daughter of mine, Mary. Lucifer has claimed you for one of his own.

Gene Sisco is right. You are lost.

You are Satan's slut.

Ashamed to be,
        Your mother

Date: March 5, 2028
To: 1stLady@whitehouse.gov
From: mary@voice_of_reason.com
Subject: Re: How dare you?

Mother (whether you like it or not):

I'm sorry you've apparently chosen to disown me. But what hurts even more is that you are obviously so brainwashed that you cannot accept even the idea that my decisions in life are my own, not Satan's.

You know, it's bad enough that you turn your back on me, but you betray the sanctity of a woman's own mind by supporting The Saviors. And yes, I said "mind." Forget about the body; you're really opposed to a woman's right to make the choice itself, even more than you're opposed to the actual abortion. It's a mental game, not a physical one.

You and Father both support the vilification of anyone whose ideas do not agree with your own, including ideas that are not a threat to you whatsoever. This would include mine, of course.

Are you so insecure with your own sexuality that mine puts you in a state of frenzy? Are you so insecure in your own faith that you perceive mine as being dangerous?

You've always been a control freak, Mother. I'm only now realizing that the person you exert the most control over is yourself. You don't allow yourself to do anything "outside the box," including the exercise of any brain cells.

I know you've got some. Pity you don't actually use them.

Mary

Date: March 9, 2028
To: heyjude@beatles4ever.ws
From: mary@voice_of_reason.com
Subject: Hey

Hi, hon!

It was nice talking to you on the phone tonight. I've missed the sound of your voice.

I've been thinking about what you said about the media. I hope you're right. It would be nice if one of the newspapers or TV stations would have the guts to stand up to my dad. But I'm not holding my breath.

So... let me run an idea by you. As you know, both of us really had a great time while you were here. And maybe I've never said it before, but I do consider you to be my best friend. Aside from Vicki, of course.

I don't know that I ever gave any sort of thought to you being more than just that. Until we spent time together, anyway. And the thought has definitely crossed my mind a time or two.

But regardless of that, the truth of the matter is that I don't like the fact that we're separated by the vast majority of the 50 states. I'd like to have you around, y'know? Vicki feels pretty much the same, though obviously her feelings for you aren't as deep as mine.

Of course, she now knows you pretty darn well. Did I tell you I've saved printed copies of every email you've ever sent me? It's true. And she's read them all. All our conversations. Yeah, even the ones we had about her, when I was still questioning my emotions. (I'm still being teased about that.)

I guess what I'm trying to say is that if you could possibly be convinced to do so, we'd both love for you to move out here.

I know I'm not giving you much incentive. But you're one of the most important people in my life. It feels somehow incomplete to not have you around, in person.

Please think about it, okay? You don't need to decide right now. As I said, it's just an idea for the future.

Well, gotta run. I'm giving Vicki an aromatherapy massage tonight. Write back soon!
    hugs

    Mary

Date: March 12, 2028
To: mary@voice_of_reason.com
From: heyjude@beatles4ever.ws
Subject: Re: Hey

Mary:

Um... wow. I thought I was beyond being shocked by things people could say to me, but you've proved me wrong. I'm utterly stunned.

Then again, I saw your sexuality page on the Voice of Reason. You never told me that you consider yourself poly.

Okay. I'm not stupid. I can read between the lines. And I'm amazingly flattered that you're so... um... what's the term? Infatuated with me? I know you didn't stress this in your email, but the part that leaped out at me was the little bit that has "crossed your mind" now and then.

I'd be lying if I said I wasn't attracted to you, Mary. But I have concerns. For one thing, I'm twenty-six years old. There's a big difference between us, at least on a physical level. I think you're far more mature than your years. I've always thought so, even when we first met. But I just don't know.

I also have concerns about how such a relationship would work. Though I identify as a polyamorous person, I've got no personal experience with it. Nor do you. And I don't think Vicki does, either. It would certainly not be an easy arrangement.

And, okay... I admit it... I'm intimidated as all get-out about the possibility of being "involved" with the President's daughter. There. I said it.

Can you blame me, though?

That being said, I'm not saying "no." I just want to explore what it is we've got, first. To see exactly what it is, and what it isn't. Give me some time to come to grips with this. Okay?

And man... if my reading between the lines of your email was wrong, I'm going to be too embarrassed to even email with you ever again!

And today in Beatles history:
1971:   Lennon's "Power to the People" released as single in U.K.

Jude

March 15, 2028

Well, Jude jumped right on the whole "more than friends" thing. Guess I wasn't as coy as I thought I was being.

And he's right, of course. None of us has experience with non-monogamy. And he's also right about the fact that he and Vicki need to know each other better. I mean, I think they'd get along great. And even though it sometimes makes me feel uncomfortable inside, I could see them being intimate, eventually. But I hesitate to think what could happen if we were to move forward without really working out the details.

So we'll give it time. I know he and Vicki are exchanging emails regularly. They'll talk on the phone, too. Eventually, we'll either know we can do it, or know we shouldn't try.

In the meantime, I'm sure busy! Doing my pages for the Voice of Reason site sure takes a lot of time. I'm still getting lots of email, but not as much as when I first started at the site.

Jefferson Paine has been wonderful. He's so polite and accommodating. I told him up front that he can edit my work, but he's put everything on just as I sent it to him. He answers all my questions and never seems at all put-out by my "intrusion" on his sacred cyberspace.

He also keeps me apprised of the activities of the Freethought Underground, and has even suggested that I join one of the groups on the road, so I can talk to the public live and in person. The very idea terrifies and excites me. Maybe I'll take him up on it, but not right now.

Still, if I want to be an activist, that would be great experience...

322

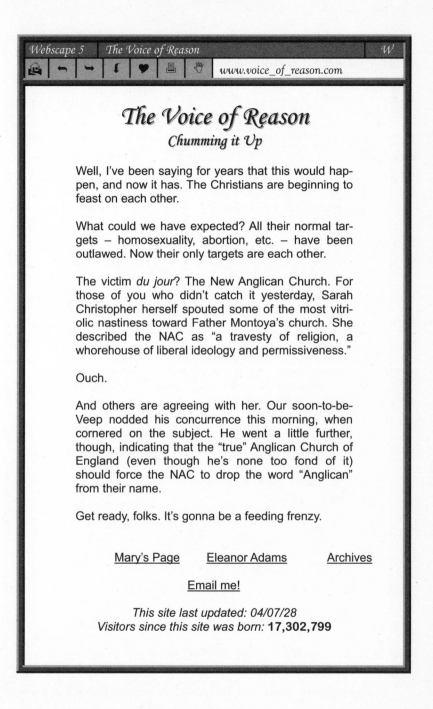

The Voice of Reason
Chumming it Up

Well, I've been saying for years that this would happen, and now it has. The Christians are beginning to feast on each other.

What could we have expected? All their normal targets – homosexuality, abortion, etc. – have been outlawed. Now their only targets are each other.

The victim *du jour*? The New Anglican Church. For those of you who didn't catch it yesterday, Sarah Christopher herself spouted some of the most vitriolic nastiness toward Father Montoya's church. She described the NAC as "a travesty of religion, a whorehouse of liberal ideology and permissiveness."

Ouch.

And others are agreeing with her. Our soon-to-be-Veep nodded his concurrence this morning, when cornered on the subject. He went a little further, though, indicating that the "true" Anglican Church of England (even though he's none too fond of it) should force the NAC to drop the word "Anglican" from their name.

Get ready, folks. It's gonna be a feeding frenzy.

Mary's Page   Eleanor Adams   Archives

Email me!

This site last updated: 04/07/28
Visitors since this site was born: **17,302,799**

Mary's Page

Okay. So my mother's an opinionated flake. Who *didn't* know this?

And she's apparently not stopping with her blasts against the NAC. Like many extremists, she's aiming her sights on anyone who doesn't agree with her 100%. That's a lot of people.

And in case you're wondering, no... my father won't do anything to shut her up, or urge her to apologize for offending such a large number of people. In case you hadn't noticed, my father isn't really much of a diplomat.

Father Montoya happens to be a friend of mine, and I admire him a great deal. I don't agree with his religious views, but so what? He doesn't agree with mine, either. But we're still friends. Either one of us would do anything for the other.

If any of you care about restoring religious freedom to this country, the first step is to promote acceptance. Not "tolerance." That has such a negative connotation. You shouldn't "tolerate" something. You should "accept" it, whether or not you personally agree with it.

So speak out! Talk to everyone you know. Tell them it doesn't matter what anyone else believes, as long as they're not hurting anyone. Maybe if enough people realize that, we'll be on our way to healing this nation.

<u>Mary's Pagan Page</u>   <u>Mary's Sexuality Page</u>

<u>Email me!</u>

8 April 2028

Sarah's outbursts are becoming problematic. And Mary's words on The Voice of Reason are accurate. I'm not a diplomat. Never have been, probably never will be.

I just don't understand people. Sarah is conservative, yes. And yes, she feels passionately about matters such as abortion. But she's never before been so... hateful. Yes, that's the word.

She's withdrawn so much this past year. Mary's emancipation never sat well with her, and everything since then has just added to her misery, especially Mary's online activities. She told me about the unpleasant email exchange she had with Mary several weeks ago.

Were I prone to psychobabble, I'd say she's lashing out at others, by proxy. She's really lashing out at herself for her "failure" as a mother. But I'm not inclined to armchair analysis.

After I chose Dowd as my Vice President, Gene tended to avoid me. He said it was due to his own activities. But now that Dowd's running against me, Gene's cozying up like a hungry cat.

Sometimes I wonder if Jefferson Paine is right. Is it truly Gene's goal to set himself up as a dictator? I've seen sides to his personality over the past couple years that I'm not very comfortable with. I agree with many of his goals, and I cherish his friendship, but what if he's not really the man I think him to be?

Date: April 8, 2028
To: 1stLady@whitehouse.gov
From: mary@voice_of_reason.com
Subject: Sorry

Mom:

I just wanted to write and let you know that I'm really sorry about the tone of my last email to you. I was deeply hurt by your email to me, and angry, too. And I reacted while in a negative state. I shouldn't have allowed my emotions to get the better of me. I should have waited before replying, and if I hurt you, I'm sorry.

I know you didn't really mean what you said about me, either. At least, not in full. You rarely ever tell me that you love me. You've never been very open with your emotions, really. But I've always known. And I hope you've always known that I love you, too. We don't have to approve of each other's lifestyles or political views in order to love each other.

I hope we can put those email exchanges behind us. I want us to have a better relationship. We can agree to disagree, but we're still mother and daughter, dysfunctional though we may be.

Drop me a line, if you're so inclined.

Mary

Crucifying the Saviors
MOTHER JONES *Speaks Out*

So just what is the goal of The Saviors in this era? When a group continues to rally for the abolition of things that have already been declared illegal, what does that say about the group?

Isn't it about time to move on? Shouldn't they find some other still-legal "sin" to abolish? Well, no one's saying they won't. But The Saviors have spent so many years stumping against homosexuality, abortion, pre-marital sex, and other such things, that they really don't know how to do anything else.

Can anyone really picture Sarah Christopher touring public schools talking about the evils of cigarette smoking, or drinking alcohol? Of course not.

Nearly half a million people die every year from smoking related illnesses. About 25,000 die annually in the United States alone from drunk driving accidents. About 400,000 are non-fatally injured. (And that's not taking into account the deaths due to alcohol-related diseases.)

No, you see, The Saviors must go after gays, pro-choicers, and others because these are the "sinners." These are the ones doing things that don't hurt others, but somehow hurt God. (Shouldn't that be impossible?) The Saviors are not interested in helping humans. They're only interested in "protecting" God.

So you'll never see this group, or any like it, helping to ease world hunger (starving isn't a sin), working to improve education (religion prefers stupid people), or any of a thousand other activities that would actually be useful.

The Saviors aren't interested in *you*, after all. They're only interested in their own righteous indignation. It makes them feel superior. Which means, according to shrinks, that they've got a collective inferiority complex.

Surprise.

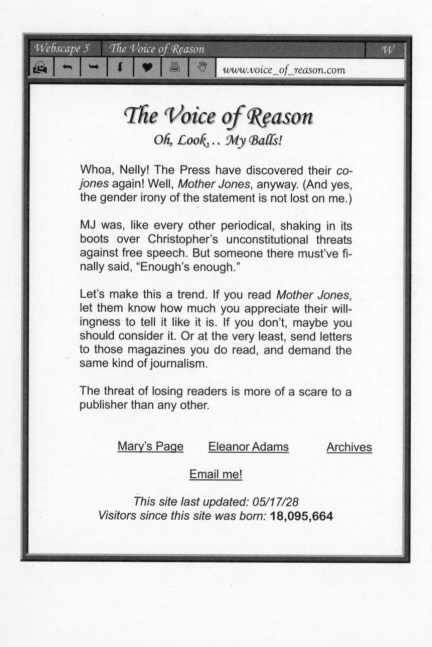

The Voice of Reason
Oh, Look... My Balls!

Whoa, Nelly! The Press have discovered their *co-jones* again! Well, *Mother Jones*, anyway. (And yes, the gender irony of the statement is not lost on me.)

MJ was, like every other periodical, shaking in its boots over Christopher's unconstitutional threats against free speech. But someone there must've finally said, "Enough's enough."

Let's make this a trend. If you read *Mother Jones*, let them know how much you appreciate their willingness to tell it like it is. If you don't, maybe you should consider it. Or at the very least, send letters to those magazines you do read, and demand the same kind of journalism.

The threat of losing readers is more of a scare to a publisher than any other.

Mary's Page   Eleanor Adams   Archives

Email me!

This site last updated: 05/17/28
Visitors since this site was born: **18,095,664**

20 June 2028

Sarah is at her wits' end. Mary's criticism of her on The Voice of Reason website is not something my dear wife is able to tolerate. She is insisting that I get this site shut down.

I've explained to her that I've tried, that a special team has been working on nothing but this task ever since the site first went online. I've even met the head of this team, a Dr. Nutt, and I understand the reasons behind the failure of the team. Apparently, Paine is a whiz kid who's utilized more than twenty privacy programs, including at least one of his own design, in order to make his site anonymous. While my task force is quite capable of defeating any or all of them, Paine (or whoever designed his privacy system) has inserted a randomizer into each program. This apparently changes something in each program at regular intervals. Our Department of Defense uses a similar strategy on their computers, in fact.

I don't understand it, or pretend to, but the practical effect is that by the time our experts can blast through ten or twelve of the privacy guards, the first one or two have already cycled to another random configuration, which renders the hack job useless. In order to gain access to the system, our computers would have to disable all twenty-odd privacy programs in a very short period of time. So far, we've only come close once or twice. Our experts say it's basically a waste of time, that this guy knows what he's doing.

But Sarah wants it shut down, not because of Jefferson Paine's incessant rants, but because this is our daughter out there ridiculing both of us. Yet another Commandment she's breaking.

Nothing would please me more than to see that site gone. But short of Jefferson Paine dropping dead, I can't see how it's going to happen.

Well, there is Gene's long-standing recommendation on how to nuke the site, but I've always considered it far too extreme. Still, maybe I should reconsider. I'll have to see what the experts think.

Date: 07/22/28
To: T. Bannister, CO BB Proj.
From: E. Nutt, CP BB Proj.
Subject: Re: Boston Project

Sir, I must voice my objections over the so-called "Boston Project." I do not believe enough consideration has been given to this plan.

Yes, recent advances have allowed us the ability to create small, localized EMPs. But even though these are "clean" pulses, there are three major reasons why deploying one is still a bad idea:

1. Since we do not know the exact location of Paine's servers, a "local" EMP would have to be large enough to affect the entire city and surrounding suburbs. And while all vital electronics are protected against EMPs, the vast majority of consumer wares would be damaged or destroyed. Chaos is virtually certain to ensue, including injuries, possibly even deaths.

2. The chance that Paine has left his own systems unprotected is incredibly slim. I protect my personal systems against EMPs, and I would be amazed if he hasn't got at least double the protection I've laid in.

3. Even if this plan succeeded, it would only be temporary. I predict the site would be back online within days, if not hours. He surely has full backups located far from the home system.

Given all this, and your continued insistence on going forward with the plans, I am left to think that you are doing so only because this is what the President wants, despite the scientific problems presented, not to mention the highly questionable ethics of the situation.

I cannot be a party to such a plan, and if you still insist on proceeding, it will be without my assistance.

CC: P. Christopher

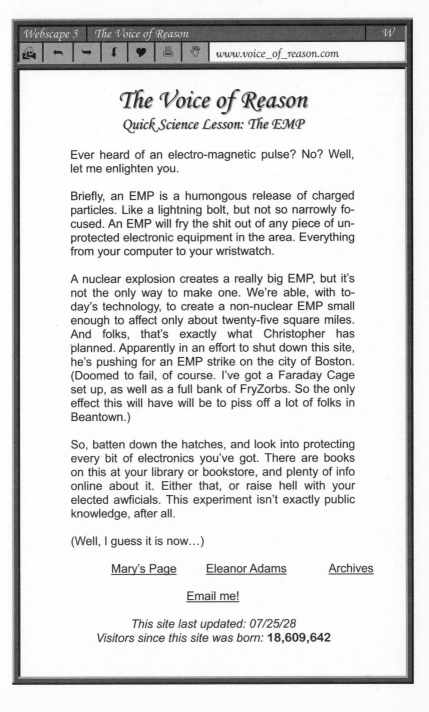

The Voice of Reason
Quick Science Lesson: The EMP

Ever heard of an electro-magnetic pulse? No? Well, let me enlighten you.

Briefly, an EMP is a humongous release of charged particles. Like a lightning bolt, but not so narrowly focused. An EMP will fry the shit out of any piece of unprotected electronic equipment in the area. Everything from your computer to your wristwatch.

A nuclear explosion creates a really big EMP, but it's not the only way to make one. We're able, with today's technology, to create a non-nuclear EMP small enough to affect only about twenty-five square miles. And folks, that's exactly what Christopher has planned. Apparently in an effort to shut down this site, he's pushing for an EMP strike on the city of Boston. (Doomed to fail, of course. I've got a Faraday Cage set up, as well as a full bank of FryZorbs. So the only effect this will have will be to piss off a lot of folks in Beantown.)

So, batten down the hatches, and look into protecting every bit of electronics you've got. There are books on this at your library or bookstore, and plenty of info online about it. Either that, or raise hell with your elected awficials. This experiment isn't exactly public knowledge, after all.

(Well, I guess it is now...)

<u>Mary's Page</u>   <u>Eleanor Adams</u>   <u>Archives</u>

<u>Email me!</u>

This site last updated: 07/25/28
Visitors since this site was born: **18,609,642**

Date: July 26, 2028
To: The_Prez@whitehouse.gov
From: mary@voice_of_reason.com
Subject: Are you insane????

Dad:

Please tell me you're not really going to zap a whole city just to shut me up. I know that's what it is. It's one thing for an anonymous guy to write inflammatory things about you, but for you own daughter to ridicule your policies and Mother's actions... that's too much, isn't it?

Well, good. I'm glad. Lately I've been taking a close look at the things you've done while in office, and it turns my stomach. I can't believe I once thought like you.

But this business makes me actually ashamed to be your daughter. To think that you're willing to wreak havoc on a major metropolitan area, just so you can perform an act of censorship! I don't want to believe you're capable of such an immoral act. Is this that jerk Sisco's influence? I can't believe I ever thought fondly of him.

Take a look at what you're planning on doing before it's too late. People could die because of this insanity. Do you really want that on your conscience?

Mary

Washington—The White House issued a press release this morning stating that reports of a deliberately planned electro-magnetic pulse aimed at Boston were unfounded.

Tyrone McAllister, head of the Big Brother project, says, "It is no secret that we've been trying to shut down *The Voice of Reason* site for some time. It is also true that our chief programmer on this project was recently let go, for reasons I cannot disclose. It is obvious that he has concocted this ridiculous story in an effort to slander the President and his Administration."

The White House expressed profound regret over any concerns the people of Boston may have suffered due to this deliberate misinformation.

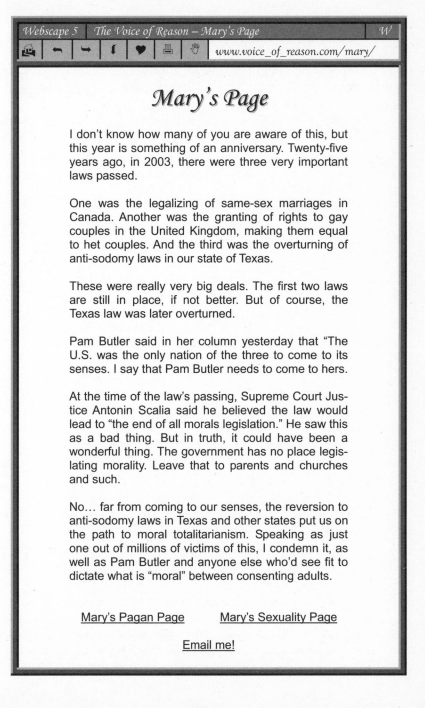

Mary's Page

I don't know how many of you are aware of this, but this year is something of an anniversary. Twenty-five years ago, in 2003, there were three very important laws passed.

One was the legalizing of same-sex marriages in Canada. Another was the granting of rights to gay couples in the United Kingdom, making them equal to het couples. And the third was the overturning of anti-sodomy laws in our state of Texas.

These were really very big deals. The first two laws are still in place, if not better. But of course, the Texas law was later overturned.

Pam Butler said in her column yesterday that "The U.S. was the only nation of the three to come to its senses. I say that Pam Butler needs to come to hers.

At the time of the law's passing, Supreme Court Justice Antonin Scalia said he believed the law would lead to "the end of all morals legislation." He saw this as a bad thing. But in truth, it could have been a wonderful thing. The government has no place legislating morality. Leave that to parents and churches and such.

No… far from coming to our senses, the reversion to anti-sodomy laws in Texas and other states put us on the path to moral totalitarianism. Speaking as just one out of millions of victims of this, I condemn it, as well as Pam Butler and anyone else who'd see fit to dictate what is "moral" between consenting adults.

Mary's Pagan Page   Mary's Sexuality Page

Email me!

2 August 2028

Mary's last email still haunts me. To think that she's ashamed to be my daughter... That's harsh.

But she's right. What was I thinking, listening to Gene's idea? It was completely irresponsible. Still, we have plausible deniability, and I think we've got damage control in hand.

Why do I listen to everything that man says? He's been causing me nothing but headaches for months. I have to admit, though, he makes a good running mate. His ability to stump for us through his television and radio shows, newsletters and magazines, is truly a blessing.

I even wished Dowd good luck with his campaign. He'll need it, and plenty of it, to do more than look like an idiot. If he carries even his home state, it'll be a miracle.

September 10, 2028

It's been an interesting couple months. I've been contacted by many people, thanking me for speaking out on the web. It's nice to know I'm making a difference. But I feel I could be doing more.

I'm still angry with my father for the blatant lying he's doing. I guess it's true what they say. Power corrupts. He wasn't like this before he became President. And still no reply from my emailed apology to Mother. Guess she's holding a grudge.

Other than that, things are great. Vicki and I are quite happy. We're still nagging Jude to move out here, but he's not biting. Yet. We both email regularly with him.

School is great, and I have the feeling this will be my last year there. The staff has hinted that I'm "ready for the world," so to speak. Question is, is the world ready for me?

I really don't know what I want to do after I graduate. College? Maybe. Or maybe not. I don't really have a particular profession in mind. But I'll need some sort of income.

I don't know if I have what it takes to be a lecturer. Vicki says I'd be sure to get jobs, but of course, my father's policies have made the things I'd talk about (acceptance of alternative lifestyles & religions) illegal. So I wouldn't really have a market.

Maybe someday...

9/13/28

Today I did something out of the ordinary for me. I spoke with Gene about Mary. He's seemed somewhat back to his normal self lately, so I felt it might be worthwhile to speak to him, in his role as a servant of God. I explained that I was torn between being offended by her lifestyle and so on, and my maternal bond to her.

I expected some sort of wisdom from him, as befitting a man of the cloth. But he dismissed it almost with disdain. He said Mary was lost to Satan and nothing he or Paul or I could do would change this. He said it was best to act as though she had never been born, that I should not consider her my daughter at all, but just another heathen sinner.

Though it was a good six hours ago that we spoke, I can't rid myself of the feeling of revulsion.

I can't help but think I'm doing wrong in God's eyes by shutting Mary out of my life. Children are a gift from God, and no matter how much trouble they prove to be, they are still God's creations.

But it is so hard.

I know I should not give up trying to bring her back to the light, but every time I try to contact her, I just lose control. I berate her and condemn her, when all I really want to do is hold her and help her.

I pray to God every night to give me strength, to reveal to me how I may reach her and bring her back to His word. So far, He has been silent. I trust this means that I already know the answer, but must find it within myself.

Mary speaks of acceptance on her website, but I cannot. I cannot accept her fallen ways. I cannot accept that she has intimate relations with another woman. I will never accept it.

Yet as much as I hate the sin, I must love the sinner. And I do love her; she is my daughter. But clearly, my love is not strong enough.

The Voice of Reason
Freedom of Religion Means All Religions

If you're not already following Vice-President Dowd's campaign, you should be. I don't agree with every single thing the guy says, but quite a lot of it, I do.

For example, he's very big on the First Amendment. While he hasn't said anything about deregulation of the Internet, or anything about Freedom of the Press, he's definitely made mention of Freedom of Religion. Dowd is urging freedom of *all* religions, which is a damn sight better than the freedom of one (or two) religions to run roughshod over all the others.

The question on the lips of many, though, are: Will he offer this freedom to religions such as Wicca, and What about freedom *from* religion?

I have no clear answer yet on the latter question. But for an answer to the first, please visit Mary's Page.

Mary's Page   Eleanor Adams   Archives

Email me!

This site last updated: 09/15/28
Visitors since this site was born: **19,396,241**

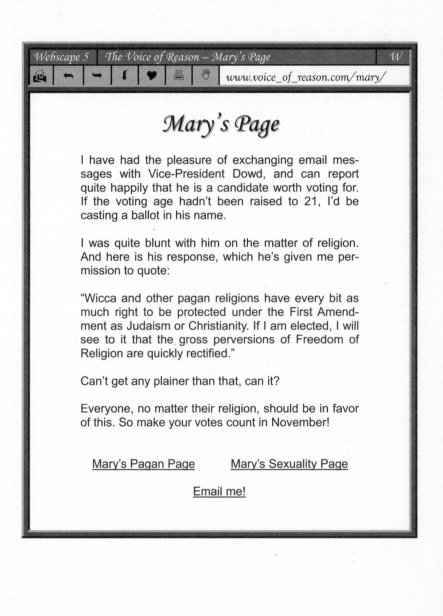

www.voice_of_reason.com/mary/

Mary's Page

I have had the pleasure of exchanging email messages with Vice-President Dowd, and can report quite happily that he is a candidate worth voting for. If the voting age hadn't been raised to 21, I'd be casting a ballot in his name.

I was quite blunt with him on the matter of religion. And here is his response, which he's given me permission to quote:

"Wicca and other pagan religions have every bit as much right to be protected under the First Amendment as Judaism or Christianity. If I am elected, I will see to it that the gross perversions of Freedom of Religion are quickly rectified."

Can't get any plainer than that, can it?

Everyone, no matter their religion, should be in favor of this. So make your votes count in November!

Mary's Pagan Page   Mary's Sexuality Page

Email me!

Date: September 25, 2028
To: jefferson_paine@voice_of_reason.com
From: Veep@whitehouse.gov
Subject: Re: Freedom from Religion

Mr. Paine:

I apologize for the delay in responding to your request. It has taken me some time to decide how best to respond to you.

In truth, I have long believed that freedom OF religion did not equal freedom FROM religion. But over the past months, I have come to conclude that your perspective is the right one. Without freedom FROM religion, there really can't be a true freedom OF religion. It's like the old saying, "No one is free when others are oppressed." Why this simple truth eluded me for so long, I cannot say.

Your friend Robert Green and I have exchanged several emails over the recent months, and this is one of the many issues we've discussed. He's very intelligent, and has explained succinctly the difficulty of being a non-believer in our society today. I'm ashamed to realize that my previously-held views were partly responsible for the prejudice against you and other non-theists. For what it's worth, I offer my apologies.

More than that, I offer you my word: If elected, I will do everything in my power to see that discrimination against the non-religious is stopped, and that a strict separation of church and state is upheld. And yes, you may quote me on that.

T. Dowd

Date: October 14, 2028
To: mary@voice_of_reason.com
From: heyjude@beatles4ever.ws
Subject: Re: Well???

Mary:

Man, you two never let up, do you? I haven't been hounded like this since my cousin joined Amway.

All right, let's put an end to this once and for all.

I'll consider moving to your rainy, chilly, sun-deprived part of the country. But it won't be for a while, yet. And even once I'm there, I make no promises about what'll happen.

In case you don't realize it, just yet, you've got a very busy life ahead of you, and won't have much time for a new relationship. It'll be strain enough for you and Vicki to maintain your existing relationship, let alone stressing about adding me to the mix.

We'll get there, though. One day. And when that day arrives, and when you're able to focus on it, we'll try it.

Hope that's enough for you at this juncture. I love you.

Hugs to Vicki.

Jude

October 21, 2028

I suppose I should be elated at the prospect of Jude eventually joining us. And I am. Well, not so much "elated," but I'm definitely "content." It'll be great having him near. He's been my support network for a long time, and I hate the idea of keeping that relationship virtual, to say nothing of building a different sort of relationship with him.

As for that other relationship, well, the more I've thought about it, the more drawn I am to it. I sometimes daydream about the three of us living together as a family. It's a nice dream.

But Jude's right, as usual. Things are pretty weird for me right now, and are only going to get weirder over the next few years, I'm sure. I really don't have the time to devote to forming a family of any sort. It's been rough on Vicki and me, but we make sure to devote as much quality time to each other as we can, even if we have to schedule it. It can only get worse, but we'll make it work.

The election is approaching fast, and it's virtually guaranteed that Dad will win again. I'm happy for him, but a bit frightened for the country. Especially because this time, Gene Sisco will be Vice-President. I know the vice-presidency has always been a position largely devoid of any real responsibility. But still… Even as a figurehead, I can't stand the idea.

I keep thinking back to my years at Camp Sonlight and get sick to my stomach every time I do. At the time, I never thought much of it, but in truth, they were little brainwashing camps. Every day, we were fed anti-gay rhetoric. Every night we sang songs around the campfire that subtly belittled everyone except Christians. How could I have missed these incredibly bigoted views before?

Washington—The 2028 election is, on several fronts, a history-making election. President Paul Christopher was elected to a third term yesterday by a margin of 51 electoral votes. Christopher becomes only the second President in U.S. history to be elected to more than two terms.

Reverend Gene Sisco, Christopher's running mate, now becomes the first ordained minister to serve in the nation's second-highest office.

Vice President Thomas Dowd, to the surprise of many, carried four states: Oregon, Massachusetts, Ohio, and Hawaii. Dowd is the first Libertarian to carry any states in a Presidential election. Dowd told reporters that he will definitely run again in 2032.

Year Nine

2029

January 1, 2029

I've never really taken to the idea of making New Year's Resolutions before, but I think I'll make one this year.

I resolve to make a difference. Specifically, I resolve to take advantage of my name and become an outspoken activist for the causes I believe in. Namely: paganism, freedom of and from religion, and complete freedom of choice in matters of a sexual or relationship nature.

I'm going to use the notoriety of my section of The Voice of Reason, as well as the fact that I'm the daughter of the President, to become an activist that people will want to listen to. Candace Gingrich did the same thing back when her brother Newt was Speaker of the House. There's no reason I can't do what she did.

I've been putting together a press kit online and will be contacting local schools and organizations. Surely someone would want to have me do lectures and whatnot.

Of course, a part of me says I'm being pretentious, that I'm not really qualified to speak with authority on any of these subjects. But I'm trying to maintain a positive outlook. Let's face it, I'm so far outside the realm of "acceptability" in our society that it's not even funny. I'm a poly-inclined, bisexual Wiccan who believes in the total separation of church and state, a woman's right to choose abortion, and a host of other "evil" concepts.

I know I'm not totally alone in my views. It's just that the ultra-conservative faction has been better organized and more vocal than their opposition for the past several decades. It's time for change. And I think I can be instrumental in instituting it.

Folks:

Things are really going to change, now. Sisco is sworn-in as Veep next week, and you can believe that he's not going to be the standard stick-in-the-mud Vice President. Christopher will give him all sorts of power and influence.

But we can't let this intimidate us. We have some serious power of our own. In addition to *The Voice of Reason* website, we have Mary Christopher positively itching to become a high-profile activist. We've also got, believe it or not, Thomas Dowd. Yes, you read that correctly. He's sworn to dedicate himself to restoring sanity to this country, and thinks we're doing a great job.

And of course, we've got all of you, who've been out there in the trenches for years now. The work you're doing is phenomenal. At last tally, there were 64 Freethought Underground "cells" in 38 states. There are over 125,000 people on our email list. That's pretty impressive.

Now all we have to do is continue what we've been doing, and not be frightened by the fact that Sisco has nearly accomplished his ultimate goal. Keep up the good work, everyone!

Paine

Leave me a message

Washington—President Paul Christopher officially began his third term today, this time with a new Vice-President, Reverend Gene Sisco. The ceremony was solemn with religion. An invocation was given before the ceremony, and a prayer service was held afterward.

Meanwhile, two thousand miles away, the President's daughter, Mary Christopher, today announced via press release her availability to speak on First Amendment issues nationwide.

Three national publications also chose this day to announce their plans to resume publication, years after being shut down by the Christopher Administration. *Queer and Now*, a publication of American Queers, will have its first new issue in February. The magazine will be available only online.

Similarly, *USAtheist*, a publication of Atheists USA, and *PagaNation*, from Pagan Pride, will produce digital magazines beginning in March and April, respectively.

How these sites will avoid the wrath of Big Brother is open to speculation, though Internet experts hypothesize that Jefferson Paine will be responsible for maintaining the sites. Paine's site, *The Voice of Reason*, has been evading Big Brother's grasp for well over seven years.

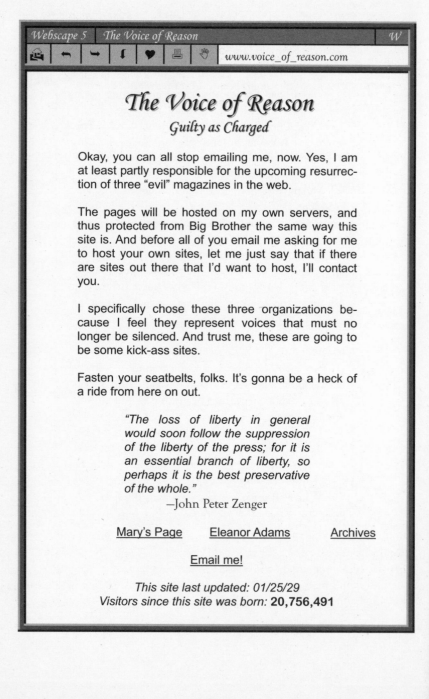

Webscape 5 · *The Voice of Reason* · *W*

`www.voice_of_reason.com`

The Voice of Reason
Guilty as Charged

Okay, you can all stop emailing me, now. Yes, I am at least partly responsible for the upcoming resurrection of three "evil" magazines in the web.

The pages will be hosted on my own servers, and thus protected from Big Brother the same way this site is. And before all of you email me asking for me to host your own sites, let me just say that if there are sites out there that I'd want to host, I'll contact you.

I specifically chose these three organizations because I feel they represent voices that must no longer be silenced. And trust me, these are going to be some kick-ass sites.

Fasten your seatbelts, folks. It's gonna be a heck of a ride from here on out.

> *"The loss of liberty in general would soon follow the suppression of the liberty of the press; for it is an essential branch of liberty, so perhaps it is the best preservative of the whole."*
> —John Peter Zenger

Mary's Page   Eleanor Adams   Archives

Email me!

This site last updated: 01/25/29
Visitors since this site was born: **20,756,491**

January 31, 2029

Wow. When I make a resolution, I make a resolution!

Polly Wright and Sam Hain have asked me to write content for the premiere "issues" of their 'zines. Naturally, I agreed.

I've also been invited to speak at a gathering of pagans and others up in Nevada City. Kinda like preaching to the choir, I think. Nevada City is called "Nirvana Silly" by some who think "new age" stuff is too weird for words. (These are the same folks, of course, who pronounce "new age" to rhyme with "sewage.") But I'll do it, though, since I need the practice and because these people are allies. We need all those we can get.

I've received my share of brutally nasty emails lately, of course. I don't care. I don't even read the flames anymore. I've got spam filters set up to automatically delete such things.

I've also gotten some really nice emails. All my old friends, it seems, have written their words of encouragement. Cat, Father Montoya, and Lorelei have offered to help in any way they can. They're such great people. I miss Cat and especially Lorelei. I should go visit them when I can.

Date: February 4, 2029
To: mary@voice_of_reason.com
From: heyjude@beatles4ever.ws
Subject: Re: Should I do this?

Mary:

Yeah. I think you should.

You said you wanted to become an activist. Well, this is your opportunity to get out there and learn from the pros. The Freethought Underground has been canvassing the nation for years. They're very good at what they do. I know you want to be more in the spotlight than the Underground, but this would be a great learning experience for you. So accept their invitation. Go "on tour" with them. What have you got to lose?

Jude

February 5, 2029

Well, Vicki and Jude both agree that I should basically take over for Sam Hain and Polly Wright. They'll both be busy with their online forums, and someone will be needed to be the visible "leader" representing alternative sexuality and paganism.

I tried talking Vicki into handling some of that responsibility, but as she so correctly pointed out, someone's gotta pay the bills here at home.

So I guess I've committed to this. Father Montoya will pick me up next Monday and off I'll go.

The staff at school is being very supportive of this. I don't think it's surprising any of them that I'll be leaving.

Damn, I'm going to miss Vicki while I'm on the road.

2/7/29

Gene Sisco. What kind of man is he, really?

This is the question that's been uppermost in my mind ever since our talk about Mary last September. And I've been asking the question of others, including many of my closest friends in The Saviors.

The answers I've been receiving are mixed. While there are some who obviously consider him to be above reproach, there are others who consider him a sham as a true Christian.

These folks consider him to be nothing more than a power-hungry zealot. And more than one has said they would not trust him as far as they could carry him.

From the days before Internet regulation, I recall seeing sites devoted to denigrating Gene and his ministry. The word "sociopath" was bandied about quite a bit. Could these heathens possibly have been onto something? Could Jefferson Paine be close to the truth?

I admit my own feelings toward Gene have soured over the years, but has his true nature been something neither Paul nor I have seen as anything more than the most casual glimpse?

I think I'll keep a closer watch on my old friend from now on.

Queer and Now

Editorial by
Mary Christopher

You know, it's true what they say: The firmer the fist of repression is clenched, the more things will slip through the fingers.

Look at how things are today. My dear father (and I don't use that word sarcastically; at heart, he's a wonderful man and I love him) is still in office, a vicious gay-basher is his VP, our civil rights are eroding more and more every day... And yet, here we are. Online. Preaching acceptance and understanding of the non-heterosexual lifestyle.

The work of dedicated activists over the past several years has made this possible, and damn it, we can make a lot more than this possible, too! Look how far the GLBT movement came. In the fifty years after the Stonewall Riot, acceptance of gays in the mainstream world grew by leaps and bounds.

And we can do it again.

Get back out of the closets, my friends. It's time to stop hiding. Hiding only encourages the continuation of oppression. Only by standing up to it can we liberate ourselves. This premiere issue of *Queer and Now* contains a wealth of information on how each and every one of us can be an activist. Read it. Be inspired by it. Be motivated by it.

[Enter]

This site uses Early Bird Protection.
Who's Afraid of the Big, Bad Brother?

February 12, 2029

I'm currently in southern California with Father Montoya. We're in the town of Lake Elsinore for the night. We've been working our way south from Sacramento. He's been stopping at New Anglican Churches along the way, mostly just to check on things and introduce me around, but occasionally he'll do a service.

He's a very gifted preacher, very sincere and amiable. I just can't swallow everything he says. Though to be fair, he hasn't really been doing much preaching of the Bible, but has been preaching universal acceptance of others. When he introduces me during his sermons (if you can call them that), he actually has me say a few words about Wicca. Much to my amazement, I'm finding the NAC folks are pretty okay with it. Or rather, they're okay with me believing it.

And that's really his point. He's trying to show his congregations that other religions aren't necessarily a threat. That's a fantastic thing, I think, because that's really the root of the problems we have: misunderstandings and feelings of being threatened, whether true or not.

We tend to make assumptions, too. We lump people into these big, faceless groups and give those groups particular traits. I think by doing that, we sometimes forget that a group is made up of individuals, and individuals are unique. But worse, it makes us stop thinking of them as actual human beings! It's so easy to just think of a group as "the enemy." It's a lot harder to do that when you think of them as individual people, rather than masses of creatures with the same label.

Would we even have any huge problems if we stopped doing this? Would we have prejudice? Would we have war? I tend to doubt it.

Well, that got deeper than I expected it to! Anyway, Father Montoya and I will leave tomorrow for San Diego, and from there, we'll cut across to Arizona. Polly Wright is in Phoenix, and I'll meet up with her there. She's apparently got a live chat arranged on her site. Dunno what's up with that.

I miss Vicki like crazy. We talk on the phone every day, but still… I need her close to me.

Queer and Now Chatroom

Powered by Early Bird Chat

Now Chatting:

BigJohn
Lucky13
MaryC
MSNBC
PollyW
Rainbo
Str8Guy

MSNBC
Mary, your mother calls homosexuality an abomination. How does that affect your chosen lifestyle?

Str8Guy
You faggots make me sick.

MaryC
My lifestyle isn't "chosen" any more than Str8Guy's is. Do you recall a conscious moment when you deliberately chose to be straight, Str8Guy?

Rainbo
Str8, you're an asshole.

Str8Guy
Better to be one than to fuck one.

MSNBC
Be that as it may, Mary, you've got quite a lot of public opinion going against you.

BigJohn
How do you know, Str8? Let's give it a try and then you can decide.

PollyW
Mary wouldn't have such an uphill battle if the press would quit being so cowardly. The fact that you're here at all, MSNBC, impresses me.

Lucky13
Good one, Johnny!

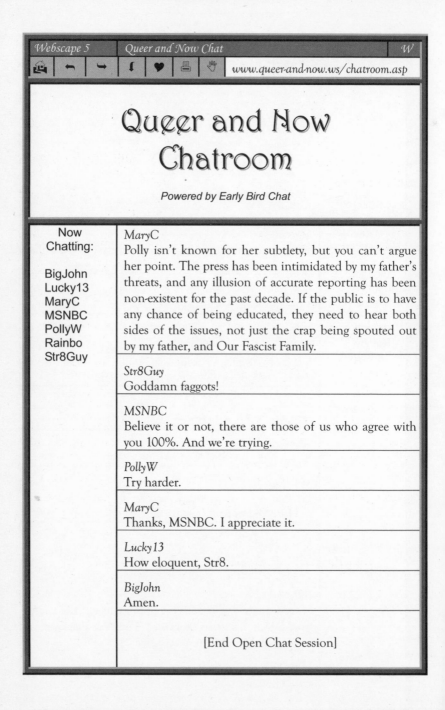

Webscape 5   *Queer and Now Chat*   *W*

www.queer-and-now.ws/chatroom.asp

Queer and Now Chatroom

Powered by Early Bird Chat

Now Chatting:

BigJohn
Lucky13
MaryC
MSNBC
PollyW
Rainbo
Str8Guy

MaryC
Polly isn't known for her subtlety, but you can't argue her point. The press has been intimidated by my father's threats, and any illusion of accurate reporting has been non-existent for the past decade. If the public is to have any chance of being educated, they need to hear both sides of the issues, not just the crap being spouted out by my father, and Our Fascist Family.

Str8Guy
Goddamn faggots!

MSNBC
Believe it or not, there are those of us who agree with you 100%. And we're trying.

PollyW
Try harder.

MaryC
Thanks, MSNBC. I appreciate it.

Lucky13
How eloquent, Str8.

BigJohn
Amen.

[End Open Chat Session]

February 23, 2029

Ah, Amarillo. Seems I'm retracing the route that took me to California in the first place.

Much to my surprise, Lorelei met Polly and me in Flagstaff. She's joined me for a while on this cross-country trek. I'd wanted to head down to San Antonio to see Cat, but she was one step ahead of me, and met us here in Amarillo!

The three of us have been having a blast for the past few days, hitting all the malls and hanging out in coffee shops talking half the night away. I love these women. If I could choose my own family, I'd want Cat as my mother and Lorelei as my sister.

There was some sad news, though. Cat told me that Black Eagle passed away last year of cancer. I was stunned. I remembered talking with him as he drove me across New Mexico and Arizona. I may have only known him for a couple days, but when Cat told me he'd died, I actually got tears in my eyes.

Anyway, tomorrow night is a big freethought rally in Martin Luther King, Jr. Park, and I'm giving a speech. I'm nervous, but with these friends behind me, I know I'll do fine.

I haven't been on email much at all. Jude and I have exchanged only very brief hellos.

I spoke to Vicki on the phone tonight and nearly cried, I miss her so much. If I could afford it, I'd fly home to spend a weekend with her before continuing my "tour."

But that doesn't look like it's in the cards for a while.

"I have to admit to being more than a little nervous up here. This is, after all, a Brights' rally. And when I hear the word 'Bright,' I think of atheists and agnostics, primarily. And I'm neither of those things.

"As such, I'm probably not what many of you think of as a Bright or freethinker, either. But a very dear friend of mine, an atheist, once told me that a true freethinker was someone who doesn't allow dogma to affect his or her views on anything. Not just about religion.

"So I guess that's why I'm here tonight. I've come before you in order to ask your help. I'm here to ask all of you to really be freethinkers in the broadest sense.

"You see, the people who are oppressing you—and by that, I naturally mean my father and the vermin he hangs out with—are the same people who are oppressing many others in our country.

"Now, many of you are aware of this. And many of you are already doing what you can to support these other minorities. And we all appreciate that. But there must be more.

"It's easy for them to look at gays and say, 'It's only a small percentage of the population.' Or to look at Wiccans and say, 'It's an even smaller percentage.' But remember... there's a reason that the gay movement later became the gay and lesbian movement. And later, the gay, lesbian, and bisexual movement. And later still, the gay, lesbian, bisexual and transgendered movement. And recently, the gay, lesbian, bisexual, transgendered, and poly movement. The reason is because there is strength in numbers. And all these groups shared a common enemy, a common persecution.

"Add up all the people in these alternative sexuality communities. Add in all the practitioners of non-Judeo-Christian religions. Add all the Brights: the atheists, agnostics, humanists, non-theistic Unitarians, Taoists, et cetera... And soon you'll have a number that's not such a small percentage of the population anymore.

"Our enemies are, at heart, bullies. And bullies only pick on those smaller than themselves. They don't like being stood up to.

"With a united front, we can stand up to these bullies. But without such a front, the persecution will continue. And not one of us here tonight wants such a future. For any of us.

"Please. Become what my friend called 'true freethinkers.' Join with the rest of us and make a stand. Our future depends on it. Let's make it a Bright future."

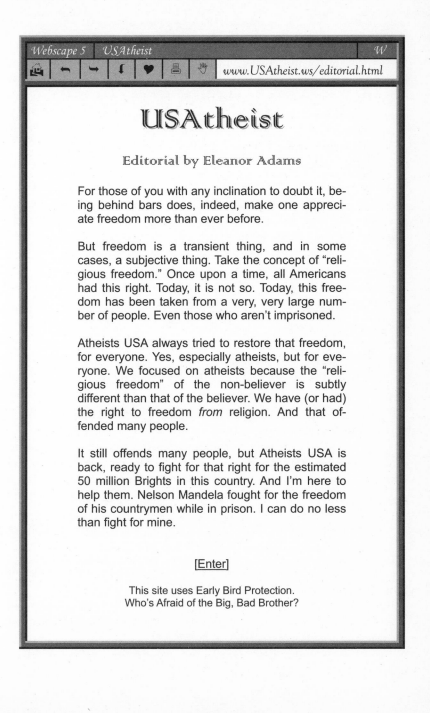

USAtheist

Editorial by Eleanor Adams

For those of you with any inclination to doubt it, being behind bars does, indeed, make one appreciate freedom more than ever before.

But freedom is a transient thing, and in some cases, a subjective thing. Take the concept of "religious freedom." Once upon a time, all Americans had this right. Today, it is not so. Today, this freedom has been taken from a very, very large number of people. Even those who aren't imprisoned.

Atheists USA always tried to restore that freedom, for everyone. Yes, especially atheists, but for everyone. We focused on atheists because the "religious freedom" of the non-believer is subtly different than that of the believer. We have (or had) the right to freedom *from* religion. And that offended many people.

It still offends many people, but Atheists USA is back, ready to fight for that right for the estimated 50 million Brights in this country. And I'm here to help them. Nelson Mandela fought for the freedom of his countrymen while in prison. I can do no less than fight for mine.

[Enter]

This site uses Early Bird Protection.
Who's Afraid of the Big, Bad Brother?

March 24, 2029

Ever since Cat told me of Black Eagle's death, I've been thinking a lot about our days together and the talks we had. We talked a lot about marriage laws, and why ours have become so restrictive. I don't think back then I really understood what he meant, but I do now. I'm a lot more educated about things than I was then.

And I understand now why he was bothered when people say marriage is under attack, or that the institution is being undermined by such things as the idea of gay marriage. I get irritated, too. Because no one has ever been able to explain to me just what het married couples "lose" if a gay couple, or a group of people, is allowed to marry. No one can give any real explanation of how marriage is being "destroyed." There's no harm being done that I can see.

Black Eagle pointed out that it wasn't so terribly long ago that the same things were being said when interracial couples wanted to marry. It's the same old prejudices, the same small-minded zealotry.

And the irony is that the "institution" of marriage isn't anywhere near as sacred or traditional as these people believe. Black Eagle told me about the history of marriage in our culture, and (amazingly) I still remember much of what he said.

I remember he told me that in the early years of American history, the wife became a sort of possession when she got married, losing some of her rights. She couldn't own property anymore, or sign contracts. Any money she earned had to be given to their husbands.

He said the nature of marriage itself has changed a lot over the centuries, largely due to economy. When people lived off the land, marriage was very different than it is today. Things like dowries and arranged marriages were common.

And pretty much any type of arrangement you can think of has been institutionalized somewhere/somewhen in the world. Didn't destroy those cultures, so what are we afraid of?

My own research has revealed that the "tradition" of marriage has even changed a lot within Christianity. Before the 15th Century, the church didn't even stress the importance of consent with a married couple, and before the 16th it wasn't even required by the church to have marriages performed by a priest and witnessed by others.

There's simply never been a universal "norm" when it comes to marriage, and it's just asinine for people today to insist on its sacredness!

So why do they?

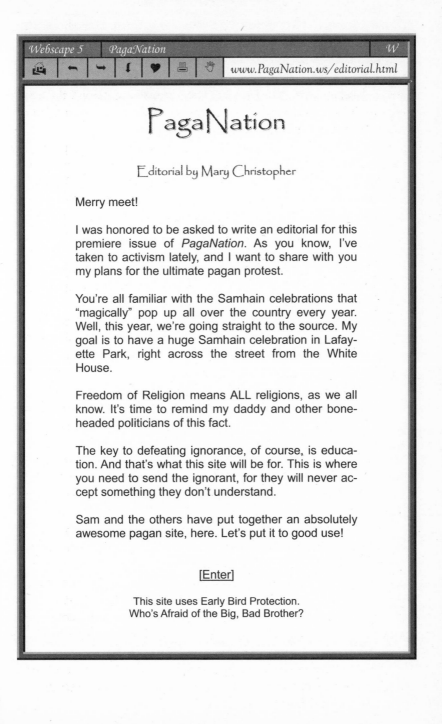

PagaNation

Editorial by Mary Christopher

Merry meet!

I was honored to be asked to write an editorial for this premiere issue of *PagaNation*. As you know, I've taken to activism lately, and I want to share with you my plans for the ultimate pagan protest.

You're all familiar with the Samhain celebrations that "magically" pop up all over the country every year. Well, this year, we're going straight to the source. My goal is to have a huge Samhain celebration in Lafayette Park, right across the street from the White House.

Freedom of Religion means ALL religions, as we all know. It's time to remind my daddy and other bone-headed politicians of this fact.

The key to defeating ignorance, of course, is education. And that's what this site will be for. This is where you need to send the ignorant, for they will never accept something they don't understand.

Sam and the others have put together an absolutely awesome pagan site, here. Let's put it to good use!

[Enter]

This site uses Early Bird Protection.
Who's Afraid of the Big, Bad Brother?

The Voice of Reason
Lemme Show You Pictures of My Kids

Boy, I tell ya… This feels good.

Okay, yes… I'm proud of some of the articles I've put online here. And I'm glad I've been able to provide a forum for Mary Christopher's budding activism. And certainly, I'm happy that I've been able to help the Freethought Underground by allowing them the use of my site for private communications.

But this… This feels good.

I'm referring, of course, to the fact that I am partly responsible for not one, not two, but three very important voices of American minorities to once again be heard. The launches of *Queer and Now*, *USAtheist*, and *PagaNation* all went without a hitch. Oh yes, Big Brother came a'knockin'… but he went away with his tail between his legs.

And you wouldn't believe how many hits those sites are getting. It's inspiring. I'm very proud to have been able to help out.

<u>Mary's Page</u>   <u>Eleanor Adams</u>   <u>Archives</u>

<u>Email me!</u>

This site last updated: 04/05/29
Visitors since this site was born: **22,609,491**

Sacramento—Mary Christopher has become something of an American institution in her own right. Being the President's daughter has certainly helped her notoriety, but her impassioned speeches on civil rights for oppressed minorities, including alternate sexualities and religions, have garnered her the recognition and admiration of many civil rights leaders across the country.

Tonight she will receive recognition from the newly resurrected ACLU. In a special ceremony, Ms. Christopher will be lauded in the ACLU's First Annual Activist Awards. The awards will be, as explained by ACLU President Bruce Clark, "...to recognize those individuals in our country who work to support civil liberties of the oppressed, often at their own peril."

Others scheduled for recognition tonight are Father Emilio Montoya of the New Anglican Church, Polly Wright of American Queers, Jefferson Paine of The Voice of Reason, and the imprisoned Libertarian Presidential Candidate Michael Lee and Atheists USA founder Eleanor Adams.

While the ceremony will not be televised, it will be able to be seen live tonight on The Voice of Reason website, www.voice_of_reason.com, at 6:00 P.M. Pacific Time.

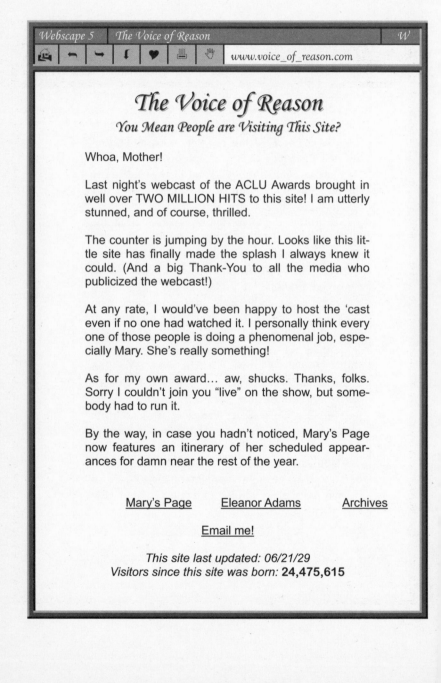

The Voice of Reason
You Mean People are Visiting This Site?

Whoa, Mother!

Last night's webcast of the ACLU Awards brought in well over TWO MILLION HITS to this site! I am utterly stunned, and of course, thrilled.

The counter is jumping by the hour. Looks like this little site has finally made the splash I always knew it could. (And a big Thank-You to all the media who publicized the webcast!)

At any rate, I would've been happy to host the 'cast even if no one had watched it. I personally think every one of those people is doing a phenomenal job, especially Mary. She's really something!

As for my own award… aw, shucks. Thanks, folks. Sorry I couldn't join you "live" on the show, but somebody had to run it.

By the way, in case you hadn't noticed, Mary's Page now features an itinerary of her scheduled appearances for damn near the rest of the year.

<u>Mary's Page</u>   <u>Eleanor Adams</u>   <u>Archives</u>

<u>Email me!</u>

This site last updated: 06/21/29
Visitors since this site was born: **24,475,615**

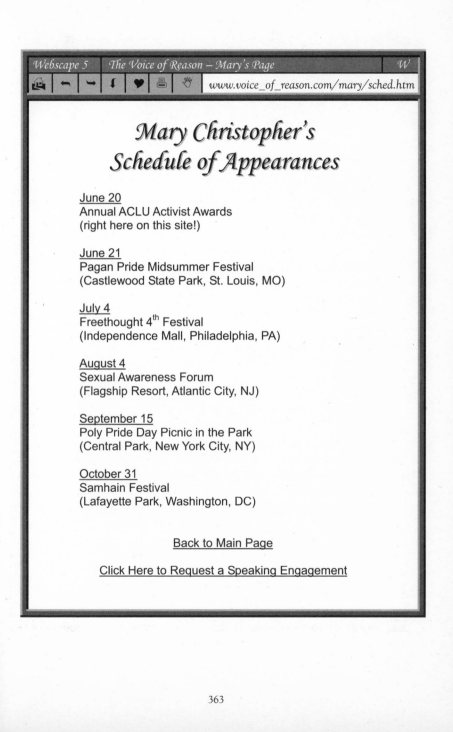

Mary Christopher's Schedule of Appearances

June 20
Annual ACLU Activist Awards
(right here on this site!)

June 21
Pagan Pride Midsummer Festival
(Castlewood State Park, St. Louis, MO)

July 4
Freethought 4th Festival
(Independence Mall, Philadelphia, PA)

August 4
Sexual Awareness Forum
(Flagship Resort, Atlantic City, NJ)

September 15
Poly Pride Day Picnic in the Park
(Central Park, New York City, NY)

October 31
Samhain Festival
(Lafayette Park, Washington, DC)

Back to Main Page

Click Here to Request a Speaking Engagement

Date: July 1, 2029
To: biwitched1@anon-e-mail.com
From: mary@voice_of_reason.com
Subject: Re: Miss You!

Vicki:

Oh, honey, I miss you, too. Y'know, I'm actually beginning to make money doing this. Maybe you can quit your job soon and join me on the road? Even before the big Samhain festival.

Things are really, really busy for me. I'm in New Hope, Pennsylvania right now, doing the autograph thing. This is a really cute little town. You'd like it. It's like Guerneville crossed with Nevada City, except it's ninety-some degrees outside with eighty percent humidity. I swear, you walk ten feet out your front door and you're soaked with sweat! How can people live with this?

Anyway, New Hope has lots of little witchy shops and whatnot, and that's where I'm drawing the biggest crowds. You'd love this place. But in the fall, I think. Not summer.

Wednesday is the big Freethought 4th celebration. Robert Green will be there, as will lots of freethinkers from the Philly area, including Delaware and New Jersey.

Frankly, I'm amazed that we're not encountering more in the way of opposition. I've often wondered if my father really did call off the bounty hunt for Underground leaders. Maybe he really did. But even if he didn't, it's not like it was back when Eleanor was captured. The Underground has got some damned impressive "security" forces. No way is some schmuck with a pistol gonna drag any of us off to the nearest FBI office.

I'll call you Wednesday night and let you know how everything went. Love you!

Mary

Pocatello—Three people were killed and over one hundred others injured, some severely, in a riot in Ross Park, where a freethought rally was being held.

Leslianne Buckwalter, 24, of Pocatello; Henry Tilson McGentry, 48, of Sun Valley; and Erin Marie Cheng, 16, of Salt Lake City, Utah, were pronounced dead at the scene by rescue personnel. All three had been beaten severely.

Among the others injured was Father Emilio Montoya, who remains in critical condition in Pocatello Regional Medical Center.

Witnesses say the riot was instigated by ten to fifteen individuals who infiltrated the event and attacked the assemblage of atheists and other Brights. Names have not been released, but it is rumored that they were members of Our Father's Family, the ultra-conservative Christian organization headed by Vice-President Gene Sisco.

The White House has thus far refused to comment.

8/27/29

Lord forgive me for thinking such a thing if I happen to be wrong, but was this horrible turn of events in Idaho actually Gene's doing? I must be mad. To think that Paul's closest friend could be responsible for such a terrible thing.

But the words of my friends keep coming back to me. "Fiend," one called him.

Surely there are those with resources who've been keeping close watch on his activities. I wonder what they could know.

Sounding OFF
By J. E. Cooper

Tracking Gene Sisco and Our Father's Family Since 2015.

Issue No. 28   **Summer, 2029**

OFF Responsible for Riot in Pocatello

It was, friends, one of the most disturbing things I've seen in my entire life.

Responding to a tip from one of *Sounding OFF's* subscribers, I attended the freethought rally in Pocatello this past weekend. (Hence the slightly late mailing of this issue.) The tipster had heard that OFF members would be infiltrating the rally in the hopes of disrupting it somehow.

At last count, four dead (three at the scene and a fourth the following day in the hospital). Scores are still hospitalized.

At least three known OFFicers were identified by rally attendees. I, myself, recognized Feldon Reese, whom I'm sure you'll remember is a frequent tool of Sisco. I last wrote of him after the 2022 "disturbance" at a Wiccan faire in Vermont that put over 100 folks in the hospital with food poisoning. Reese later allegedly bragged that he'd dumped a vial of salmonella bacteria into a large vat of stew.

Unfortunately, then as now, no one caught him in the act of doing anything that could directly implicate Sisco or OFF. But I certainly don't doubt their guilt.

Witnesses have described seeing the OFFicers instigate the violence. It began with heckling of speakers, escalated to mild roughhousing, and ultimately to outright battery. Some witnesses mention seeing the use of weapons, which may have been baseball bats or even metal pipes.

The injuries to the deceased, according to my buddy in the Pocatello Police, were severe. Broken bones, one crushed skull, and so on. Not the work of fists, in other words.

From what I was able to see, Feldon Reese acted as coordinator of the violence. I never saw him assault anyone personally, but he was clearly directing some of the action, so to speak.

(Continued on p. 3)

Inside This Issue...

29 August 2029

Gene's followers have certainly done it now. I spoke to him about it this morning, and to my amazement, he showed only the faintest hint of remorse. I told him a press conference was in order, so he could condemn the assault (for that's really what it was). But he declined, stating that he would address it in his next television broadcast.

I told him this was not good enough, but he insisted that it was a matter that involved his organization, not his position as Vice President.

Perhaps true, but issuing an apology and condemnation from the White House would, I think, do more to make amends and defuse any potential problems that could come of it. But when I told him this, he laughed in my face. "Since when do you care about the potential problems that could exist for these infidels?" he asked.

Again, he's right. I never have given much attention to the matters involving non-religious people. But that doesn't mean I think they deserve to be beaten with baseball bats.

Gene's attitude toward this situation is just one more indication that I may have erred in judgment when making him my running mate.

8/29/29

This is unbelievable. There are many in The Saviors who are utterly convinced that Sisco was responsible for the riot in Pocatello, that he ordered it to happen!

I spoke to Paul about this tonight, but he glared at me as though I'd just told him that I'd been unfaithful. His devotion to Sisco is so strong. I know now that I can never broach this subject with him again.

But what do I do? Report him to the police? The FBI? He's the Vice-President. No one would take me seriously.

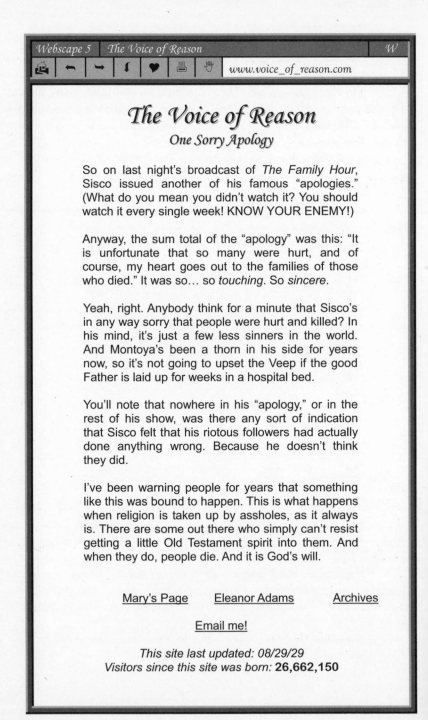

The Voice of Reason
One Sorry Apology

So on last night's broadcast of *The Family Hour*, Sisco issued another of his famous "apologies." (What do you mean you didn't watch it? You should watch it every single week! KNOW YOUR ENEMY!)

Anyway, the sum total of the "apology" was this: "It is unfortunate that so many were hurt, and of course, my heart goes out to the families of those who died." It was so… so *touching*. So *sincere*.

Yeah, right. Anybody think for a minute that Sisco's in any way sorry that people were hurt and killed? In his mind, it's just a few less sinners in the world. And Montoya's been a thorn in his side for years now, so it's not going to upset the Veep if the good Father is laid up for weeks in a hospital bed.

You'll note that nowhere in his "apology," or in the rest of his show, was there any sort of indication that Sisco felt that his riotous followers had actually done anything wrong. Because he doesn't think they did.

I've been warning people for years that something like this was bound to happen. This is what happens when religion is taken up by assholes, as it always is. There are some out there who simply can't resist getting a little Old Testament spirit into them. And when they do, people die. And it is God's will.

<u>Mary's Page</u>   <u>Eleanor Adams</u>   <u>Archives</u>

<u>Email me!</u>

This site last updated: 08/29/29
Visitors since this site was born: **26,662,150**

August 30, 2029

I'm still heartbroken over the events in Pocatello. I saw the vids of those poor people being beaten, and I can't get the images out of my head.

I'm so relieved that no one I personally knew was killed. I was terrified of that. But poor Father Montoya. I can't believe anyone would attack a priest in such a fashion! He's such a lovely human being... I pray that he recovers quickly.

Jefferson said he'd do some digging and find the addresses of the families of those who died. I want to do something for them, but don't know what.

I've got two weeks before my next speech, in NYC. Then six more weeks of canvassing before the Samhain gig.

I have to admit I'm nervous about that particular event. As with every event I've attended, there have been protesters. But with this one, I half expect my mother to be in the front of the crowd, carrying the biggest picket sign.

MRS. CHRISTOPHER >STOP<

REASON TO BELIEVE DAUGHTER IN DANGER >STOP<

THIS IS NOT A THREAT >STOP<

IT IS A CONCERNED WARNING >STOP<

PARCEL AT MCPHERSON STATION POST OFFICE >STOP<

CHECK WITH POSTMASTER >STOP<

THIS IS NOT A JOKE >STOP<

PLEASE DO NOT DISREGARD >STOP<

*"Love withers under constraint: its very essence is liberty: it
is compatible neither with obedience, jealousy, nor fear: it
is there most pure, perfect, and unlimited where its votaries
live in confidence, equality, and un-reserve."*

"That's from Percy Bysshe Shelley, one of my girlfriend's favorite poets. I think everyone here can agree with his sentiment, can't we? Today, we're here to celebrate that sentiment, to proclaim pride in loving unconstrained.

"Now, I'm the furthest thing from an expert on this subject. I've only recently come to think of myself as poly-oriented. I have no actual poly experience, and can't guarantee I ever will. But I definitely am poly-positive. I know it's not unnatural, that it's not deserving of the ridicule so often heaped upon it.

"There are so many misconceptions about polyamory out there in the world. Lots of people still equate it with swinging or with polygamy in the sexist religion sense. And there's also a severe discomfort factor. Many straights, gays and lesbians used to be uncomfortable with the notion of someone loving both sexes, hence their dismissal and/or condemnation of bisexuality. Likewise, many monogamists today – no matter their sexual preference – are often uncomfortable with the notion of someone loving multiple people.

"The discomfort and misunderstanding are almost entirely based on unfamiliarity. We humans tend to fear or hate what we don't understand. But once we learn about things, the fear and hatred disappear for the most part. This is always the way to deal with phobias, stereotypes and negative impressions. Learn about them.

"This has always been one of the main tasks of the Freethought Underground, incidentally. And as you all know, I have made it my goal to unite all the different factions that are being discriminated against by our government. The alternative sexuality group might be fairly united now, with bisexuals and polys welcome under the old rainbow, but we still hold others at arm's length. Many polys are pagan of one stripe or another, and that's pretty great. But many polys are uncomfortable with Christians. Many are uncomfortable with atheists. Some are even uncomfortable with monogamists.

"But we can't allow this to continue. At the risk of sounding like a recording loop, I have to stress this. We must have a unified front, cemented by mutual understanding and acceptance. So I urge you all to put aside whatever feelings of discomfort you may have, and reach out your hands to help support everyone who's up against the same wall as you."

9/21/29

It's like something out of a bad detective story. The parcel was waiting, as the telegram said. The contents were disturbing. First was a letter signed by "J. E. Cooper," saying that Gene Sisco has become increasingly angered by Mary's activities, and plans to "deal with her."

Also in the packet were copies of a newsletter this Cooper person evidently publishes. It's amateurish, no doubt printed on a home computer and mailed anonymously to a private list. There were several of them, dating back nearly a decade. It's essentially a smear sheet against Gene and his group's activities. It's disturbing to think that anyone would devote so much time to such an endeavor.

Part of me just wants to write this man off as disturbed, paranoid, and maybe even dangerous. Certainly, that's how Paul would see him, which is why I shan't bring this to his attention.

But another part of me (my maternal side?) is afraid what Cooper says is true. If even a couple of the items detailed in his newsletter are accurate, then Gene Sisco is nothing less than reprehensible, if not – as one of the newsletters asserted – a dangerous psychopath.

No. I cannot disregard this warning, even though I find it hard to believe that Gene even considers Mary's activities to be threatening, let alone warranting some sort of "dealing with." But I would rather be wrong about that, embarrassingly so, than to pay no attention and have Cooper's warning come true.

The problem is that he has given me no details! No time, place, or method of whatever is supposed to happen. He claims he will contact me again when more information is available, and that I should alert the White House switchboard to accept his call and to put him through to me immediately.

I can easily do that. I want to do more, but cannot. It is infuriating!

"Everything began just fine. Yeah, there were protesters there, but everyone expected that. Mary was on stage, and after the cheering died down, she gave her speech. And right in the middle of it... It was unreal." –*Elsbeth Morgan, Wilmington, DE*

"I really didn't see it happen. I was distracted by people next to me screaming. I heard the shot, but never saw anything until I saw her lying on the stage." –*Holly Kline, 29, Frederick, MD*

"Mary was on the stage, talking about Samhain. Then there was this big commotion and uproar at the front, and then I saw her mother running across the stage, screaming her name. There's a lot of yelling, then a gunshot. Even as far back as I was, the crowd just went nuts. Next thing I know, I'm on the ground. Got stepped on six times before I got back up. By that point, I couldn't see anything on the stage, there were so many people there." –*Bill Dent, 18, York, PA*

"I was off to the side. I saw everything. She was shot right in the chest. I mean, boom. Right dead center in the middle of the chest. Goddess, there was just so much blood." –*Lindsay Diamond, 23, Dover, DE*

"After Pocatello, who could possibly be surprised by this? It's a terrible shame. Just awful." –*J. T. Carlson, 65, Atlantic City, NJ*

"Why? That's what I wanna know. Sure, lots of people don't like what she's done, but why would anyone want her dead?" –*Al Shafer, Richmond, VA*

Washington—First Lady Sarah Christopher is dead, killed by a single gunshot to the chest.

The tragedy occurred last night, as the Freethought Underground, led by Mary Christopher, hosted a Halloween Celebration in Lafayette Park, across Pennsylvania Avenue from the White House. This was done over the objections of the Vice-President, Reverend Gene Sisco, who called the celebration "Satanic."

After firing the one fatal bullet, the alleged gunman was subdued by several celebrants around him. Police have the man in custody, a Mr. Feldon Reese. At this time, no motive has been suggested.

Speculation exists, however, about whether Sarah Christopher was, in fact, his intended victim.

The White House has issued no further comment at this time.

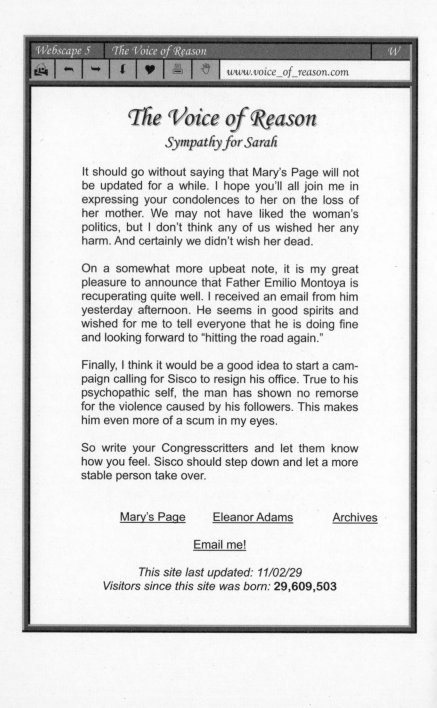

www.voice_of_reason.com

The Voice of Reason
Sympathy for Sarah

It should go without saying that Mary's Page will not be updated for a while. I hope you'll all join me in expressing your condolences to her on the loss of her mother. We may not have liked the woman's politics, but I don't think any of us wished her any harm. And certainly we didn't wish her dead.

On a somewhat more upbeat note, it is my great pleasure to announce that Father Emilio Montoya is recuperating quite well. I received an email from him yesterday afternoon. He seems in good spirits and wished for me to tell everyone that he is doing fine and looking forward to "hitting the road again."

Finally, I think it would be a good idea to start a campaign calling for Sisco to resign his office. True to his psychopathic self, the man has shown no remorse for the violence caused by his followers. This makes him even more of a scum in my eyes.

So write your Congresscritters and let them know how you feel. Sisco should step down and let a more stable person take over.

Mary's Page   Eleanor Adams   Archives

Email me!

This site last updated: 11/02/29
Visitors since this site was born: **29,609,503**

4 November 2029

Oh, God, why have you allowed this to happen? Sarah was as devout a woman as they come. Yet you permitted this atrocity. Am I supposed to be grateful that Sarah had a productive and mostly happy life? If so, then you must help me to focus on that, for all I feel now is rage and grief.

Gene warns me not to become angry with you, and I am trying. But you are not offering any explanations, either, and I am becoming more despondent daily.

Gene himself is little help. He continues to hint in his utterly unsubtle fashion that he is quite capable of taking on the mantle of the Presidency, should I consider myself "too distraught to function properly."

I'm half tempted to let him do so. I confess my mind isn't on the job. It's only been four days since Sarah's death, but I can't imagine ever not feeling this way again.

November 5, 2029

It makes no sense! Why was she there? To protest? It didn't seem that way. And where were her stupid Secret Service goons?

The bullet must have been meant for me. No one would have any reason to think she'd be there. She probably saved my life.

I should have taken Vicki's advice and invested in body armor. I will, assuming I ever speak in public again. Reese could've been just a lone crackpot, but who knows?

Vicki arrived yesterday, and I'm so glad she's here. But she wasn't comfortable staying in the White House with me, so she took a hotel room. Guess I can't blame her. Dad's been pretty much unapproachable, except from me.

He's devastated by this. I've never seen him so upset. So fragile. Seeing him this way, it's hard to remember the stressful times between us. Right now, he's just my daddy. And he's hurting the same as I am.

"My fellow Americans...

"First of all, I want to wish each and every one of you a safe and joyous holiday season. Secondly, I wish to thank the millions of you who have sent their condolences. Cards and emails are still pouring in, and I want you to know that they all mean a lot to me, and to Mary.

"Sarah was a remarkable woman, in many ways. Most of her detractors saw only one side of her, as detractors often do. I hold no ill feelings toward them. It's virtually impossible to get to know all about anyone in the public eye.

"As the press has already informed you, the authorities have concluded that Mary was the actual target of the assassin. I can only conclude that Sarah learned of this, somehow, and for reasons known only to her, chose to intervene personally. These may be mysteries forever unsolved.

"I can understand how many do not agree with my daughter's politics, with her lifestyle. Obviously, I have problems with them, myself. But I don't think I'll understand, as long as I live, how someone could have hated her enough to want to kill her.

"I disagree with the politics of liberals, but I do not wish any of them dead. This is America, and we're each entitled to our own opinion, whether or not our neighbor happens to like it.

"Well. Again, thank you for your condolences. Now for the purpose of this broadcast.

"This event weighs heavily on my heart. So heavily that I find I cannot devote my full energies to my duties. I had hoped that I would be able to put this atrocity behind me. But Sarah was my wife. My partner. Much of what I am is because of her.

"I am now, and ever shall be, significantly lessened without her. Because of this fact, I am increasingly of the opinion that I cannot carry out the duties of my job as you have come to expect.

"Therefore, effective noon tomorrow, I am resigning the office of President."

Year Ten

2030

Sounding OFF
By J. E. Cooper

Tracking Gene Sisco and Our Father's Family Since 2015.

Issue No. 29   **Winter, 2030**

No Regrets

It was, of course, not supposed to go that way.

I tipped off Sarah Christopher as soon as I received information. But by the time I was able to contact her, there was less than an hour before the Halloween bash was to begin. And she was supposed to send others in to protect Mary, not go herself.

We'll probably never know why she didn't, why she chose to go there in person. All we do know is that she's dead because of that decision.

Because of that, Mary's still alive. I'm glad of that, of course, but am sorry her mother died.

Do I regret sending her the information? Do I regret that fateful phone call that prompted her to rush out on stage and catch a bullet meant for her daughter? Of course not. I'm deeply sorry she's dead. But I'd do it again in a heartbeat.

I'm just glad she actually believed me, or at least played it safe by heeding my warnings, whether she thought they were correct or not.

Now, if only her husband had paid attention to all the material I've been sending him over the years. Or the police, for that matter.

Of course, he probably never received it, and the cops almost certainly passed it off as paranoid ravings. I'm sure his mail is screened very closely, and my stuff never makes it to his desk. One of these days, though, he'll figure it out.

Here's something a bit weird, though. Now that Sisco has gotten his dream, the Presidency, I'm not as worried as I have been in the past. I think he's finally snapped. He's finally screwed up to the point that people are going to see through his mask. He's on the verge of total

(Continued on p. 4)

Inside This Issue...

January 5, 2030

How different life is, already. Mother's been gone only a couple months, but it seems much longer. I know it's because we weren't exactly close for quite a while. I can't decide if that fact makes her death easier to take, or harder.

Dad and I began re-establishing our relationship right away. Nothing like a tragedy to bring people closer. But by the time Thanksgiving neared, he'd grown more and more quiet. By Christmas, he was closed off even from me. Before New Year's, he flew to Portland and then drove to the beach house on the Oregon coast. Wouldn't surprise me a bit if he decides to live there permanently. I haven't spoken to him for a few days.

The press cares nothing about what he's going through. They're too busy playing armchair psychologists, trying to figure out why he resigned. "Christopher's having a nervous breakdown," they say. Or worse.

I wish I could say they're wrong, but I honestly don't know if they're not at least partially right.

I'm back in Sacramento, now. Vicki quit her job, since Mother had a rather sizeable insurance policy, with me as the sole beneficiary. We won't be hurting for money for a while. Definitely not the way I wanted to become financially independent.

And the speaking offers are pouring in, many of which are paying gigs. I have no desire to do this for the rest of my life, but with Sisco now in the Oval Office, my activism is more important than ever. At least I'll be able to have Vicki with me as I tour the country.

20 January 2030

I have been sequestered here in Rockaway Beach for two weeks, but to no avail. I had hoped the ocean would clear my mind, as it so often has in the past. There has always been something about the wildness of the Coast that cleanses me. But my mind continues to feel as foggy as the weather here.

I keep thinking of the same things, over and over. First and foremost are the words I heard, which still ring in my ears. "There's been an incident." I can't even remember now which staff member told me. "There's been an incident." Such an understatement. Then, of course, I think of Sarah's loss and the emptiness is overwhelming.

And then I think of Mary, and I truly hate myself, because I'd very nearly succeeded in losing her, too, by shutting her out of my life. And I suppose I'm still doing it.

My own words haunt me. "This is America, and we're each entitled to our own opinion, whether or not our neighbor happens to like it."

Why has it taken me so long to understand this? I don't think I ever really understood until that press conference, until the words came unbidden and unexpectedly from my lips, that this is what Mary has been telling me all along. This is precisely what she's been crusading for. And, much to my shame, I realize that it's what those I've labeled "enemy" have been fighting for, too, since day one.

I have fought against them, against my daughter. I pasted her with labels meant to insult. I pushed her out of my home, out of my life. I have emotionally molested her. I'm a failure as a father.

Somehow, I must make amends. But I don't know how.

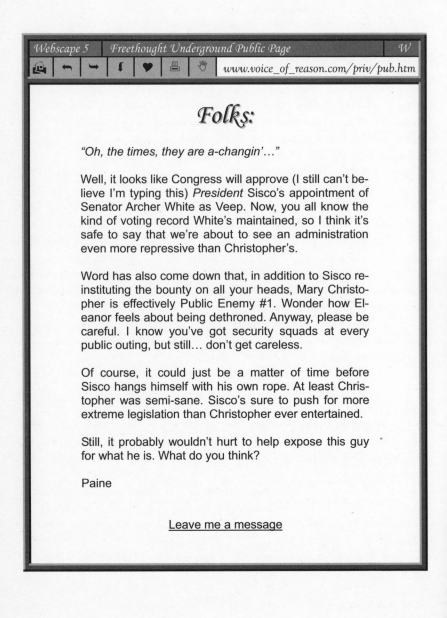

Inside the browser window:

Webscape 5 — *Freethought Underground Public Page* — *W*

www.voice_of_reason.com/priv/pub.htm

Folks:

"Oh, the times, they are a-changin'…"

Well, it looks like Congress will approve (I still can't believe I'm typing this) *President* Sisco's appointment of Senator Archer White as Veep. Now, you all know the kind of voting record White's maintained, so I think it's safe to say that we're about to see an administration even more repressive than Christopher's.

Word has also come down that, in addition to Sisco reinstituting the bounty on all your heads, Mary Christopher is effectively Public Enemy #1. Wonder how Eleanor feels about being dethroned. Anyway, please be careful. I know you've got security squads at every public outing, but still… don't get careless.

Of course, it could just be a matter of time before Sisco hangs himself with his own rope. At least Christopher was semi-sane. Sisco's sure to push for more extreme legislation than Christopher ever entertained.

Still, it probably wouldn't hurt to help expose this guy for what he is. What do you think?

Paine

<u>Leave me a message</u>

Date: January 25, 2030
To: heyjude@beatles4ever.ws
From: mary@voice_of_reason.com
Subject: Thanks.

Jude:

Thanks for your offer to come spend some time here. But I'm not going to be around Sacramento much over the next few months. I've got several offers for speaking engagements, and I'm going to accept a few of them.

Vicki will be coming with me. If we're in your neck of the woods, we'll let you know.

We're going to spend a few days in Guerneville, I think. I need to spend some time in the trees and reconnect with Mama Gaia. It's been too long since I've done that. So if I'm incommunicado for a while, that's why. I need a break from everything.

I'll call you next week, sweetie.

Mary

January 26, 2030

Vicki and I are pretty determined to move. Sacramento has been good for us in a lot of ways. Our living situation is good, and I couldn't have hoped for a better educational experience. But it's too crowded for us. We want to be in an area much less urban. We thought about Guerneville, but we both are really attracted to the idea of living in an intentional community, and there isn't one near there.

Actually, Southside Park is a co-housing IC. The folks here have all been very friendly to us, and have been very understanding about my situation. But I guess what Vicki and I are looking for is something with a great deal of close-knit intimacy. We want a community that is more like a family than just very friendly neighbors.

We've scheduled tours of a few ICs further north in California and in Oregon, over the next two months. Hopefully one of them will strike our mutual fancy.

February 2, 2030

As I write this, I'm lying in a sleeping bag in a redwood grove. Vicki and I spent three days in Guerneville with Margot. It was great to see her again, and we held an Imbolc ritual with the coven. It was nice, but I really wanted to have some solitude.

So this morning, we just started driving north. Eventually, we reached Rockefeller Forest. This is, Vicki tells me, the largest grove of old growth redwoods in the world. Being February, many of the campsites were vacant. We took one as far from the occupied sites as we could find.

It's pretty chilly, I have to say. But it's fantastic.

It's a new moon tonight, so it's very dark. But the sky is overcast, so even if we could see through the branches above us, we wouldn't see any stars.

Vicki built a cozy little fire and we held our own little ritual around it. It was very soothing. I'd been feeling so out-of-sorts, ever since mother's death. But now I feel more centered.

The fire feels wonderful; the air is so clean and fresh. I love these trees. I don't think I could ever be happy if I lived too far away from them. Visiting here has made my desire to move even stronger. I can't wait for our IC visits.

Soon it will be time to rejoin society, though, and dive back into being Ms. Activist. There's a rally in Portland in about three weeks. Afterward, I think I may visit Dad. It's not a very long drive from there to Rockaway Beach. And it's a beautiful drive, at that.

I'm getting so tired, though. I don't know how full-time activists do it. Of course, most of them are protesting some faceless concept or group. I've been protesting against people I love. It's been very hard, and frankly, I'm not sure I want to continue. I've already lost one parent.

Of course, with Dad being out of office, my protests will now be aimed mostly at Sisco, and that's not something I'll lose any sleep over.

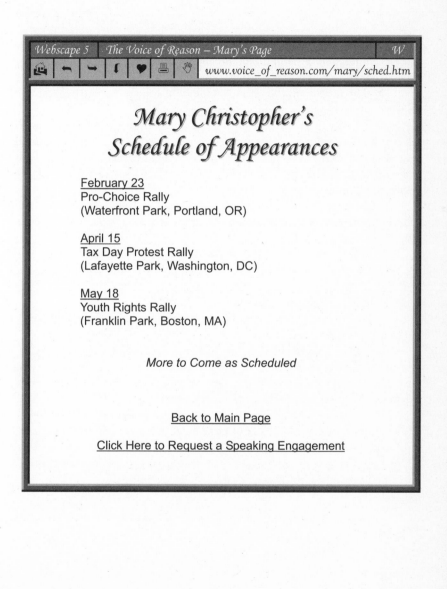

Webscape 5   *The Voice of Reason – Mary's Page*   *W*

`www.voice_of_reason.com/mary/sched.htm`

Mary Christopher's
Schedule of Appearances

February 23
Pro-Choice Rally
(Waterfront Park, Portland, OR)

April 15
Tax Day Protest Rally
(Lafayette Park, Washington, DC)

May 18
Youth Rights Rally
(Franklin Park, Boston, MA)

More to Come as Scheduled

Back to Main Page

Click Here to Request a Speaking Engagement

"Here's a quiz for you. Which of these two events is the more dangerous? Undergoing a natural childbirth in a modern healthcare facility, or undergoing an abortion at the same facility?

"The truth is that natural childbirth is a much more dangerous endeavor than having an abortion.

"Surveys taken from two hundred major hospitals during the years 2005 and 2006 – the last years such data were collected – show the rates of complications during pregnancy were in the range of twelve percent, with maternal death rates being in the neighborhood of a tenth of a percent, or one death in every one thousand births.

"By comparison, using the same hospitals and the same years of data collection, the rate of complication during abortion was a remarkably low one percent, and zero deaths.

"These are rates of complications and deaths *during* these events. It is true that the rates of complications and deaths during the year *following* the birth or abortion are different. The rates are higher for those having had abortions than having given birth.

"But if we combine them for an overall picture, abortion still comes out as the safer procedure.

"I'm not sharing these figures with you in order to promote abortion. I'm doing this because there is a large population of people under the mistaken impression that our ban on abortion has saved the lives of countless mothers. This is yet another lie by the anti-choice crowd.

"Today we'll be examining the anti-choice movement in great detail, and looking at ways in which we can make a difference in returning a woman's right to choose what to do with her body.

"We've got an impressive lineup of speakers today, including former Surgeon General Jo-Lynn Young. Thank you for coming."

24 February 2030

Mary surprised me today by coming to visit. She was in Portland, at a speaking engagement.

Vicki was with her. I confess I was disturbed initially. When she came to Washington after Sarah's death, I didn't see her. So this is the first Vicki and I have seen each other since she was evicted from the White House. Seems like a hundred years ago. Seems like yesterday.

I was taken aback, though, when she immediately hugged me tightly and, with tears in her eyes, expressed her condolences for Sarah's loss. Vicki knows quite well that Sarah couldn't stand her, or even the thought of the relationship she and Mary share. And she certainly has every right to hate me, all things considered.

But this girl... this caring, forgiving girl... actually comforted me as she would a friend. For the rest of their visit, I felt self-conscious and ashamed.

When we spoke of Sarah, Vicki squeezed Mary's hand in hers. It was one of the most touching gestures, and it made me choke up inside.

The truth is, their love for each other is so real it is palpable. Just watching how they interact is proof enough of that. They are as much like a married couple as Sarah and I had been. Maybe more than we had been, toward the end.

I don't think it ever occurred to me that this could be true. I think I'd always regarded their relationship... all same-sex relationships... as nothing more than perverted lust. Real love? That was never part of my perception of it.

They stayed overnight. I allowed them to share the guest room. I felt a bit of a hypocrite in doing so, condoning their ungodly relationship in such a fashion. But the feeling was fleeting.

And now, hours after their departure, I miss their presence. And I wish them all the happiness in the world.

Dear Dad,

I received your letter the other day, and have been mulling over how to respond ever since. You asked me how it was that I lost my faith. That's not an easy thing for me to explain, to be honest. To answer your direct question, I did not abandon my Christian faith just because of my years of emailing with Jude. To explain why I did may not really make a whole lot of sense to you, but I'll try as well as I can.

My conversations with Jude did do one very important thing. They made me realize that a literal belief in the Bible is something I could no longer hold to. You and Mother raised me to believe that this book was infallible, that every single thing in it was literally true. But I think deep down I never really believed that. I find it hard, in fact, to accept that anyone truly does. Such a belief strikes me as being in denial of reality, and certainly in denial of a large quantity of evidence in the world around us.

I could say that from that realization onward, it was simply a natural progression to abandon my belief in the god of the Bible entirely. And, to a point, that's true. For example, I began to question many aspects of the book, and became very disturbed by what it said, especially the atrocities in the Old Testament. But even with all that, I just found Christianity itself to be... I don't know how to really say it any other way... I found it a bit hollow.

Maybe I don't really understand what the Bible says, Dad. I don't know. But I found that even reading the passages I used to find so enriching left me feeling like it was missing a lot.

Yes, the Bible tells me to love my neighbor, but it also condemns large segments of the population, even to the point of promoting abuse of them. This made no sense to me, and I couldn't abide that.

I guess when it comes down to it, I just needed a spiritual life that was more fulfilling for me than Christianity was. I look back on my days as an evangelical and realize that I only thought I was spiritual. In reality, I was just repeating what you and Mom and Gene Sisco kept saying. I was acting the way the Bible told me to act, but not how I felt I really needed to act.

I never once considered myself an atheist, I want you to know. Jude may have helped convince me that the god I once believed in wasn't real, but I've always felt there must be something.

Vicki introduced me to Wicca, and eventually something about it just clicked. This religion made more sense to me. It doesn't presume so many things about our Creator, as so many Christian sects do.

Christianity never made me appreciate the wonder of our world. Dad, I feel so connected now, like an integral part of this world. As the saying goes, life is a web, and each and every one of us is a strand in that web. We're all connected, to each other and to the world around us. And I'm sorry, but your belief system never conveyed that to me. Perhaps it does to you, but I don't think you really get that from your faith. And I know very well that Gene Sisco doesn't.

I guess I just reached a point where spirituality became really important to me. And I knew I needed something different. It would be more accurate to say, Dad, that I didn't "lose" my faith. I just redirected it. Because I do believe in something. But I can't name it, and I certainly can't describe it. It has no personality, no edicts. But I believe it to be very real, whatever it is.

I don't know if I'll be Wiccan for the rest of my life. I might find something tomorrow that makes even more sense to me. But I'll concern myself with that when and if it happens. For now, I'm happy.

This life is too precious, too short, to be angry with and condemn our fellow humans. My faith now emphasizes accepting one another, nurturing one another. And that just makes sense to me.

Perhaps most importantly, it stresses individuality and privacy. "'An it harm none, do what ye will." I believe this with all my heart, Dad, and I find this creed makes much more sense than anything Christianity ever offered. It even makes more sense than the Golden Rule. At least, to me. You might (and probably do) disagree.

So there's your answer. Again, it may not make much sense, and I'm sure I could've said it more clearly. But it's the honest truth.

I want to thank you again for becoming accepting of me and Vicki. It means more to me than you can know, and we had a wonderful visit with you. I've missed you, Dad. I'm glad we're becoming friends again. And I love you very much.

Hope to hear from you soon.

Love always,

Mary

19 March 2030

I phoned Gene this evening. I'm not sure why. I guess I just needed to hear his voice. I forget, sometimes, that we were friends long before we were political partners.

To my surprise, he invited me to be a guest on The Family Hour next month. He broadcasts live from the White House once a month. I accepted the offer.

Before we hung up, I did ask him if he thought I'd made a mistake by resigning. After all, I hadn't discussed it with him until I'd already made my decision. But he said I'd done the right thing. He understood perfectly.

And he pointed out that I wasn't really a politician at heart. I probably never would've had the urge to run for any office whatsoever, had he not planted the idea in my head. Nor would I, as he pointed out, have been elected, were it not for his "family."

He's right, of course. His horde of followers wields incredible power, and I owe them the years I spent in office. But of course, Gene isn't a politician, either. Why does he think he's qualified to be President?

Ah, well. No matter. It's not like I want the job back, anyway. I'm quite enjoying my quiet time alone, and getting reacquainted with my daughter.

I also, it seems, have the option of getting to know Sarah a little better, too. This afternoon I went through the boxes of her personal effects. In one of them, I found her diary. I hadn't even known she'd kept one.

Is it wrong of me to read it? Is it still an invasion of privacy once the author is deceased? I've been wondering that ever since finding it. I scanned the first couple pages. They're very old entries, from before she and I even met. It's quite a thick book. It will be a very long read. But I've decided to do it. Perhaps it will help me in the grieving process.

April 1, 2030

I think we've found it!

Vicki and I just returned from our third intentional community. And we loved it!

We weren't all that crazy about the first two we went to see. The one about an hour or so north of here was a big farm, and everyone there worked on it. The people were really, really nice. But neither of us is exactly agriculturally inclined.

The next one, which was outside of Brookings, Oregon, was more interesting. Again, the people were fantastic. They answered our questions with enthusiasm and seemed to like us a lot. It was mostly self-sufficient and eco-friendly. But we were a bit concerned over continual references to one of the founders of the place. He appears to be considered the "leader," for lack of a better term. And maybe he's a nice guy (we never met him), but we're looking for a strictly egalitarian living arrangement. We don't want any "leaders."

So when we found Clearwater, an IC just outside of Trinidad, we were blown away. First of all, Trinidad is on the coast, right along Rte. 101. So we've got the ocean and the redwoods right there. Beautiful!

Clearwater itself is an eco-village that is entirely self-sufficient, egalitarian, and friendly to pagans and those of alternate sexuality. They produce all their own food and even a form of "green fuel," which is a byproduct of the composting toilets, of all things. And speaking of toilets…

The housing units were arranged in a large circle, and each unit's "back door" led into the middle of the circle, which was a tremendous greenhouse. I swear it must have been a hundred meters across. Anyway, the "bathrooms" were in the greenhouses! You walked into your own private section of the greenhouse, and there was a composting toilet built in.

There was also a little tile floor with a drain. A showerhead was mounted above this. They use eco-friendly shampoo, since the water is recycled in something they call a "gray water system." I'm not sure how it all works. But there was this little waterfall that came down an incline of moss and stone, also emptying into the shower drain. You could see little bubbles from the shampoo coming down the waterfall, too. It was way cute.

Everything there was recycled, it seemed. They're totally off the power grid, using solar, wind, and hydrogen fuel cells (using hydrogen produced there) for all their electrical needs.

We had the grand tour of all the technology, but I don't remember most of it. What I do remember (aside from having a jungle for a bathroom) is the community. They were amazing. Like a family.

And of course, that's what we want.

We made no secret about the nature of our relationship, but no one seemed to think anything of it. We mentioned the possibility of a third person joining us one day in the future, as part of our family (or at least a roommate). Here, there was slight trepidation, but not because of the poly nature of things. Rather, it's because every potential member of Clearwater must be approved by the rest of the community. (That would be on the order of three dozen people right now.) Vicki and I – and Jude, should he eventually choose to join us – will have to go there and get to know all of them. Afterward, they'll have a group meeting and give the yea or nay on us.

My own reputation has preceded me, of course. It's not like when I moved into Southside Park. Then, I'd cut and dyed my hair and wore glasses rather than contacts. But today, my hair is back to its natural blondish hue, it's halfway down my back, I've ditched the glasses, and my face is being seen in newspapers and magazines on a regular basis.

Despite that, they still didn't seem opposed to having me as part of their community. In fact, I think they like the things I've been doing.

Vicki and I are really excited about this. I hope it comes through!

When we got home, there was a message on our answering machine. It was Dad. He sounded very odd. Distraught, almost.

I tried calling him back, but got no answer. All he said was, "I found out the truth. I'm not sure what to do or who to go to. But I'm still going to do the show."

I have not a clue what he meant. Hopefully, I'll be able to reach him tomorrow and find out.

Date: April 2, 2030
To: emsdad@anon-e-mail.com
From: jefferson_paine@voice_of_reason.com
Subject: Re: A couple questions

Sir:

I must admit, I never expected to receive another email from you. Oh, and there's no need to apologize for the tone of your last message to me. I understand what you were going through.

I also understand what an effort it must have been for you to contact me, of all people. But don't be afraid to talk to your daughter about this. She's not a little girl anymore. I find her to be a very impressive young woman. It's been an honor working with her online. In fact, I think it's clear that her assistance in this matter would probably be more effective than my own.

By the way, I know it's late in coming, but my sincerest condolences on the loss of your wife. I can't imagine how awful that must have been for you.

But to address your inquiries...

I don't really like the word "evil," but I do think Sisco is a hateful example of humanity. I don't think he's mentally stable. Dangerous? In certain ways, absolutely.

No, of course the Freethought Underground will not stop making Americans aware of how dangerous a man he is. Why do you worry about us stopping? And what did you mean by, "no matter what happens"?

Your tone concerns me.

Jefferson

SISCO: Good evening, and welcome to The Family Hour Live. We're coming to you directly from the Oval Office in the White House. Our special guest this evening is a man who was last on this show six and a half years ago, but who occupied this very chair less than one year ago. Please welcome my dear friend, Paul Christopher!

[Camera pulls back to reveal Christopher sitting near Sisco. He nods soberly at the camera.]

CHRISTOPHER: Thank you.

SISCO: Thank you for being here. Now, you and I are friends of long standing, and we've remained in contact since you left office. But to our friends out there, you've practically vanished off the face of the earth. Considering the trauma of dear Sarah's tragic death, this is understandable. But please tell us what you've been up to. I understand you're living in Oregon.

CHRISTOPHER: Yes, on the coast. It's a vacation home Sarah and I purchased some years back. It's now my primary residence. I spend most of my time reading. And visiting my daughter.

SISCO: Ah, yes. Mary has become quite... outspoken.

CHRISTOPHER: Indeed she has. I'm quite proud of her.

SISCO: Proud? Well... You are her father. And parents often support the actions of their children in order to impart self-esteem. But the things she promotes...

CHRISTOPHER: Yes, they're just awful, aren't they? She promotes equality for all people, regardless of their age, gender, religion, sexual preference, race, or anything else you care to name. Vile stuff.

SISCO: [Clears throat.] Sarcasm, old friend? Am I to understand that you agree with her?

CHRISTOPHER: It's taken me a long time to realize it, but yes, I do.

SISCO: [Obviously taken aback.] But... *bisexuality*, Paul? Is it true that she has a female lover?

CHRISTOPHER: Victoria is a compassionate, intelligent young woman. I admit I'm still not entirely comfortable with the nature of their relationship, but I've grown quite fond of her. She's practically a second daughter to me.

SISCO: Well. You mentioned that you do a lot of reading. What's on your bedside table, old friend, *The Satanic Bible?*

CHRISTOPHER: It's funny you should mention books, because I do want to discuss one with you. I have a question for you before we begin. Do you remember exactly when we became friends?

SISCO: Oh, you're pushing my memory with that one. *Exactly* when? I'm afraid not. It was over twenty years ago.

CHRISTOPHER: I can't remember the precise occasion, either. But I do know exactly when we stopped being friends.

SISCO: [Laughs nervously.] We've stopped being friends?

CHRISTOPHER: March thirty-first. Just last week. [Pulls a small book from his jacket pocket.] That was the day I read this.

SISCO: I don't understand. A book has caused you to dismiss our friendship?

CHRISTOPHER: It's my wife's diary. I'd like to read from it.

SISCO: Her *diary?* Now, Paul... Sarah's private thoughts shouldn't be shared with millions of viewers on live television. And certainly, there's nothing she could write that should in any way turn you away from a twenty year friendship.

CHRISTOPHER: Well, there's this entry from last September. She writes, "I hesitate to tell Paul of my suspicions. He'll just tell me I'm paranoid. He and Gene are too close for me to be able to convince him that this man has no scruples when it comes to getting his way. My friends in The Saviors say Sisco has his eye on the Presidency."

SISCO: [Laughs.] As Vice-President, that would be expected.

CHRISTOPHER: Oh, of course. I fully anticipated turning over the reins to you one day. And I did, didn't I? But then, with term limits repealed... your idea, you'll recall... it didn't look like I'd be going anywhere soon. Especially not with my popularity ratings.

SISCO: What are you insinuating?

CHRISTOPHER: In a later entry, Sarah refers to some documents given to her by a reporter. I found them. I read them. They're the stuff Pulitzers are made of, Gene. Nothing rock solid, but pretty clear ramifications. They paint a very ugly picture of you, my old friend. The irony is that, by my own orders, the press is forbidden to write incriminating things about the President. That was your idea, Gene. One of many you planted in my head over the years.

SISCO: Paul, don't make me cut to a commercial early.

CHRISTOPHER: [Closes the book.] Well, if you're going to be that way about it...

SISCO: Thank you.

CHRISTOPHER: Feldon Reese acted under your orders! You ordered him to murder my Mary, you sick son of a—

[End of transmission.]

Washington—Former President Paul Christopher, taken into custody by White House Secret Service after a dramatic outburst on live television last night, was turned over to the FBI this morning. In yesterday's broadcast of *The Family Hour,* Christopher accused President Sisco of being responsible for targeting activist daughter Mary Christopher for assassination, an attempt that resulted in the death of his wife Sarah.

According to Christopher, his wife's diary and documents allegedly given to her by an as yet unidentified reporter implicate President Sisco as being responsible for the attempt, as well as the Pocatello riot and other acts of violence around the country.

The White House has denied all allegations.

Christopher is slated for release this afternoon. The diary and other documents remain in the custody of the FBI.

April 8, 2030

My mind is completely blown. Sisco ordered me to be killed. I just can't believe it.

Well, I suppose I can, on an intellectual level. But not on an emotional level. It's just too much. I mean, no matter our differences of opinion on religion, this is a guy I grew up calling "Uncle Gene." To think that he'd want me dead is more than I can even imagine.

I spoke to my dad this morning. I couldn't believe what he did! I guess he can't, either. He says he doesn't know what came over him. He said that when he read Mom's diary and learned what she suspected, he realized he had to do something.

He said Sisco was too powerful and popular, and Sisco's "Family" would ridicule normal, legal accusations. But if the charges were made on live television, while his "Family" was watching, and if they could hear it from the lips of someone they still thought highly of, then it might go a long way to undercutting Sisco's power base.

Before going on the show, he sent the reporter's documents to the head of the FBI by courier. He kept copies for himself, though. He also sent Mom's original diary. The one he took on the show was actually just a blank book into which he'd copied a few passages. Good thing, since Sisco's goons took the book from him immediately after cutting transmission.

He says the press has been hounding him ever since he was released from custody. I can imagine, as they've been pestering me to the point where I had to turn off the ringer on the phone. Apparently, Dad made more photocopies of relevant sections of Mom's diary and has given them to any reporter who's asked. He says that even though the FBI has the actual diary itself, he thinks a good investigative reporter will turn up information more quickly than a government agent. He's probably right. And he's handed them something so juicy that no media outlet in the country would hesitate to run after it, whether or not it'll get them in trouble.

I'm not sure, but I think my dad may have just made himself into a hero.

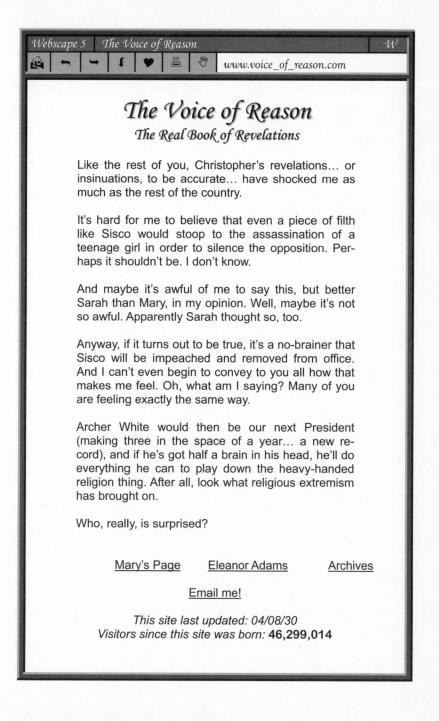

The Voice of Reason
The Real Book of Revelations

Like the rest of you, Christopher's revelations... or insinuations, to be accurate... have shocked me as much as the rest of the country.

It's hard for me to believe that even a piece of filth like Sisco would stoop to the assassination of a teenage girl in order to silence the opposition. Perhaps it shouldn't be. I don't know.

And maybe it's awful of me to say this, but better Sarah than Mary, in my opinion. Well, maybe it's not so awful. Apparently Sarah thought so, too.

Anyway, if it turns out to be true, it's a no-brainer that Sisco will be impeached and removed from office. And I can't even begin to convey to you all how that makes me feel. Oh, what am I saying? Many of you are feeling exactly the same way.

Archer White would then be our next President (making three in the space of a year... a new record), and if he's got half a brain in his head, he'll do everything he can to play down the heavy-handed religion thing. After all, look what religious extremism has brought on.

Who, really, is surprised?

Mary's Page   Eleanor Adams   Archives

Email me!

This site last updated: 04/08/30
Visitors since this site was born: **46,299,014**

"It won't surprise any of you when I say I don't know much about taxes. I'm a couple weeks shy of twenty. And the only thing most people my age know about taxes is that they are one of only two things that are certain in life.

"I'm told, though, that the purpose of taxes is to pay for the benefits of government. In this fashion, I guess the government fancies itself some sort of business, a provider of services for a fee. But there are two huge problems with this picture.

"First, when a business provides a service, the user of the service pays for the service. But government taxes one and all for all services provided, whether used or not.

"And second, the government does not provide services that meet the expectations we have, based on the amount of money we are robbed of every year.

"Yes, I said 'robbed.' The government cannot function without money, and since the government generates no income of its own, funding has to come from somewhere. And given that the common person knows the excesses of government and would never willingly give their hard-earned cash to such a poorly run organization, our money is taken from us by force. Call it whatever you like. It's still taking something without permission.

"But I'm not here to talk about theft. I'm here to say that there are many other ways to do this. The truth, my friends, is that government does not need to tax us. They do it because they've done it for so long, they don't know any other way to survive. And of course, there are those of us who really don't want to see it survive in its present form, anyway.

"Today you're going to hear half a dozen speakers talking about how we can have a more effective government, providing all the services we need them to provide (and there are very few, really), and doing so without taxing us, and in fact, generating wealth all by itself! Wouldn't that be grand?

"I'm happy to state that our keynote speaker is none other than former Vice-President Thomas Dowd, who will speak on the subject of the income tax, and alternative taxes such as flat taxes, national sales taxes, and his own tax plan, the 20/20 plan. Also today, we have Dr. David Freedman speaking on how welfare creates poverty; Dr. Elizabeth Tate on the Social Security Tax; Dr. William Earl on corporate tax breaks; Gen. Louis Mitchell on the privatization of the military, to end its reliance upon taxes; and somewhere in there, I'll be back to talk with you about whatever's left.

"Thank you."

Washington—In response to an FBI statement alleging evidence in support of Paul Christopher's recent claims, the House Judiciary Committee has announced the beginning of an active investigation.

William Walters has been appointed Independent Counsel in charge of the investigation.

In a press conference immediately following the announcement, Walters said he would "stop at nothing to discover the truth of the situation."

It is expected that Walters will question selected members of Our Father's Family, the Saviors, and Feldon Reese, the man convicted of killing Sarah Christopher.

Anyone with information pertinent to this investigation is urged to contact the nearest FBI office.

27 April 2030

I feel as though a great weight has been lifted from my shoulders. I confess that I had my doubts as to whether the House would actually support an investigation. But they have, and when the connections they're looking for are found, they'll have no choice but to grant the authority to conduct an impeachment inquiry.

Nothing, of course, will make up for the fact that Gene and his followers robbed my dear wife of the rest of her life. But this, at least, will go a ways toward balancing the scales.

I just wish I had not been so devoted to Gene that Sarah believed me (probably accurately) to be unapproachable with her suspicions about the man.

It makes me feel no better than any of the gullible sheep over the years who have blindly followed fools and madmen. Just because someone is charismatic does not mean he is the keeper of Truth. I learned that about Gene the hard way.

And about myself.

May 10, 2030

We got it! Jeff at Clearwater called to tell us we've been accepted! We're actually going to be living right in amongst the redwoods! It's even better than it was in Guerneville.

Trinidad's little... the population isn't even five hundred. And I can deal with that. I'm growing tired of the public life and could easily learn to appreciate long days of lying in a hammock with a good novel. Maybe I'll take up sailing. Heck, Humboldt State University is only about fifteen miles away, in Arcata. Maybe I'll go to school. It might be a pleasant change from being a public activist.

This next rally has me concerned. I mean, you'd think the tax protest would've been my big fear, since I've only recently begun to understand how pervasive our tax laws are. I didn't really feel qualified to speak there.

But It's so difficult for me to believe that the United States is the only industrialized nation in the world that has not accorded any sort of rights whatsoever to minors. It's shameful. Kids are people, too. And I should know, since I was one not all that long ago.

I'm brushing up, though, using the 'net to get access to some really great documents about the abuses American kids are subjected to, without much recourse.

In other news, the investigation into Sisco has apparently pieced together how Mom happened to intercept a bullet meant for me. It seems she received a tip from her mysterious reporter friend, not long before the event. Mom apparently dispatched the Secret Service to get over there and protect me. But it seems the S.S. goon she gave the order to was in Sisco's pocket, and he ignored the order.

When she got over there herself, she saw there were no Secret Service around. That's what caused her to run on stage. I guess she was coming to warn me. I don't think she actually saw Reese and deliberately jumped in front of me. But I suppose anything's possible.

The whole thing makes me sick to my stomach, just thinking about it.

Sunday is Mother's Day.

Goddess, I miss her.

"The Convention on the Rights of a Child was adopted in 1989. Its basic premise is that all human beings under the age of eighteen have the same freedoms and fundamental rights that older human beings have.

"For some reason, our own country, The United States of America... land of the free... has not ratified this Convention. Though we signed the Convention thirty-five years ago, ratification has still not happened. We are the only advanced nation on the face of this planet that has not done so. This fact truly astounds me.

"But maybe it shouldn't. It took us over thirty years to ratify the Convention on the Prevention and Punishment of the Crime of Genocide. And the Convention on the Elimination of All Forms of Discrimination Against Women also still has not been ratified, though it was signed *fifty* years ago. But that's a rant for another rally...

"America has never been rapid in ratifying conventions such as these. But this is ridiculous.

"I speak to you today as someone who's felt the discrimination of being a minor in America. But I was lucky. I came from a very privileged family, and was fortunate enough to acquire my own emancipation. I was able to escape what so many others have been trapped by. Of course, I escaped only to continue to be discriminated against on the basis of my religion and my sexuality, but that's another story altogether.

"Or is it?

"Discrimination is discrimination. Throughout America's history, there have been movements and legislation geared toward ending or easing discrimination against people on the basis of race, gender, sexual orientation, religion... just about everything, including old age. Everything but *young* age.

"Unless, of course, you're talking about age in negative numbers. The unborn in this country actually have more rights than the just-born, or the almost-eighteen. What kind of sense does this make?

"Personally, I have no idea. Even if I were more knowledgeable on the subject of rights, I still don't think it would make sense. And neither do the scholars here today. The stories they have to tell will make you wonder, too, why this Land of the Free is so selective in the freedoms it confers."

"Fellow Christians:

"Over the past two months, many hurtful allegations have been made about my possible involvement in the unfortunate death of my dear friend Sarah Christopher. An investigation is, as you know, underway, which will establish completely that I had nothing to do with this terrible event.

"But despite my innocence, I am sorry to say that the scope of this affair has begun to impact negatively on my ability to perform the duties of my office. And so, I have decided that it would be in the nation's best interest for me to stand aside temporarily, while the investigation concludes.

"Tomorrow morning, I will tender a letter to the President *pro tempore* of the Senate and the Speaker of the House. This letter states that, due to these circumstances, I am unable to properly carry out the duties of my office. And, according to the provisions of the Twenty-Fifth Amendment to the Constitution, Vice President Archer White will assume the mantle of Acting President until I say otherwise.

"I have no wish to see this investigation impeded in any way. And once I have been fully exonerated, I shall return to carry on the sacred duties to which I am sworn to fulfill. For they are my duties, and no one else's. I believe one should never have someone else do for you what you can and should do for yourself. So I will return immediately upon the completion of this investigation."

Washington—At noon today, President Gene Sisco voluntarily vacated the Oval Office, making Archer White the Acting President.

Sisco, along with Chief of Staff Mitchell Ross, Press Secretary Donna Woodley, and several others, left for Camp David shortly thereafter.

Meanwhile, the House Judiciary Committee will hold its next hearing beginning Monday morning.

9 July 2030

In the time since confronting Gene, I've tried to figure out just what caused me to do it in such a fashion, and the only conclusion I can come up with is that it was God's doing. I finally got the message God had been sending me for the past several years.

All throughout my Presidency, many Christian organizations protested my policies. At the time, I passed them off as being foolish, or not "real" Christians. But I see now that Gene Sisco was not truly doing God's will (nor was I, when I was following him). God sent me many messages, in the form of these good Christians who beseeched me to change my mind, and even the Freethought Underground, who belittled and mocked me for being such a fool.

Two very effective methods of conveying a message, yet I was blind to both. Even Mary. She was a messenger from God, too. And still I turned my eye away.

Is that why Sarah never confided in me? Did she think I was too close to Sisco to listen to her concerns and fears about him? Undoubtedly, yes.

But God knew. God knew Sarah was the only one to reach me. And maybe her death was his way of scolding me for not paying attention to Him. She had to speak to me from beyond the grave in order for me to pay attention.

But I did, and now I have done God's work in deposing Sisco, a man who professes to represent the will of God, but is only interested in self-glorification.

I am very happy, today. I think I am truly beginning to understand God's will for the first time in my life. And it's nothing like I'd thought for so many years. People like Sisco are corrupted by baser human instincts and are actually doing the work of Satan, even though they don't realize it.

God's message really is love, but it's unconditional love. That's something people like Sisco can never understand, because everything is conditional with them.

More's the pity.

Date: September 14, 2030
To: emsdad@anon-e-mail.com
From: jefferson_paine@voice_of_reason.com
Subject: Some cautionary thoughts.

Sir:

I'm sure it hasn't escaped your attention that Sisco is a control freak. You must realize that this is an integral part of his personality. And he is used to being in control. He's been in control of big things for a long time, from Our Father's Family, to being the man with the most influence on the President, to being Vice-President, and finally, President himself.

But now the White House is lost to him. He is under investigation, and has been steadily losing credibility among his own followers. This cannot possibly be easy for him to stomach.

Sisco is also a narcissist, believing he can do no wrong. This is reinforced by his conviction that he is doing God's work. He will, believe me, never accept that what has happened to him is in any way his fault. He will blame others. And the most obvious target of that blame is you.

Some might think Mary is the obvious target. After all, he tried to have her killed. But her "crime" has been far eclipsed by your own.

Let me put it into an analogy I'm sure you'll relate to.

I, and others like me, have always represented the Serpent in the Garden of Eden that is Sisco's mental world. Your daughter is Eve, tempted by the serpent. You have always been his Adam, the alpha male in his creation. But Mary corrupted you as Eve did Adam.

Exit Adam (you) from Eden (the White House). Enter Sisco (Christ) to save the day. But you went one step further. You betrayed him. You are now his Judas.

Carry the analogy as far as you like. The point is that you humiliated him in front of his followers, causing him to leave office. Your "sin" is far greater than Mary's, in his eyes.

I honestly believe you are in danger. Sisco is not going to sit still for this. I have no doubt that he will try to exact vengeance. He may not utilize his followers, as he did in Pocatello and with the tragedy on Halloween. Those didn't go so well. Now he'll take it upon himself to finish the job. I honestly don't think he's going to sit quietly in Camp David watching the squirrels run up and down the trees.

I suggest you leave Rockaway Beach. Go somewhere he can't find you. And I'll urge Mary to do the same.

J. P.

Date: September 16, 2030
To: jefferson_paine@voice_of_reason.com
From: emsdad@anon-e-mail.com
Subject: Re: Some cautionary thoughts.

Mr. Paine:

Your analogy was very creative and entertaining, but I think you are exaggerating Gene's neuroses. Leave? No, I think not. I am not afraid of Gene Sisco, even were I to put stock in your little scenario. I have come closer to the Lord, lately, and that makes me stronger than Gene Sisco could ever be.

I thank you for your concern, though. It's very thoughtful of you.

P. C.

Webscape 5 · *Freethought Underground Public Page* · *W*

www.voice_of_reason.com/priv/pub.htm

Folks:

Okay, time to go into protection mode. Christopher may have made life hell for us for most of a decade, but we should probably try to keep an eye on him for his own good.

Those of you in the Pacific Northwest, please coordinate amongst yourselves and be prepared to get to Rockaway Beach. Some of you may want to be ready to head to Trinidad, since it's just as possible that Sisco may try to harm Mary.

Rumor has it that prior to abortion being outlawed, there was an underground network to help clinic bombers and doctor killers get around the country. Ten bucks says plenty of O.F.F. members were part of it, and will help Sisco any way they can. Anyone know a thing about this?

Paine

Leave me a message

September 16, 2030

Jefferson emailed me today, expressing some concern about the possibility that Sisco might try to harm me. After all, he did once, why not try a second time?

I suppose I should be worried about that possibility. If I were still under sixteen, I'd have Secret Service goons to protect me. Glad I don't, though. Those guys always creeped me out. Even without them, though, I'm not very concerned. I'm not sure why, exactly.

I called Dad, who told me Jefferson had emailed him, too. And while he thinks the threat is unlikely, he suggested maybe I should go visit him. So I will.

I berated him (again) for not accepting Secret Service protection. Why on earth would anyone turn down ten years of free bodyguards? Maybe they creeped him out, too.

Anyway, I urged him to call the FBI, the police, or anyone who will be able to protect him. But I doubt he'll follow my advice.

The main reason I'll go to Oregon is that I'd hate to think I'm endangering others here in Clearwater just by my presence. Of course, at this point, it's all just paranoia. Sisco is up in the mountains in Maryland, and certainly isn't a threat to me here in California.

"September 18, 2030. J.E. Cooper, here, beginning yet another hair-raising investigative journey.

"This lovely wooded area you see in this vid is a tiny section of Catoctin Mountain Park in Maryland, home to the Presidential retreat, Camp David. It is, of course, restricted property. No civilians allowed. It says so right there, on the main gate.

"But restrictions rarely stop intrepid reporters such as myself.

"Why am I here, shooting footage of a bunch of trees? Well, our President happens to be somewhere amongst them: Gene Sisco, currently under formal investigation concerning the shooting death of then-First Lady Sarah Christopher on Halloween of last year.

"He's guilty as sin, by the way, if you'll pardon the irony. I'm here in the admittedly vain hope that I'll catch a glimpse of him and possibly get a chance to corner him on the subject.

"Time will tell."

"September 19, 2030. The building currently receding on your screen is a ranger's station. I just left there, after being fined for violating Park Service Regulation 36CFR, subsection 4.12. That's the section that spells out the fact that peons such as myself are not allowed to 'accidentally' go down a restricted path into Camp David.

"Fortunately for me, neither the ranger nor the Marines who escorted me to the station searched my possessions very thoroughly. When they determined I had no weapons, they seemed satisfied.

"I am unsure what my next action should be. For now, it's back to the Super 8."

"September 22, 2030. I am sitting in the rear row of pews in Pioneer Baptist Church on the outskirts of Thurmont, Maryland. Why? Because it occurred to me that Sisco just might be the sort to drop in and check out the local talent, so to speak. The Yellow Pages revealed two Baptist churches in Thurmont, Pioneer being closer to the edge of town than the other. My instinct (which I always heed, despite its poor track record) told me this was the one he'd visit, if he visited any.

"Pay close attention to the figure in the center of my PenCam's frame. Ignore the facial hair. Mentally remove the heavy-framed glasses. And then picture that head topped with the familiar graying hairdo of Gene Sisco.

"I'm virtually certain it is him.

"What is he doing here? My thought now, after seeing this disguise, is that it is a test to see if he'd be recognized if he decided to leave Camp David. And it seems to be successful. The locals don't seem to know who he is. Only the fact that I was specifically looking for him allowed me to see through the disguise.

"I'm not sure at this point how I'll be able to keep tabs on him. I'm convinced, though, that if and when he leaves Camp David, it'll be in disguise, and almost certainly by car, rather than helicopter.

"Perhaps I should head back up to Catoctin and find a place to watch the main gate through binoculars."

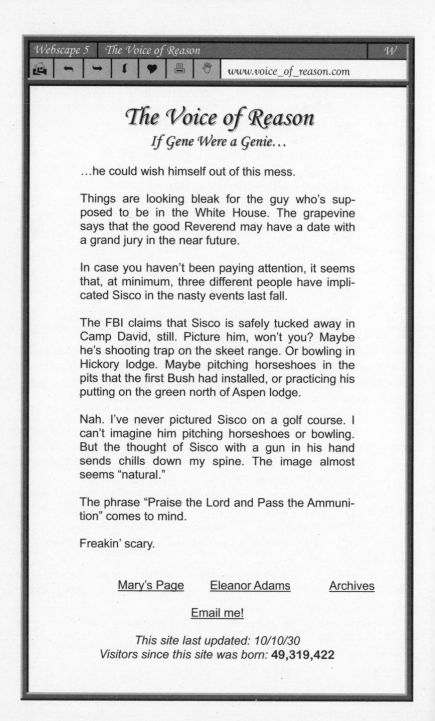

The Voice of Reason
If Gene Were a Genie...

...he could wish himself out of this mess.

Things are looking bleak for the guy who's supposed to be in the White House. The grapevine says that the good Reverend may have a date with a grand jury in the near future.

In case you haven't been paying attention, it seems that, at minimum, three different people have implicated Sisco in the nasty events last fall.

The FBI claims that Sisco is safely tucked away in Camp David, still. Picture him, won't you? Maybe he's shooting trap on the skeet range. Or bowling in Hickory lodge. Maybe pitching horseshoes in the pits that the first Bush had installed, or practicing his putting on the green north of Aspen lodge.

Nah. I've never pictured Sisco on a golf course. I can't imagine him pitching horseshoes or bowling. But the thought of Sisco with a gun in his hand sends chills down my spine. The image almost seems "natural."

The phrase "Praise the Lord and Pass the Ammunition" comes to mind.

Freakin' scary.

Mary's Page   Eleanor Adams   Archives

Email me!

This site last updated: 10/10/30
*Visitors since this site was born: **49,319,422***

13 October 2030

Mary arrived today. And a few hours later, four members of the Freethought Underground showed up, claiming they were here to "protect" us.

Lord knows why they think we're in danger, but I noticed at least two of them are armed. I admit it makes me a tad nervous. After all, I don't know these people, let alone trust them around me with guns. Ironic, since I was such a friend to the pro-gun lobby.

Still, they are very polite toward me, even friendly. But they are, I've noticed, very watchful. According to Mary, Paine warned them that some of Gene's "Family" may decide to drop in for a visit.

I'm allowing them the use of two of the guest rooms. Apparently, they will take turns keeping an eye on the house and watching out for suspicious characters.

Let them have their fantasy, I say.

Still... better safe than sorry. I put in a call to Wes Noonan at the FBI, to see what he could tell me, if anything. He assured me I was in no danger. Then he asked if I wanted them to come round up "those damned freethinkers." He used the last word like an epithet. I hung up feeling uneasy.

Half my brain says to listen to Wes. I've known him since college, and he certainly wouldn't steer me wrong. But the other half can do nothing but remind me of Sarah's written words, of the fact that Gene ordered his followers to start the riot in Pocatello, and that he ordered Feldon Reese to kill my daughter.

JUSTTHEFAX JUSTTHEFAX JUSTTHEFAX JUSTTHEFAX

FEDERAL BUREAU OF INVESTIGATION

Date: October 13, 2003

From: W. Noonan, Special Agent

To: Chief of Police

Re: Freethought Underground

It has come to the attention of the Federal Bureau of Investigation that the "Freethought Underground" may be planning to contact law enforcement agencies in and around Rockaway Beach, Oregon, with claims that President Sisco and/or members of his organization, Our Father's Family, are about to make attempts on the lives of former President Paul Christopher and/or his daughter, Mary.

We have it on the authority of the Secret Service that President Sisco is still sequestered at Camp David, and that this is nothing but a grandstanding ploy by the Freethought Underground in an effort to gain national attention and besmirch the President's good name.

Should you be contacted by anyone claiming that such an "attack" is about to take place, I urge you to take action. You are expected to learn all information about the caller, including name and location, and then move in to make arrests.

Please do not for a moment assume there to be any truth to their allegations. This is, after all, an organization notorious for spreading falsehoods on any number of topics.

Should you apprehend any members of this organization, you will receive all due gratitude from your government.

Feel free to contact me directly with any questions about this.

October 18, 2030

Sometimes it amazes me that Dad enjoys it here in Rockaway Beach so much. I mean, yeah... he's got a stunning ocean view from the house here. And certainly privacy. But the town itself is such a tiny little place. Okay, so it's got about triple the number of people as Trinidad, but despite that, you can't even get a decent selection of groceries unless you drive to another town.

We went down to Tillamook today and toured the cheese factory and the air museum there. It was kinda cool.

When we got back, we stopped in at Neptune's Corner again. The proprietor makes his own chocolate, and I'm sure that's why these are the best mochas I've ever had. I've been on an almost constant caffeine and/or sugar rush since arriving.

Dad and I talked a lot today, and of course the conversation turned to Gene Sisco. Dad assured me that he was no threat, and that his friend in the FBI promised that they had everything under control.

But there's a little voice in my head telling me that I should take nothing for granted. Maybe it's just paranoia, or maybe it's that I value Jefferson Paine's opinions and Jude's advice.

Dad and I also talked about Jefferson and the Freethought Underground. He's been pretty nice to the ones that are here, even though they're not really around us much. I think his opinion of them has changed a lot. From things he said, I think he's begun to really understand why they're doing what they're doing. And why I'm doing what I'm doing. Mom's death really caused him to stop and take a hard look at things. It did that to me, too, but I was satisfied with what I saw. Evidently, Dad wasn't.

Anyway, speaking of Jefferson and Jude... The other night I was reading over a lot of old emails and stuff, and I noticed that their writing styles are really similar. Even some of the expressions they use are the same. I can't believe I never suspected until now that Jude is really Jefferson Paine!

At first I was really annoyed with him for not telling me, but then I realized that I wasn't exactly up front with him about my own identity. I can't be that much of a hypocrite. Still... let's see how long it takes him to confess to me.

"November 2, 2030. We're outside of a hotel in Bend, Oregon. Sisco and his two Secret Service men stopped here for the night. I consider it nothing short of amazing that I've followed them this far without being discovered.

"This is their latest vehicle. They abandoned the Cherokee in Boise and are now traveling in this Suburban. Sisco's new disguise, with the mutton chops, kinda makes him look like Elvis, don't you think?

"I'm now convinced that their destination is Rockaway Beach. We've been making a beeline for Oregon for so long, and now we're halfway across the state.

"Earlier today, I phoned the Rockaway Beach police, only to be told that they'd been 'warned' about me. The deputy read some fax from the FBI insisting that Sisco was still in Camp David. I guess I shouldn't be surprised at who all is in Sisco's pocket, but sometimes I still am.

"Should I contact the FBI? Can't see how that would help. Try to track down Paul Christopher's home number? I'll try, but I'm sure it's unlisted. Maybe I should just get there before Sisco does and warn him in person. Because that's the only reason Sisco could be coming here: to get revenge on his predecessor.

"Yes. That's the plan. I'll grab a couple hours of sleep, then get back on the road."

"November 3, 2030. As you can see, I was apparently wrong in thinking I'd not been discovered. I woke at four A.M., planning to make Rockaway Beach by mid-morning. But it doesn't look like that's going to happen with four slashed tires.

"The car rental places won't be open for hours, yet. And the worse news is that the Suburban is gone. God only knows how much lead time they've got on me."

"November 3, continued...

"The uniformed gentleman now walking away from the camera is Officer Penis-dick, who stopped me for speeding.

"Notes to self. One. Never, ever, get a speeding ticket in Oregon again. Holy shit, is it expensive. Two. Perhaps think twice before deciding to film every little thing that happens to you. Oh, and three. Next time, make entirely sure the person you're calling a penis-dick is totally out of earshot.

"At any rate, I'm now near the town of Sweet Home, which apparently indicates that I've made a wrong turn and ended up in Alabama. Go figure.

"With luck, I should hit Rockaway Beach in under three hours, depending on traffic and highway patrol. Of course, I still have no idea how to find Christopher's house..."

Date: November 3, 2030
To: biwitched1@anon-e-mail.com
From: mary@voice_of_reason.com
Subject: Stuff

Vicki:

Hey, sweetie... Just thought I'd drop a line while Dad's in the shower. We're going out for an early breakfast today, then I'm going to church with him. Yeah, I know. I'm not into the idea all that much, but I'm doing it as a favor to him.

I really miss you, and wish you'd have come with me. I know you didn't feel comfortable with the idea, but Dad's become much more accepting of you. Okay, maybe not enough for this. But he has asked about you and said to send you his respects. That's good, right?

I'm not sure how much longer I'm going to stay here. I guess it depends.

Gotta go. Someone's at the door.

Love you!

Mary

COOPER: November 3, continued... Okay, this long driveway is to Paul Christopher's house. I was able to locate online the tax assessor's lot division information for Tillamook County. It didn't take long to find the biggest lot with the surname of Christopher on it.

Ah-ha. The familiar white Suburban, which appears to be empty. Getting out of my car... Looking up the hill, we see the Christopher house. Whoa. Very nice. Let's see if anyone's home. Stairs up from the driveway are over here.

This is a great area, secluded from the neighbors by quite a lot of trees and at least two acres on either side of the house. Surprised it's not gated, though.

Top of the hill. Wow. Look at that view. That is *sweet*.

It's pretty quiet, though... Wait a moment. What's that? Oh, Jesus... Someone's on the ground. [Running.] Damn, that's a lot of blood.

Hey! Are you okay? Let's roll you over... oh. Dear God.

[Head-mounted camera focuses on cell phone as 9-1-1 is dialed.] C'mon... Answer the damn... Yes! I'm at Paul Christopher's house and we need police and ambulances.

What? Oh. Okay.

[Cell phone beeps as connection closed.] Someone called them just a minute ago. That's encouraging news, I guess.

Okay, so the shots came from toward the house. Stupid as it sounds, that's where we go. C'mon, Coop. It's for the Pulitzer. It's for the Pulitzer.

Oh, Christ. [Camera focuses on two more figures on the lawn, both with handguns lying nearby.] Okay, that one is clearly one of the Secret Service guys who accompanied Sisco. No idea who the other one is, or that last one. [Cooper leans down to check for vital signs.] Both dead.

The cops would fry me if I got my prints on the guns, so I guess I'll leave them be.

Getting close to the house, now. I can hear voices coming from inside, but can't make out anything being said. [Audible moaning is heard off camera.] That came from over near the garage. I'll check around the corner...

[Two young people, one male, one female, are propped against the wall of the garage. The girl is clutching her bleeding leg and sobbing over the boy, who is clearly dead. Cooper rushes to her side.]

COOPER: How bad is it?

GIRL: [Sobbing.] He's dead!

COOPER: Yeah. I'm sorry. But I meant you.

GIRL: Who are you?

COOPER: I'm a reporter. What happened here?

GIRL: They showed up about half an hour ago. Two guys...

COOPER: Secret Service?

GIRL: I don't know. We saw the car pull up and tried to warn Paul and Mary, and to make whatever defense we could.

COOPER: Mary's here, too? Damn. Listen, the police should be here soon. What about the Christophers?

GIRL: After they shot us, they brought Sisco up. He went into the house a few minutes ago.

COOPER: Okay. You just wait here for the EMTs, all right?

GIRL: There's still another one out there!

COOPER: Right. [Turns toward house.] Okay, so we'll take the steps up to the porch. Let's see if we can see anything in the window.

[Camera focuses inside the house and scans the room, but finds no one. A noise is heard and the camera view swivels to the right, revealing another Secret Service agent with a gun pointed at Cooper. Two rapid gunshots are heard. The Secret Service agent jerks and falls through the window with a loud crash. The camera turns again to focus on the wounded teen, who continues squeezing the trigger, though the gun is out of ammunition. Then she collapses, exhausted.]

COOPER: *Jesus!*

                 I am *definitely* sending her a get well card.

                 I guess that accounts for all the Secret Service. Now to find the man himself. The door is around this side of the house, I guess.

                 [Whispering.] There's a pounding noise coming from somewhere. Let me get through the living room, here. There's a hallway over there.

                 Uh, oh. [Camera perspective moves toward a bare foot protruding from a doorway.] Damn. Blood all over... Oh, shit.

[Paul Christopher is lying on his back on the floor of a bathroom. He is clothed only in a bathrobe. His torso is covered with blood, as is the floor.]

                 Sir! Sir, can you hear me?

CHRISTOPHER: [Weakly.] Yes.

COOPER: Oh, man... What happened?

CHRISTOPHER: Gene. Came in. Shot me. Just... shot me. Mary! He's... [Christopher grits his teeth in pain and falls silent.]

COOPER: Help is on the way. Just lie still. I'm going to find him.

                 [Back in hall.] What *is* that damn banging? Sounds like it's coming from upstairs.

                 [Softly.] Okay, at the top of the stair, now. The banging is much louder now. A quick peek around this corner...

Bingo. Sisco's in front of a door, apparently trying to break it down. But is that...? Jesus. He's hammering on the doorknob with a big metal crucifix. Must've grabbed it off the wall. Kinda dumb. Guess no one ever taught him how to break down a door. Luckily for Mary.

Stands to reason that it's her room. Man, he looks pissed. He's obviously gone totally over the edge. He gets through that door and Mary's as good as dead.

I don't know if I could stop him. He's awfully big, unlike myself, and that's one mother of a piece of metal in his hands.

Room's gotta have a window. I'll head back outside...

[Camera goes black, then powers up again, outdoors.]

The camera's now on the telescoping wand. I've got a portable mike. I'm approaching the window. It's open, too. And now I can see why she doesn't just jump. You can't see them from this angle, but there are jagged ornamental rocks just below her window.

Mary's near the door, holding something in her hand. A tennis racquet. Let me turn up the gain on the camera's mike in case there's anything to hear.

[Sirens can be heard in the background.] About time they show up!

Oh, man. The doorknob is shaking, coming loose. She can't really expect to do much with the racquet, can she? Oh! There it goes! The door's open! Sisco is... What's he doing? He's propped the crucifix against the wall. Oh, hell. He's pulled out a gun! He's stepping into...

Whoa! Mary just smacked him in the face with the racquet! He's dazed... She's swinging again.

He caught it! Sisco caught the fucking racquet! Now he's torn it from her hands! He's pointing the gun at her! Oh, God, oh, my God...

MARY: You shot my father, you bastard!

SISCO: Of course. He betrayed me, just as you betrayed him.

MARY: I never...

SISCO: Everything you are is a betrayal of the way your father and mother raised you.

MARY: Don't you *dare* mention my mother, you bastard!

SISCO: Shut up! It's *your* fault she is dead.

MARY: What!

SISCO: It was you, Mary, who bewitched her. You caused her to run in front of you at the exact moment Reese pulled the trigger. You deliberately sacrificed her to save your own evil little life.

[Sirens increasing in volume.]

COOPER: Come on, girl. Keep him talking...

MARY: Goddess, you're a crazy son of a bitch.

SISCO: "*Goddess.*" You mean Satan, so just say it. Don't pretend otherwise. A devil by any other name is still the Prince of Lies.

MARY: You hypocrite. You claim to spread the word of Jesus, the Prince of Peace. Yet you are a killer. You killed my mother. You probably killed my father. And you mean to kill me. How very *Christian* of you.

SISCO: "*But those mine enemies, which would not that I should reign over them, bring hither, and slay them before me.*" So said Jesus. You and your father betrayed me, and in so doing, rejected Christ. You are the enemy, child. You must die.

MARY: Fine. Then get it over with, already.

COOPER: No! That is *not* the thing to say! Oh, shit. Sisco's raising the gun. Mary's just standing there...

SISCO: In Jesus' name...

MARY: Dad!

[Sisco lurches forward, struck from behind by the crucifix he'd discarded. His gun fires; Mary screams and falls to the ground. Paul Christopher stands in the doorway. Sisco turns, raising the gun. Christopher swings again. Blood flies as the crucifix smashes into Sisco's face.]

COOPER: Sisco is down! Christopher has fallen to his knees. He's looking at the blood-covered crucifix. Now he's... he's clutching the cross to his chest, almost embracing it, and... I think... I think he's crying.

POLICE: You! On the ground!

The Voice of Reason
Fade to White

I trust you've all seen (probably more often than you'd like) J. E. Cooper's vid. It could be marketed as a slasher flick, don't you think?

How many of you went to Sisco's funeral? Yeah, me neither. Quite a slugger Paul Christopher turned out to be. The second blow didn't really look deadly, but then, you just never know when it comes to head trauma.

Speaking of Christopher, he's expected to make a full recovery, according to my source. He'll be hospitalized for at least another week, though. When he gets out, I'm gonna see if I can get him to try out for the Sox. They could've used a hitter like him this year.

And speaking of my source, Mary says thanks to all of you who've sent such touching emails to her. Her shoulder is healing well and the doctors say she'll not have any loss of use.

She and I both also wish to express our profound condolences to the families and friends of the three Freethought Underground members who gave their lives trying to protect Mary and her father. They will certainly not be forgotten.

Mary's Page   Eleanor Adams   Archives

Email me!

This site last updated: 11/19/30
*Visitors since this site was born: **51,009,442***

December 8, 2030

Jude phoned late this evening. He'd just returned from the vigil/celebration in Central Park, commemorating the 50th anniversary of John Lennon's murder. He says it was an amazing event, with thousands of people there. I wish I could've been there with him, but couldn't, for obvious reasons.

He still hasn't owned up to being Jefferson Paine, either, the brat.

Dad's going to be released from the hospital in a few days. I've convinced him that the place to rest and recuperate is here with me and Vicki in Clearwater, not in Rockaway Beach. In fact, I'm going to urge him to sell that house. How anyone could live in their home after such events is beyond me.

I'm still a bit nervous. Though Dad and I have been getting along well lately, there's still a part of me that's afraid of how he's going to react when he's around me and Vicki full-time. Will he grow more tolerant of our relationship, or will it disturb him?

But I want him with us. I've come to realize just how important family is to me, between losing my mother and nearly losing my father... that was just too much. I need my dad in my life, and this is a good way for us to really reconnect.

I wish I'd had the opportunity to mend the rift between me and Mom. Dad let me read her diary, and it about broke my heart. I hate that I only saw her superficially. Underneath the obsessed, anti-choice "Savior" was a very loving woman. The things she wrote about how our estrangement hurt her... it was almost too much to bear.

And reading her passages about her suspicions about Sisco, and how she couldn't let any harm come to me... I cried.

Why wouldn't anyone listen to her? She wrote of talking to the chief of security, only to have him wave off her concerns as paranoia. In the end, she felt so sure that something was going to happen, that she resolved to stop it all by herself, if she had to.

I miss her.

The Voice of Reason
Archer D. White. That's D for "Duh."

Archer White has got to take the prize for being the most clueless guy we've had in the White House in more than twenty years.

I mean, if every opinion poll over the past three months has shown that the public has become highly suspicious of religious zealots in office, it's just not smart to say, "This Administration will continue in its efforts to bring this nation to God, one way or another." Am I wrong?

White's popularity has plummeted from a "high" of 32% to its present 17%. I can't help but laugh.

Still, what's on the horizon is no joke. We've managed to oust the demagogues. But now we lack any kind of leadership in the White House. Normally, that's not an issue, since the country doesn't usually *need* a leader. But we're a very confused and volatile nation right now, and having a strong presence in office would be a good thing.

Sadly, we're out of luck on that front for a couple more years. Tighten those seat belts, my friends. We're still in for a bumpy ride.

But hey… a bumpy ride can still be a fun one, right?

Mary's Page   Eleanor Adams   Archives

Email me!

This site last updated: 12/17/30
*Visitors since this site was born: **52,009,405***

426

30 December 2030

J've not kept up my journal since leaving the hospital. J suppose J can be forgiven, though, as J am having the most joyous time here. Clearwater is a lovely community, and the people have been exceptionally friendly toward me.

J've been here for two weeks. My recuperation is going well. J spend a lot more time off my feet than J'd like, but the doctors said this is to be expected for a while. So J've been reading a lot, writing letters, and enjoying the company of my daughter and Vicki.

Vicki truly is almost a second daughter to me, and J have grown less and less uncomfortable with the fact that she is Mary's lover. Should this please me or cause me guilt?

J was a bit concerned when the girls insisted J join them in their Yule celebration. As Wiccans, they do not celebrate anything having to do with Christ during this season. But Mary assured me that it would be enjoyable and not offensive to my sensibilities. How sad, J think now, that she needed to even say such a thing to me. Further, she said she and Vicki would be happy to observe a traditional Christmas service with me, if J would observe theirs with them. And J agreed.

Their Yule celebration was... J hesitate to use the word "enchanting," given the connotations, but J must admit the word fits. Jt was nine days ago, but the whole experience is still fresh.

Preceding the ritual, Vicki explained that it was expected that we should each spend some time outdoors in nature, to "connect" with the earth, and to quiet our spirits. So the three of us strolled through these magnificent redwoods, idly chatting. J asked questions about what was to come, but J was told to just wait. Eventually, Vicki went her separate way. J'd thought it was to allow Mary and me some private time, but then Mary, too, went off alone. Jt was truly to be private time, she said, equivalent to private prayer.

So that's what J did, when she was gone. J sat among these ancient trees and prayed. Or rather, J talked. Aloud. J did not bow my head. And J spoke to God, apologizing for what J now know was arrogance on my part. And yet, even as J did so, J knew J had forgiveness from the ones who mattered most. Mary and, yes, Vicki. Both had accepted me into their lives. So J thanked God for that. Later, of course, J also thanked the girls.

Some of the things I said to God were far more straight-forward than I'm used to being. Ever since Sarah's death, I've not been as timid in addressing the Lord as perhaps I should be.

Probably because Mary and Vicki's relationship was on my mind, I asked... no... I demanded that He give me a clear sign that the love they share is wrong. Something unmistakable, something new. Something incontrovertible. I'm still waiting.

I also spoke freely of myself, and of what I see of myself in my daughter. Mary has retained a very keen sense of optimism, undimmed by the tragedies she's experienced over the past year or so. I remember that feeling, of being able to look the world straight in the eye without feeling intimidated. I, however, seem to have lost it somewhere along the way, and hadn't even realized it was missing until I saw it in Mary.

And I regret losing it. That flame was so much a part of who I was. It was probably a good part of what attracted Sarah to me in the first place. So I asked God if He might be inclined to spare a little optimism for me, or at least to tell me how to get it back, myself. Though, perhaps I should simply ask my daughter.

After I'd said all I had to say to God, I returned to the community. Mary and Vicki returned shortly thereafter.

The Yule ritual itself took place right in the center of the enormous greenhouse that is common to all the living quarters. There was an altar draped with red cloth, and decorated with real holly and mistletoe, long stretches of ivy, and candles of various colors. Behind the altar stood Sam Hain, dressed in a red velvet robe. He was there by Mary's invitation, and is quite an imposing fellow, brooding in his looks, but with a kindly twinkle in his eye. When Mary introduced us, I was somehow unsurprised when he shook my hand and welcomed me. I said it was nice to meet him. And I meant it.

I confess to having some trepidation about the ceremony, despite Mary's assurances. I have believed for so long that all pagan faiths are Satanic in nature, and never really swallowed the story of them being "earth centered." But if this celebration is typical of what these pagans do, what they believe, then I am once again ashamed.

At the beginning, Sam lit a Yule log. He explained that it represented the year now coming to an end. At the end of the ritual, when the log was nearly extinguished, a second was placed on top. This represented the year just about to begin.

Over the intervening hour, there was much singing and candle lighting, chanting and gesticulating. But all focused on "mother Earth, father Sun," and so on. At no point did I actually believe they were speaking of or to literal deities as Christians do, but rather to figurative spirits, as embodied by these celestial fixtures. But then, I could be wrong. I did not ask. I was so relieved to hear no mention of devils or demons, probably, that I just sat back and enjoyed the singing.

My daughter has a lovely voice.

And the food! Perhaps not as impressive as the gourmet meals I became accustomed to in the White House, but still very impressive. We feasted on fresh roasted turkey with stuffing, squash, cookies, even fruitcake. And to drink, we had this delicious hot spiced apple cider with lemon and orange. The produce was grown in the greenhouse. The turkeys were purchased from a local breeder, not from a frozen supermarket case.

After the feast, we engaged in several different activities in small groups. Mary, Vicki and I spent our time making a Yule wreath. I was touched, since Sarah loved fresh wreaths. The smell of evergreens always filled our home at Christmas.

The wreath the girls and I put together was, I think, the most impressive wreath I've ever seen. Or maybe I think this because I had a part in making it. Assembling a wreath is not as easy as it looks. It definitely takes the hand of an artist. Fortunately, Vicki has two such hands.

We started with a base of entwined dried vines, and then secured tiny boughs of redwood, holly, and fir. We decorated it with cones. Amazingly, the cones of the redwood tree are only about the size of a thimble! This astounded me. But they were quite nicely sized for our wreath, when grouped together in pairs and more. When it was finished, we hung it on the door to Vicki and Mary's home.

We exchanged a single present for each, the girls happily agreeing to hold off on the rest until Christmas. And they kept to their word. They went with me to a small church in town for a Christian ceremony on Christmas Eve.

It was, by all accounts, a very nice sermon, and a pleasant service all around. Not too long, not too short. But there seemed to be something missing from it that was present in the Yule ceremony. For several hours afterward, I could not place what it was.

Not until after the girls and I had opened the rest of our presents and had some wonderful leftovers did I figure it out. It was Nature. It was the sounds, the smells... everything... about being surrounded by the wonderful world that God created for us.

And maybe that's all pagans are really celebrating: Creation. Christians celebrate the forgiveness that Christ brought us. Pagans celebrate the very world itself, God's ultimate gift to us. Without it, there would be no life, after all.

I'm ashamed of how I used to view my daughter's religion. Of course, there are those in my own faith who would assert that Mary and her friends are brainwashed, that they are really worshiping Satan, whether they realize it or not. I can no longer accept this view.

I have learned so much from Mary, things I never would have learned on my own. I'm beginning to understand more about human nature, and just maybe, beginning to truly understand my daughter.

Who says miracles don't happen anymore?

December 31, 2030

I've been thinking a lot lately about the last decade or so. About how turbulent it's been, not just for me, but for the whole country. I suppose every decade is turbulent in one way or another, but this is the one I think I'll remember as "my" decade. I can't imagine ever going through another span of time in which I will grow as much, or change as much, as I have over these last ten years.

Or so I say now. I suppose it's possible that in thirty or forty years, I'll read over this diary entry and laugh, saying, "Girl, you have no idea what you're headed for." But for right now, I just can't conceive of events more profound than those I've just lived through.

I worry about the future, but less than before. In truth, I think we lucked out. Things could have become much worse than they did.

I asked my father just the other day to tell me the real reason he resigned. I had my suspicions, and apparently, I was right. When Mom was killed, lots of things started to click in his head. He saw all the hatred and resentment in society being exacerbated by the policies he'd implemented. He realized just what kind of lousy society he'd helped create. And he knew that Sisco would hang himself, if only he had enough rope. So Dad gave him that rope, by giving him the Presidency.

You can say many things about him, but you can't say my father's stupid. In fact, I'm saying some pretty nice things about him, these days. I'm amazed at the changes I see in him. He treats Vicki almost like his own daughter, and I love him so much for that.

Still, we don't push our luck. Vicki and I are careful not to display too much affection for each other in his presence. One step at a time.

Steps...

A journey of a thousand miles begins with a single step, as Lao-Tze said. And it's sure true. I look back and think of all the little steps taken to get me from there to here, all the steps taken to get the country from darkness to something resembling light. And it's amazing.

What was my first step? I don't really know. Was it in opening my mind to what Jude told me about religion? Or was it something even before that? Was I destined to take these steps? Had I not met Jude, would I still have begun questioning things? I don't know. How could I?

And what of the future? "Jefferson Paine" is right—the coming years will definitely be bumpy. The economy has been showing signs of going into the toilet. It's been declining for a decade, but it's getting worse.

He's talked about sharing his site with more guests, too, including Libertarian leaders and other activists. But he's also said he's going to take leave of the site for good when Archer White loses the next election to Thomas Dowd, who's going to run on the Libertarian ticket.

And no one thinks he's wrong about Archer White losing the next election. The man is incompetent. Whatever respect he had as a Senator is being wiped out by his insistence upon keeping to the visions of Gene Sisco.

So I look forward to when Dowd is sitting in the Oval Office. Under him, I think we'll see more focus on civil liberties. He's already said he'll release all political prisoners, including Eleanor Adams, Michael Lee, and others. But even with him firmly on the side of the oppressed, the fight to restore what's been lost won't be won quickly.

Some are saying my dad should run for office again. But he's not interested. I'm kinda glad. We're doing so well on becoming close again. I don't want to lose him to his job again. Call me selfish.

I plan on continuing the speaking circuit. But I don't just want to rage against the machine any more. I want to present messages full of promise and constructive ideas. Outrage only gets you so far, after all.

Vicki and I are thinking Beltane, 2032, for our handfasting. We thought about going up to British Columbia to get legally married, but since the U.S. doesn't recognize Canadian same-sex marriages, what would be the point? There are ways we can obtain many of the same benefits using some fancy legal footwork. And we've talked about adopting, sometime after that.

Anyway, that's enough about the future. Right now it's New Year's Eve, time to make resolutions for 2031. Generally, I feel life is too unpredictable for such things, but I do have one in mind.

I resolve to live my life as the precious gift that it is. Not just for me, but for everyone. It's so easy to fall into the delusion that we, as individuals, are the axis around which the world spins. But we're not.

The world spins all by itself, oblivious to the lives we all lead. And it's up to each of us to make our time here as good as it can be. And living self-centered lives will never accomplish more than a superficial version of that.

Sometimes we have to try to see the world through the eyes of those who appear to be our enemies. I guess I did that, when I met Jude. I tried to see the world from the perspective of a non-believer. And I didn't like what I saw. It was a harsh, oppressive world, and not one that brought much happiness.

Of course, it wasn't the world itself that was oppressive, but the society we'd created. That realization was truly eye-opening. And I think I'd begun to see that by the time I was just getting to know Vicki. And ever since, I've been able to see the world through the eyes of others pretty easily.

Even now, I can still see the world through the eyes of people like Gene Sisco. I can actually understand why he was so frustrated and angry about so many things.

But life is a long string of compromises. It must be, for there to be peace. When our nation was run in accordance to Sisco's warped visions, millions and millions of people were miserable. Because Sisco was unwilling to meet anyone halfway.

Those of us who have lived through this past decade are not likely to forget the widespread loss of freedoms suffered. Hopefully, future generations will learn from this period of history, and always be vigilant. We can never allow this sort of thing to happen again.

It's like Margaret Mead said: "Never doubt that a small group of thoughtful, committed individuals can change the world, indeed it's the only thing that ever has." I think we've demonstrated that pretty well recently.

We're moving now, slowly but surely, toward the kind of society that we should've had all along, I think. Maybe we'll never really achieve that Utopian ideal, but it's worth trying for.

If we keep sight of that ideal, and never allow closed minds to hold sway over reason, we might just stand a chance. With luck, there will always be people who will educate and agitate... people who'll make a stand... people who will fight for liberty... and justice... for <u>all</u>.

I know I'll be one of them.

About the Author

Vincent M. Wales has lived in Pennsylvania, Utah, and California, and has been an activist for alternative lifestyles and freethought issues for several years. His *Polyamory Awareness and Acceptance Ribbon Campaign* has been online since 1997, and *The Atheist Attic* has been a popular haven for non-theists since 1998. He was also the founder of the Freethought Society of Northern Utah and general thorn in the side of the prevailing theocracy there. Online, he answers questions on AllExperts.com on the subjects of polyamory, atheism, and writing books, and teaches a series of fiction writing classes at The Learning Exchange in Sacramento, California, where he lives currently.